THE END OF
RUSSIA'S WAR
IN UKRAINE

TED HALSTEAD

BOOKS BY TED HALSTEAD:

The Second Korean War (2018)
The Saudi-Iranian War (2019)
The End of America's War in Afghanistan (2020)
The End of Russia's War in Ukraine (2020)

All four books, including this one, are set in a fictional near future. Some events described have happened in the real world, and others have not.

To my wife Saadia, for her love and support over more than thirty years.

To my son Adam, for his love and the highest compliment an author can receive- "You wrote this?"

To my daughter Mariam, for her continued love and encouragement.

To my father Frank, for his love and for repeatedly prodding me to finally finish my first book.

To my mother Shirley, for her love and support.

To my granddaughter Fiona, for always making me smile.

All characters are listed on the very last pages, because that's where I think the list is easiest to find for quick reference.

CHAPTER ONE

SS-24 Mod-2 Test Site, Ukraine, USSR
July 30, 1986

Private Pofistal Arbakov gaped as he looked up at the SS-24 on the launch pad. Over twenty-three meters tall, the missile looked like it was straining to be released from the pad and into space.

And then to fall upon the Soviet Union's enemies, no matter where in the world they might be. The USSR spanned over ten thousand kilometers from Leningrad in the west to Vladivostok in the east. The SS-24 could be launched from anywhere within those ten thousand kilometers, and its range was eleven thousand kilometers.

Yes, Pofistal thought to himself with awe. Nobody could attack his beloved country without knowing a devastating response would follow.

"Hey, Kosta, who's the new guy?" a nearby Sergeant asked.

"This is Private Arbakov. Excuse me, Sergeant Bannik, this is Private Pofistal Arbakov," Sergeant Konstantin Estrin replied with a sly grin.

Arbakov groaned inwardly but said nothing. He'd had to live with jokes about his name during his entire short life. Pofistal was short for "Pobeditel fashisma Iosif Stalin," or "Josef Stalin, defeater of fascism."

What made it much worse was that his father had named him Pofistal over a decade after Stalin's death.

His father hadn't just stopped with the name. Throughout Arbakov's life until he'd enlisted in the Soviet Strategic Rocket Forces, his father had told him Party first, country next.

It went without saying that Arbakov and every other individual Soviet citizen came dead last.

Yet, somehow, Arbakov had never been bitter. Instead, he'd accepted everything his father said, even after Mikhail Gorbachev came to power in 1985.

"Pofistal, huh?" Bannik said thoughtfully. "So, have we got a true believer on our hands?"

Estrin's grin widened. "Well, he's only been here a short time. But so far, all signs point to yes."

Bannik shrugged and looked Arbakov over. "Well, at least he has the good sense to keep his mouth shut when the sergeants talk. That's more than I can say for most of these new privates."

Estrin nodded. "True enough. Oh, did I mention that Private Arbakov didn't wait for his draft notice, and volunteered instead?"

Bannik just stared at Estrin, speechless. Finally, he said, "I can't remember the last time that happened."

Estrin laughed and said, "I'm not sure it ever has, at least while I've been in the Service."

"Well," Bannik said, "I think you've just solved my problem. I was going to ask if you had a Private who could help me move the rest of the test warheads back to storage. I guess I've found him."

Estrin looked at Arbakov and asked, "So, Private Arbakov, willing to volunteer for some extra duty with Sergeant Bannik here?"

Arbakov didn't hesitate. "Of course, Comrade Sergeant."

Turning to Sergeant Bannik, Arbakov said, "I will be back in a moment wearing my anti-radiation gear. Shall I bring a set for you as well, Comrade Sergeant?"

Estrin looked like he was fighting hard not to laugh, while Bannik was both frowning and puzzled.

Both Estrin and Bannik could see that none of these reactions made any sense to Arbakov.

Bannik slowly said, "Private, you were told that these were test warheads. What makes you think we need anti-radiation gear?"

Arbakov replied immediately. "Sir, one of the key aspects of a nuclear missile test must be whether the electronics that control navigation and detonation continue to function despite the radioactivity emitted by the nuclear payload. So, test warheads would have to be exactly as radioactive as a real payload."

Bannik's frown deepened. "Must be," he repeated. "Did you learn this in your training?"

Arbakov shook his head. "No, sir. I thought it was obvious. Am I wrong, sir?"

Now Estrin had to laugh. "No, Private, you're not wrong. You've just spoiled Sergeant Bannik's little joke. You were supposed to go with him to the test warheads, and then be sent running all the way back to collect the anti-radiation gear that you were too dumb to know you needed."

Arbakov's reaction was the last one either Sergeant expected. He said, "Yes, sir. That would have made sure I'd never forget those test warheads are radioactive."

Bannik snapped, "Attention!" Arbakov immediately followed the order.

Bannik then slowly walked around Arbakov, shaking his head. Tall, sandy hair, blue eyes, clean-shaven. Or, maybe too young to need a shave. He looked like an absolutely typical Private.

Finally, Bannik turned to Estrin and asked, "What do you think, Kosta? Was he grown in a lab?"

Estrin laughed and replied, "I think we have to face the possibility that somehow a Private has been assigned to us with an IQ in triple digits, and at least some common sense. After all, future Sergeants have to come from somewhere."

Bannik grunted. "So, Private, do you think you'll be with us long enough to become a Sergeant some day?"

Staring straight ahead, Arbakov said, "Sir, I plan to be in the Service as long as I can be of use to the Soviet Union."

Bannik nodded. "Very well, Private. Go and collect two sets of anti-radiation gear."

Arbakov saluted and moved off at a brisk pace to carry out the order. Once he was gone, Bannik turned to Estrin.

"Do you really think he'll make Sergeant?" he asked Estrin.

Estrin shrugged. "Arbakov is the first Private I've met who I think I could end up having to salute someday."

Pervomaysk, Ukraine
January 4, 1992

Colonel Valery Rozum looked out his office window at the sprawling base and sighed. When he had arrived for his assignment two years ago, it had been buzzing with activity on a nearly non-stop basis.

Ukraine's Declaration of Independence had been ratified in a popular referendum by a margin of over ninety percent just last month. In response, many of the Russian-speaking officers and troops at Pervomaysk had requested and received transfers to bases within Russia.

Pervomaysk Strategic Rocket Base had become a much quieter place.

"Sergeant Pofistal Arbakov reporting as ordered, sir," Arbakov said.

Rozum turned away from the window to the soldier at the door.

"At ease, Sergeant. In fact, have a seat," Rozum said, gesturing towards one of the chairs facing his desk.

Sitting down behind his desk, Rozum opened Arbakov's personnel file.

"Sergeant, you are now the senior noncommissioned officer remaining at this base. So, my first question for you is, do you plan to remain here, or instead to join the other Russian-speaking soldiers who have requested a transfer to bases within Russia?" Rozum asked.

Arbakov shook his head decisively. "I'm not leaving, sir. I was born here. My wife was born here, and so was my son. The new Ukrainian government has promised no discrimination against Russian-speakers. If we all flee, who will hold them to it?"

Rozum grunted. "Well, I've made much the same decision. But it's easy for me since I'm just a few years from retirement. I expect to serve out those years here."

Then Rozum paused. "You know the Ukrainians will probably give up the SS-24s at this base, and I don't see Ukraine trying to remain a nuclear power by developing its own weapons. So, what will you do with the rest of your military career?"

Arbakov shrugged. "Colonel, I will do my job, whatever the officers over me decide that should be. If it means maintaining Tochkas, so be it."

Rozum couldn't help wincing. There were several Tochka ballistic missile variants, and the most recent had just been deployed. Even it, though, had a range of only one hundred eighty five kilometers.

The Tochka, called the Scarab by NATO, was a far cry from the SS-24s now at Pervomaysk.

"Well, for now, we have the SS-24s. Do you still have sufficient men and supplies to maintain them?" Rozum asked.

Arbakov nodded. "Yes, sir. Of course, they've been off-line for months. The permissive action links needed to fire them were always controlled from Moscow, and they have now been disabled. Given current political realities, I see no chance they will ever be restored. So, we will carry out maintenance as a safety measure. But I doubt the forty-eight SS-24s deployed here will ever resume operational status."

Rozum grimaced with distaste. "Agreed. We spent so much time and effort to develop the first truly reliable solid-fueled ballistic missiles, and had just finished deploying them here when..."

Rozum waved his arms towards the window. Arbakov knew Rozum was referring to everything happening in the world outside his office and nodded with understanding.

It was indeed, frustrating. But what could anyone do about it?

CHAPTER TWO

Pervomaysk, Ukraine
July 27, 1994

From a respectful distance, Colonel Valery Rozum observed Sergeant Pofistal Arbakov working with a swearing, sweating squad of soldiers to remove a warhead from an SS-24 missile. It had been many years since Rozum had laid hands on a ballistic missile. Looking at the array of equipment around the SS-24 in the blazing summer heat, Rozum thought to himself that he was glad he could keep it that way.

One of the talents that had helped Rozum advance to the rank of Colonel was knowing when to leave well enough alone. It took nearly another hour while Rozum waited in his air-conditioned staff car. Finally, though, warhead removal was completed by Arbakov and his men. Arbakov's crew then moved the warhead to the nearby weapons bunker to be prepared for shipment to Russia. Everyone but Arbakov had gone with the warhead.

Rozum left the car and walked to where Arbakov was putting away equipment, still wearing his anti-radiation gear. As Rozum drew near, Arbakov stopped and saluted.

Rozum smiled and saluted back. "At ease, Senior Sergeant," he said.

Arbakov's eyes widened, and Rozum laughed. "Yes, it's official. Now that you're nearly done removing all the SS-24 warheads at this base, even the brass at headquarters finally had to agree you deserve the promotion. Even if you are a Russian speaker."

"Thank you, sir. I appreciate everything you've done for me," Arbakov said. Waving his arm towards the silos behind him, Arbakov asked, "What do you think they'll do with all these, sir?"

Rozum shrugged. "According to the terms of the arms control agreements with the Americans, they should all be destroyed. Ukraine has lots of uranium and plenty of scientists who know how to build nuclear weapons. But hardly anyone in the Ukrainian government really wants to rejoin the nuclear club. So, I think Tochkas will be the biggest thing you'll be working on after this, and they don't need silos."

Arbakov nodded silently. The SS-24's warhead component, with its ten independently targeted warheads, was, by itself, double the weight of the entire OTR-21 Tochka. In fact, every Tochka that Arbakov had seen had been mounted on a vehicle.

Yes. Silos wouldn't be needed.

Aloud, Arbakov said, "I've said before that I have no problem working on Tochkas, sir, and I meant it. If the Americans are getting rid of the same number of missiles, maybe that's a good thing. It might mean my son will live in a safer world."

Rozum just raised his eyebrows and said nothing. When he saw Rozum's expression, Arbakov couldn't help himself.

Both of them roared with laughter until they were gasping for air. Finally, wiping tears from his eyes, Rozum said, "Well, Senior Sergeant, I'm not going to miss the Cold War. But if I'm sure of anything, it's that Ukraine still needs soldiers. It's lucky to still have a few men like you with a little common sense, who are willing to stick around despite everything."

With that, Rozum smiled and said, "Carry on, Senior Sergeant."

Grinning, Arbakov replied, "Yes, sir!" and saluted. Rozum returned the salute automatically, and then went back to his staff car and drove off.

Arbakov continued putting away equipment for several minutes, as he thought about how happy his wife Natalia would be with his promotion. The extra money wouldn't be that much, but it would certainly come in handy.

Arbakov's thoughts darkened as he realized that once the SS-24 transfer to Russia was complete and Rozum retired, this would probably be his last promotion. Part of the problem would be discrimination against him as a Russian speaker.

But only part. A bigger problem was that in the newly independent Ukraine, the military would not be very important. After all, Russia had enough problems just keeping order inside its still vast territory, and could hardly be considered a threat. Neighboring countries like Hungary and Moldova certainly had no interest in attacking Ukraine.

Every indication so far suggested that the new Ukrainian government would not use the military against its people. Arbakov was glad that was true and would have quit if one of the newly elected leaders tried to establish a dictatorship backed by military force.

Still, that left Ukraine's military with little to justify its existence, aside from the possibility that a threat could emerge with little warning. For example, maybe someday Russia would manage to restore its military. It was hard for Arbakov to imagine, though, that Russia would ever attack Ukraine.

Russia. Arbakov felt a sudden rush of anger. The SS-24s he was now shipping off to Russia had been designed and built by the Yuzhnoye Design Office in Dnipro, Ukraine. He and many other Ukrainians had spent nearly a decade making sure that they were ready to protect the homeland. It was just wrong that he was now being forced to turn over the weapons he and so many other Ukrainians had worked so hard to design, build and maintain.

But what could he do about it?

Later, Arbakov would look back at what he did next and have to admit he couldn't explain his actions. He had no plan and was risking years in prison and severe hardship for his family.

But Arbakov didn't think about any of that.

Instead, all that consumed Arbakov's thoughts was an overwhelming feeling of injustice—combined with blind rage.

Arbakov walked to the weapons bunker and punched in the code that secured the door. He walked in and saw, as he expected, that the SS-24 payload they had just removed was on a large metal work table. Another crew had already been scheduled to prepare and crate the warheads for transport.

Arbakov took out two of the ten warheads from the SS-24 payload with the equipment on-site in the bunker. Then he placed each of the warheads on the edge of the massive work table.

Next, Arbakov went to a large metal storage locker set in the bunker's back right corner. It occupied nearly a fifth of the bunker's space, and several soldiers over the years had asked Arbakov what it contained. Each time he had smiled and answered honestly.

Nothing you'll ever need.

The only items in the locker were the ten dummy warheads left over from the SS-24 tests Arbakov had witnessed in 1986. They had been moved here from the test site as soon as the second launch had been declared a success. Arbakov remembered Sergeant Estrin telling him success was never to be taken for granted in such a test firing, and that the launch of the first SS-24 version had been a failure.

Arbakov had never been told whether there was a reason to keep the test warheads and had never asked. He had always assumed that someday he would be asked to dispose of them, but no orders had ever come. Many years had passed since the test. With the collapse of the Soviet Union, Arbakov wasn't surprised everyone else had forgotten about these dummy weapons that no longer served a purpose.

Well, that wasn't right, Arbakov thought. Two of the test warheads would now prove useful.

Arbakov used the bunker's equipment to remove one of the test warheads and place it where one of the real warheads had been just minutes ago. Then, he repeated the procedure with the second warhead.

Moving the two real warheads to the spaces in the weapons locker vacated by the test warheads was even quicker. While Arbakov had to be careful to place each of the test warheads precisely in the newly vacant spaces in the SS-24 payload, such care wasn't necessary for the storage locker.

After all, Arbakov had the only key to the locker. He knew nobody else could know that anything about the locker's contents had changed.

Arbakov did have to think about how to place the real warheads so that he could distinguish them from the test warheads. He settled the problem by making use of the gap he had created when he had removed two of the test warheads. Arbakov placed the real warheads slightly to the left in the locker. Though only about ten centimeters separated them from the eight test warheads, Arbakov was confident he'd have no trouble distinguishing the real ones.

Arbakov had no idea what he would do with the warheads. He hadn't planned that far ahead.

But he was sure he would think of something.

CHAPTER THREE

April 30, 2008
Russian Nuclear Weapons Disposal Plant

Andreas Burmakin sighed as he began disassembling yet another nuclear warhead. Today he was working on what he'd been told were the very last ZBV3 model 152mm projectiles left from the old Soviet stockpiles. Atomic artillery shells with one kiloton warheads designed to be fired from the 2A65 "Msta-B" howitzer, they had been withdrawn from service and stockpiled in 1993, a few years after the Soviet Union's collapse. In 2000, Russia had announced that it had destroyed "nearly all" of its nuclear artillery shells.

Burmakin sighed as he looked at the pile of artillery shells still left to disassemble. Well, he supposed that "nearly all" was vague enough to cover just about any number.

Then Burmakin smiled, as he looked across to where Vitaly Dreev was glumly beginning the disassembly process for another SS-24 warhead. Yes, it could always be worse. At least the artillery shells were relatively small and easy to handle. With an explosive yield five hundred times the one contained by his shells, Dreev had to use more complex and cumbersome equipment.

And since they were the only ones here today, there were no bosses to care whether the air conditioning worked. Not, of course, for the workers. For the bosses, since every supervisor Burmakin had ever met was fat, and badly needed cold air flowing through the vents.

Disassembling warheads with nuclear protection gear on was uncomfortable work with functional air conditioning. Without it, it was utterly miserable.

On the bright side, the gear did protect them from an annoyance that had astonished both Burmakin and Dreev when they started work at the plant. The smell. Almost identical to rotten eggs, the stench had washed over them like a noxious wave as soon as they entered.

Burmakin had asked and been told that the source of the smell was ironically the same as from old eggs. Decomposition. The complex components inside all nuclear weapons decayed over time, and every munition they were working on was at least a decade old.

Some were much older.

The smell wasn't just annoying. The outgassing of decayed nuclear weapon components contained compounds that could injure or even kill, depending on their composition and exposure time. The truth was that nobody had asked Soviet weapons designers to predict what would happen when their creations were taken apart.

Well, now they were finding out using the usual Russian method, Burmakin thought with a grim smile.

Learn by doing.

"Hey, how much longer do you think we'll be stuck with the worst shifts?" Dreev asked.

Burmakin had to think about that one. They were the only ones working today because everyone else but the guards at the entrance gate had taken the day off, as well as May 2. Since May 1 was a holiday, and May 2 was a Friday, everyone else got off five days in a row and only had to use two days of leave.

Naturally, Burmakin and Dreev were also the only ones scheduled to work on Friday.

"Well, we're the only ones who failed to meet our quotas, so I suppose if we step up the pace, we'll get better shifts," Burmakin said. Not because he meant it, but due to his longstanding belief that everything he said at work was being recorded.

Fortunately for both of them, on this particular day, that wasn't true. Not because the equipment to do so wasn't in place. It was. However, today there were no supervisors present to turn the system on.

Dreev scowled and shook his head. "You know that's not right. We've both been stuck with quotas that are impossible to meet. The people who set them don't know anything about these weapons."

Burmakin said nothing in response but shrugged with resignation. It was true. Their quota was for total uranium extracted, and they had the toughest tasks in the entire facility, for very different reasons.

Burmakin's problem was the relatively tiny amount of uranium extracted per artillery shell. Whoever had set his quota had entirely miscalculated how long it took to open each round without setting off its explosive component, and then remove the uranium. Burmakin had no intention of risking either the explosion of one of the shells or exposing himself to radiation.

But slow and steady meant falling behind his quota.

Dreev obtained much more uranium per SS-24 warhead, but disassembling each was a highly sophisticated operation.

Dreev frowned with concentration as he applied a solution of dimethyl sulfide (DMSO) to remove a stubborn bit of explosive that had fused to a metal warhead component. When Dreev had started work at the plant, every worker had been physically scraping off explosive residue when necessary for disassembly. Twice the results had been...unfortunate.

So, the arrival of DMSO had been received by all the plant's workers as a godsend. Dreev had heard a rumor that they had the Americans to thank for the idea to use DMSO, but wasn't sure whether to believe it. Although the Americans were buying all of the highly enriched uranium Dreev and his fellow workers were extracting from these old Soviet weapons.

Dreev had heard fantastic sums, like a billion dollars a year, had been paid by America to Russia for the uranium.

Shaking his head, Dreev snorted with disgust as he completed disassembly of the third of the SS-24's ten warheads. If Russia really was getting all that money, he sure wasn't seeing much of it.

As he began work on the fourth warhead, Dreev had a sudden thought. Could it be that whoever set his quota had simply failed to account for each SS-24 having ten warheads?

No, he thought with a sigh. His quota wasn't that far off. But the complexity of the disassembly process... Dreev thought that might be a more promising avenue to pursue with his supervisor. Removal of the tritium bottle and neutron generator from each warhead were not tasks to be safely rushed.

No sooner had Dreev had the thought when he completed the removal of the warhead's metal casing to find neither one. No tritium bottle. No neutron generator.

There were no internal warhead components at all.

Instead, there was just a solid metal mass. Frowning, Dreev ran his instruments over the metal.

Well, he had no way to know what the metal was, but it was undoubtedly radioactive. The readings were very close to the ones Dreev was used to seeing from standard SS-24 warheads.

"Hey, what's up over there? Find a problem?" Burmakin asked.

Dreev and Burmakin both had a rhythm to their work that, over the last few months, had become familiar to them. Spotting a disruption in that flow had become easy.

Dreev hesitated for an instant but quickly decided he needed advice. If he couldn't trust Burmakin, then who?

"I've found a dummy warhead. It's got enough radioactive metal to give off the right readings until you open the casing. But inside, there's nothing but metal. No mechanism at all," Dreev said.

Burmakin grunted. "Very odd. Never heard of anyone finding a dummy warhead. Is it just the one?"

"I've done three others from this SS-24 that were completely normal. I won't know if there are any more dummies until I'm done," Dreev said.

Burmakin nodded absently. "We had dummy artillery shells that we used in training. You have to make sure that the new troops know the basics of loading and firing before moving on to harder stuff, like aiming. But why would you need a dummy warhead in an ICBM?"

Dreev scowled, but for a moment, said nothing.

That was an excellent question.

Like Burmakin, Dreev had worked with the weapons he was now disassembling when they were still in use. Even in Russia, where so often reality defied logic, the plant managers had done the obvious. Who better to take weapons apart than the men who had used them?

Maybe more to the point, they no longer had jobs once the former Soviet military shrunk to a Russian ghost of its old self. That made men like Burmakin and Dreev eager to take even the meager salaries offered by the disassembly plants.

Finally, Dreev looked up. "OK, I did hear about dummy warheads once. But they were only used for tests of new ICBM models. All the warheads coming to us were operational. And, even if somehow a mistake was made and someone sent us a test SS-24, then all the warheads would have been dummies. There wouldn't be a dummy mixed in with working warheads."

"That makes sense," Burmakin replied. "But couldn't there have just been a mistake that nobody caught, and one dummy got loaded because someone was careless? After all, you said you couldn't tell the difference until you opened the warhead casing."

Dreev shook his head vigorously. "No way. We tested the firing circuits in the warheads every month. The dummy would have sent back zero signals. Could that have been missed once? Maybe. But every SS-24 was tested dozens of times from when it was deployed until it ended up here. There's no way this dummy warhead was missed that many times."

"OK, you've convinced me. It couldn't have been an honest mistake," Burmakin said with a shrug. "Then how do you explain it?"

Another excellent question. Dreev frowned and sat silently as he tried to find an answer.

Several minutes later, Dreev finally looked at Burmakin and said, "There's only one explanation that makes sense. Someone stole the warhead, and replaced it with a dummy."

Burmakin held up both hands and replied, "Whoa, there. Slow down! How did you come up with that?"

"Think about it. The dummy warhead wasn't in the SS-24 when it was in its silo, or it would have been detected. Same story if the warhead had simply been missing. That means while deployed, there were ten working warheads in this SS-24. Now there's a dummy warhead where the real thing used to be."

Dreev paused. "You tell me. If it wasn't stolen, what happened to the real warhead?"

Burmakin swore softly, which earned him a grim smile from Dreev in response.

"Exactly. So that leaves us with just one question. What do we do now?" Dreev asked.

Now it was Burmakin's turn to think. Both of them sat silently, trying to think about what to do next.

Then Burmakin sighed and said, "There are just two choices. Report it, or don't. If we do, there will be many questions for both of us about whether we had something to do with the missing warhead."

Dreev nodded gloomily. "Yes. Especially since we just happened to discover it was missing on a day when we were the only ones working here. We both know that's just a coincidence. The bosses aren't likely to believe it."

Burmakin nodded back. "Agreed. I thought about trying to point out that smuggling out an entire SS-24 warhead would be impossible, but that won't stop the bosses from blaming us anyway. Otherwise, the finger might get pointed at them."

Dreev grunted agreement. The plant was ringed with razor wire-topped fences, sensors, and cameras monitored by a guard force far better paid than the workers inside the plant. The sensors were designed to detect the radiation emitted by a few grams of weapons-grade uranium, never mind an entire SS-24 warhead.

But Dreev knew that an appeal to logic was unlikely to work. The bosses would only care about saving their skins.

And that meant finding someone else to blame.

Dreev slowly said, "Something else just occurred to me. We're the only workers who failed to meet their production quota. Because of that, we've been forced to work over a holiday weekend. Wouldn't disgruntled workers be the first ones you'd suspect if something turned up missing?"

Burmakin winced and then nodded. "You're right. Shooting the messenger is an old tradition. For us, I think the only question is whether we'd get a blindfold."

"Then it's settled. We keep our mouths shut," Dreev said flatly.

Burmakin frowned, and asked, "What about the dummy warhead? Isn't someone likely to ask what it is and where it came from?"

"Well, yes, if I just drop it on top of the production pile like a star on a Christmas tree. To avoid that, I'm going to need your help," Dreev replied.

Burmakin sighed, but then nodded. It was the only way.

The "production pile" was a large, lead-lined metal container where all the weapons-grade uranium extracted at the plant was placed. Once filled, it was covered, secured, and then put on a truck. The truck would take it to the Russian factory where it would be reprocessed from ninety percent weapons-grade enrichment down to the under five percent used as reactor fuel. Then the reactor fuel would begin its long journey to America.

They would have to move the uranium already in the container to make a hole large enough to drop in the dummy warhead and then cover it with uranium extracted from regular warheads.

"One other thing. Let's make the hole nice and big, in case this isn't the only dummy warhead I find," Dreev said.

Burmakin groaned. "Well, you are a ray of sunshine! But I can't say you're wrong. OK, let's get this over with."

It wasn't easy, but working together, Burmakin and Dreev were able to use the plant's equipment to ready the dummy warhead's concealment.

"There," Burmakin said with satisfaction. "That should be enough room for three or four of the cursed things."

Dreev shivered. "Bite your tongue. I'm hoping this is the one and only. Now, let's get back to our normal work. We don't want to draw attention by falling further behind on our quota. In fact, by the time this weekend is over, we'd better be caught up."

"You're right. We're going to be a lot later than usual clocking out tonight, and the only explanation the bosses will like is that we were catching up on our quotas," Burmakin said.

With that, they both got back to work. Several hours later, they were both exhausted but could see they had done nearly enough for the day.

"So, no more dummies?" Burmakin asked.

Dreev shook his head. "No. I've got just one left to do, and all the other warheads have been normal."

"Good," Burmakin said. "You know, I've been thinking about what you said. That the warhead was stolen. I'm worried that somebody out there has a half megaton weapon. One is bad enough. I don't think I could handle sitting on the news that more than one is out there somewhere."

Dreev nodded. "I know. I've had the same thought. But remember that it's been over a decade since these weapons were taken out of deployment. So the theft happened long ago. If anybody had set it off since then, I think it would have made the news."

"Yes, I'm sure you're right," Burmakin replied. "But who knows when they'll strike?"

"Look, I don't like it any more than you do. But after all the years that have passed since the theft, the real warhead could be anywhere. We've already talked about what's likely to happen if we report the dummy warhead. Are you changing your mind?" Dreev asked.

Burmakin sighed. "No. But I don't like it."

"Well, there we're agreed. I don't like anything about this business either. Look, why don't you go home. I'll finish up here," Dreev said.

"Are you sure?" Burmakin asked. Dreev nodded to himself as he saw Burmakin getting up while he asked the question. Dreev didn't blame him. Burmakin had served in artillery all the way to retirement and was at least a decade older than Dreev.

"Yes," Dreev said. "After all, properly speaking, this is my mess. I appreciate what you've already done to help me clean it up. Go home, old man," Dreev said with a smile.

Burmakin didn't need to be told again. In minutes, Dreev was alone in the plant.

Dreev began work on the last of the SS-24's ten warheads.

And swore bitterly, as he discovered it was another dummy.

At the same time, Dreev realized that he had one reason to be thankful. Burmakin was already uncomfortable with hiding the theft of one warhead. He certainly wouldn't have kept quiet about two.

Dreev had no such problem. Burmakin's wife had divorced him years ago, and he had no children. Dreev, though, had a wife and child depending on him. Reporting the thefts would mean losing this job at best.

Prison started a long and unpleasant list headed "at worst."

It was also fortunate that Burmakin had helped him to move the uranium in the container to make room for the dummy warheads at the bottom. It would have been a lot harder on his own.

Two hours later, Dreev was finally done. Looking at the container, he nodded with satisfaction. By the time the weekend was over, they would have extracted enough uranium to fill the rest of the box and meet their quotas in the process.

Then the container would be on its way. When its top was lifted, and someone finally worked their way to its bottom, they might report the dummy warheads.

But maybe not. The warheads were definitely radioactive and probably made of uranium.

Since the entire dummy warhead was metal, but probably a uranium alloy, it would have to be processed less than the uranium from a working SS-24 warhead.

Dreev thought so, anyway. The uranium they extracted was reprocessed to reduce its enrichment to the level used for reactor fuel. So the dummy warheads...would just make that task a little easier?

Dreev shrugged. No use worrying about things he couldn't control. Whoever found the dummy warheads would either report them or not. What mattered most was that by then, tracing them back to Dreev would be impossible.

He hoped.

CHAPTER FOUR

Five Kilometers outside Donetsk, "Donetsk People's Republic"
Several Years From Now

Boris Kharlov knew that many in both the West and Ukraine called him a "warlord," which he had always found amusing. The term sounded so...medieval.

In one respect, the term fit. The vast, perfectly manicured grounds that stretched in front of his imposing white marble mansion looked just right for a man of wealth and power. Not that Kharlov cared about a single blade of grass, bush, or flower.

No, Kharlov mused as he looked over the grounds from his second-story study, dominated by an enormous carved wooden desk. Appearances mattered when it came time to settle on the payments he was due. Nobody handed over millions to a man operating from a tin shack.

Appearances mattered for Kharlov himself, too. Most women considered him handsome, though some thought it better not to find out if he was as dangerous as he appeared. Kharlov's suits were made in London, and his black beard was neatly trimmed. Regular workouts kept him in the same combat-ready shape as when he had served in the military.

Kharlov had been called many other things besides "warlord." Brutal. Cunning. Treacherous. He had no problem with any of those adjectives.

However, Kharlov considered all these traits incidental. First and foremost, Kharlov thought of himself as a modern Russian patriot. As he looked out his study window, Kharlov took a moment to reflect on how he had arrived at this point. Now that so much was likely to change.

And quickly.

Patriotism had motivated Kharlov to volunteer for service in the Russian Army, and then go through the grueling selection and training process necessary to become a member of the Spetsnaz, as Russia called its Special Forces.

The extraordinary aptitude Kharlov demonstrated in training had led to his first assignment to the Special Weapons Company at Brigade Headquarters. There he had mastered a broad range of weapons and explosives, many only available to Spetsnaz, sometimes because their purpose was highly specialized.

In most cases, though, it was because the very best weapons cost far more to make than models produced for both ordinary Russian soldiers and export.

In both the old Soviet Union and its successor Russian Federation there was a simple reason for spending the money. Spetsnaz were far more likely to see combat than regular troops.

Since its formation in 1976, the 22nd Special Purpose Brigade had been deployed to Afghanistan, Angola, Azerbaijan, and Chechnya. Kharlov had joined just in time for their last deployment in the Second Chechen War. He had been fortunate to miss the first years of heavy fighting, which had seen the deaths of many of the brigade's best soldiers.

Instead, Kharlov was present for the Chechen conflict's final years. A combination of bribes and carefully targeted assassinations swung a critical mass of the Chechen insurgent leadership to acceptance of "autonomy" as a solution. In practice, this meant that surviving Chechen insurgent leaders acceptable to Moscow would indeed be able to run Chechnya on a day-to-day basis.

But Moscow would still have its troops in Chechnya, and taxes kept being collected by the Russian federal government and the "autonomous" local government. The Russian flag continued to fly in Chechnya, and everyone there was still a Russian citizen.

Kharlov's signature contribution to this victory was the assassination of a critical Chechen leader adamantly opposed to negotiations with Russia, Khasan Idrisov. Kharlov carefully and painstakingly molded a small shaped explosive charge inside a cell phone, while still leaving the phone functional.

It took experimenting with five different cell phone models to finally get it right.

But that wasn't the hardest part. Finding someone close to Idrisov willing to take a bribe proved impossible. So, Kharlov was forced to use another strategy. Kidnapping a close associate's wife and infant daughter.

Kharlov's greatest success was convincing the man that he had only been ordered to find a way to open negotiations with Idrisov. Kharlov could see the man really cared for his wife and daughter and was eager to believe he could get them back.

When the man turned on the phone, and it worked, he was satisfied Kharlov was telling the truth. Kharlov never forgot the lesson he learned that day.

Always make it possible for people to believe what you want them to hear.

Later the same day, Kharlov called the phone, which was then handed to Idrisov by his associate without explanation. Without thinking, Idrisov hit the button accepting the call and put the phone to his head. Then Kharlov heard Idrisov ask, "Who is this?"

Kharlov was in a former village post office ten kilometers away. The bottom level had been burned, but the concrete structure was still intact. The windows on the upper floor had been shot out long before, so the smell of smoke wasn't too bad.

All it took was a small generator and some folding tables to make it a field headquarters, and let Kharlov set up the few pieces of equipment he needed. Two other soldiers were with Kharlov, one guarding the traitor's wife and daughter and the other standing watch outside.

Kharlov answered Idrisov's question with the word that would make him a Spetsnaz legend.

"Dasvidaniya."

At nearly the same moment, Kharlov pressed the trigger.

It was indeed a very final goodbye. A loud bang was immediately followed on Kharlov's end by silence.

Kharlov learned later that Idrisov had been killed instantly, but that everyone else in the room had been left untouched.

This was particularly unfortunate for the traitor, whose death took place several long and agonizing days after Idrisov's.

Kharlov had rules he was determined to follow. One was not to kill women or children unless they were firing a weapon. So, he kept his promise to the traitor and released his wife and infant daughter just before he left to report to his superiors on the operation.

The soldiers with Kharlov raised no objections, and Kharlov thought no more of the matter. A year later, he learned one of the soldiers had followed the two released prisoners and killed them both.

By then, both soldiers had been killed in the war, so there was little Kharlov could do.

Except ask his commander, Colonel Leonid Shipov, whether he agreed with his order to let the prisoners go or the other soldier's decision to kill them.

Shipov had nodded thoughtfully and took so long to answer that Kharlov had started to think he never would.

Finally, he'd said, "Kharlov, you're a good soldier, and you get results. You'll always have a place on my team. But sometimes you forget that most men fighting here have just one thing on their mind. Survival."

Shipov had paused and looked at Kharlov, who'd nodded his understanding but said nothing.

"You didn't see that woman and her infant daughter as a threat. But the woman knew the building you'd used to launch an operation, correct?" Shipov had asked.

Kharlov had nodded. "Yes, sir. But we all left almost immediately. Or at least, I did, and I had ordered both of the other soldiers to leave right behind me."

Shipov had smiled. "I know that area. You were using that old post office because it's one of the few buildings still standing. What do you think the chances are that at some point we'll use it again? And if that woman had lived to tell the Chechens what she knew, that they might leave a present or two for us when we do?"

Kharlov had nodded sullenly but stayed silent.

Now Shipov had laughed. "Come now, Spetsnaz don't pout! I know you think that any decent soldier should be able to spot a Chechen booby trap. But the key word is 'decent.' There are plenty of conscripts here fresh out of basic training. We have to think about them, too."

This time, Kharlov's nod had been more thoughtful. Finally, he'd shrugged and said, "You're right, sir."

"But that's not all," Shipov had said. "That woman had a father, uncles, and so on. Someday her body might be discovered in the woods. Who knows who did it? There are plenty of ordinary thieves and murderers around, not to mention stray Chechen bullets."

Shipov had paused and shaken his head. "Now imagine that she goes home with the story of your successful mission to eliminate Idrisov. Along with a detailed description of you and your men."

Kharlov had stirred and begun to speak, but Shipov had held up a hand to stop him. "Yes, I know, you had to keep her close in case the traitor demanded to speak to his wife. But I read your report. She was close enough to hear everything that happened, wasn't she?"

Kharlov had frowned and slowly nodded.

"So, you tell me. If she had made it back to tell her story, do you think you'd be standing in front of me right now? Or would a Chechen sniper have made adding you as one more notch to his rifle stock a special priority?"

Kharlov had sat still for a moment. Then, he'd said, "Colonel, you've given me a lot to consider. In particular, I see I need to give a higher priority to operational security."

Shipov had grinned and clapped Kharlov on the shoulder. "Good man. Keeping your mind open to new lessons is the best way for any soldier to stay alive."

Kharlov shook himself awake from his reverie. New lessons. Yes.

The Russian government had just announced that it would broker a settlement between Novorossiya and the Ukrainian government. "Novorossiya" or "New Russia" was shorthand for the combined territory controlled by the "Donetsk People's Republic" and the "Luhansk People's Republic." That area of eastern Ukraine bordering Russia had been out of the control of the central Ukrainian government since 2014.

The Ukrainian government, of course, recognized neither "Novorossiya" or "People's Republic" as legitimate names for these territories. Instead, Ukraine and its friends in the West called it "Donbas" as a shorthand for "Donets Basin," since the Donets River flowed from one end of the region to the other.

Novorossiya existed because Russian-speakers in eastern Ukraine had longstanding grievances against Ukrainian-speakers, who they said discriminated against them in many ways both subtly and overtly. In particular, very few of Ukraine's most powerful politicians were Russian-speakers.

The Russian government had covertly encouraged Russian-speakers to seek independence, while publicly sympathizing with their grievances and urging the government in Kyiv to give them "autonomy." Everyone expected that either "autonomy" or independence would be a prelude to eastern Ukraine's absorption by Russia, with which it shared a long border.

Novorossiya had only been able to avoid the return of Ukrainian central government control thanks to Russian military and financial support.

After Chechnya, Kharlov had become dissatisfied with the low pay provided by the Russian military. Maybe even more important, with no conflict on the horizon to replace the action he had seen in Chechnya, Kharlov had also been bored.

As it happened, due to no more than random chance Kharlov had been assigned to the 22nd Special Purpose Brigade, at Stepnoy in Rostov Oblast. That happened to be the Oblast, or administrative district, bordering what would shortly become the Donetsk People's Republic.

Seeing the possibilities offered by Novorossiya's creation, Kharlov had deserted. It had taken less than an hour from his post at Stepnoy to cross the border to the new land of opportunity.

Opportunities Kharlov had seized with both hands.

Russia had already demonstrated its appetite for Ukrainian territory by annexing Crimea in 2014. Part of its justification for the seizure was that Crimea had been Russian territory until 1954, when Soviet General Secretary Nikita Khrushchev had transferred it from Russia to Ukraine.

The leaked outlines of Russia's proposed new settlement were far more favorable to the Ukrainian central government than any of the previous failed agreements. They included the withdrawal of all Russian forces and military equipment from Ukrainian territory.

Except, of course, for Crimea.

In effect, it would mark the end of Russia's war in Ukraine after over a decade of on-again-off-again fighting.

Yes, Kharlov would need a radically new approach to survive Ukraine's reassertion of sovereignty over its eastern territory.

Or stop it from happening.

But how?

CHAPTER FIVE

FSB Headquarters
Moscow, Russia

Anatoly Grishkov looked at the sturdy red leather sofa that domi-nated the office of FSB Director Smyslov. It was currently occupied by Mikhail Vasilyev and his new bride, Neda Rhahbar. Both had been deeply engrossed by the files each of them held, and each looked up as he entered like divers coming up for air.

Despite that, Grishkov knew he was grinning. Partly because he was genuinely happy to see both of them again after all they had survived to-gether on their last mission.

But a larger part was his pleasure at seeing how natural and...content they both seemed together. Even sitting together reading mission files, Grishkov could tell that they weren't just married.

They were happily married.

Grishkov had the good fortune to also be in such a marriage. He had always counted himself lucky to find a good woman like Arisha to put up with his looks and stubbornness. As Grishkov aged, he looked more and more like his father, who had also been a policeman. Like him, he was shorter and more muscular than the average Russian, with thick black hair and black eyes.

Grishkov's son Sasha was fourteen, and his other son Misha was twelve. Though both had black hair, otherwise they thankfully looked more like Arisha.

Grishkov had worked together with FSB Colonel Alexei Vasilyev, Mikhail's father, on his first two missions. Before that, he had been the lead homicide detective for the entire Vladivostok region, but after their first mission, FSB Director Smyslov had put him on "indefinite special assignment" as a Captain in the Moscow Police Department. After Alexei Vasilyev died during their second mission, Smyslov had assigned Alexei's son Mikhail as Grishkov's new partner.

This assignment was no coincidence. Smyslov knew that Grishkov was close to insisting on returning to police work after his second mission, simply because he thought his luck was unlikely to last for the third encounter with rogue nuclear weapons. He also knew Grishkov was not concerned for himself, but that he felt a strong responsibility to Arisha and his two sons. Grishkov had only agreed to volunteer for his third mission because of the deep respect he had even now for Alexei Vasilyev and his nearly superstitious belief that his son Mikhail would help Grishkov survive it.

His third mission, which had taken Grishkov to Pakistan and Afghanistan, had nearly killed him. Though he had been cleared to return to duty after a lengthy hospital stay, Arisha had begged him not to do this fourth mission.

And she had cried, which had shocked Grishkov. Arisha was a woman Grishkov genuinely believed stronger than himself, and he had never seen her cry. He had finally ended the argument by promising to make this his last mission.

Grishkov had every intention of keeping that promise.

Like his father had been, Mikhail Vasilyev was in excellent physical condition. Also, like him, Vasilyev was a firm believer in the value of hand-to-hand combat skills. Vasilyev was only a bit taller than Grishkov but was even thinner than his father. His full head of dark brown hair and his perpetual air of detached amusement had helped Grishkov recognize Vasilyev immediately as Alexei's son.

That recognition had come only after Alexei's death. Alexei had been worried that knowledge of his son's existence would be used against him by the many enemies he routinely encountered in his assignments abroad, a worry which only intensified once Vasilyev defied him and also began working for the FSB.

Grishkov had met Vasilyev's wife, Neda Rhahbar, when she was fleeing Iran. The wife of Iran's leading nuclear scientist, she had defected to Russia when she learned her husband was making three nuclear test devices available for an attack against Saudi Arabia. An accomplished nuclear scientist herself, Neda had been recruited to work in the FSB after her defection.

Neda's first marriage ended when her Iranian husband died voluntarily while setting off one of his nuclear creations.

Neda's expertise with nuclear weapons and language skills had served Grishkov and Vasilyev well on their last mission in Pakistan and Afghanistan. That mission had also left her with the scar that was clearly visible on one cheek, as well as a smaller one on her forehead.

Neither scar appeared to trouble Vasilyev, who had married Neda soon after their last mission concluded. Grishkov wasn't surprised since even with the scars, Neda was still a strikingly beautiful woman with long dark hair and flashing dark eyes. He also knew that the sort of danger they'd shared could do a great deal to drive people close together in a remarkably short time.

It also gave them a certainty that many couples never achieved. That no matter what, they could count on each other.

FSB Director Smyslov launched himself at Grishkov like a bearded missile as soon as he saw him come through the door. No sooner had Grishkov had the thought than he was wrapped in an embrace that once again made him think of the term "bear hug." With his stout, towering frame, and dark bushy beard, Smyslov reminded nearly everyone who met him of the Russian bear stereotype.

Finally releasing him, Smyslov held him by the shoulders at arm's length and critically looked him over. The strength of his grip reminded Grishkov that there was a lot of muscle in the Director's stout frame. Smyslov had risen through the ranks as an agent, and there were many stories still told about his time in the field.

"So, you seem in much better shape than the last time I saw you!" Smyslov exclaimed.

Grishkov tried to shrug but found that thanks to Smyslov's grip, he couldn't.

Instead, Grishkov smiled and said, "Since the last time you saw me I was flat on my back in a hospital bed, I guess that's no surprise. I give most of the credit for my speedy recovery to Arisha. There's nothing like home cooking and the love of a good woman to bring a man back to his old self."

Satisfied, Smyslov clapped Grishkov on the back and said, "Good, good! Have a seat! First, business, and then a proper lunch."

Grishkov was able to skip through much of the file thanks to his service in the Russian Army. He was already familiar with Soviet ICBM models and their capabilities, and the program for extracting their uranium and exporting it to the United States. Grishkov frowned and looked up at Smyslov when he came to the report explaining how the FSB had become aware of a missing Russian thermonuclear warhead.

"So, we only learned of this theft because of a literal deathbed confession. Any chance we can speak to this man again to try to get more details?" Grishkov asked.

Smyslov shook his head. "No. One detail not in the files you're all holding is that the man did indeed die earlier today. I received the call with that news just before you all arrived."

Grishkov nodded. "So, then, this fellow...Vitaly Dreev...is the only one who might be able to tell us more. Especially because he was an SS-24 technician before he started work at the disassembly plant."

Smyslov nodded. "Correct. But, as you see in the file, though we've been looking for him for the past several days, we've had no luck."

"I'm not surprised," Grishkov said with a shrug. "At his age, with no family, there's a good chance a former soldier would be homeless and drinking himself into an early grave."

Into the sudden silence, Grishkov said defensively, "I'm not saying that's what I think should have happened to him. If I hadn't met Arisha, that could have been me. But remember that I spent years as a policeman and then detective. Nobody spends that much time on the street without encountering men like Dreev. Anyway, I'm sure I can find him and know I can do it tomorrow."

Smyslov's bushy eyebrows flew upwards. "Really? How can you be so sure?"

Grishkov tapped a page in the file. "It says here that his last recorded address was right here in Moscow, but that he's not there anymore. If I'm right that he's homeless, he'd have no money to go anywhere else. He probably has no bank account. So, he'll have to collect his small pension in person, and would ask for cash. There's only one office where he can do that here in Moscow, and I know where it is. Pensions are paid the first of the month. That's tomorrow."

Smyslov grinned broadly. "Excellent! Now, how do you think you can get him to talk to us? I can already authorize an amnesty for his failure to report the theft earlier, but I doubt that will be enough."

"I think the fastest way will be to solve his biggest problem. He needs a place to live. Let's give him one," Grishkov said flatly.

Smyslov grunted and then looked thoughtful. "There are, of course, public housing apartments owned by the government. The waiting list for them is normally long, and the rent is low but not free. But you're proposing we just give him an apartment, correct?"

"Yes," Grishkov replied. "However, besides the need to get information quickly, this will be a cheap way to do it. Dreev was forced to leave his last apartment almost a year ago. After that long on the street at his age, he won't be around much longer. And Dreev has no family to leave the apartment to, so it will revert to the government once he dies."

Another silence followed, just as deep as the first.

Exasperated, Grishkov said, "Look, I know I'm blunt, but we don't have the luxury of sentimentality in the police. Director, you'll have to pry an apartment loose from a different government department by close of business today, and what I'm saying about Dreev should make it easy."

Seeing Smyslov's frown, Grishkov added, "Or, easier anyway. I think it's our best chance of getting Dreev to talk, and to be sure that he's telling us everything."

Smyslov cocked his head. "And how can you be sure of that?"

Grishkov shrugged. "Simple. I'll tell him that if we discover he's left out any details, we'll take away the apartment."

Smyslov nodded. "Very well." He lifted his phone from its cradle and began tersely giving orders. A few minutes later, he turned back to Grishkov.

"I'll know before you leave today whether the apartment will be available. My staff will make it clear that this is a matter of national security, so I am optimistic," Smyslov said.

Now Vasilyev tapped the file in front of him and said, "If we are successful in tracking down this SS-24 warhead, we'll need more information than I see here to deal with any device someone may have made with its nuclear core. Neda told me such technical information was critical to her success in defusing the bomb the Taliban created from a stolen Pakistani nuclear weapon."

Neda pursed her lips and frowned. "Even with such technical details, all I can do is guess. But with such information, at least it will be an educated guess."

Smyslov grinned. "Here, at least, I have anticipated your request. Complete details on the SS-24 are available right here in Moscow. Grishkov, you will remember where I believe."

Grishkov groaned and then gave a resigned nod. "Strategic Rocket Forces Headquarters."

Vasilyev's expression made it clear he was confused. "But surely they will cooperate once they understand what's at stake!"

Smyslov shook his head. "On the contrary. If they understand why you're there, you won't be allowed anywhere near the documents you need. A thermonuclear warhead stolen from the Strategic Rocket Forces? Incompetence is the kindest word that could be used to describe allowing such a theft. Other terms would include dereliction of duty and criminal neglect. No, the authorization papers I've prepared will simply say you need the information for unspecified national security reasons."

Vasilyev nodded. "Understood. Is Neda included in the authorization request?"

"I'm afraid not. Neda's naturalization as a Russian citizen was expedited at the President's direction after her outstanding performance in your last mission, and she now has one of our highest security clearances. But none of those details can be shared outside this agency, and so her appearance alone will preclude cooperation from the...conservatives...at the Strategic Rocket Forces," Smyslov said.

Grishkov nodded. "The Director is right. When I walked into their headquarters building last time with Alexei, I felt like I was traveling back in time to the 1980s. We had trouble getting any information last time, even with your father leading the way."

Neda's expression was impassive, but Vasilyev was clearly unhappy with this response.

"So, will they allow us to make copies of documents with the SS-24's technical specifications? And if not, how are we going to get any useful information to Neda?" Vasilyev asked.

Grishkov smiled. "The answer to your first question is no. However, your father had a solution. Tell me, did Alexei leave you anything after his passing? Cufflinks, for example?"

Now Vasilyev could see that Smyslov was smiling as well, but had no idea why.

"Well, yes, now that you mention it, he did. I've never worn shirts that use cufflinks, though. What do they have to do with this?" Vasilyev asked.

Grishkov nodded. "It will be easier to show you than to explain. I'll stop by your apartment after we're done here if that's OK with both of you."

Vasilyev glanced at Neda, who smiled and nodded. Grishkov was careful to keep a smile from his lips as he saw the rapid exchange. It boded well for the longevity of his friends' marriage.

Only then did Vasilyev say, "Of course! We look forward to having you visit."

"Excellent!" Smyslov beamed. "Now that we've finished our business, on to the most important phase of mission preparation!"

Right on cue, two of Smyslov's staff wheeled in a cart groaning with Russian delicacies. There was pelmini, dumplings filled with minced meat and wrapped in a thin dough, then topped with sour cream. Pirozhki, puff pastries packed with potatoes and cheese, were flanked by shashlyk, Russian kebabs with chicken and vegetables. Blini, a wheat pancake, was served rolled and filled with caviar.

Grishkov smiled when the smell from the large pot of solyanka hit him. His favorite soup, this version contained beef as well as cabbage, carrots, onions, and potatoes, and was topped with chopped pickles. Many side dishes and sliced loaves of warm, dark bread completed the feast.

Grishkov and Vasilyev had both already had the good fortune to receive this traditional Russian send off for a dangerous mission. Neda, who had never seen this much food in one place in her life, sat wide-eyed in astonishment.

Now Smyslov turned to Neda and said, "Don't think I've forgotten your religion! There's no pork lurking anywhere in these dumplings and pastries. For me, that's no sacrifice, since I've always preferred beef anyway."

Neda gave Smyslov a smile that was warm and genuine. "I appreciate you remembering, nevertheless." Pointing at the blinis, she asked, "Do I see caviar at the ends of these pancakes? I had it once in Iran many years ago, but it's been impossible for a long time to find it there at a reasonable price."

Smyslov grinned. "Indeed, it is. This is Beluga caviar, the best in the world. Though the wild Caspian Sea sturgeon that is the ordinary source of Beluga caviar is endangered, you can enjoy it here without guilt. The sturgeon that provided the caviar at this table are responsibly farmed right here in Russia and produce the finest caviar I've ever tasted. Now, enough talking! Eat!"

None of his guests had to be told twice.

Finally, everyone had finished their meal and were nibbling on one of their favorite desserts. Neda had picked a Napoleon cake, a pastry similar to the French millefeuille. It had been created by the Tsar's bakers in 1912 to celebrate the centennial of Russia's victory over Napoleon. All the men had settled on vareniki, Russian dumplings filled with cherries and topped with sour cream and powdered sugar.

Pausing to sip some strong black tea, Neda sighed and turned to Vasilyev. "So, will you still love me if I can no longer fit in my dress?"

Vasilyev grinned and whispered his answer into Neda's ear. She reddened and immediately slapped away Vasilyev's hand, which had found its way to her knee, much to Grishkov's and Smyslov's amusement.

Minutes later, they were finished, and all evidence of the meal had been removed. Each had a single shot glass before them in its place, and in the table's center was a bottle of Stolichnaya Elit vodka.

Smyslov poured each of them a shot. He raised his glass and said, "Success to us all, and confusion to our enemies!"

They all raised their glasses, cheered, and drank their shots in a single motion.

Grishkov was particularly impressed by Neda's form. She looked as though she'd been downing shots since college, though Grishkov knew she'd never touched alcohol before arriving in Russia.

Grishkov nodded to himself with approval. In this and many other ways, Neda had shown she would do whatever was necessary.

Yes, Grishkov thought to himself as he looked around the table. We have the skills and the determination.

We will indeed succeed.

CHAPTER SIX

Strategic Rocket Forces Headquarters
Moscow, Russia

Mikhail Vasilyev looked at the grim concrete edifice before them with a distinct lack of enthusiasm and then turned to Anatoly Grishkov.

"I see what you meant about feeling like you were back in the 1980s," Vasilyev said.

Grishkov arched one eyebrow. "Wait until you get inside. Since you are by far the better-dressed agent, I'll let you do the talking."

Indeed, Vasilyev was resplendent in his new, custom-fitted suit and fine cotton shirt. With, of course, French cuffs held together by his father's cufflinks.

The previous day, Grishkov had shown Vasilyev how they worked. Vasilyev's father Alexei had the cufflinks custom made by a friend who dated from his KGB days. There his friend had worked in the Seventh Directorate, which among other things, produced surveillance equipment. Like Alexei, he had continued in the new FSB, but now with access to better technology.

Each cufflink contained a tiny optical lens concealed in the cufflink's black "stone" surface. The image collected was stored directly to an SD card, embedded within the cufflink.

Alexei had told Grishkov that the challenging task for his friend had been writing the software that stitched and sharpened the two images from the cufflinks together. This software was necessary because the cufflinks were intended to work in tandem, capturing images side by side as each hand moved down the page.

They walked through the entry door and were immediately before a lone receptionist, a burly man who sat behind bulletproof glass next to a heavy metal door. It was the only one leading inside the building from this entrance.

Vasilyev said calmly, "Captain Vasilyev to see Comrade Pavel Golovkin, accompanied by Captain Grishkov. We have authorization papers."

The receptionist frowned, and said, "I remember those names, though I don't remember you. And the names I remember were from men with the FSB."

Vasilyev nodded. "Yes, you're right on both counts. We are with the FSB. You don't remember me because the last time it was my father who came with my colleague, Captain Grishkov."

"Humph," the receptionist said. Pulling a lever that slid a metal drawer towards them from below the glass, he added, "Papers, please." Vasilyev and Grishkov both handed over their FSB IDs, to which Vasilyev added a thick sheaf of authorization papers.

The receptionist picked up the phone. "Comrade Golovkin, please. Yes, FSB Captains Vasilyev and Grishkov are here to see you. Yes, they have authorization papers to conduct research. Very well, I will have them wait for you to escort them to the archives."

The receptionist pulled out two plastic cards with the word "Visitor" on them in large letters, each attached to a metal chain. Pulling on the lever, the metal drawer slid towards them again, and the receptionist said sharply, "All phones, cameras, weapons, and metal objects of all types must be deposited with me until your departure from this building. You will pass through a metal detector before you are allowed entry past this lobby, and any metal objects detected will be confiscated permanently."

Once they had dropped everything they were carrying in the drawer, it went back and then returned with the visitor cards and Vasilyev's authorization papers, but not their IDs.

"Wear these at all times while you are inside this headquarters. You must remain in the company of your escort at all times. Failure to do so is a breach of security regulations. You will retrieve your IDs and possessions when you return your visitor cards."

Pointing to two hardcast plastic chairs that appeared to have been in place since the building opened, the receptionist added, "Sit, please, and await Comrade Golovkin."

Once they were sitting, Grishkov leaned towards Vasilyev and said in a near whisper, "Spooky, like he was some kind of robot. Everything that receptionist said was the same as the last time I was here with your father."

Vasilyev gave Grishkov a faint smile. "And why would it be any different? He's probably said the same thing to visitors hundreds of times. Maybe thousands."

At least they didn't have to wait long. After just a few minutes, the heavy metal door opened, and Senior Academic Researcher Golovkin was gesturing to enter.

Grishkov thought to himself that the man looked just as he had the last time. A mole in human form, right down to the blinking eyes and skittering walk. A crooked bow tie, gold wire-rim glasses, and a perfectly bald head completed the picture. As Grishkov had suggested based on his father's performance during their last visit, Vasilyev spoke to him with deep respect as they walked down the halls.

"Comrade Golovkin, it is a genuine pleasure to meet you. My father told me a great deal about you, in particular, how helpful you were during his last visit," Vasilyev said.

Golovkin blinked and picked up his already brisk pace. Grishkov thought to himself that he'd never imagined a speedy mole. Unless something was chasing it?

Golovkin confirmed Grishkov's guess. "It won't be long until my boss finds out you're here. We have to be done before that happens. What do you need?"

Vasilyev hadn't expected Golovkin to get to the point quite so quickly but didn't hesitate.

"We need technical data on the SS-24 warhead," Vasilyev said.

Golovkin nodded and turned a corner. "Warheads," he said absently. "There were ten on each missile. But then you probably knew that much, at least."

Without waiting for a reply, Golovkin settled to the task of unlocking the door to the record archives, which took several steps. First, Golovkin placed his hand on a scanner and bent towards a lens that appeared to examine his right eye for a retinal scan. Finally, he entered a code onto a keypad and gestured for the others to follow as the door slid open.

Rows of plain metal file cabinets marched in ranks that to Vasilyev's eye appeared to number in the dozens. Seeing his expression, Golovkin laughed. "Captain Grishkov may remember what I told him on his last visit. We've disposed of all records relating to weapons that were destroyed either due to replacement with more advanced models or due to strategic weapons agreements with the Americans. Naturally, that includes the SS-24."

Seeing the look of confusion and dismay that was now on both Vasilyev and Grishkov, Golovkin shook his head. "Don't worry. That's just what I told my boss. I doubt you're here for the records that really were destroyed, like maintenance schedules. Technical schematics and operational instructions, yes?"

Vasilyev and Grishkov both nodded.

Golovkin walked directly to an unmarked filing cabinet about halfway through their massed ranks. Then he pulled a large key ring from his pocket and began fishing for the right ones. A metal bar passed through the drawers' handles, making it physically impossible to open them without removing the padlock that secured the bar at its top.

Vasilyev and Grishkov exchanged glances, but both remained silent. Yes, the contrast between the technology at the entrance and now here at the source of the information they needed was striking. But at least it was nearly in their hands.

Grishkov was impressed with how quickly Golovkin found the right key and extracted the heavy metal bar from the cabinet. Practice, he supposed.

"Here's the file you need. I see you have your father's equipment," Golovkin said, pointing at Vasilyev's cufflinks and then at a nearby small wooden table. "Use it to copy the file there. Hurry."

Vasilyev was only partially successful at keeping astonishment away from his expression but wasted no time following Golovkin's instructions.

While Vasilyev worked to copy the file, Grishkov couldn't help asking Golovkin, "Why are you helping us? And aren't you risking trouble with your boss?"

Vasilyev's frown told Grishkov he didn't like his questions. Grishkov saw, though, that his queries didn't stop Vasilyev from his methodical work copying the file.

Golovkin shrugged. "When you were here the last time asking about the nuclear 'suitcase' weapons used by Spetsnaz forces, it was evident that one or more had gone missing. I assume the same is true for the SS-24 warheads."

Grishkov nodded but said nothing.

"Good. The less I know, the better," Golovkin said with a smile. "As to why I'm helping you, that should be obvious. I've dedicated my life to preserving records on the weapons that have kept us safe from enemies like the Americans. If any of those weapons were stolen and not recovered, that protection could unravel very quickly."

Grishkov looked at Golovkin directly. "And the risk to you?"

Golovkin gave a short, dry chuckle in response. "Not so great as you might imagine. Replacing me would not be easy, as my boss well knows."

Golovkin waved at the ranks of label-free cabinets and smiled.

"No, as long as I've followed the rules, my boss will bark but can do little to bite," Golovkin said confidently.

As though summoned by repeated mention, the door to the records storage room flew open to admit the same corpulent figure Grishkov remembered from his last visit. While he now understood that the "mole man" persona Golovkin had adopted was an act, he was sure the same wasn't true of his boss.

Just as before, the man's wobbling neck fat made Grishkov think of an angry bullfrog. If anything, the man's beady red eyes and the stench of vodka that preceded him like a cloud made it clear the intervening years had done nothing to improve him.

"Golovkin, what are they doing here! After the last time these FSB men came poking their noses where they have no business, I told you never again!" Golovkin's boss said in an angry roar.

Grishkov had to swallow a smile at Golovkin's transformation back to the hesitant, hunched figure he'd presented at the start of their visit.

Blinking through his thick glasses, Golovkin answered in a quavering voice.

"Yes, Comrade Director. I tried to reach you, but your secretary said you were unavailable. These FSB men do have proper authorization papers, and I knew you wouldn't want me to take action contrary to regulations without your direct order. Shall I tell them to leave now, sir?" Golovkin asked.

As the man's eyes bulged and the veins in his neck throbbed alarmingly, Grishkov thought for a moment that a stroke might solve Golovkin's problems on the spot. After a moment, though, the full meaning of Golovkin's words penetrated.

If he tried to do anything to Golovkin, he might be asked why he had been unavailable for Golovkin's call. Since the only answer was to be found in the vodka bottle he kept in his bottom desk drawer, it would be best to wrap this up.

Collecting himself with a visible effort, the Director said in a lower voice. "Yes. They must leave immediately. Did you give them copies of any documents?"

"No, sir. That would be completely contrary to regulations!" Golovkin said in a mildly indignant tone. He then pointed to Vasilyev and Grishkov, whose hands were clearly empty.

The Director's eyes narrowed. "Secure that file," he said, pointing at the file on the desk. "Then escort them out. Once they're out of the building, come to my office."

"At once, Comrade Director," Golovkin replied.

Moments later, Vasilyev and Grishkov were trailing behind Golovkin as they approached the exit.

"Did you get what you needed?" Golovkin asked in a near whisper.

Vasilyev nodded. "I finished seconds before your boss arrived. Should I have our Director call yours to explain why we were here?"

Golovkin snorted with laughter. "That might be the only way to get me fired. No, leave it to me. I've outlasted five Directors, and this one is no real challenge. I'll still be here long after he's drunk himself into an early grave."

With that, he opened the exit door. "Good luck to you both," Golovkin said in a low voice as he closed the door behind them.

CHAPTER SEVEN

Myrhorod Air Base, Ukraine

Captain Josh Pettigrew sat at his classroom desk and looked around the room at the fifteen young Ukrainian officers he would be training.

They all looked back with frank curiosity.

Pettigrew had to suppress a smile. Since he'd been given this assignment with almost no notice, Pettigrew knew none of his students could have had time to find out much about him.

Of course, given how his last few assignments had gone, it would be alarming if any of his students had learned much about Pettigrew. Most of his file was now classified as Sensitive Compartmented Information (SCI), which meant even few of his fellow US Air Force officers could find out more than basic details on his career.

At least this assignment promised to be a quiet one. Yes, Ukraine's conflict with Russia continued to simmer. But peace talks appeared to be on track, and it had been months since Ukraine's Air Force had seen any real action.

Yes, a few times in the past year, Russian fighter jets had "strayed" into Ukrainian airspace. But they'd quickly retreated across the border when approached by Ukrainian fighters.

Pettigrew was willing to bet those were incidents generated by local Russian commanders. Or young pilots bored with drilling holes in the air and hoping for some action.

If that was the worst that happened during this tour, Pettigrew was looking forward to some downtime. He'd read about many sights and activities available here on the multiple long commercial flights into Ukraine.

Compared to his last overseas assignment in Saudi Arabia, this one promised to be a vacation.

Pettigrew stood up and introduced himself. The Ukrainian students all had military regulation haircuts, were all in their twenties, and in excellent physical condition. Thankfully, the students were also all wearing standard flight suit coveralls, with their names and ranks visible on their left chest.

And in the Roman characters Pettigrew was used to, rather than the Cyrillic ones in use just about everywhere else in Ukraine. Pettigrew correctly guessed that this was part of Ukraine's push to join NATO.

That wasn't happening until peace with Russia was not only accomplished but likely to last.

"Lieutenant Bondar, who do you expect to face in combat?" Pettigrew asked.

Bondar hesitated, and finally said, "Separatists, sir."

Pettigrew nodded. "And who is arming those separatists, Lieutenant?"

"Russia, sir," Bondar replied.

"Correct," Pettigrew said. Then he pointed to a man in the back of the classroom.

"Lieutenant Melnik, how many aircraft of all types has Ukraine lost to hostile fire during this conflict?" Pettigrew asked.

"I'm not sure exactly, sir. I think about twenty or so," Melnik replied.

"You think correctly," Pettigrew said. He clicked on his first Power-Point slide.

It showed small icons for different types of aircraft. Next to the images were numbers.

"Losses have been five Mi-8 and five Mi-24 helicopters, one Su-24, four Su-25s, two MiG-29 fighter jets and one each of An-26, An-30 and Il-76 transport aircraft. The total is twenty," Pettigrew said.

The room was quiet as the Ukrainian officers looked at the slide.

Pettigrew knew they were thinking about the lost aircrew represented by each icon and number.

His next slide showed an autocannon.

"This is a 23mm anti-aircraft twin autocannon. It accounted for some of the aircraft shot down on the previous slide. Can anyone identify the model?" Pettigrew asked.

Several hands went up. Pettigrew pointed to a man on the far left. He walked close enough to see that it was Lieutenant Smirnova.

"It's a ZU-23, sir," Smirnova said.

"Correct," Pettigrew said. "We happen to be very familiar with this weapon because it accounted for many of our aircraft shot down during the Vietnam War."

The next slide showed a large tracked vehicle painted in a dark green camouflage pattern.

"This is a Russian medium-range surface to air missile system. Does anyone know the name of this system?" Pettigrew asked.

"That's a Buk, sir," Melnik replied immediately. Pettigrew was glad the look Melnik sent the image wasn't directed at him.

"Yes. We call the original Buk the SA-11 Gadfly and the improved version the SA-17 Grizzly. And this systems' most notorious target, Lieutenant?" Pettigrew asked quietly.

"Malaysia Airlines Flight 17," Melnik replied.

"Correct," Pettigrew said. "Over three hundred passengers and crew killed, still the single deadliest shootdown incident in history. Now, can anyone tell me if any equipment besides the examples I've just shown you have shot down aircraft over Ukraine?"

"Iglas, sir," said Bondar.

"That's an important one," Pettigrew said. "Why haven't I put an Igla on a slide?"

"Because you're sure we've all seen one," Melnik said.

"That's one reason," Pettigrew said, nodding. "Accurate and giving next to no warning, the Igla is top of the nightmare list for any pilot flying lower than eleven thousand meters. Which is everyone here, right?"

All the students nodded.

"The other reason I haven't bothered showing you an Igla is that they're small enough to be man-portable, which means they're tough to find from the air. Not impossible, but you're much more likely to spot a ZU-23 autocannon or a Buk surface to air missile carrier," Pettigrew said.

Pettigrew paused. "I know you haven't been told which drone you'll be training on for this class. Part of that was security. Part of it was a last-minute change to what you're getting."

Laying the control for the slide display on the table next to him, Pettigrew asked, "How many of you passed up the chance to train on the Bayraktar drone to get into this class?"

Every single hand went up.

Pettigrew nodded. "The Turks did a good job on the Bayraktar. It can loiter at an altitude of fifty-five hundred meters for about a day and can go even higher if you're willing to sacrifice some endurance. And of course, it's armed with munitions that have proven effective on the battlefield."

Pettigrew picked up the control and clicked for the next slide.

The reaction from the students to the image on the screen was... silence.

Well, Pettigrew hadn't expected them to be thrilled.

"I'm hoping you'd already guessed that given the political realities of supplying an American combat system to a country fighting a nuclear-armed enemy, we weren't going to sell you an armed drone. But there's more to this drone than you may expect," Pettigrew said.

The continued silence suggested his audience would need some convincing.

"The RQ-21 Blackjack uses a catapult launcher, and so doesn't need a runway. It weighs just sixty-two kilos. It only uses one kilo of fuel per hour, so can stay on station for up to seventeen hours, with a range a little under a hundred kilometers," Pettigrew said.

Smirnova raised his hand, and Pettigrew nodded.

"Well, sir, something that small can't carry satellite communications equipment. So, we'll have to control it from fairly close range, right?" Smirnova asked.

"I'm glad you asked that, Lieutenant. Now we come to that last-minute change I mentioned," Pettigrew replied, bringing up the next slide.

It showed a close-up of part of the Blackjack.

"Up until recently, the standard satellite communications package would indeed have exceeded the Blackjack's total payload capacity. However, recent advances have enabled us to include satellite control as part of every Blackjack we've sold to Ukraine," Pettigrew said.

An excited murmur from the students told Pettigrew this was what they wanted to hear.

"The original Blackjack could generate full-motion video day or night, plus infrared and electro-optical imagery. All of that data was processed through an automatic identification system. The original Blackjack could also be used for laser range-finding of targets," Pettigrew said.

Pettigrew grinned. "The version we've sold you can do all that. Now, it also includes a sensor integrating a new electro-optical camera, wide-area imager, short wave hyperspectral imager, and high-resolution inspection camera."

"Sir, what sort of support equipment does the Blackjack need?" Bondar asked.

"An excellent question, Lieutenant," Pettigrew replied. "What we call a single Blackjack system consists of five Blackjack drones, two ground control centers, and associated launch and recovery equipment. That one system could give you complete coverage of every inch of Donbas, but of course, you're getting more than one system."

Pettigrew paused and smiled. "At some point, the operators need to sleep."

The students all laughed, and Pettigrew relaxed a bit. As he'd hoped, the students' initial disappointment was visibly giving way to enthusiasm.

"That brings us to our next slide," Pettigrew said.

The image showed a vehicle with a two-wheeled trailer behind it.

"You can see here just how small the catapult system is that's used to launch the Blackjack. Now, let's look over the other system components..."

CHAPTER EIGHT

Ministry of Defense Pension Disbursement Office
Moscow, Russia

Mikhail Vasilyev and Anatoly Grishkov sat in a plain dark sedan parked across the street from the pension disbursement office. Each of them had a file photo of Vitaly Dreev, the man that Andreas Burmakin had identified as the coworker who had discovered the missing SS-24 warhead.

Vasilyev shifted uncomfortably in the sedan's driver's seat. The vehicle was not a luxury model.

"So, tell me why we can't just wait for Dreev in the building's lobby?" Vasilyev asked.

Grishkov smiled. "First, let me note that I've apprehended quite a few people over my police career, so when I suggest an approach, I'm drawing on experience."

"Granted," Vasilyev replied. "So, let me benefit from your experience. Why are we here?"

"Well, we'd be immediately spotted by anyone in the lobby as officials of some kind, probably police. That word would be passed on by the first pensioner to spot us to others outside the building," Grishkov said.

"Understood," Vasilyev said. "But this pension is Dreev's only source of income. If your guess is right that we haven't found him so far because he's homeless, isn't he likely to come in anyway to get his money? After all, he has no reason to think we'd be there for him."

Grishkov nodded. "True. So let's suppose he does come in the lobby despite being warned. We look at the photos we each have and spot him as he comes in. Then what?"

"Well, we wouldn't approach him right away. Maybe wait until after he's at the counter getting his money," Vasilyev said.

"Good," Grishkov said with a smile. "And do you think you'd be able to control your 'aha, there's the man we've been looking for' reaction while Dreev was sauntering up to the counter?"

"OK, maybe not. But even if Dreev does run, do you doubt that we could catch him?" Vasilyev asked.

"Well, maybe. But have you ever seen a movie or TV show where police are chasing someone who tries to cross a street without looking and is run over by a car?" Grishkov asked, gesturing towards the heavy traffic between their car and the target building.

"Yes, I have," Vasilyev said. "But does that happen in real life?"

Grishkov nodded. "As a patrolman, I saw it happen twice. The first suspect escaped with minor bruises. The second wasn't so lucky. Even worse, it turned out he wasn't the one who committed the crime. Ever since I've vowed not to repeat that experience."

Just a few minutes later, Dreev walked up to the building entrance. He was not easy to recognize from his military file photo, but a glance between Vasilyev and Grishkov confirmed they agreed. Older, thinner, and with less hair. But still Dreev.

As planned, they waited until Dreev entered the building. Then Vasilyev and Grishkov crossed the street and waited outside the entrance.

This time their wait was longer. But after half an hour, Dreev exited the building. Vasilyev and Grishkov converged on him, with Grishkov to his front.

Flipping open his FSB identification card and badge, Grishkov said, "Vitaly Dreev, we have some questions for you. We just need information. You are not a suspect, and you do not face any charges."

Dreev's eyes darted back and forth between Grishkov and Vasilyev, and the heavy traffic at his right elbow. Grishkov could see Dreev was calculating his chances of escape.

"In fact, there may be a reward if you can give us the information we seek," Grishkov said.

Far from being reassured, Dreev's eyes narrowed with suspicion. "Government agents bearing gifts? Please. Why don't you just tell me what you want here and now?"

Grishkov spread his arms. "This was my idea. I served too, and I think a lot of Soviet veterans got a raw deal. You're not in cuffs, are you? Why not come with us and hear me out? If you don't like what I have to say, you can leave then."

For a moment, Vasilyev thought that Dreev would try to run after all. Then, Dreev shrugged. "All right. I'll hear what you have to say."

As Vasilyev drove, Grishkov asked Dreev just one question.

"When we were unable to find you, we thought you might be homeless. But it looks like you've been living indoors, yes?" Grishkov asked, gesturing towards Dreev's clothes. Though plain, they were clean, as was Dreev himself.

Dreev grimaced. "Who told you that, my soon to be ex-wife? Yes, when she kicked me out, I'm sure she thought I'd end up on the streets. I've been couch surfing for some time now. But I'm close to running out of friends ready to put up with me. It probably won't be long before she's proved right. My pension certainly won't cover renting an apartment."

A few minutes later, their car pulled up in front of a tall apartment building. Grishkov had to swallow the question that immediately came to mind as Vasilyev parked the sedan.

Was Vasilyev sure this was the right address?

There had been no time for Grishkov to check on the apartment Smyslov had arranged to put in Dreev's name. One of Smyslov's staff had passed him a folder filled with documents and handed him a set of keys.

He'd just said, "The Director said to tell you this was the best he could do."

Based on that comment, Grishkov had been expecting Soviet-era public housing.

This building was not that.

It was all glass and steel and looked like it would have been more at home in a city like London or New York.

Well, Grishkov thought, that was the exterior. Maybe once we're inside, it will prove to be no more than a facade.

The lobby was dominated by a chrome and glass reception desk. Seated there was a fit man with dark, close-cropped hair and a bearing that shouted "ex-military" to Grishkov.

A man in a suit sitting on a nearby leather sofa was reading a newspaper. Another more casually dressed man was looking over a digital display mounted to the wall on the far left corner of the lobby. From this distance, Grishkov couldn't be sure, but the screen seemed to be showing vacant apartments for rent.

Grishkov was sure, though, that if he made one wrong move, three weapons would be pointed at him. And quickly.

So, "the best he could do" was another example of the Director's sense of humor.

Grishkov sighed. Well, the carrot would be juicy. Now to see if it would do the trick.

Sliding his ID folder and the file folder containing the apartment's papers to the receptionist, Grishkov waited mutely for questions.

There were none.

"Captain Grishkov, Captain Vasilyev, Mr. Dreev," the receptionist said with a smile. "Welcome. We've been expecting you. Please, go right up. The elevators are straight ahead."

Grishkov saw several reactions from Dreev. First, that he'd been impressed by what he'd seen so far. Next, that he'd also seen the effort to disguise the three armed security guards in the lobby.

Finally, that Dreev was becoming more suspicious by the second.

They stepped into one of the four elevators, which quickly whisked them to the twelfth floor. As they exited, Dreev looked back at it and shook his head.

"Two things make that elevator different than any other I've seen in a Moscow apartment building. First, it worked. Second, it didn't smell like piss."

Pointing at Grishkov, Dreev said, "I'm not going one more step without another look at that supposed FSB ID." Then he jerked his chin towards Vasilyev. "His, too."

Grishkov looked at Vasilyev and nodded. They both handed their IDs to Dreev and silently stood while Dreev examined them both.

Finally, Dreev shrugged and handed the IDs back. "OK, if they're fakes, they're excellent ones." Then he looked at Grishkov. "One thing that convinced me was that your ID's not that old. But seeing you now, it's obvious the last couple of years weren't easy ones."

Grishkov nodded. "You're right. Now, the apartment where we'll talk is right there," he said, pointing two doors down.

The professional in Grishkov nodded with approval as the key slid into the door's sturdy lock. No easily spoofed key cards here, and he knew the lock's model. Though any lock could be defeated by a professional with the right tools, Grishkov doubted he could do it quietly enough to avoid alerting the apartment's occupants.

Grishkov swung the door open and held his breath. After all this buildup, would the apartment itself prove a disappointment?

No.

Furnishing the apartment was a detail that had occurred to Grishkov only on the ride to the building. He'd thought wryly that this failure would have come as no surprise to his wife, Arisha.

Fortunately, Smyslov's staff had not forgotten. Not only was the apartment furnished, but it also appeared to have been decorated by a professional told that its occupant would be a single male. Wood and leather dominated living spaces, while granite and stainless steel could be seen in the kitchen to the left. The floors were a light-colored wood.

Grishkov could see Dreev's eyes going first to the large digital TV mounted in the living room. Grishkov casually gestured in that direction, saying, "Let's have a seat and talk."

Dreev shrugged and walked forward, finally gingerly sitting on the large dark leather sofa. He sighed as the smell of new leather washed over him.

"I always figured the secret police lived well," Dreev said. "I never imaged how well," he added, shaking his head.

Grishkov sat on the sofa next to Dreev, while Vasilyev sat in a matching leather chair on the other side of the heavy wood coffee table in the middle of the room.

Passing the file folder to Dreev, Grishkov said, "Before we start with questions, have a look at these papers."

Dreev shrugged and began looking through the papers. Very quickly, his look of puzzlement was replaced with anger.

"Is this some kind of a joke?" Dreev asked. Before he could say any more, Grishkov interrupted.

"Look through all the papers, including the stamps and seals at the end," Grishkov said quietly.

Dreev clearly wanted to say more, but finally frowned and looked through the entire lease.

"So, if I called Moscow city authorities, they'd confirm that I'm the legal owner of this luxury apartment?" Dreev asked.

Grishkov silently slid a cell phone towards Dreev across the coffee table. Dreev looked at it and then shook his head.

"If this is some elaborate ruse, I'm sure they're in on it too," Dreev said thoughtfully. "So, what's the catch?"

Grishkov nodded. "A good question. There are several."

Dreev visibly relaxed. "That's more like the FSB I know. What are they?"

"First," Grishkov said, "You aren't actually the owner of this apartment. You are a tenant with guaranteed free occupancy for the rest of your life. You may not sell it, or its contents and all rights to its use revert to the government upon your death."

Dreev nodded. "That's fine. My children are grown and have moved away from Moscow. They have their own places and their own lives. I hardly ever hear from them anymore. Next?"

Grishkov handed Dreev a new cell phone. "This is a secure cell phone. My number is the only one programmed. Use it if you think of anything relevant after we finish speaking today. Also, you are to keep it charged and ready to respond to my call at all times if we have more questions."

Dreev shrugged. "Fine," he said.

"Here's the part you have to listen to most carefully. If your answers to any of the questions I'm about to ask are false or incomplete in any way, you lose this apartment. We will be the sole judge of whether your cooperation has been satisfactory," Grishkov said.

Dreev nodded again. "Anything else?" he asked.

Grishkov shook his head. "No. Now, why do you imagine we want to talk to you?"

Dreev gave a short, bitter laugh. "I'm not an idiot. I suppose you've already talked to Burmakin? How's he doing? I haven't heard from him since we worked together on warhead disassembly."

"Other FSB agents did talk to him, and he told us about the missing SS-24 warhead. I'm sorry to inform you that he subsequently died. Cancer," Grishkov said.

Dreev shrugged. "Deathbed confession. That sounds like him. After all the warheads we worked on, I always thought cancer would be what got me too."

His eyes narrowed. "So, your gift might not cost you as much as I thought. This is starting to make a lot more sense."

Grishkov shook his head. "You look fine to me. For all either of us knows, you'll live another thirty years. Now, what can you tell us about the missing warhead?"

Dreev paused and finally said, "OK, I'm going to take a chance and tell you everything. You already know enough to lock me up if that's what you want to do, so I guess I've got nothing to lose. First, it's not warhead. It's warheads. Specifically, two."

Grishkov and Vasilyev both looked at Dreev with dismay. "Two?" Grishkov asked. "Both five hundred kiloton SS-24 warheads?"

Dreev nodded. "Yes, from the same missile. Burmakin didn't tell you about the second one because he didn't know. I found it after he left that day."

"Do you have any idea who could have stolen the warheads?" Grishkov asked.

"I have an excellent idea," Dreev said with grim satisfaction. "And I hope you catch the bastard."

'Yes?" Grishkov prompted.

"Pofistal Arbakov," Dreev said.

Grishkov's eyes widened, and he had to suppress a laugh. "Well, I was going to ask if you were sure of the name, but I can see how you managed to remember it."

Vasilyev frowned. "I don't understand. What's so special about the name?"

Now Grishkov did laugh, and Dreev did too. Grishkov explained the meaning of 'Pofistal' and saw Vasilyev's expression quickly change from confused to incredulous.

"Stalin, defeater of fascism? I'm too young to have any personal knowledge of Stalin's cult of personality, but I have trouble believing it went that far. I've also never heard the name 'Pofistal' before," Vasilyev said.

Grishkov shrugged. "I'm guessing that just about everyone still living who was born with the name has changed it by now. Except for this fellow, it seems. Probably tells us something about him."

Turning to Dreev, Grishkov asked, "How do you know it was him? And do you have any idea where we could find him?"

Dreev opened his hands wide and said, "I'm going to be as clear as possible here. I don't know anything for sure. But I said I had a good idea because I pulled the documents for that SS-24 missile's warheads from the administration office. Burmakin knew nothing about that either, since I did it two days after I found the missing warheads, once he went off shift. There was nobody else in the building because we were the only ones working on a holiday weekend."

Dreev paused. "I guess you know from my file that I was an SS-24 crewman before they put me to work disassembling them. I'd bet anything that the only person who could have stolen two of the warheads was the man in charge of pulling them from the missile. And the signature on the documents was Pofistal Arbakov," he concluded.

Grishkov nodded. "Do you have the documents?"

Dreev shook his head. "No. I put them back to make sure they wouldn't be missed. I thought about making a copy, but only two details in the file mattered, and I knew I'd never forget them. Besides, we were thoroughly searched every time we left the plant, and any copies would have been discovered."

"And where could we look for this man?" Grishkov asked.

"Right," Dreev said. "That's the second detail. Pervomaysk, Ukraine. That's where the missile was based. But with a name like Pofistal, you can bet he's a Russian speaker. A lot of them have left Ukraine for Russia."

Grishkov grunted. "But from your experience, how easy would it be to transport two SS-24 warheads undetected from Ukraine to Russia?"

That made Dreev stop and think. "You're right. I don't see how he could do it, especially alone. At least at first, he must have hidden it at the same base where the warhead was initially removed. There'd be equipment there that would let him later load the warheads on a truck."

Dreev paused and then shook his head. "But how would he offload them at the other end? Never mind the problem of hiding something the size of two SS-24 warheads from a border checkpoint. No, without help, those warheads would probably still be somewhere in Ukraine."

Grishkov and Vasilyev both nodded but sat quietly.

Finally, Dreev scowled. "So, if I knew all this, why did I say nothing? Well, until a few years ago, when they moved out, I told myself it was to protect my children. Then to protect my wife. When she kicked me out, I thought about reporting this. Then I asked myself whether that would be fair to Burmakin."

Dreev looked at Grishkov bleakly. "The truth is, though, that I was just a coward who didn't want to go to prison. So, what now?"

Grishkov reached into his pocket and removed the set of keys he'd used to enter the apartment. Another key on the set opened the apartment's mailbox.

Then he put the keys on top of the folder holding Dreev's apartment papers.

"We made a deal, and I will honor it. Make sure you honor it too, by calling me if you think of anything else that could help us find the warheads," Grishkov said.

"I swear I will," Dreev said. "I have no reasons left to hide anything, and every reason to tell you all I know," he added, looking around the apartment in wonder.

Grishkov nodded, and a few moments later was standing next to Vasilyev waiting for the elevator to take them downstairs.

"So," Vasilyev asked, "Do you believe Dreev has told us all he knows?"

Grishkov nodded absently. "Yes. Some small detail may come to him later, but today I think he's told us everything he could remember."

"I think we should check with Neda to see if she's been able to make use of the SS-24 technical data we passed her. Then, all travel together to Ukraine," Vasilyev said.

"Agreed," Grishkov replied. "And who knows? Maybe we'll find both warheads sitting in storage right where Arbakov left them."

As the elevator door opened, Grishkov and Vasilyev entered and looked at each other.

And then began laughing uncontrollably.

By the time the elevator doors opened, and they both emerged, Grishkov and Vasilyev were just managing to return to normal. The receptionist looked at them curiously, but said nothing and just nodded politely.

Yes, Grishkov thought, it was good to laugh now. It would probably be their last opportunity for some time to come.

CHAPTER NINE

En route to Domodedovo Airport, Moscow

"Explain why we're doing all this, please," Grishkov grumbled. "It makes no sense to me."

Vasilyev sighed. "When I called Neda to tell her we were en route and to see what she'd learned as you suggested, she said there was no time to waste. That we had to get to Ukraine right away. And that we would talk on the way, once we pick her up."

"OK," Grishkov nodded. "Then why do we have to take two flights to get to Kyiv? I've been there before, and it was a nonstop flight that just took a couple of hours or so."

"Well, that must have been years ago, because nonstop commercial flights in both directions between Russia and Ukraine ended after our...reunification with Crimea. Getting clearance for a nonstop diplomatic charter flight would have taken longer than two flights, so..." Vasilyev's voice trailed off.

"So we're taking Belavia, one of the 'baby Flots' born from the old USSR version of Aeroflot. Well, I checked, and at least we're not on an old Tupolev. Both our flight to Minsk in Belarus and the onward flight to Kyiv are on Boeing 737s. Versions built before the one that had so many problems, thank goodness," Grishkov said.

"I'm glad you approve of that much," Vasilyev said with a smile.

"OK, so why do we need a driver? I'm perfectly capable of driving to the airport." Looking forward to the front seat, Grishkov quickly added, "No offense."

The driver glanced up at the rearview mirror and gave a quick smile. "None taken," he said mildly.

Vasilyev shook his head in exasperation. "You understand that we'll all need suitcases for this trip so as not to appear conspicuous upon arrival in Kyiv, yes? Neda is preparing them and will have them ready by the time we stop at our apartment. Which happens to be on the way to the airport."

"Now I have you," Grishkov said triumphantly. "We're hardly the same size."

Grishkov saw the driver's eyes dart to the rearview mirror and heard his poorly concealed snort of amusement. Vasilyev was, indeed, both taller and thinner than the heavily muscled Grishkov.

"The clothes in your suitcase will be just for show. Since they'll be mine, though, I would like to have them back," Vasilyev said.

Grishkov's eyes narrowed. "So, either I'll be running around Ukraine naked, or clothes will be given to me after we get there. Let me guess - spy games of some sort?"

Vasilyev grinned. "We have people at our Embassy in Kyiv working on that now. Of course, we were only able to get visas quickly enough for our flights because we're accredited to the Embassy as temporary personnel."

With that, their car pulled up in front of Vasilyev's apartment building. The lobby door opened immediately, and Neda emerged, dragging a suitcase and a carryon behind her. All three men in the car exited quickly to help her.

"There are two suitcases still in the lobby," Neda said as they approached. Handing a suitcase to Vasilyev, she said, "Everyone gets one."

Moments later, the car was loaded and on its way to the airport.

Vasilyev gestured towards the driver. "You may recognize him as the same man the Director assigned to drive us to the airport for our last mission. You may speak freely."

"Very well," Neda said. Then she sat still for a moment gnawing on her lower lip, clearly unsure how to begin.

Hoping to help, Vasilyev asked gently, "Do you have any drawings to show us?"

On their last mission, Neda had filled pages with freehand drawings of possible nuclear weapon designs. The atomic cores of stolen missiles had been used to power weapons with new detonation mechanisms.

But Neda shook her head, and whispered, "No. There will be no drawings of various possible detonation mechanisms. This time they're not needed."

Vasilyev frowned. "Why not? Do you need more information than we were able to obtain from Strategic Rocket Forces Headquarters?"

Neda shook her head again. "That's not it. I have all the information I need to tell you that whoever has the weapons doesn't need to extract their nuclear cores and fashion new detonation mechanisms. He can use them just as they are. And obtain their full five hundred kiloton yield. Each."

A stunned silence settled over the car, finally broken by a soft oath from the driver. "Sorry," he said, with a backward glance.

"I don't blame you," Vasilyev replied.

"But how?" Grishkov asked. "When the Taliban stole Pakistani nuclear weapons, they had to remove the nuclear cores to make new weapons. You told us that's because the Pakistanis had arming codes that had to be transmitted to the weapons, which the Taliban couldn't access. Don't tell me that's not true for our weapons!"

"It's not that simple!" Neda replied. "I don't know if I'll have time to explain before we get to the airport, but I'm going to try."

Neda drew a deep breath and continued. "OK, first, you know these missiles were designed in the early 80s, and pulled from their silos in the early 90s, right?"

Vasilyev and Grishkov both nodded.

"Good," Neda said. "Now, did either of you have a personal computer in the early 90s?"

Both shook their heads.

"OK, do you remember the first one you did have?" Neda asked.

Vasilyev and Grishkov both nodded.

"How would you compare them to a computer you could buy today?" Neda asked.

Vasilyev laughed. "My first computer didn't even have a color screen," he said.

Grishkov nodded. "And mine had no hard drive."

"Exactly," Neda said. "In the decades since the SS-24 arming mechanism was designed, computer hardware and software capabilities have advanced tremendously. By comparison, the Pakistani scientists who designed their nuclear missiles had access to the latest technology."

Neda paused. "But that's not the only reason I'm sure whoever has the SS-24 warheads will be able to arm them."

Vasilyev and Grishkov both looked at Neda with alarm but silently waited for her to continue.

"The missiles that had their warheads stolen were pulled from silos.

However, there was also a rail-mobile version of the SS-24. The arming mechanism and code type were the same for both versions," Neda said grimly, shaking her head.

Vasilyev and Grishkov looked at each other in confusion. Vasilyev asked first. "Why is that so important?"

Neda frowned. "Sorry. Of course, that's not obvious to you. Look, for a fixed silo-based missile, you can have a dedicated underground cable carry the arming code, and that's just what they did. But a rail-mobile missile has to receive its arming code by radio. That means the code has to be relatively short, or you risk part of the code being missed in transmission and arming failure. This is especially so if an enemy nuclear weapon had already detonated nearby."

Grishkov snorted. "Surely no one thought these rail-mobile missiles could survive a near-miss by an American nuclear weapon!"

Neda smiled. "The files you obtained included the results of a Soviet test conducted in 1991 when one hundred thousand TM-57 antitank mines were detonated between four hundred fifty and eight hundred meters away from the SS-24 train."

Grishkov paled. "I know the TM-57 from my time in the Army! They had over six kilos of explosives! That means..."

"That's right," Neda said. "The total explosive yield of the antitank mine pile was about a kiloton, though of course without a nuclear weapon's radiation or electromagnetic pulse."

"Madness!" Grishkov said, shaking his head. "Did the train survive?"

"Yes, and though there were injuries, there were no deaths, and the simulated launch of the train's missiles was successful," Neda said.

"But shortened codes and ancient software aren't the only reasons I'm sure these SS-24 warheads can still be used," Neda added.

Grishkov and Vasilyev both looked at Neda in dismay. This time Grishkov asked first.

"OK, what else?" Grishkov asked.

"Well, all the rail-mobile SS-24s were in Russia. With those, the files show the decommissioning of each missile was done properly. By that, I mean the arming component was removed from each warhead before they were sent to a plant for uranium extraction. The same for the silo-based SS-24s within Russia. But there is nothing in the files about arming component removal from the SS-24s in Ukraine, and I don't know why," Neda said.

Grishkov shook his head. "I don't know either, but I can guess. You said that the arming code for those missiles would be sent through an underground cable from Russia, right? Well, they knew no code would be sent. And the warheads were physically removed from the missiles and shipped to Russia soon after the Soviet Union's collapse, right?"

"That's all correct," Neda said.

"Well, you're both too young to remember what things were like after the USSR ended, but I'm not. I may have been a child, but I'll never forget the near chaos of those days. A detail like removing the arming components of warheads being pulled and shipped back to Russia anyway was missed? I'm far from surprised," Grishkov said.

Vasilyev nodded. "It also may not have been an oversight. Given a choice between removing the arming component while the weapons were still in Ukraine and getting the warheads back to Russia as soon as possible, they may have made a conscious choice just to do warhead removal."

Neda shrugged. "Maybe. But the bottom line is that the files say the arming component is present on both of these particular SS-24 warheads. Only a mobile-standard decades-old arming code stands between their present owner and warhead use."

"So, is that it?" Grishkov asked. "Whoever has them could set them off anytime?"

"Maybe, but maybe not. Only one real obstacle stands in the way of their use. First, they'd need to build an emulator, and that would take some real technical skill. Plus, ideally, knowledge of the software used to write the arming component software," Neda replied.

Grishkov frowned. "What's an emulator?"

"Sorry, I forgot to explain that. The easiest way to defeat any code, especially an old one that has been shortened for mobile use, is brute force. You just use a fast, modern computer to throw every possible code combination at the software until you get the right one. You can't do that with the actual arming component unless you have the disarming code, which they don't," Neda said.

Grishkov nodded. "So you'd need to create a software copy of the one used by the arming component. But surely, the software had code that didn't allow multiple arming attempts?"

"I'm sure it did. So, the person copying the software would have to omit that code from the emulator," Neda said.

Vasilyev frowned. "There can't be many people still living who worked on the SS-24's arming software. We must get a record search underway immediately!"

Now Neda looked uncomfortable. "I've already asked the man on the Director's staff assigned to support us on this mission to do that. I would have talked to you first, but I think minutes may count here. Remember our last mission."

Yes, Vasilyev thought to himself, they had cut that one pretty close.

Aloud, he said, "I agree with your decision in this instance. But, please do consult with me when time allows."

Neda's relief was evident in her expression. Then she startled Vasilyev by leaning forward and kissing him on the cheek.

"You know I will," she said.

Neda and Vasilyev smiled at each other as the car pulled up in front of the terminal.

Grishkov nodded to himself. So far, they evidently had team harmony. Good.

It sounded like they'd need every advantage to get through this mission.

Chapter Ten

Myrhorod Air Base, Ukraine

Captain Josh Pettigrew was pleased with his students' rapid progress. He strongly suspected the Ukrainian Air Force had made a real effort to send both their best young pilots, and their best English speakers, to Blackjack training.

Pettigrew held up a stack of paper and announced, "You all passed the classroom portion of Blackjack training!"

As Pettigrew expected, the classroom erupted in cheers and clapping.

But he didn't expect what happened next.

Lieutenant Melnik stood up, holding a softcover book. "Sir, the class has a small gift for you."

Pettigrew gestured for Melnik to come forward.

Holding the book so Pettigrew could see the cover, Melnik said, "We thought it was important to recognize the important role the US Air Force has played in helping us fight off foreign invaders. So, we are presenting this book to you to show we understand this."

Pettigrew saw the book's title was simply, Myrhorod Air Base and the US Air Force. A photo of a B-24 Liberator bomber illustrated the cover.

The first page was blank and had the signatures of all the students.

The rest of the pages were photos of B-24s, along with many of their crewmen. Pettigrew recognized the insignia of the Eighth and Fifteenth Air Forces.

Many of the B-24s had visible damage. One was a smoking wreck that had obviously failed to land safely.

"I knew our planes had flown into Ukraine during World War II. I had no idea, though, that we'd used this very base," Pettigrew said.

"Yes, sir," Melnik said proudly. "American planes flew from England and Italy to attack Axis targets in Eastern Europe and then flew here to repair, refuel and rearm. Then they would attack more targets on the way back. The main American base in Ukraine was at Poltava, but this base saw heavy use from June through September 1944."

"Thanks to all of you for reminding me of this important chapter in our history, and for this very handsome book," Pettigrew said, shaking Melnik's hand as the other students clapped.

"Now, who's ready to fly a Blackjack?" Pettigrew asked.

More laughter and cheering answered him.

Pettigrew thought that after everything he'd been through over the past few years, it was a relief to have lucked into such an outstanding assignment.

Borispol International Airport, Kyiv

Grishkov frowned as he walked with Neda and Vasilyev to the terminal exit, each with a bag in hand.

"It feels like everyone here is staring at us," he grumbled.

Vasilyev nodded solemnly. "I would say, no more than half."

That earned him a glare from Grishkov and a punch in the shoulder from Neda.

"Ow," Vasilyev said, grinning at Neda and rubbing his shoulder. "You're stronger than you look."

Neda sniffed. "You'd do well to remember it. I've warned you about flippancy."

"So you have," Vasilyev said with a nod. Turning to Grishkov, he said, "You're right, of course. We entered Ukraine with our Russian diplomatic passports, and as far as the government here is concerned, we're...well, not at war, but not far from it. Truthfully, I'd be astonished if we weren't being watched."

Grishkov shook his head and said in a low voice, "Then how are we supposed to accomplish, well, anything?"

"Well, your friend will have those answers, I hope. She's supposed to be waiting for us just outside," Vasilyev said.

Now Grishkov scowled. "I've indeed been here before, but I made no friends. And Arisha would certainly not approve of any female friends, here or elsewhere!"

Vasilyev shrugged. "Well, she told me she remembers you. Let's see if her face jogs your memory," he said, as they exited the terminal building.

Sure enough, the tall blond woman Vasilyev knew as Alina was waiting next to an idling official limousine. Vasilyev noted automatically that most men would have called her beautiful, but there was a coldness to Alina's manner that immediately put him on guard.

Smyslov had told Vasilyev he was putting them in the hands of one of their most capable agents. Looking at her now, he believed that.

Alina also looked as though she'd had to make some hard decisions to earn that reputation.

As Alina opened the rear door, they could see two ranks of seats facing each other. She sat in the one closest to the front and pointed impatiently at the ones closest to the rear.

Vasilyev had expected recognition from Grishkov and was not disappointed. Once they'd taken their seats and the limousine got underway, Grishkov thrust his hand towards Alina and growled, "Good to see you again, Alina. It's a relief to see someone in charge here who will do whatever is necessary for mission success."

Alina gave Grishkov a warm smile that, for an instant, let Vasilyev see a glimpse of what she must have looked like years ago.

"I'm glad to see you here, too," Alina said. "Someone with military experience will be very helpful on this mission."

Then her smile disappeared, and she turned to Vasilyev.

"I was sorry to hear about your father. I only hope I die so well," Alina said.

Without waiting for an answer, she immediately turned to Neda. Vasilyev had noticed that Neda had seemed to freeze when she saw Alina, but had no idea why.

"Don't blame your husband. He did not know our history. I told the Director having been your debriefing officer in Tehran wouldn't be a problem. Was I right?" Alina asked.

Neda sat quietly for a moment and finally shrugged. "Well, I won't lie. When I saw you, my first memory was of you threatening to turn me over to the Iranian secret police if I didn't tell you everything I knew about the nuclear weapons my husband had designed."

Then Neda paused. "But I'm not the same meek, fearful woman I was then."

Alina's answering smile was thin but genuine. "Yes. The Director gave me access to your file or at least part of it. Enough to see your performance in training, and enough of your last mission to make me grateful you'll be part of this one."

Alina then glanced at the thick plexiglass partition between their seats and the driver.

"We can speak freely. This partition renders our seats soundproof, and I had this car swept for listening devices just before we left. We're on our way to the Embassy, where our first task will be to brief you fully on what we've been able to learn about the stolen weapons. By then, it will be evening, so after dinner and sleep, we'll leave the Embassy first thing in the morning. Of course, we'll have to rid ourselves of Ukrainian surveillance," Alina said, and then paused.

Pointing first at Vasilyev and then Grishkov, she said, "I know you've been through that routine from your files. Neda, disguise was covered in your training, but you've never done it in the field. Are you able to use contacts?"

Neda shrugged. "Yes, you're right that they were part of training. They never gave me any trouble."

Alina smiled. "Good. I've always hated sticking them in my eyes, so you're ahead of me there."

Vasilyev looked out the car window. "I see we're not far from the Embassy, so I'll just ask one question. We know the weapons were stolen from Pervomaysk, a base that was closed years ago. Do you know where the rest of the test weapons they were swapped with are supposed to be now?"

Alina nodded. "Vasylkiv Air Base, home of Ukraine's Air Command Central. The test weapon records should be there too. It's less than an hour's drive from the Embassy, so maybe we'll be able to wrap this up quickly."

Seeing the expressions on the three people in front of her, Alina had to smile.

"Very well. Understood. No tempting fate."

CHAPTER ELEVEN

Russian Embassy, Kyiv, Ukraine

Grishkov was still rubbing his eyes when Vasilyev and Neda joined him in the Embassy cafeteria for breakfast. The basement where the cafeteria was located had no windows, but Grishkov had seen on his way down the stairs that it was still dark outside.

Vasilyev smiled when he saw the food laid out in front of Grishkov. "Well, good morning! It's nice to see you haven't forgotten to feed all those muscles!"

Indeed, Grishkov had missed little among the choices laid out in the buffet line. A bowl of kasha, a multi-grain porridge, came first. Beside it were butterbrots, a buttered slice of toast, and two fried eggs. So far, he had touched none of it and was instead cradling a cup of black coffee in both hands.

"You should both do the same," Grishkov said soberly. "No telling what the day ahead holds, and my time in the Army taught me never to pass up an opportunity to eat a decent meal. Besides, think of how lucky we are! No exotic foods testing our stomach here," Grishkov said, waving at the food in front of him.

"Well, first, good morning," Neda said with a smile. "I hope you're not waiting for us to start eating. Don't let your food get cold!"

Grishkov shook his head. "We've had this conversation before. My mother raised me better than that. I can wait for a few minutes. Besides, I need some of this coffee in me to really wake up at such an hour."

A few minutes later, Vasilyev and Neda were seated across from Grishkov. Vasilyev's choices were identical to Grishkov's, while Neda had just butterbrots and tea.

"So, what do you think of Alina's plan?" Vasilyev asked Grishkov.

At first, Grishkov was surprised Vasilyev appeared to be ignoring his wife and looked at Neda for her reaction.

Then Grishkov kicked himself. Of course, Vasilyev and Neda had already discussed this. He still wasn't quite used to the fact that his other two team members were sharing a bed.

Grishkov took a long pull from his coffee mug while he thought. Finally, he shrugged.

"A lot will depend on whether the man Alina says works for us is at the front gate when we show up. And whether she's right about where the weapons locker is on base. We need to get in and out fast. All it will take is an alert officer to check our papers directly with the Ministry of Defense here in Kyiv to find out we're imposters. A lot is riding on Alina's acting skills."

Vasilyev nodded, and then they all concentrated on finishing their breakfast. As Grishkov pushed away his last plate, he looked up and was startled to see Alina standing next to him.

She smiled at his reaction. "Good morning! I hope you show the enemy no more mercy than that breakfast," Alina said, gesturing towards the collection of empty dishes in front of Grishkov.

Grishkov scowled. "And I hope you can convince our Ukrainian friends you're one of their officers. We can all follow most of what's said in the language, but none of us can pass for Ukrainian speakers."

Alina nodded and said something rapidly in Ukrainian.

Grishkov smiled. "If I got all that, you said you were born in Ukraine and lived near Kharkiv until you started middle school when your family moved to Moscow. That would explain why I couldn't hear a Russian accent. My estimate of our chances has just gone up considerably."

"Well, you three being Russian speakers isn't as big a handicap as you might think. There's still a substantial Russian-speaking minority here, even outside the region bordering Russia. Most Russian-speaking Ukrainian soldiers aren't assigned to combat in this war, so seeing them in rear echelon duty like an inspection squad won't surprise anyone," Alina replied.

As they walked up the stairs into the Embassy working space, Grishkov noticed the sun still wasn't up.

Alina pointed down the hallway. "Vasilyev, your barber is waiting at the second door on the right. Grishkov, you were good enough to keep your old Army haircut, so you may go directly to fitting for your uniform, first door on the left. Neda, come with me."

By the time Alina had finished Neda's transformation, Vasilyev and Grishkov were waiting in an office next door. Both men were in Ukrainian Air Force uniforms, Vasilyev as a First Lieutenant and Grishkov as a Sergeant. Vasilyev's hair was considerably shorter than it had been minutes before, but otherwise, his appearance was unchanged.

Grishkov had never really altered his military haircut and bearing after leaving the Russian Army and looked completely at home in uniform.

Both men, though, caught their breath when Alina walked into the room with Neda at her side. Alina's long dark blond hair had been swept up into a neat bun, pinned above her Ukrainian Air Force uniform collar. Neda was also in a Ukrainian Air Force uniform as a First Lieutenant.

She was completely unrecognizable.

Neda's short blond wig was several shades lighter than Alina's natural hair color and ended just above her collar. Her contacts were a shade of cornflower blue that set off her blond hair perfectly.

Neda's eyes narrowed as she saw the reaction of the two men, and perhaps not surprisingly focused on her husband.

Gritting her teeth, Neda bit out, "Not. One. Word."

Vasilyev and Grishkov demonstrated the survival instincts that had kept them alive through numerous missions, and just nodded.

Alina smiled and said, "I'm glad to see you both approve of my work. Let's get to our transport."

None of them were pleased to see the windowless gray van waiting for them in the Embassy's sub-basement, but it was obvious Alina had expected their reaction.

"Get inside, and I'll explain our next steps on the way," she said.

Bare metal seats were bolted to both walls of the van, and sacks of mail occupied much of the available space. The van's driver started the engine as soon as they were all seated. As soon as the van emerged on the street, through the windshield, they all noticed a small dark sedan idling to the right.

The van turned left, and the sedan was no longer in view.

"As you've probably guessed, all vehicles leaving our Embassy are followed by the Ukrainians. Their version of the FSB is the Security Service of Ukraine, which everyone calls by its Ukrainian acronym, the SBU. To give you an idea of their size, they have six times as many staff as the combined British MI5 and MI6. Thankfully, they aren't nearly as well trained," Alina said with a smile.

Grishkov frowned. "So, this is a regularly scheduled Embassy transport?"

"Exactly," Alina nodded with approval. "The twice-weekly mail run to our Consulate in Odessa, which has followed the same schedule for over a year. We've opened the van and unloaded it in the parking lot at the Consulate during that time, so SBU surveillance cameras across the street could see sacks of mail was all we were carrying. For the first three months, SBU agents followed the van the entire seven-hour drive to Odessa."

"But after that, only half-way," Vasilyev said.

"Correct," Alina said. "Then, for only an hour. For the past month, they've followed this van no farther than the outskirts of Kyiv. Of course, we're sure they still log the van's arrival time in Odessa. If that were to change, I'm sure we'd be back to full-time surveillance. Happily, Vasylkiv Air Base is in the right direction, straight down the E95 highway."

Vasilyev nodded. "So, once that sedan behind us loses interest and turns off, we'll switch to a car with the appropriate Ukrainian Air Force decals for the remaining distance to the airbase."

"Just so," Alina said with a smile. "With luck, we'll get to the base well before dawn. I'm hoping the Ukrainians won't have their A team manning the gate at this hour, and that whoever's there won't be at their best."

Grishkov grunted approval. It was true. People were at their least alert in the hours just before dawn, even if they were technically awake.

On the one hand, Ukraine had been on a war footing for years. On the other, Vasylkiv Air Base was hundreds of kilometers from the front lines.

Well, they'd see soon enough just how alert the Ukrainians really were.

Vasylkiv Air Base, Ukraine

The upper half of the substantial guard booth fronting the airbase was made of plexiglass. Grishkov was sure it was bulletproof. The bottom half was made of reinforced steel that appeared more than capable of stopping a rifle bullet. Cameras ringed the booth's top.

There was still over an hour to go before dawn. Lights were angled to provide adequate illumination to the booth's entire front, not just the road leading to the base.

The professional soldier in Grishkov approved. The current FSB agent Grishkov hoped the men now inside the booth were less competent than its designers.

As Alina had predicted, the SBU surveillance sedan had peeled off once they'd left Kyiv, and their transfer to a car with Ukrainian Air Force decals had taken place without incident minutes later. As their car rolled to a stop at the gate, Alina lowered her window and thrust a sheaf of papers at the startled guard.

"I am Captain Rudenko, here to conduct a surprise inspection. I need to speak to the senior officer at this booth immediately!" Alina barked.

The guard gulped, saluted, and scurried inside the booth without saying a word or taking her papers.

Alina smiled to herself. So far, so good.

Seconds later, the guard re-emerged. "Please come inside, Captain. The others in your squad too."

With that, the guard stood to the side of the booth's entrance door and watched nervously as Alina and her team entered.

"I am Lieutenant Boyko," the officer now standing before Alina said. "Papers, please. And all your IDs."

There was barely room inside the booth for all of them, mainly because it had already held two officers. Besides Boyko, a Ukrainian captain sat in the far corner smoking a cigarette, with a half-finished coffee cup sitting on the counter beside him. He said nothing and was plainly entertained by the spectacle in front of him. His lined, weather-beaten face proclaimed it had seen quite a bit that amused it over the years.

Alina handed over her papers, and each of the team passed Boyko their IDs.

Boyko read through the papers and compared each ID to the person in front of him. Alina smiled to herself as Boyko's gaze lingered a bit too long on Neda. Well, Boyko was a healthy male in his early twenties, and distraction had been one of her goals in Neda's makeover.

With a visible effort, Boyko turned his attention back to Alina.

"These papers say you are here to conduct a surprise inspection of our munitions storage. They say I am to notify the officer in charge of munitions, and no one else. I must confirm these orders with the base commander," Boyko declared.

Now the Captain sitting in the corner coughed discreetly.

"Yes, Captain Moroz?" Boyko asked nervously.

Moroz put down his cigarette. "Well, Lieutenant, you're in command of this booth. That means the responsibility for handling these visitors rests with you. But the orders say you're to notify only the responsible officer. That's so if something is wrong, nobody has the chance to cover it up. So, up to you," he said with a shrug.

Alina nodded shortly. "The Captain is correct. Of course, we expect your officer to accompany us to munitions storage, and to remain with us while we conduct our inspection. Please notify him immediately. As specified in these orders, no one else on base is to be notified until we have completed our inspection."

Boyko stood still for a moment and then made his decision.

He pulled out a folder with names and phone numbers and then reached for the nearest phone.

"Colonel Klimenko? This is Lieutenant Boyko at the front gate. I have a surprise inspection team here with orders. They want you to join them at the front gate and escort them to our munitions storage. Their orders say no one else is to be notified until their inspection is complete," Boyko said.

Boyko paused. "Yes, sir, I have read through their orders carefully, and examined all their IDs."

Another pause. "Very well, sir," Boyko said, and put down the phone.

"Please return to your vehicle. Colonel Klimenko will be with you shortly," Boyko said.

Alina nodded, and they all got back in their car.

Grishkov said in a low voice, "So, Captain Moroz is your man inside the base?"

Alina shrugged. "More like he was. Once they check on us, and at some point they will, that Lieutenant will remember who suggested letting us in was a good idea. Moroz will have to be long gone before then."

Alina paused. "With luck, us too."

A few minutes later, a car rolled towards them and flashed its lights. Then it turned around and began to go back the same way it had come.

Alina smiled. Good. The less conversation, the better.

Minutes later, both vehicles were in front of a large single-story concrete bunker, with a massive double-sided metal door in its center. Blazing lights on all sides made it easy for her to see Colonel Klimenko's next actions. He walked up to a wooden guard booth staffed by a single soldier, who snapped to attention at Klimenko's approach and saluted.

Klimenko returned the salute and gestured to the door. The guard hurried forward to unlock and open the door and then swung it open. In the meantime, Alina parked their car next to Klimenko's sedan.

Klimenko gestured for Alina and her team to join him. Alina strode towards Klimenko purposefully, saluted, and then passed her orders to him. "My orders, Colonel."

Klimenko nodded. "Tell your team to get started with their inspection. Come to my office, and we'll discuss what it is you're trying to find."

As they walked to Klimenko's glass-walled office, Alina studied the man. There were no young Colonels, but this one's gray, thinning hair told Alina he couldn't be far from retirement.

On the other hand, Klimenko's office looked much newer than the rest of the structure. Glass made up the top two-thirds of the office walls, signaling that the occupant wanted to know what was going on outside it.

Klimenko would have to be handled carefully.

Gesturing for Alina to have a seat in front of his desk, Klimenko sat down and began reviewing Alina's supposed orders.

A few minutes later, Klimenko grunted and looked up. "So, not a word here about why we've been singled out for this inspection. Care to explain?"

Before Alina could reply, Klimenko's eyes narrowed, and he pointed outside the office.

"That blond lieutenant is carrying what looks very much like a Geiger counter. I haven't seen one of those in use since I was a lieutenant myself. Ukraine has had no nuclear weapons on its soil for decades. Just what are you looking for, Captain?"

Alina was spared having to invent a reply by Neda's frantic waving of her right hand above her head.

"Well, Colonel, let's see if that lieutenant has an answer for your question," Alina said, rising from her chair.

Klimenko nodded sharply and followed.

Neda stood in front of a large metal weapons locker set against the bunker's back wall, studying the Geiger counter's readings. It was chattering steadily.

Alina gestured towards the padlock in the center of the locker. "Do you have a key for this lock, Colonel?" she asked.

Klimenko shook his head with a frown. "No. When I assumed command here, I reviewed the inventory papers for this locker, which described its contents as inactive test weapons. There was a further notation that the weapons were obsolete and scheduled for disposal. I had planned to do just that, but with a war going on didn't make it a priority. Are you telling me there are nuclear weapons inside this locker?"

Alina shrugged. "I'm not telling you anything, Colonel. That is," she said, gesturing towards the chattering Geiger counter.

Grishkov strode forward beside Alina, holding a large bolt cutter.

Alina smiled. "Colonel, my sergeant has brought us a universal key. Shall we see what's inside that locker?"

Klimenko nodded silently.

"Very well. Sergeant, please proceed," Alina said.

Seconds later, Grishkov had cut the padlock and opened the locker.

The Geiger counter objected loudly, going from "chattering" to "screeching" in an instant.

"Turn that thing off, Lieutenant," Alina said calmly. "I think we've got the message. Am I right to guess that we'll be OK for a few minutes of exposure?"

Neda frowned but slowly nodded.

"We need to take pictures for my report, Colonel. Any objections?" Alina asked.

Klimenko shook his head. "They look like missile warheads. I count eight. Do you think they're live?"

Alina shrugged. "We'll need to get a team with anti-radiation gear here to remove the warheads and take them to a properly equipped facility to answer that question. But my guess is no. Just as your inventory papers say, I think they are obsolete test weapons."

Then Alina looked at Vasilyev, who had lowered his camera. "Finished, Lieutenant?"

Vasilyev nodded.

"Good," Alina said. Then she gestured towards Grishkov. "Let's close this up, Sergeant."

"One last thing, Colonel. Do you have the inventory papers for this locker to hand?" Alina asked.

Klimenko nodded absently. "Yes, they are in my office."

A few minutes later, they were back at Klimenko's office, and shortly after that, he pulled a yellowing file from a metal filing cabinet.

"May I make a copy for my report, Colonel?" Alina asked.

Klimenko nodded and gestured towards the nearby copier.

Once Alina had finished making copies of the inventory papers, she handed back the original documents to Klimenko.

"Thank you for your cooperation, Colonel," Alina said. "You can expect to hear from the team that will remove the warheads within the next several days. In the meantime, as specified in my orders please do not discuss this matter with any other officer for security reasons. I also recommend that you replace the padlock we cut, and be sure to keep the locker doors closed."

Klimenko nodded, and then said slowly, "Your squad isn't very chatty, is it, Captain?"

Alina nodded calmly, although her heart rate had actually picked up considerably.

"Yes. They're all Russian speakers, and experience has taught them that it's smart to keep their mouths shut. As you know, we keep most Russian speakers away from the front lines, so inspections are an area where we can still get some use from them," Alina replied.

Klimenko frowned but finally nodded. "Makes sense, especially the part about keeping their mouths shut. Very well, Captain. I'll look forward to getting these warheads out of here. Do you have a card?"

Alina nodded and handed Klimenko a card with the Inspector General's office logo and her supposed name and number.

Klimenko stood up and offered his hand. "Good work, Captain. Nice to see someone's still on the ball in Kyiv."

Alina shook Klimenko's hand, saluted, and left.

Minutes later, she was back in their car, with Grishkov at the wheel.

"Drive," Alina said tersely.

As the gate came within view, Alina's phone buzzed. Looking at its display, she sighed.

Seeing the looks from the others in the car, Alina shrugged.

"That text message told me Klimenko called the number on the card I gave him. Of course, it was staffed by one of our agents, who had an appropriate script."

Vasilyev frowned. "Do you think Klimenko bought whatever your agent had to say?"

As they came up to the gate, Alina replied, "We're about to find out."

They idled in front of the gate, and through the guard booth's plexiglass could see Lieutenant Boyko on the phone.

Seconds later, the gate went up. Grishkov wasted no time moving through it.

All of them looked straight ahead until the guard booth was out of sight.

Finally, Vasilyev looked behind them. Nothing.

Alina tapped the file folder in her lap. "I'd been hoping that there was some other name on that inventory record besides Pofistal Arbakov's. There wasn't. He was the one who signed off on the weapon locker's transfer to Vasylkiv Air Base. And he removed the two warheads before that transfer."

Alina paused. "I've had agents looking for Arbakov ever since we learned of a stolen warhead. When you discovered two were stolen, I ended all our other operations and had our agents follow every lead that might lead to Arbakov, no matter how remote. I hope one of you has an idea of what to try next because I don't."

Grishkov nodded. "I do. First, as you briefed us last night, we'll go to the safe house in Markhalivka, switch cars, and get out of these uniforms. Then we'll go to Arbakov's house, while you go back to the Embassy and brief Moscow on what we've learned."

"What we've learned?" Alina repeated bitterly. "I've risked you all for nothing."

Vasilyev shook his head. "On the contrary. We are now certain the weapons are not at Vasylkiv Air Base, and since he signed the inventory transfer papers, we know Arbakov is the last person on record to have them."

"I was a detective for a long time, and supervised other detectives, too. When they came up empty, I always told them to go back to the beginning. For us, that means Arbakov's house," Grishkov said.

Alina shook her head. "He hasn't been there for weeks. We turned the house inside out, looking for clues. Do you really think you'll find something we missed?"

"No disrespect intended. But we've simply got different skills. I could have never managed what you just did in getting us onto and, more importantly, out of that Ukrainian airbase. Believe me when I say that if I look for a suspect, I will find him," Grishkov said.

Alina glanced at Grishkov, who was making the turn for the safe house in Markhalivka and shrugged. "Very well. You have Arbakov's address near Malynivka, right?"

Grishkov nodded.

"Fine. You won't make it there before dark, and Arbakov's house no longer has power. I suppose he hasn't paid the electric bill since he left. So I'll make reservations for all of you at a hotel in the nearest large town, Pokrovsk, and text you the details," Alina said.

"Good," Grishkov said. "Stay by your phone. By tomorrow afternoon, I'll have a lead to follow on Arbakov's whereabouts."

Vasilyev and Neda in the backseat both looked at each other and smiled.

Grishkov looked in the rearview mirror and growled, "Do you doubt me, back there?"

Vasilyev did his best to suppress a smile but failed completely. "No, sir, Senior Detective, sir!"

Grishkov shook his head but finally smiled himself. "Well, we'll see tomorrow, won't we?"

Vasilyev nodded, and as they pulled up to the safe house, he felt a confidence he couldn't explain.

No, that wasn't right. He could. Grishkov never promised a result he couldn't deliver.

The only real question was whether they'd find Arbakov too late.

CHAPTER TWELVE

Donetsk, "Donetsk People's Republic"

Avel Karpenko was not what anyone would call a handsome man. His short, squat frame was crowned with a matted tangle of greasy black hair that appeared to rarely encounter either soap or comb. His close-set brown eyes peered out from a pockmarked face left behind after a childhood illness he'd barely survived.

But Karpenko had responded to these defects with hard work, shrewd intelligence, and an absolute absence of what others might call "moral standards."

If something was good for Karpenko, it was...good. Period.

In particular, Karpenko had discovered that with enough money, female companionship was guaranteed. Yes, it took considerable funds to overcome the revulsion usually prompted by his appearance.

But, as his fortune grew, he was able to afford women with better skills at acting. Among other skills.

The separatist movement in eastern Ukraine had been a godsend. Karpenko's criminal enterprises had been lucrative, but their scope had been limited by a Ukrainian police force that was reasonably competent.

The creation of the Donetsk and Luhansk "People's Republics," or Novorossiya for short, had changed all that.

First, many Ukrainian-speaking police officers in Novorossiya left with their families to areas within Ukraine unaffected by the fighting.

Then, many Russian-speaking police officers left to join the new militias formed to fight the forces of the central Ukrainian government.

Finally, as the fighting hit the economy of Novorossiya tax revenues began to dry up. And started missing paychecks for all government employees, including the police.

Russia began quietly sending funds to prop up Novorossiya. But not before many police officers began looking elsewhere for the money they needed to feed their families.

Karpenko had seized the opportunity. He'd actively recruited police officers for what he called a "people's militia" to maintain public order.

In the West, it would have been called a "protection racket."

Those businesses still open and with goods worth stealing were approached, as well as wealthy residents who had not yet fled.

The proposition was simple. Pay us, and you will be safe.

Don't, and if you're lucky, you'll just be robbed. Arson and murder were also on the table, especially for those who complained to the authorities of the "People's Republics."

Karpenko was careful to keep the "enlistment" side separate from the "enforcement" side of this operation. He knew many former police officers would object to the threats being used to recruit clients.

But several factors worked in Karpenko's favor. First, calling the regular police for help often resulted in either a late response or none at all.

Second, Ukrainian territories in rebellion were awash in both weapons and those who were newly unemployed, with no work prospects.

Unsurprisingly, property crime skyrocketed.

Finally, the Karpenko approach to law enforcement appealed to many former police officers. There was no arrest, trial, or prison for anyone caught in the act or credibly accused of committing a crime against a paying client.

There was simply immediate execution.

Success bred success. Karpenko used the money from protection to expand his smuggling activities, particularly drugs, as well as trafficking women and children for the sex trade.

A former Spetsnaz commander named Boris Kharlov already had smuggling of hard currency, weapons, cigarettes, and luxury goods sewn up. At first, this hadn't troubled Karpenko, who already had enough to manage. Plus, Kharlov had been willing to sell him weapons and anything else on the same reasonable terms as everyone else.

As Karpenko gained a handle on the sudden expansion of his organization, though, he cast his eye more and more enviously at the smuggling activities Kharlov controlled.

Karpenko also bitterly resented Kharlov's attacks on his sex trade shipments. Taking the women and children to sell himself, he would have understood.

But freeing them? That was just wasting money.

Who was Kharlov to decide smuggling weapons was better than trading in people? After all, the women and children Karpenko moved would kill no one, unlike Kharlov's munitions.

Karpenko hesitated to move against Kharlov, though.

Kharlov kept the best weapons for himself and his men. And many of Kharlov's men were ex-military. Karpenko knew they were more than a match for his band of criminals and ex-police officers.

No, a frontal assault was out of the question. But Karpenko was a patient man.

First, he quietly recruited informants within Kharlov's organization. Though some were discovered and shot, many were not.

His next step took years, but finally, he had achieved it. With payments to the right men in the "People's Republics" Karpenko had subsequently attained recognition as the leader of a legitimate militia. This recognition meant he could openly pressure even more clients to sign up for protection, increasing the funds available to recruit more men and buy more weapons.

The trade-off was that Karpenko was often called on to help push back incursions by the Ukrainian military against the territory of Novorossiya.

Well, there were those Karpenko suspected of disloyalty or who were merely poor performers. He always had men he was willing to order to the front.

Now that Karpenko had covered himself with the Novorossiya authorities, he was ready to make his first move against Kharlov.

His next sex trade shipment would contain a surprise for Kharlov.

Karpenko smiled grimly.

He just hoped Kharlov would lead the attack personally.

CHAPTER THIRTEEN

Near Malynivka, Ukraine

Mikhail Vasilyev looked out the front passenger window at the passing countryside and shook his head. "Amazing to think that a man with two thermonuclear warheads lived out here in the middle of nowhere."

Anatoly Grishkov took his eyes off the gravel road for a moment to glance toward Vasilyev. "For years, apparently. The file says Arbakov lived here from retirement until very recently. He inherited the property years before that from his father."

Neda Rhahbar stirred from the back seat, where she had been studying an SS-24 technical schematic.

"Come on, you two. Where was Arbakov going to hide two thermonuclear warheads in a Kyiv apartment? On the balcony?" Neda asked.

Vasilyev and Grishkov both laughed at the image. Finally, Vasilyev shook his head.

"Of course, you're right that Arbakov needed plenty of space to hide the weapons, and being far from prying eyes was a bonus. No, it's that city Russians like us tend to think of rural countryside like this as having nothing besides crops, farm animals, and the simple folk who tend them.

Not where you'd expect to find some of the most powerful weapons ever created."

"Well, hang on there," Grishkov said. "Simple might be right in some respects. Most here won't have traveled far from where they were born, for example. But when I was put in charge of a team of detectives responsible for investigating homicides in the entire Vladivostok region, my first lesson was that simple didn't equal stupid. While rural folk may not know as much about the wider world as urban dwellers, I found they often had a better understanding of people. Especially their neighbors."

Vasilyev nodded. "So, though Alina's agents interviewed Arbakov's neighbors, you think it's worth having another go at them."

"Correct," Grishkov said with a smile. "In particular, the widow in the house directly across from Arbakov's property. The report just says she had no idea where Arbakov went, and that's probably true. I'm betting, though, she knows a lot more than that. And here we are," he said, making the turn onto the dirt road leading to the widow's house.

Grishkov didn't park the sedan as close to the house as he could have. And when Vasilyev and Neda moved to unbuckle their seat belts, Grishkov gestured for them to stay still.

"Let's give her a moment," Grishkov said. "I'm sure the widow Kulik gets few visitors. She'll need a moment to make herself presentable, and to look us over. We'll see her soon enough."

Grishkov was right. After only a few minutes, the front door opened, and an older woman emerged onto the porch. Her hair was gray and held back by a colorful handkerchief. Though she was leaning slightly on a cane, there was still a keen intelligence looking out from her blue eyes.

Kulik gestured sharply for them to come forward.

Grishkov unbuckled his seat belt and said calmly, "You two stay right where you are. I don't want to overwhelm her."

Without waiting for a response, Grishkov opened his door and strode at a slow but steady pace toward Kulik, giving her plenty of time to look him over. He walked right up to the porch steps, but no further.

Looking up, Grishkov said, "Babushka, a good morning to you. My name is Anatoly Grishkov. I am here with my friends to ask you a few questions about your neighbor Pofistal Arbakov. I hope you can spare us a few minutes, but we can come back another time if you're too busy."

Kulik's bright blue eyes glittered as she looked hard at Grishkov and said nothing for a moment.

Then, Kulik cocked her head and shifted her grip on her cane.

"So, you're Russian. But these old ears can't quite place from where, and that puzzles me," Kulik said.

Grishkov nodded. "I was raised in a village a few hours drive from Moscow, but back then, we were still far enough away that we saw few people from the capital. Then I served in Chechnya. Next, I was in Vladivostok with my family for many years. The last few years, I've lived in Moscow."

"That explains it," Kulik said with a satisfied nod. "You've lived in both ends of Russia, and smack in the middle. No wonder I couldn't place your accent!"

Kulik paused and looked again hard at Grishkov. "I believe you when you say you served in Chechnya. But you didn't stay in the military, did you? Police?"

Grishkov smiled and nodded. "Yes, babushka. For many years."

Kulik shrugged and made her decision. Waving her cane at Grishkov, she said, "Very well, you'd better come inside for tea. And tell your friends to come, too."

With that, Kulik turned and went back inside the house, leaving the door open behind her.

Grishkov waved at Vasilyev and Neda and waited for them to join him. Then, they all entered the house.

There were no lights on inside, but there was plenty of sunshine coming in through the sparkling clean windows. The living room furnishings were old but sturdy and well made. An ancient Russian Rassvet-307 TV set sat silently on a stand against the wall.

They could hear clattering from the kitchen nearby. Next, they heard Kulik's voice.

"You men, have a seat. Young lady, please come and help me."

Vasilyev and Grishkov both looked at Neda and smiled. Vasilyev silently mouthed, "You're up," as he made a show of sitting and relaxing on the nearby couch.

Neda smiled back and shook her head the same way Grishkov had seen his wife do when his children Sasha and Misha did something foolish, but not worth punishing.

Even more than the living room, walking into the kitchen made Neda feel that she was stepping back in time. Though everything she could see was spotlessly clean, Neda was certain every appliance was older than her.

Neda could immediately feel Kulik's keen eyes on her and lowered her gaze in response.

"Child, that blond wig must be uncomfortable. Please remove it and put it over there," Kulik said, pointing to a small table in the corner.

Neda did so, and then removed the net that had kept her hair in place under the wig. Her dark hair tumbled free.

"Much better," Kulik said. "But, now, I see that your eyes are all wrong." She reached into a cabinet and removed a large ceramic platter. Putting it on the table next to the wig, she said, "Get those things out of your eyes. Use the platter to make sure you don't lose them."

A few minutes later, Neda was back to her old self.

"Well, you're a beauty! What's your name, child?" Kulik asked.

"Neda, ma'am," she replied.

Kulik nodded. "And the tall man, he's your husband, right? What's his name?"

"That's right, ma'am. His name is Mikhail," Neda replied.

"You have a few years on him, don't you, dear?" Kulik said with a smile.

Neda just shrugged.

Kulik laughed and said, "Good for you. It's about time we ladies had some fun. You haven't been married long, have you?"

Neda shook her head.

"Could see it in the way he looked at you," Kulik said. Pointing at the wig, she lowered her voice and said, "Hold onto that, though, dear. Could come in handy later," Kulik said with a wink.

Neda blushed and mutely nodded.

"Now, dear, I can see that Mikhail is as Russian as I am. But though you speak Russian well, you come from farther away, right?" Kulik asked.

"Yes. I was born and raised in Iran, but I'm a Russian citizen now," Neda replied. "That citizenship was given to me by the President himself," she added.

Neda immediately kicked herself for the addition. She had no idea why she'd said it, especially since she'd kept it to herself so far from everyone except her husband and Grishkov.

Well, Neda couldn't really count Director Smyslov, since he was the one who'd told her.

"Is that so?" Kulik asked thoughtfully in a way that made it clear she didn't expect an answer. Neda realized Kulik didn't doubt her word but was instead reevaluating her based on the new information.

Some spy I am, Neda thought to herself bleakly. Maybe the FSB would be better off hiring this old woman as an interrogator!

The tea kettle began to whistle on top of the stove, which thankfully interrupted Kulik's stream of questions and observations.

Kulik handed a large tin to Neda and pointed to an even larger metal serving tray on the nearby counter. "Please put some of the cookies in the tin on the tray while I make the tea. At least two apiece," she said.

A few minutes later, Neda put the tray on the coffee table in front of the sofa where Vasilyev and Grishkov were waiting and sat down between them. Kulik lowered herself carefully into a large overstuffed chair on the other side of the table and gestured towards the tray.

"Neda, please serve the men first. I know I'm old fashioned, but at my age, I don't think that should come as a surprise," Kulik said with a smile.

Neda served an amused Vasilyev first. "Don't get used to this," she said under her breath.

Kulik's answering smile told Neda that old or not, there was nothing wrong with her hearing.

Once they were all sipping tea, Kulik said casually, "So, you're here to ask me about Pofistal Arbakov. I suppose the men who were here before told you I said I don't know where he is. I was telling the truth then, and still am now."

Grishkov nodded. "I believe you. I'm just hoping to get some background on your neighbor. For example, did you ever speak with him?"

Kulik nodded, and then her eyes narrowed. "Those other men showed me IDs saying they were Ukrainian police, though their Moscow accents told me otherwise. Now, you at least didn't insult my intelligence with fake IDs. I won't insult yours by asking who you really work for, and instead just guess some part of the Russian government. Am I wrong?"

Grishkov shrugged, and said, "You're not wrong."

Kulik nodded again and then sighed. "Poor Pofistal. Such a hard life he's had, including that wretched name. And you know his son died from the flu when he was still just a boy. Mind you, Pofistal's a good man. Always has been. A very hard worker. But ever since his wife Natalia died, there's been a darkness in him I thought would lead to trouble. And you three coming to see me means it's serious trouble."

Kulik paused and then shook her head. "But yes, I should answer your question. Pofistal has helped me many times over the years. Just about all my appliances have been on his truck at one time or another."

Grishkov raised his eyebrows. The file had said the only vehicle registered under Arbakov's name was a sedan. A nationwide lookout issued through an FSB agent working undercover in the Kyiv police force had failed to turn up any sightings.

"Can you tell me anything about his truck?" Grishkov asked.

"I can tell you exactly what it was. A Ural-4320. We don't see many of those beasts here, I can tell you," Kulik said.

Grishkov nodded. The Ural-4320 had been in continuous production for Russian military and civilian use since the 1970s. A massive 6x6 all-wheel-drive diesel truck with excellent ground clearance, it would have no trouble moving the stolen SS-24 warheads even over poor roads.

"I've heard of them used as fire trucks, or for transporting logs. What did Arbakov use it for?" Grishkov asked.

"Well, he used it to move appliances and other things he was repairing, mostly. Pofistal was always good with his hands. Never any excuses. He could fix anything. But he always refused to take my money for it, even when I insisted. Said it was the least he could do for a neighbor. Cookies and cakes, that's all he'd accept," Kulik said.

Kulik paused and added, "He told me once he only used the truck around here. Said he was saving it for when he really needed it."

Grishkov nodded. "I'm sure the truck wasn't cheap. Do you know how he got it?"

"As a matter of fact, I did ask him about that. Pofistal told me he got a really good price on it when an airbase where he worked closed. It was declared surplus, along with many other things the military decided were too much trouble and expense to move. He said he stuffed the truck with things he spent his life's savings to buy."

Then Kulik cocked her head and looked thoughtful. "You know, Pofistal said nobody would believe what a good deal he'd been able to get, with a funny smile I didn't understand at the time. Said when he drove it all right off the base, nobody even looked. It's the only time I ever heard him laugh."

Grishkov and Vasilyev exchanged glances. Kulik had just answered several of their questions, without even knowing it.

Neda was looking at Kulik. She could see Kulik was deeply troubled.

"So, Pofistal took something from that base he shouldn't have, like weapons or explosives. Whatever it was, isn't my business. I know you have to get it back. But I hope you'll try to do it without hurting him," Kulik said.

Grishkov nodded gravely. "We don't want to harm him. Only, as you say, to recover property he shouldn't have taken. I'll go even further and say we have been ordered to find and detain him, but to do so without causing him serious injury."

That was stretching the truth a little, but not that much. A dead or unconscious Arbakov wouldn't be able to reveal the location of the SS-24 warheads.

Kulik appeared to be convinced of Grishkov's sincerity.

"Very well. There are two other things you should know. When I talked about how Pofistal changed after Natalia's death, you should hear the reason. He was convinced the Ukrainian government was to blame.

Natalia had cancer, and Pofistal thinks she got poor care because she was a Russian speaker," Kulik said.

Grishkov raised his eyebrows but said nothing.

"Was Pofistal right? I have no idea. I think all that matters is that he believes it," Kulik said.

Kulik paused. "The last thing I'm going to tell you may not mean anything. But after those other men asked me about Pofistal, I couldn't get my last conversation with him out of my head. He mentioned what he called the woodpecker, with a strange look in his eyes. Pofistal said that everyone would hear from it again, but this time its song would be different, and they'd have to listen."

Grishkov quickly glanced at Vasilyev and Neda and could see that "the woodpecker" meant nothing to them either.

"Well, thank you very much for your help," Grishkov said, standing along with Vasilyev and Neda.

Kulik rose as well, clutching her cane.

Grishkov handed his card to Kulik. "In case you think of something else, please let me know."

"I will. And I will say a prayer for Pofistal tonight," she said soberly.

Yes, Grishkov thought to himself as Vasilyev and Neda said their goodbyes.

Prayer might be a good idea.

CHAPTER FOURTEEN

Mariyinsky Palace
Kyiv, Ukraine

President Babich finished rereading the SBU report, an old technique for trying to spark new thoughts.

This time, it wasn't working. Nothing about the report from the Security Service made any sense.

Babich took off his glasses and tiredly rubbed the bridge of his nose. He'd been told many times that he looked like a President, and no doubt this had helped him win in the last election.

But his wife Sofia was becoming more and more worried by the new lines etched in his face, and the gray that was creeping into his thick black hair. A few nights before, she had jokingly made a show of dragging him from this desk to bed.

Well, that didn't end with him getting much rest, but he was certainly not complaining.

No, Sofia was right, he thought. He needed to finish concluding peace with the Russians, and quickly before his hair turned gray altogether.

If this report was accurate, though...

Babich shook his head. If anyone could make sense of the report, it ought to be someone like him, the former head of an SBU Directorate. The problem was that his Department K had been outside the SBU mainstream since its founding.

Most of the SBU had the same missions as the old KGB. Surveillance of enemies of the regime. Counterintelligence. Criminal investigations beyond the scope of local authorities.

To that the SBU had added counterterrorism, which had helped justify the creation of special operations units called Alpha in every Ukrainian province.

But Department K had only one mission. Rooting out the corruption which had been a part of Ukrainian politics all the way back to Soviet days. Babich was no historian, but wouldn't have been surprised to learn that Ukraine's corruption went back even further.

When he'd resigned to run for President, Babich's men had presented him with an oversized framed Department K emblem, which now occupied a prominent place on his office wall. It was a vertical sword with the letter "K" imposed on it.

The Ukrainian word for corruption was "korruptsiia," and Babich had always imagined the emblem showed the sword cutting through it.

Against all expectations, including his, Babich had succeeded in bringing cases that held up in court against several Ukrainian household names.

Including the Prime Minister, who had been forced to resign.

Several prominent opposition politicians had seen their chance. Run Babich for President on an anti-corruption platform, and then continue to run things from behind the scenes. After all, what did Babich know about politics?

To their dismay, it turned out the answer was - more than they did.

Babich didn't just win. It turned out he wasn't interested in limiting anti-corruption investigations to the other party. Everyone, including his backers, was fair game.

Several politicians went from backers to inmates in a matter of months.

Babich also concluded early on that peace was a necessary precondition for eliminating corruption. War, declared or not, was too often used to justify breaking all sorts of rules. For example, no-bid contracts and associated kickbacks were often justified by "military necessity."

No, you couldn't eliminate corruption without following the rules.

But not everybody wanted peace. The head of the SBU, for example, had been vocal in his belief that the Russians couldn't be trusted.

Director Shevchuk had also repeatedly pointed out that the Russians refused even to discuss returning Crimea, the first European territorial change made at gunpoint since World War II.

Well, one thing at a time, Babich thought to himself with a sigh.

Babich had been tempted several times to simply fire Shevchuk. As President, he had the authority.

And it would have been very satisfying. Shevchuk had been his boss when Babich had been the head of Department K. He'd made no secret of his disdain for anti-corruption work, but Babich had turned that to his advantage.

Shevchuk wasn't interested in his activities? Well, then there was no need to brief him, was there?

By the time Shevchuk realized how wide-ranging Babich's investigations were, the Prime Minister had been charged, and they were too late to stop.

The truth was, though, that Shevchuk was good at his job. At least, the parts he considered necessary.

And, despite ample opportunity, Shevchuk lived on his official salary. Babich believed privately that this wasn't due to any particular virtue. Instead, material possessions just didn't matter to Shevchuk.

As Shevchuk was shown into his office, Babich was careful to keep a smile off his face. Yes, Shevchuk was wearing one of the same threadbare gray suits Babich remembered from his Department K days. It was, at least, a good match for Shevchuk's sallow complexion.

No, fancy clothes and fast cars didn't interest Shevchuk. Power and authority did.

Well, better the enemy he knew, Babich thought.

"Good to see you, Shevchuk. Please, have a seat," Babich said.

"Mr. President," Shevchuk said with a stiff nod, as he sat in one of the chairs in front of Babich's desk.

"I've read your report, and have a few questions," Babich said.

"Yes, sir?" Shevchuk replied.

"It says a team of four Russian agents breached our security at Vasylkiv Air Base, and that at least one of them was assigned to the Russian Embassy. Don't we keep all Russian Embassy personnel under surveillance?"

Shevchuk had to struggle to keep his expression impassive, but managed.

"Yes, Mr. President. They evaded our surveillance," Shevchuk replied.

"Interesting. Do we know how?" Babich asked.

"That's under investigation. Once we know for sure, I'll send you a follow-up report," Shevchuk replied.

Babich nodded. "The report says the Russian agent assigned to the Embassy was identified based on a photo match. Based on a six-pack, or a single photo?"

A six-pack was six similar photos, with one of them being the suspect. It was a much more accurate method than a match made based on a single photo, as every investigator knew.

"I don't know, but will find out," Shevchuk replied, succeeding in keeping his expression and tone neutral.

Barely.

Babich had to work hard himself to keep from smiling. Very well, he'd tortured Shevchuk long enough.

"So, let's assume for a moment that these were Russian agents. I'm surprised they were able to get on one of our airbases. What about this Captain..."

Babich made a show of looking up the name on the report, though he remembered it perfectly well.

"Moroz. Without his intervention, it seems likely the base commander would have been notified. But I see nothing about this Captain being interviewed in the report."

"Yes, sir. By the time our investigators arrived at the base, Moroz was on previously authorized leave. The report was high priority, and so was completed based on what we knew then. I did have investigators attempt to locate Moroz," Shevchuk said.

Babich's eyebrows rose. "Attempt?"

"Yes, sir," Shevchuk said with a scowl. "I have put out an all-points notice. By now, though, Moroz could be anywhere."

Babich nodded. "Like Russia. Now, we've always suspected the Russians have agents in place in key locations like our military bases. But I know you're making every effort to find them."

Time to throw Shevchuk a bone. Besides, Babich knew it was true.

"So, the Russians wouldn't burn such a valuable asset without an excellent reason. But what these agents did at the base makes no sense. Are we sure they left with nothing but photos and document copies?" Babich asked.

"Absolutely, sir. They were under observation by Colonel Klimenko the entire time they were in the munitions bunker. He has conducted a complete inventory in the base commander's company, and nothing is missing," Shevchuk said.

"These test warheads. Are we sure they are truly inactive? Your report said they had been sent for expert examination, correct?" Babich asked.

"That's right, sir. The Yuzhnoye Design Office in Dnipro. They designed and built several nuclear weapons while Ukraine was part of the Soviet Union. This morning I received their report. It confirms that they were inactive warheads, used to test the SS-24 ICBM," Shevchuk replied.

Babich nodded. "So, the Russians took photos of these test warheads and copied documents about those same warheads. And that's all they did. Is that right?"

Shevchuk shrugged. "I see your point, sir. It seems like a lot of trouble for very little."

"Yes. It means we're missing something. What about the woman, the agent you say is assigned to the Russian Embassy? Where is she?" Babich asked.

Shevchuk reddened. "I don't know, sir. We had two teams following her, but she somehow managed to lose them both. For the second time."

Babich let the silence that followed linger for a few seconds, but not too long.

It was apparent Shevchuk already knew how badly this failure reflected on the SBU.

"We disagree on whether the Russian peace offer is genuine," Babich said.

Seeing Shevchuk begin to speak, Babich held up one finger to stop him.

"But we agree on one thing. The Russians aren't fools. They wouldn't have gone to these lengths without an excellent reason. We need to find out what it is."

Babich tapped Shevchuk's report on his desk.

"I look forward to your follow up report," Babich said evenly.

Shevchuk rose and said stiffly, "Yes, Mr. President."

Once he was alone, Babich pulled the report open again and started to read it for the third time.

The answer was there somewhere. If he could just find it.

CHAPTER FIFTEEN

Near Bryanka, "Luhansk People's Republic"

Boris Kharlov manned one of the two PKP Pechenegs his squad would use for the ambush. Lighter than most 7.62x54mm machine guns, it was still accurate and easy to control. In particular, Kharlov preferred its bipod mount over the cheaper PKM Pecheneg used by most Russian Army units.

No, Kharlov mused, sometimes you just had to spend the extra money.

Kharlov had chosen his spot carefully. He'd learned in Chechnya that most battles were won or lost before they even started. He and all his men were dug in on each side of low hills overlooking a dirt road leading to Highway T0504. Not many kilometers away, that highway led out of the "Luhansk People's Republic" to territory controlled by Ukrainian authorities.

Today, though, these smugglers wouldn't be reaching Highway T0504.

Not that Kharlov had a problem with all smugglers. Far from it. Smuggling was how he'd made most of his considerable fortune.

It was the type of smuggling carried out by the men he was about to ambush.

Women, boys, and girls for the sex trade, mostly destined for Western Europe where prices were higher.

Kharlov knew that many of his men considered such missions quixotic at best, and a dangerous waste of time at worst. But, he paid far better than his few remaining competitors and gave his men better weapons too.

So, they stayed and put up with Kharlov's eccentricities.

Kharlov cursed as he saw the long-bed pickup truck in the lead of the smugglers' convoy. Triple-mounted to its bed was a DShKM heavy machine gun, with a thick metal plate in front shielding the gunner. At the first sign of trouble, this machine gun nicknamed "Dushka" could lay down a rate of heavy caliber fire guaranteed to cause casualties in his squad.

Apparently, the smugglers were learning from his previous successful attacks.

Kharlov frowned. Karpenko was the so-called "militia leader" behind these shipments of women and children.

Kharlov had believed he had a lock on weapons smuggling to the "People's Republics."

It seemed that wasn't true, because he certainly hadn't sold a Dushka to Karpenko.

Assuming he survived his encounter with this one, Kharlov resolved to learn how Karpenko had acquired the Dushka.

And what else he might be missing.

Kharlov forced his mind back to the present. How was he going to deal with the Dushka?

Kharlov saw only one slim chance. Tapping his head-mounted

radio's switch twice, he sent the prearranged signal for his squad to hold in place.

Bouncing and lurching over the rough road, the Dushka and its gunner were coming up fast. Behind it was a small truck that Kharlov was sure held the captive women and children.

Bringing up the rear was a large SUV with heavily tinted windows, that Kharlov thought probably contained heavily armed shooters.

Kharlov was about to break one of the cardinal rules of an ambush.

Once you're in place, don't move.

No matter how careful Kharlov and his men had been to camouflage their positions, an alert gunner could still spot movement from a considerable distance. And with a Dushka firing at the rate of six hundred rounds a minute, he'd only need to aim toward that movement's approximate location.

Kharlov eased his right hand towards the sniper rifle he'd placed at his side and moved it towards him. Chambered in the original 7.62x54mm, the Chukavin was a considerable improvement over the Dragunov SVD sniper rifle Kharlov had used in Chechnya and that was still in use by most Russian Army snipers.

The Chukavin was simply too expensive to deploy all at once. Kharlov had paid a steep premium to get this one. But, he thought to himself, his current situation demonstrated it was money well spent.

Kharlov carefully switched his left hand as well to the Chukavin. He'd paid plenty for the German-made Schmidt and Bender riflescope he was looking through as well. As the Dushka came quickly into focus, he thought, "worth every dollar."

Germans weren't interested in rubles.

Right now, the metal plate protecting the Dushka's gunner filled the scope. A few seconds after the pickup truck moved past him, his view would be blocked by the small truck behind it.

Kharlov would get one split-second opportunity.

This gunner was no fool. The Dushka swung slightly back and forth, as the gunner examined the low hills on either side.

He could see this would make an excellent ambush site.

The driver evidently realized the same thing because he accelerated even more, making the pickup truck buck up and down even harder over the potholed dirt road.

Kharlov snarled with frustration. Hitting the Dushka's gunner as he jerked back and forth would now have more to do with luck than skill.

There! Now or never.

Kharlov squeezed the Chukavin's trigger.

Yes! The Dushka's gunner was down.

"Execute, execute, execute," Kharlov said calmly into his radio, as he switched to his PKP Pecheneg machine gun.

The machine gun on the other side of the road beat him, but only by a few seconds. Less than thirty seconds later, all three vehicles had come to a stop. The front and rear vehicles' tires were shredded by machine-gun fire, while there was no room for the truck carrying the smugglers' cargo to get past the pickup holding the Dushka.

The drivers of the front and rear vehicles were also dead.

The truck with the women and children was untouched. All of Kharlov's men knew the penalty for firing a stray round into it.

There were still a few survivors in the rear SUV, though. Both the front and rear passenger side doors opened, and men bolted from both, emptying their submachine guns wildly at the hillsides.

They hit nothing but brush and trees, and seconds later were face down in the road, dead from multiple rounds.

"Proceed. Overwatch," Kharlov said into his radio. His men knew this meant to move towards the vehicles below, while he kept watch through his rifle's scope.

The only survivor among the smugglers was the driver of the small truck. He was holding his hands up and babbling that he wanted to surrender.

Kharlov's men pulled him out of the truck and marched him into the brush on the road's side.

A single shot rang out.

Kharlov would never let his men take people like this driver as a prisoner. As far as Kharlov was concerned, men who had anything to do with enslaving women and children deserved only one fate.

Several of Kharlov's men waved an "all-clear" signal in his direction. Kharlov moved down the hill, leaving every weapon but his pistol behind for the moment. He had a small bag in one hand.

Kharlov nodded towards the two men on either side of the small truck's rear doors. Two other men stood behind them with pistols drawn, in case the smugglers had a man inside the truck's cargo bed.

One of Kharlov's men had a bolt cutter, which he now used to cut through the padlock securing the truck's rear doors.

The smell that came from the now open truck made it clear the smugglers had provided their victims with no bathroom breaks.

Kharlov's men lowered their pistols, as they could quickly see no smugglers were hiding among their cargo.

Several of the children and two of the women were crying as Kharlov reached the truck's back.

"Do any of you know how to drive a stick shift?" Kharlov asked.

One woman looked up from trying to comfort one of the children. "I can," she said in a confident voice.

Good, thought Kharlov with relief. So far, every truck he'd rescued had contained at least one woman capable of driving it.

He didn't want to give any of his men the temptation that would come with driving such a truck.

Kharlov thought he might be worrying too much, as he looked at the expressions of the men standing around him. True, he had seen how they had acted in nightclubs with women just like the ones in the truck.

But now the expressions of his men were a mixture of outrage and compassion.

And anger. Well, there was no way to make these smugglers pay more than they had already.

"Come forward," Kharlov said to the woman. "I need you to drive this truck."

A few moments later, the woman was standing in front of Kharlov. Older than the other women in the truck at what Kharlov guessed was her mid-twenties, she defiantly looked back at him. Kharlov noted the prominent bruise on her right cheek and guessed there were others concealed by her dress.

She hadn't gone into the truck willingly. Excellent.

"What is your name?" Kharlov asked gently.

"Yana," she said evenly. "So, do we work for you now?" she asked contemptuously.

"No," Kharlov replied. "No women work for me. At least not the way you mean. You will go to some people who will see that you are all safe."

Yana's eyes narrowed. "What tall tale is this? How will I even know how to get there?"

"Come with me," Kharlov said, pointing to the truck cab.

Once they were there, Kharlov gestured towards the driver's seat and stood aside.

He knew Yana wouldn't welcome a hand up.

Nor did she need it. Seconds later, she was checking to make sure the keys were in the ignition. They were.

Kharlov reached into the bag he was carrying and withdrew a GPS attached to a stand, and set it on the truck's dashboard.

"Have you ever used one of these?" Kharlov asked.

Yana shook her head. "No, but I know what it is. The vehicle symbol in the center shows where I am, and the blue line where I should go."

Then she frowned. "The blue line is ahead, but there's just white space all around us."

Kharlov nodded. "This dirt road isn't on the map loaded in this GPS. However, to reach the blue line, all you have to do is drive straight ahead about two kilometers and then turn right when you reach Highway T0504. All the other turns will be shown on the GPS. The drive should take no more than an hour."

Yana still looked dubious. "How will we get past the checkpoints? I've heard they're on both sides."

"You're right. But both the Luhansk and the Ukrainian guards have been well paid to let you pass. If either squad betrays me, they know the penalty," Kharlov said, gesturing towards the smuggler bodies littering both sides of the road.

Yana swallowed hard as her eyes followed the gesture. But there was also a grim satisfaction in her eyes.

Well, Kharlov didn't blame her for that.

"Very well. One last question. Who are these people waiting for us on the other end of this blue line?" Yana asked, looking at the GPS as though it might hold the answer.

Kharlov shrugged. "They call themselves a 'nongovernmental organization.' I think you would call them a charity. They exist to help victims of the sex trade, and years ago, many of them were victims too. But no longer. This won't be the first time they've helped me with people I've rescued."

"Well, then, all that's left is for me to thank you. I guess we should get moving," Yana said, as she started the engine.

Kharlov's men had given a shorter version of his explanation to the women and children in the back of the truck, along with food and bottles of water. Even more appreciated had been the opportunity to use the bushes on the side of the road.

Now they all moved back into the truck while Kharlov's men closed the rear doors. One of them leaned around the vehicle to the side and gave Kharlov the "ready" signal with his right hand.

Kharlov pointed straight ahead and said, "Good luck."

Yana nodded and put the truck into gear. Moments later, the vehicle was out of sight.

On the surface, everything had gone perfectly. None of Kharlov's men had even been injured, and soon all of the women and children they'd rescued should be safe.

So, why was a small insistent voice in his head warning him of mortal danger?

CHAPTER SIXTEEN

Donetsk, "Donetsk People's Republic"

Avel Karpenko's fist came down against his desk so hard that he thought he might have broken a bone for a moment.

Rubbing the injured hand, the pain began to recede. No, it was not broken.

About the only thing that had gone right today.

First, the commander of the sex trade shipment had failed to check-in. Then, a man on his payroll in the Ukrainian military told him a truck matching the one he'd used for the delivery had crossed into Ukraine.

Alone.

Now he'd just received confirmation from the men he'd sent to check on the shipment that all the guards Karpenko had assigned to protect it were dead. And, of course, the load was missing.

To add insult to injury, an explosive charge had destroyed the Dushka he'd bought at ridiculous expense.

Well, apparently, it wasn't the way to get rid of Kharlov anyway.

But Karpenko hadn't made it where he was by always expecting success.

No, he always had a plan B.

And now that he knew Kharlov was still alive, it was time to use it.

Six Kilometers Outside Donetsk
"Donetsk People's Republic"

Boris Kharlov frowned as he saw the smoke rising in the air about a kilometer ahead.

He held up the clenched fist that signaled "hold" to the men around him.

They had pulled their vehicles well off the road a few hundred meters back and were advancing on Kharlov's mansion through the trees that surrounded its vast lawns.

The smoke told Kharlov why the squad he'd left behind wasn't answering their radios. They were probably dead, and his mansion was on fire.

But, he had to be sure.

Kharlov used hand signals to direct his men into assault position. Whoever had attacked his base could still be there.

But no. As Kharlov looked through his binoculars minutes later at the raging fire that was consuming his mansion, he could see no movement of any kind.

Just the dead bodies of his men, scattered around the grounds where they'd fallen.

Kharlov signaled his squad to move forward.

Then he swore as he recognized what had caused the fire. The blast damage to the mansion's entrance was still visible, even though the fire consuming the structure sent waves of heat towards Kharlov and his men.

The attack had included an anti-tank rocket.

Then Kharlov swore even more bitterly as he examined his men's dead bodies. Most had been hit by large caliber rounds, that guaranteed death from shock and blood loss no matter where they hit. And made body armor useless.

Karpenko had bought more than one Dushka.

Kharlov frowned as he saw a radio lying on the ground beside one of the bodies. He had received no radio message, no cell phone call.

So, Karpenko's men had equipment capable of jamming both.

Kharlov shook his head as he realized he'd severely underestimated the importance of Karpenko's new status as the leader of a recognized militia. It had opened new sources of weapons and equipment to Karpenko that had shifted the balance of power between them.

And Karpenko must have informants within my ranks. Kharlov knew there was no other explanation for the timing of the attack on his base.

For the first time in many years, Kharlov wasn't sure what to do next.

He needed help to take on Karpenko. But Kharlov had systematically eliminated everyone besides Karpenko with a criminal enterprise big enough to threaten him.

So, who could he turn to now?

CHAPTER SEVENTEEN

FSB Safe House
Troieshchyna District, Kyiv, Ukraine

Anatoly Grishkov paced back and forth through the living room like a caged tiger. Neda Rhahbar had retreated to the kitchen table to have peace for her examination of the SS-24 technical documents Grishkov and Vasilyev had been able to obtain.

Mikhail Vasilyev sat on the living room couch lost in thought, apparently oblivious to Grishkov's pacing.

Suddenly, Vasilyev looked up and pointed at the chair opposite the couch.

"Sit," he told Grishkov.

Grishkov at first looked startled, but then shrugged and sat.

"Very well, let's look at this problem logically. Our search of Arbakov's home turned up nothing except enough residual radiation readings to know the warheads were stored there. We now know Arbakov used a heavy truck to transport the warheads off the base, to his home, and then somewhere else," Vasilyev said.

Grishkov nodded. "Alina's people were able to trace the record of the truck's sale to Arbakov through a military database, once they knew where to look. It didn't appear in any Ukrainian vehicle database under Arbakov's name because he never registered the truck. So, it still has its original Ukrainian military plates."

"That's why Arbakov was careful to use it sparingly, and only in a rural area where police are few and far between. He probably had to stick to back roads to move the warheads to wherever they are now. At least, we now have a national lookout on his truck," Vasilyev said.

"For all the good that does us," Grishkov said with a scowl. "He's had days to hole up with the warheads. And we have no idea where."

"Well, at least we have one clue. That strange woodpecker story. Maybe that means something," Vasilyev said

"Like what? Alina says she ran the word 'woodpecker' through every FSB database and came up empty. Where else can we turn?" Grishkov asked.

"OK, let's think logically. We know the reference was to the past because Arbakov said 'the woodpecker's song will be heard again.' And in the past, Arbakov spent years working on maintaining SS-24s at Pervomaysk. Wasn't Dreev there for years, too, manning an SS-24 silo?"

Grishkov snapped his fingers. "Right. And he's one of the few people we can ask without security concerns since he already knows about the stolen warheads."

Moments later, Grishkov's secure cell phone was in his hand and ringing.

To his credit, Dreev picked up on the first ring. Grishkov could hear a TV in the background, which was almost instantly muted.

"Yes?" Dreev asked.

Without preamble, Grishkov asked, "Does 'the woodpecker's song will be heard again' mean anything to you? It's something Arbakov said, and we think it might have something to do with his time at Pervo-maysk. Or maybe not. Anyway, can you tell us what he might have meant? We've searched every database and come up empty."

"Let me think," Dreev replied, and for the next several seconds, there was nothing but silence on the line.

Grishkov was about to tell Dreev to call him back if he thought of something when he heard an intake of breath and the last sound he expected.

Laughter.

"If it's what I think, no wonder you found nothing matching 'wood-pecker' in any Russian or Ukrainian database. We never called it that," Dreev said, and then paused.

"I'm not an expert on this topic, but here's what I remember. We had an over-the-horizon radar called Duga designed to give us early warning of a Western ballistic missile attack. It was extremely powerful, putting out over ten million megawatts at its peak. That's one reason we were briefed about it," Dreev said.

"I don't understand," Grishkov said. "Could it have interfered with an SS-24 launch?"

"No," Dreev replied. "That wasn't the concern. Depending on the target, though, Duga could have interrupted contact with an SS-24 after launch. Of course, it's precisely after a launch that we could have expected Duga to be turned up to full power."

Grishkov grunted. "Yes, to detect answering missiles. But you said one reason. What was the other?"

"Well, I'm only guessing, but Duga was designed to give us early warning. I think we were briefed about it so that if we were ordered to launch based on that warning, we wouldn't hesitate," Dreev replied.

"Makes sense," Grishkov said. "No matter how effective military discipline might be, anyone could have trouble condemning millions to death without absolute certainty it was warranted. But you still haven't explained what this has to do with 'woodpecker' or its song."

Dreev's laugh was short and sharp. "Duga was hated in the West. It put out a signal that interfered with television broadcasts, amateur radio communications, and even commercial aircraft. The signal was heard as a sharp, repetitive tapping noise that immediately reminded any listener of a woodpecker. It became such a nuisance that TVs and radios in the West were made with 'woodpecker blanket' circuit designs. Amateur radio operators banded together as the 'Russian Woodpecker Hunting Club' to transmit matching signals in an attempt to jam Duga's signal."

"Well, for someone who says he's not an expert, you seem to know a lot about Duga. Is it still in operation?" Grishkov asked.

"No," Dreev replied immediately and then paused. "Duga's receiver was a few kilometers from Chernobyl."

Another pause. "Here's the part where I'm not an expert, because I never went to Duga. Duga's receiver was part of a complex that included anti-missile defense, space surveillance and communication, and research. The complex was all underground in order to survive a nuclear strike. One of the men who transferred to my SS-24 crew from there told me it was a city that never saw the sun, and that even silo duty was preferable. It seems we got to the surface more often."

"So, you think we need to find someone who has worked at Duga if that's where Arbakov is holed up," Grishkov said.

"Ideally, yes," Dreev replied. "There can't be many left who did, so you may have to make do with maps. Some at Duga were called upon to help deal with the Chernobyl disaster and died then. Many others suffered significant radiation exposure. And of course, enough decades have passed that many working there would have died from natural causes."

"Well, you're still around. Maybe we can find someone else from back then," Grishkov said.

Another short, sharp laugh from Dreev answered Grishkov. "True, I am still around. Sometimes that surprises me. Well, if I remember anything else about Duga, I'll call you."

After thanking Dreev for his help, Grishkov hung up and looked at Vasilyev, who had been listening to the conversation with him on speaker.

"So, did that all make sense to you?" Grishkov asked.

"Well, hiding out in a massive deserted underground complex, yes," Vasilyev said.

"But?" Grishkov prompted, seeing Vasilyev's frown.

"Arbakov had years to plan this. We definitely need to find someone who knows more about the Duga complex, or at least some maps. It certainly fits the woodpecker reference," Vasilyev said, and then paused.

"But we also need to think more about what Arbakov meant when he said the woodpecker would 'sing again, but with a different song.' Turning Duga back on makes no sense, and I can't see how he could anyway," Vasilyev said.

"Agreed," Grishkov said. "But whatever he's up to, I think Arbakov is determined to be heard."

CHAPTER EIGHTEEN

Donetsk, "Donetsk People's Republic"

Avel Karpenko smiled with satisfaction at the report he'd just received detailing his men's attack on Boris Kharlov's mansion. Only one of his men had been wounded and not even seriously. All of Kharlov's guards were dead, and the estate had been on fire when Karpenko's men left.

They had retrieved many items from the mansion before leaving, including cell phones and laptops, which would be very interesting to explore.

The attack leader had radioed to request permission to remain to attack Kharlov when he returned. Karpenko appreciated the man's enthusiasm and courage but had refused the request.

First, Karpenko always knew better than to push his luck. It was one of the reasons he'd been so successful.

More important, though, Karpenko wasn't going to risk the Javelin launcher his men had used in the attack. He only had a few of them, and he was going to use them again tomorrow morning.

Now that he'd struck Kharlov hard, Karpenko's next priority was derailing Russia's peace negotiations with Ukraine. Everyone knew without Russian military and financial support, Novorossiya would collapse. But Russia was still searching for a way to extricate itself from the fighting that avoided outright Ukrainian victory.

It looked like autonomy for Novorossiya might let Russia do just that. In return for giving up the pretense of independence, officials in Novorossiya would be allowed to keep their positions. Also, Russian would be given status as a fully recognized official language in Novorossiya.

Of course, militias like Karpenko's would have to disband and turn over their weapons.

Even worse, his protection and smuggling operations were unlikely to survive after the fighting ended, and Ukraine reestablished sovereignty over its eastern provinces.

Unfortunately, Karpenko and the other militia leaders had no voice in the negotiations. But that didn't mean he was giving up.

No, he knew the talks were delicate, and there was plenty of mistrust on both sides. So, what would happen if one side received proof of the other's treachery?

Karpenko was stirred from his musings by Osip Litvin's arrival in his office. He had known Litvin since childhood. So, Litvin was the only one of the men working for him Karpenko trusted.

Mostly.

The first lesson Karpenko had learned to survive as a criminal was to give no one absolute trust.

As always, Karpenko silently marveled at the contrast. Litvin sported coiffed blond hair, chiseled good looks, and a fit body that didn't show an ounce of excess fat. His tailored clothes fit like a glove.

Karpenko was sure Litvin had never paid a kopek for female companionship.

Litvin's looks made him perfect as the public face of Karpenko's criminal enterprise. Negotiations with officials of the "People's Republics" were needed? Send Litvin. The press had questions about militia activities? Send Litvin.

Best of all, Litvin had no taste for violence. It was one of the things that had cemented their friendship in elementary school. Karpenko dealt with any bullies who bothered Litvin. In return, Litvin elevated Karpenko's status just by being his friend.

Karpenko gestured for Litvin to have a seat in front of his desk. Litvin already knew to close the door to Karpenko's soundproofed office behind him.

"Our men are going to launch an attack tomorrow morning," Karpenko said. "I need you to spin it so the media draw the right conclusions. Newspapers, TV, online. I want everyone to get the same message."

Litvin nodded silently.

Karpenko gave him a thin smile. One of the advantages of knowing each other so long was that Litvin understood when to keep his mouth shut. He knew Karpenko would tell him everything he needed to know.

"We're going to take out four tanks tomorrow morning. I need you to make sure everyone understands the importance of this action," Karpenko said.

Litvin smiled. "That should be easy. I don't think our forces have ever knocked out that many Ukrainian tanks at one time."

Karpenko smiled back. "We're going to destroy four of our tanks."

Litvin blinked in surprise but said nothing at first.

Then, he slowly nodded. "We're going to blame the attack on the Ukrainians. And derail the peace talks with Russia."

"Yes. Now, you'll need to have our hackers upload video of the attack on a public Ukrainian military website. I'll text you the word 'ready' once the attack is complete, but right now, I can give you an approximate time. Here's the website and a rough time frame," Karpenko said, sliding a slip of paper across the desk.

It quickly disappeared into Litvin's jacket.

"Do we expect casualties?" Litvin asked.

Karpenko nodded. "Without them, it would be a much smaller story."

"We don't have so many tanks. Will you be hitting the oldest ones?" Litvin asked.

"Three T-72s and one T-54," Karpenko replied.

Litvin winced but said nothing.

Good, Karpenko thought. Yes, their side only had a few dozen of the more modern T-72s, and couldn't afford to lose any. He'd selected the T-54 because it was one of the handful of tanks provided to Karpenko's newly authorized militia.

Who would believe he'd destroy one of his tanks?

"One other thing to highlight. The T-54 we'll destroy will be the one from the Donetsk museum," Karpenko said.

"Great choice," Litvin said. "A lot of people will remember the photo of that T-54 being put on a flatbed truck by grinning freedom fighters in 2014. It's the sort of thing that will get more attention than just a few burning tanks."

Karpenko nodded. This showed once again why Litvin was so useful. He'd known destroying that T-54 would get attention, but not that it would be the headline.

The truth was, Karpenko had initially selected the T-54 because he'd resented being given a literal museum piece. At the time, he'd thought there was only one reason he hadn't been given the IS-3 tank pulled from a WWII historical monument as well.

The Ukrainians had captured it.

Aloud, he just said, "The Ukrainians will detect the hack and quickly remove the video of the attack from their public military website. We need to get the video downloaded and reposted on other sites in a way that can't be traced back to us."

"Easy," Litvin said. "We have world-class hackers who've done this sort of thing many times before. I'll see to it," he said confidently.

Another thing Karpenko liked about Litvin. No excuses, just performance. So far, Litvin had never failed him.

"Good," Karpenko said. "With luck, this will put a spike in the peace talks no one will be able to remove."

CHAPTER NINETEEN

15 Kilometers From Donetsk
"Donetsk People's Republic"

There were many reasons for Danya Shulga's recent emergence as Karpenko's top military commander.

Shulga had leaped over many other former Ukrainian officers who had switched to Karpenko's service because of what he'd brought with him. Stolen Javelin anti-tank launchers and missiles, and seven enlisted men he'd trained in their use.

In 2018 Shulga had been one of the first officers trained in the Javelin's operation. He had subsequently been put in charge of setting up training programs throughout the Ukrainian Army. Despite the success of the training program, Shulga had repeatedly been passed over for promotion.

It turned out that connections, both political and within certain families, counted for far more than performance when it came to promotion. Shulga had no such relationships, so he was facing forced retirement from the only job he'd ever had since joining the Army as an officer cadet at age eighteen.

It wasn't so much that his military pension wouldn't be enough to cover Shulga's expenses. He was intelligent and a hard worker with plenty of friends. He knew he could get some sort of work after retirement.

No, it was the rank injustice of his treatment that Shulga wasn't able to bear. It ate at him, but it took over a year and receipt of a letter informing him of his retirement date before Shulga decided to do something about it.

Opportunity had something to do with his decision, too. The first two hundred ten Javelin missiles and thirty-seven launchers Ukraine purchased in 2018 were kept under tight security. But the next one hundred fifty missiles and ten launchers were delivered in 2020 during the coronavirus pandemic.

Though Ukraine hadn't been hit as hard as some other European countries, the Army had still been deployed to provide logistical support throughout the country. At the same time, peace talks with Russia made the prospect of a tank invasion from the East appear remote.

With the Army's generals distracted by the pandemic and Shulga now in charge of the Javelin training program, it hadn't been hard to move some missiles and launchers to a training facility under his direct control. Yes, it had taken more time to reschedule the training at the facility to well after his planned departure.

It had taken even more time to get his superiors to agree to issue orders authorizing Shulga to train front-line troops in Javelin use. That finally got him to the border of Novorossiya with Javelin missiles and launchers.

But how would he get over it?

Fortunately, one of the enlisted men Shulga had recruited had the answer. One of his cousins was the customer of a Novorossiya smuggler named Avel Karpenko, who was also a militia commander.

Notified of the availability of Javelins, Karpenko had quickly responded with a detailed offer. In return for the missiles and men to operate them, Karpenko would provide more money than Shulga and his troops had been paid over their entire military career.

He would also put Shulga in command of his militia. Coincidentally, the man who'd held that job had just had an accident.

A fatal one.

Karpenko believed, correctly, that the previous commander had been plotting against him. And that the other former Ukrainian officers in his militia couldn't be trusted either.

But Shulga would be brand new, and unconnected with the other officers in Karpenko's militia.

That meant Shulga's dependence on Karpenko would be total.

Ordinarily, this would have put Shulga in great danger from his fellow militia officers, especially since none of them knew anything about the Javelin missiles Shulga was bringing.

That's why Karpenko assigned his best men to guard both Shulga and the missiles and housed them at his compound.

For an experienced smuggler like Karpenko, getting the trucks carrying Shulga's men and their missiles into Novorossiya had been easy.

Now, all the work and money required to get Javelins to Novorossiya was about to pay off.

For Karpenko, anyway.

Shulga looked through the Javelin's sight at one of the tanks they were targeting. The American who had trained Shulga had called it the "Command Launch Unit." Then, he'd called it by the acronym "CLU" and tried to joke about it, asking Shulga, "Do you have a CLU?"

It had taken quite a while for the American soldier to explain his joke. Shulga didn't laugh once.

The CLU was used to help locate and identify the target, and then fire the missile. Shulga was not happy that they were attacking during the day, but Karpenko had been precise about the time. He was forced to use the CLU as merely a magnifier since thermal mode was unavailable in daylight.

Of course, Karpenko hadn't explained that a daytime attack was essential because the maintenance depot where these tanks were located had few if any soldiers present at night. Or that he needed casualties to magnify the attack's importance.

Karpenko had instead said that the man who would be video recording the attack needed daylight, which made sense.

On the other hand, their firing position was close to ideal. A large meadow was to their front, providing an unobstructed view of the depot. Trees and brush were to their back so that it would be nearly impossible for anyone at the depot to spot them.

Until they fired, anyway.

However, Shulga was more than puzzled by Karpenko's order to attack Novorossiya's tanks.

In the end, though, he'd shrugged and decided to carry out the order. It wasn't as though Shulga had a choice at this point.

Each of Shulga's crew was wearing thin, flexible headsets for combat communications. Now, Shulga signaled each of them to prepare to fire on his command.

Shulga first locked his target. Then he gave each of his crew a few extra minutes to lock their targets, just to be sure.

Each crew consisted of one gunner and one ammunition bearer. Though a single soldier could theoretically operate the Javelin, in practice the launcher and missile were too heavy for one man to carry very far.

Plus, Shulga had brought an additional missile with him, just in case.

"Ready?" Shulga asked. One after the other, all three of the other crews radioed back, "Ready."

Shulga gave the fire command and pressed the Javelin's trigger.

Four missiles leaped forward almost simultaneously.

Each missile hit!

No! Somehow, despite all the hours of training, two of Shulga's crews had managed to lock onto the same tank.

Worse luck, someone was inside the undamaged T-72 tank. Because it was moving.

Fast.

And straight at them.

Shulga swore as his crewman loaded the second missile in his launcher. These tanks were supposed to be sitting ducks undergoing maintenance.

Well, maybe this one had just arrived at the depot.

And if it was loaded with ammo...

The T-72's main gun, which had been tilted at a side angle when the tank started, began to traverse in their direction.

Yeah, Shulga thought, as he desperately tried to get a lock on the T-72. It's got ammo.

A thunderous noise to Shulga's front, quickly followed by an impact to his far-right, told him that the T-72 had fired on his crews.

Shulga was fortunate that the T-72 was loaded with 3VBM-8 armor-piercing sabot rounds rather than explosive HEAT rounds, which could have quickly taken out two of his crews at once.

As it was, Shulga only lost one.

At last, Shulga had his lock!

The T-72's turret began to traverse in his direction.

Shulga pulled the trigger.

His Javelin leaped forward.

The T-72's turret flew upwards, accompanied by several interior explosions that rocked what was left of the tank.

No one got out.

Now Shulga could see soldiers holding rifles running towards them from the depot.

Lots of soldiers.

Time to go.

Shulga gave his surviving crewmen the command to fall back to the truck that had brought them through the forest road. Fortunately, it wasn't far away.

Even better was that Shulga was confident they would find the truck waiting for them.

Not because of any importance Karpenko placed on him or his men. But thanks to the value of the Javelin launchers they were carrying.

As he ran towards the truck, each of his remaining crewmen checked in. Shulga looked behind him and saw that Karpenko's cameraman was bringing up the rear.

Shulga had been delighted with his decision to go to Novorossiya when Karpenko's payment had registered in his foreign bank account.

Now he was wondering if he'd live long enough to spend it.

CHAPTER TWENTY

FSB Safe House
Troieshchyna District, Kyiv, Ukraine

Neda Rhahbar did her best to swear and threw down her pencil in frustration. She'd been sitting for hours with the SS-24 technical documents covering the kitchen table. Crumpled paper littering the floor around her testified to less than a complete success.

Maybe part of Neda's frustration was that her ability to swear in Russian was minimal. A phrase she'd inadvertently learned from an FSB martial arts instructor after the first time she beat him was far too strong, and Vasilyev had forbidden its use.

Instead, he'd taught her a phrase that in English might translate to "gosh darn it."

It didn't fit this situation.

Anatoly Grishkov and Mikhail Vasilyev looked at each other.

Grishkov said nothing, but his shrug was easy to translate.

Your wife, your problem.

At least that's how Vasilyev took it. However, the thoughts going through Grishkov's mind were considerably more sympathetic. He regarded Neda's ability to make any sense of nuclear weapons schematics as one short step from sorcery.

Vasilyev approached Neda carefully, knowing she was not in the best of moods.

"Maybe it would be best to take a break, and attack the problem fresh later," Vasilyev said quietly.

Neda at first glared at her husband and then sighed. "You're probably right. Anyway, I've just learned something from the SS-24 documents I should have figured out earlier. Let's go to the living room since you both need to hear this."

A few moments later, she was sitting on the sofa beside Vasilyev, while Grishkov sat on a chair across from the coffee table.

"Arbakov only needs one code to arm both warheads," Neda said flatly.

Vasilyev and Grishkov both stiffened with dismay.

"But how?" Vasilyev asked. "Didn't you say that each warhead has a separate arming component?"

"That's right," Neda replied. "But each SS-24 missile had only one module to receive and authenticate the arming code. That module then relayed that same code to each of the SS-24's ten warheads."

Grishkov shook his head. "Why? A different code for each warhead would have been elementary security."

"The problem was space. There wasn't enough of it in the SS-24's warhead to enable ten modules to receive and authenticate the arming code. Remember, we're talking about the degree of electronics miniaturization achieved by Soviet technology in the 1980s," Neda replied.

"So, once Arbakov has one arming code, he can detonate both warheads," Vasilyev said.

Grishkov cocked his head. "But would he know that?"

Neda shrugged. "If he were an ordinary SS-24 crewman, maybe not. But a sergeant who worked on the guts of these missiles for years? I'll bet he knew everything there was to know."

Vasilyev nodded and tapped his secure cell phone. "I just received the list you requested before leaving Moscow of experts with SS-24 experience who could construct an emulator capable of verifying a code that would work for Arbakov's warheads. There are only two men still alive on that list who live in Ukraine, and one isn't far from here."

Vasilyev paused. "Anyway, our agents were only able to confirm a current address for that one. They're still working on the other, who was last known to be in Ukraine but seems to have disappeared."

Neda took a deep breath and nodded. "OK, then let's go. I'm going to need more time to figure out how to defuse one of these warheads without a disarming code. Maybe it will come to me during the ride there. It's sure not coming to me here," Neda said, pointing at the crumpled paper on the kitchen floor with disgust.

Vasilyev texted Alina the engineer's name and address and a brief explanation.

If Alina could get away from the Embassy in time without being spotted, a little local backup wouldn't hurt.

Donetsk, "Donetsk People's Republic"

As soon as he saw Osip Litvin's expression, Avel Karpenko knew the news wasn't good.

Karpenko leaned back in his chair and sighed. Well, maybe it wasn't as bad as Litvin thought.

And at first, Karpenko's hopes went up.

"Let me start with the good news," Litvin said.

Well, OK. Not a complete disaster, then.

"We uploaded the video of the Javelin attack on our tanks to the Ukrainian military web site open to the public. There were multiple downloads before the hack was detected, and the video removed. We then uploaded it to many additional sites, and as expected, the video has gone viral, with millions of downloads," Litvin said.

Karpenko's eyebrows rose. Well, that all sounded great so far.

"There have been pointed questions asked about the attack in the Ukrainian legislature and press, and even the media in Russia has reported on the attack," Litvin continued.

"But?" Karpenko asked quietly.

Litvin frowned. "The Russians aren't buying it. Neither are many of our own Novorossiya officials, though so far none are saying so publicly. As expected, the Ukrainians loudly deny any involvement in the attack."

Karpenko smiled. Well, why wouldn't they? For once, the Ukrainians were, in fact, totally innocent.

"The Ukrainians are saying the Javelins were stolen, and that turncoat Ukrainian soldiers carried out the attack. They ask how real Ukrainian soldiers could have carried out the attack deep within Novorossiya and then escape."

Litvin paused. "Also, another video of the attack has been uploaded, and has now been reposted on a Ukrainian government website."

Karpenko stiffened with dismay. "Can Shulga and his men be identified?" he asked.

"No. By the time one of the soldiers at the depot pointed his cell phone at them, their backs were turned, and they were running for the forest. The video quality was also poor since it was shot at long range, and the soldier was running towards the attackers," Litvin replied.

"But they can be seen wearing Ukrainian Army uniforms," Karpenko said flatly.

Litvin nodded.

Karpenko shrugged. He'd been the one who insisted that Shulga and his men do so.

It might not have been his best idea.

He simply hadn't considered the point being made by the Ukrainians. Indeed, how could the attackers have made their way back to Ukraine through Novorossiya territory?

"But that's not our biggest problem," Litvin said.

Karpenko glared at Litvin, prompting him to add hurriedly, "The Ukrainians have released the names and photos of Shulga and his men. Our own Novorossiya officials have the bodies of two of them."

Seeing Karpenko's reaction, Litvin added even more quickly, "The bodies' condition makes a photo match impossible. However, one militia commander has suggested sending the remains to the Ukrainians for a DNA match."

Karpenko relaxed and settled back in his chair.

Litvin smiled. "As you've guessed, nobody else thought it was a great idea. First, many here don't believe the Ukrainian story. Second, even those who do, acknowledge a DNA match performed by the Ukrainians would lack credibility. Of course, we can't do a match ourselves."

Karpenko frowned and asked slowly, "What if the Russians offered to do a DNA match based on the bodies and the Ukrainian Army's DNA records?"

"They haven't offered to do that so far, or I would have heard. But you're right. If they did, the Russians are much more likely to be believed by our people," Litvin replied.

"Can we replace the bodies?" Karpenko asked.

Litvin nodded. "Maybe. I've already asked Shulga for two sets of his men's uniforms and thoroughly washed them to remove any traces of DNA. Bodies the same approximate age and size as the dead crewmen should be no problem. Recreating their current condition won't be as easy, but I think we can come close."

Then Litvin paused. "I'll have to pay several people substantial sums to get access to the bodies. After that, before long, those people will need to have accidents."

"Just get me the names," Karpenko said. He knew Litvin didn't like to get his hands dirty, which was fine.

It made it much less likely Litvin would try to replace him.

"Look, I know all this means the peace talks will go on, and stopping them was the whole point of this exercise. I have another idea for how to do that, but I have to start by saying it's a long shot," Litvin said.

Karpenko nodded expectantly. At this point, he was willing to try almost anything.

"As you know, we routinely monitor dark web traffic for anything that could help us. A few weeks back, there was a post from someone offering an SS-24 warhead," Litvin said.

Karpenko grunted. Someone was always trying to sell nuclear weapons on the dark web. Every offer they'd checked out had either been a scam or an attempt at entrapment by some country's intelligence service.

"How much did they want?" Karpenko growled.

"That's what caught my attention," Litvin replied. "They didn't want money. They said they'd trade the warhead for the services of an expert in writing software for SS-24s."

Karpenko nodded thoughtfully.

"So, maybe they have two warheads, but zero arming codes. How powerful is an SS-24 warhead?" Karpenko asked.

"Half a megaton, enough to level a major city," Litvin replied.

"And the warhead is Russian so that the blame would fall on them first," Karpenko said.

"Yes. And SS-24s used to be based in Ukraine, so it would be credible if one exploded there that it was a warhead the Ukrainians had failed to turn over to the Russians. And that it had been set off by accident," Litvin said.

"Good," Karpenko said. "Did you reply to the posting?"

Litvin shook his head. "I would never do that without your approval. Instead, I had a search made for an expert in writing software for SS-24s living in Ukraine. That person would be far easier for us to reach than one living in Russia."

"Makes sense," Karpenko said approvingly. "No point in saying anything until we have something to trade."

"Yes. We found two men, but one seems to have vanished. I have a team headed by one of our best men on the way to the other, and hope to hear from him soon," Litvin said.

"Marko Zavod?" Karpenko asked.

Litvin smiled and nodded.

"Good choice," Karpenko said.

Zavod was another recent defector, in his case from the Ukrainian Spetsnaz, a force Karpenko admired for two reasons.

He liked their slogan, borrowed from the Ukrainian prince who a thousand years ago had established what had briefly been the largest state in Europe.

Svyatoslav the Brave's slogan had been, "I come at you!"

Maybe more important was that in 2019 the Ukrainian Spetsnaz had been certified as the first special operations force allowed to participate in operations with the NATO Response Force from a non-NATO member state.

Yes. If anyone could get the job done, it would be Zavod.

Chapter Twenty-One

En Route to Nova Basan, Ukraine

Mikhail Vasilyev looked at the text on his secure cell phone and sighed.

Alina would join them, but she expected to be late. It appeared the Ukrainians were shadowing everyone from the Russian Embassy even more aggressively than usual. Throwing them off her trail would take time.

Well, Vasilyev couldn't argue with that. They certainly didn't want the Ukrainian government involved.

Grishkov was a careful driver, and kept his hands on the wheel of the large black SUV he was driving when he spoke for the first time since leaving the safe house.

"This SS-24 engineer we're going to see. What do we know about him?" Grishkov asked.

"Olek Tarasenko," Vasilyev replied. "Let me look again at what I was sent."

Then Vasilyev glanced at Neda Rhahbar in the back seat, once again immersed in SS-24 technical documents.

"Will we be disturbing your work?" Vasilyev asked Neda.

Neda shook her head absently without looking up from the document she was holding.

Vasilyev turned back to Grishkov.

"Tarasenko was a rarity, both a software and a mechanical engineer, which made him a highly valued employee. He worked his entire career for the Yuzhnoye Design Office in Dnipro, about a six-hour drive from his current residence. Yuzhnoye dates back to 1951 and produced many missiles and rockets besides the SS-24, including the SS-18, which is still in service. Their most recent rocket is the Cyclone 4M, a satellite launch vehicle first successfully launched from Nova Scotia a few years ago," Vasilyev said.

Grishkov smiled. "So, they went from building ICBMs that certainly targeted Canada to launching satellites from Canada."

Vasilyev smiled back. "Well put. I hadn't thought about it that way."

"So, unless Tarasenko enjoys twelve-hour commutes, I take it he's retired?" Grishkov asked.

"Correct," Vasilyev replied. "Since last year. He's living out in the countryside about ten kilometers north of the village of Nova Basan. His mother died giving birth to him, and he has no siblings. Tarasenko inherited the house when his father died about two years ago. His wife died six months later. He has no children."

Grishkov shook his head. "A series of heavy blows, and no family to cushion them. Not surprising that he couldn't go on at work."

"Yes. Yuzhnoye is a large company with over five thousand employees, and Tarasenko was considered one of their most valuable. No matter how much they offered him, though, they couldn't convince him to stay," Vasilyev said.

"So, we will have to find some motivation besides money," Grishkov said thoughtfully.

Vasilyev nodded. "And we'll need to find it soon. The turn for Nova Basan is just ahead."

They both sat thinking quietly, the only sound the rustling of paper as Neda switched from one SS-24 document to another, and the hum of the SUV's tires. Once they exited the highway, the quality of the roads dropped dramatically, and Grishkov found himself appreciating both the SUV's four-wheel drive and its excellent ground clearance.

Then Grishkov's eyes narrowed. "Is it my imagination, or is that SUV following us?"

"It's either following us, or it's just headed in the same direction. Take that next turn to the right, and let's see what he does," Vasilyev replied.

Grishkov had thought the dirt road leading to Tarasenko's house was terrible. The road he was on now barely deserved the name and was really more a collection of potholes.

Grishkov's attention focused on avoiding breaking an axle, while Vasilyev leaned back to examine the other SUV's reaction.

Vasilyev grunted with surprise as he was able to see the SUV's full size for the first time. A Toyota Sequoia, or something even more massive. With all the dust between them, it was hard to be sure.

But whatever it was, it didn't stop or even slow down.

Vasilyev observed as the other SUV approached the turnoff for Tarasenko's home, visible less than a kilometer ahead.

But it kept on going and was soon out of sight.

Grishkov was already maneuvering their SUV into a turn back onto the road leading to Tarasenko's home.

Grishkov and Vasilyev looked at each other.

"I don't like it," Grishkov said flatly. "That was no farmer's vehicle."

Vasilyev shrugged. "Maybe so. We will have to remain alert."

As they reached the driveway leading to Tarasenko's home, Grishkov hissed with dismay.

A sturdy metal gate set a few meters from the road barred the way forward. Mature trees on both sides of the road made driving around it impossible.

There was nothing visible showing how the gate opened. Grishkov guessed, correctly, that it was operated by remote control.

There was no intercom. Apparently, Tarasenko had no interest in visitors.

Tarasenko's driveway wound its way through the trees up to his house, barely visible about half a kilometer ahead.

Grishkov backed their SUV up to the gate. Its front was out of the road, but not by much.

Vasilyev shook his head. "I guess we walk."

"No choice that I can see. I wonder if our friends from the other SUV will be waiting when we come back," Grishkov said.

Vasilyev mutely shrugged and opened his door.

Minutes later, they were all standing in front of Tarasenko's house. Before they could approach its door, a distinctive sound made them stop.

The sound of a round being chambered into a shotgun.

From behind the door, Tarasenko's voice said firmly, "Strangers aren't welcome. Go back to the road the way you came."

Before either Grishkov or Vasilyev could say anything, Neda held up a piece of paper.

"Do you recognize this? Someone is about to use your creation unless we get your help," Neda said.

Silence followed. The door stayed closed.

Then the voice returned, less confident this time.

"How do you have that? Those documents are highly classified. Anyway, your concern is decades late. All of those warheads were destroyed long ago," Tarasenko said.

"Two of them were swapped for test warheads and hidden until now. Now the thief has decided to use them. Do you care?" Neda asked.

The silence lasted even longer this time. Finally, though, the door opened, and Tarasenko gestured silently for them to enter.

Tarasenko was dressed just as Neda would have expected if he were behind the desk at his Yuzhnoye office. Maybe force of habit, Neda thought. His silver hair made him look distinguished, not old. Certainly, Tarasenko still appeared both alert and highly intelligent.

Tarasenko's home was at least as old as Kulik's, but the contrast between them couldn't have sharper. After his father's death, Tarasenko had evidently removed every piece of furniture and decoration from the house. Even the wood flooring was new.

The furnishings Tarasenko had put in their place were functional and straightforward, but well made. There were no pictures or decorations and no television. A recent model laptop sat closed on the coffee table.

Tarasenko waved them impatiently to the sofa, while at the same time stretching his hand towards Neda.

"The folder, please," Tarasenko said.

Neda silently handed over the folder containing the SS-24 technical documents, and they all sat.

Tarasenko perched in a chair across from them and began to flip through the documents. A few minutes later, he looked up at Neda.

"So, you're all working for the Russian government. Nobody else could have given you these documents. Everything we had at Yuzhnoye on the SS-24 was destroyed decades ago. The Ukrainian government was never given copies," Tarasenko said flatly.

"You're right. So, will you help us?" Neda asked.

Tarasenko frowned. "To do what?"

Vasilyev interrupted. "First, let me explain who we are. I am Mikhail Vasilyev, and that's Anatoly Grishkov. You've been speaking to Neda Rhahbar, our nuclear expert. We all work for the FSB."

Reaching inside his jacket, Vasilyev extracted a photo. Pointing at it, he said, "This is the image that started our search. You recognize what it shows?"

Tarasenko reached for the photo and looked at it intently.

"These are SS-24 warheads. I recognize the series numbers, or at least their format. You have investigated and confirmed that this is a real image of actual missing warheads?" Tarasenko asked.

Vasilyev nodded. "Yes, we have. The first thing we need to know is whether anyone has tried to contact you about these warheads."

Tarasenko shrugged. "No. Few know where I went after retirement, and I made it clear to everyone at Yuzhnoye I wasn't interested in visitors. No one has attempted to contact me for any reason in over a month."

"Good," Vasilyev said. Gesturing towards Neda, he said, "Neda will explain why we need your expertise."

Tarasenko looked at Neda expectantly.

"The thief who put this image on the dark web didn't ask for money. He asked for a software engineer's services with SS-24 experience in return for one of the warheads," Neda said.

Tarasenko laughed with relief. "Of course! He doesn't have the arming code!"

"I notice you said code, not codes. So, the code is the same for both warheads?" Neda asked.

"Yes, but I think you'd figured out that much already. The serial numbers on the warheads aren't sequential, but they are just a few digits apart. That means they came from the same SS-24, and the documents in that folder should have told you there was only one module in each SS-24 to receive and decrypt the arming code," Tarasenko replied.

Neda smiled. "Since I have the expert before me, I thought I should check rather than assume I was right."

Tarasenko laughed even more loudly and said, "Thank you. It's been a long time since I can remember laughing at anything. Yes, when it comes to nuclear weapons, it's best not to assume anything. So, you think they need someone like me to build an emulator?"

"Exactly," Neda said. "Could you do it, and could you use that approach to obtain an arming code?"

"Yes, to both questions," Tarasenko replied.

"Do you know anyone else who could?" Neda asked.

Now all trace of amusement left Tarasenko's face, and it was hard to imagine him as the man who had been laughing just a moment ago.

"Fedir Popova," Tarasenko said, biting off each syllable as though it were poison.

Vasilyev looked at Neda and tapped his cell phone.

Neda smiled her understanding. Popova was the other name Vasilyev had received from Moscow.

The man who had disappeared.

"Do you think Popova would be willing to build an emulator for the thief?" Neda asked.

Tarasenko sat quietly for a moment, clearly gathering his thoughts.

Finally, he said, "The thief expected someone to pay an expert like Popova or me to build the emulator in return for one of the warheads. With Popova, though, it would be much simpler. He would have eliminated the need for a middleman."

Neda frowned. "Do you mean that Popova would have been willing to take the warhead in payment for building an emulator, and then sold it himself?"

"No. I mean, he would use the warhead himself," Tarasenko said grimly.

Silence descended as they all struggled to absorb Tarasenko's last statement.

"Why do you say that?" Neda finally asked.

"Because Popova is and always has been a treacherous snake," Tarasenko replied promptly. "I never trusted him. About five years ago, I was finally able to prove he was selling our technology to one of our business rivals. I tried to get him prosecuted, but all I could do was get him fired. I also made sure, with the full support of all the senior executives at Yuzhnoye, he never worked as a software engineer again," Tarasenko said.

"So, you think he would use the weapon against Yuzhnoye," Neda said doubtfully.

"Yes, if I were you, I'd find that hard to believe, too," Tarasenko said. "One other detail may change your mind, though. A couple of months ago, my old boss at Yuzhnoye called to tell me he'd heard Popova had cancer. Pancreatic. I think he believed I'd be happy to hear the news, and maybe part of me did. But that's not a fate I'd wish on anyone, even Popova."

Neda winced and nodded. A type of cancer with a notoriously low survival rate.

And a painful progression.

"How close would he need to get to be sure of destroying Yuzhnoye headquarters?" Neda asked.

Tarasenko shrugged. "Impossible to say with any precision, even if we assume the warhead is detonated at ground level. A five hundred kiloton yield?"

Tarasenko shook his head.

"Anywhere in the general Dnipro area, where Yuzhnoye has its headquarters. It's a city of about a million people. Anyone in the city would either be killed immediately or wish they had been."

Neda swallowed and sat silently for a moment.

"Can you think of anything that would help us find the warheads?" Neda asked.

"Yes," Tarasenko said immediately. Then he grabbed a notepad sitting on the coffee table and quickly dashed off a series of elements and percentages. Next, he tore off the top page and handed it to Neda.

Neda looked it over and nodded. "The exact composition of the radioactive elements in the warhead. I'm impressed that you could remember it so precisely after all this time. I was disappointed it wasn't in the technical documents."

"Why would it be? Those were operational documents. It's not as though the composition could have been changed after the warheads were made. And you can be sure of those numbers. The SS-24 was the only nuclear missile I worked on, and I remember every detail," Tarasenko said.

"This will be very helpful in picking out the warhead from other radiation sources. But once we find it, we'll have to defuse it," Neda said, handing Tarasenko drawings illustrating her most recent attempts to devise a disarmament plan.

"Once we find Popova and the warhead, we have to expect him to enter the arming code. Do you know how long we'll have until detonation?" Neda asked.

"Not long. Exactly how long would depend on the distance to the programmed target. Less time for a target like an airbase in Alaska. More time for a city like Miami. I suppose there are no surviving records that would tell you the targets assigned for each warhead in this particular SS-24," Tarasenko said.

Neda looked at Vasilyev, who shook his head.

As Tarasenko began to examine her drawings, Neda added, "These are my best ideas, but I don't think they'd work."

Tarasenko looked through Neda's drawings intently, at first frowning, and then smiling.

After several minutes, he looked up from the drawings at Neda with new respect.

"I see what you were trying to do, and I'm impressed. These approaches might have worked against some of our other nuclear weapons, but you're right. Not against the SS-24," Tarasenko said.

"Understood," Neda said. "So, how can we disable the circuitry controlling the detonation of the warhead once the arming code has been entered?"

Tarasenko looked at her blankly and then said slowly, "Oh. I see you haven't understood."

"You can't."

CHAPTER TWENTY-TWO

Pryluky Air Base, Ukraine

Fedir Popova had driven past the base's Tupolev TU-16 monument, which was still in good condition, and expected to see someone. Anyone.

No. As far as he could tell, Popova was utterly alone.

Crumbling concrete runway stretched as far as he could see.

Pofistal Arbakov hadn't been kidding when he said the base had been destroyed. Every structure in sight had either been removed down to the foundation or was nothing but rubble.

Popova remembered reading that the Americans had requested the destruction of facilities at inactive former Soviet strategic bases in Ukraine as a condition for aid.

It looked like Ukraine had kept its side of the bargain.

Popova shook his head. So, where was he supposed to build an emulator in the safety and security that Arbakov had promised?

Of course, that presumed Arbakov would show up with the promised warhead. Now that Popova had built an emulator for one of Arbakov's warheads, there was nothing to stop him from just keeping the other.

Popova looked at his watch and shrugged. Well, if Arbakov had betrayed him, there was absolutely nothing he could do about it.

To be fair, that was also true about the arming code Popova had given Arbakov. Yes, Arbakov wouldn't know whether it worked until he pressed the button on the small radio transmitter Popova had given him tuned to the warhead's frequency.

For about the tenth time, Popova asked himself whether it was essential to build another emulator. The serial numbers on the warheads backed up Arbakov's claim that they had come from the same SS-24 missile.

Popova was almost sure he remembered that the arming code for the SS-24 was the same for all of its ten warheads. Something to do with concern about radio transmissions having to be repeated for rail-mounted SS-24s subjected to a near miss by an American ICBM. About the possibility there wouldn't be enough time to send ten different arming codes by radio.

Never mind that Arbakov said this SS-24 had been silo-based. Popova knew there was no difference between the arming mechanism in both SS-24 models. Part of the design had been based on the belief that all SS-24s should be switchable between the two basing modes.

No, Popova concluded again with a sigh. He had to be sure.

Well, if Arbakov didn't show up, the question would be moot.

Almost immediately, Popova shook his head. He could use many words to describe Arbakov.

Unstable. Grim. Determined.

But not dishonest.

Popova smiled at the irony. He was self-aware enough to realize that anyone who knew his history would indeed call him dishonest. But it was precisely that fact which made him confident he could detect that quality in others.

Looking in the rear-view mirror towards the base entrance, Popova caught a glimpse of himself and shuddered. The gray hair and lined face that looked back at him belonged to someone else, not Fedir Popova.

Nothing could get him used to the transformation that disease had wreaked on his body. Or the pain that came with it.

Popova climbed down from the truck and looked again towards the base entrance.

Yes. The more he thought about it, the more certain Popova was that Arbakov would be here.

As though summoned by the thought, Popova saw a dot in the distance that rapidly grew into a truck. As it came closer, he could see it was the same massive Ural-4320 6x6 all-wheel-drive truck Arbakov had used to bring him the first warhead.

Moments later, the truck pulled up in front of him, and Arbakov gestured for Popova to follow. Nodding, Popova put his vehicle into gear and did just that.

It didn't take long, but when they stopped, Popova understood what Arbakov had meant about security for his work. There was nothing and no one visible in any direction except dirt, grass and crumbling runway.

Arbakov climbed down from his truck and walked up to Popova's as he switched off the engine.

"This is a KrAZ truck, correct?" Arbakov asked.

Popova lowered himself to the ground and nodded. "Yes, a KrAZ-6322, built right here in Ukraine."

"Good," Arbakov said, nodding with approval. "You have enough water and food for your stay here?"

"Yes. I also have the canvas cover you told me to get," Popova replied.

"Excellent. Now, show me where in the truck I'm going to put the warhead," Arbakov said.

Popova nodded and gestured for Arbakov to follow him to the back of the truck. Then, he lowered the gate and pointed to a large metal apparatus bolted to the far end of the truck bed.

"Just put it in the case at the end right against the truck cab," Popova said.

Arbakov cocked his head and looked at the apparatus. "May I?" he asked.

Popova nodded, and Arbakov walked up the ramp formed by the lowered gate and into the truck bed. A few moments later, he was crouching over the apparatus and running his hands over the mechanism.

"So, I see that the case is lifted above the truck bed on brackets, to cushion it against impacts. Also, the metal plate extending the width of the truck bed is mounted on these rails. This position will let me drive the forklift close enough to deposit the warhead into the case against the cab. Further back, and you will have plenty of room to work on the warhead. Once your work is complete, you can press the plate up against the warhead so it will be secured for transport."

Arbakov nodded towards a motor bolted to the right corner of the truck bed near the gate.

"And that is the power source for the mechanism, correct?"

"That's right," Popova replied.

Now Arbakov pointed at a metal handle, gears, and chain attached to the left side of the truck bed.

"And this crank is a manual backup in case the motor fails," Arbakov said.

Popova nodded.

"I would have kept my promise to bring you the other warhead in any case. Now I'm glad to see I didn't waste my time doing so," Arbakov said.

Without waiting for a reply, Arbakov trotted down the ramp and headed for what, as far as Popova could see, was an area of grass and weeds like all the rest around them.

Popova was astonished when Arbakov bent down and pulled aside what turned out to be a length of green canvas with grass and weeds piled on top. Now that Popova looked more closely, he could see that some of the plants were turning brown.

Arbakov saw him look and smiled. Then he said, "I'll grab a few handfuls to refresh the camouflage before I go. Anyway, it's not intended to stand up to close examination, just anyone who sends a drone overhead."

Now Popova could see a metal wheel set less than half a meter below the ground, attached to a metal hatch. Arbakov twisted it open in just a few minutes. It looks just like the entry hatch I've seen in movies about submarines, Popova thought.

Arbakov pointed down into the newly revealed hole. "Let me have a few minutes, and then I'll give you a tour of your new home. In the meantime, you can start bringing over your supplies."

Arbakov climbed down and was soon out of sight. Popova walked up to the hatch and looked down. Just as he did so, he could see a dot of light come on at the bottom.

A flashlight, Popova guessed correctly.

Popova shrugged. Nothing for it but to hope Arbakov knew what he was doing.

Drastically diminished appetite was one consequence of the cancer that was killing Popova. It meant bringing the food and water Popova expected to need didn't take long. As he finished, Popova could see light flood the hole in the earth, revealing the top of Arbakov's head approaching as he climbed up the ladder.

Arbakov exited the ladder and stood next to Popova.

Pointing at the small pile of food and water, Arbakov asked, "Is this all you have to go down?"

Popova nodded but then hesitated. "Well, except for my equipment. That's the radio transmitter, the emulator, and my laptop."

"They're in the cab of your truck, right?" Arbakov asked.

Popova nodded. "Yes. I'll need to use the laptop and emulator once you've moved the warhead to my truck for about an hour. Then they'll all need to go down with me."

"Fine. What needs to come out with you once you're done?" Arbakov asked.

Popova shrugged. "Only the radio transmitter and I can put that in my pocket."

"Good. Now, let me show you around. I'll go first," Arbakov said.

Popova noticed a metal tray attached to a rope on both sides next to the entrance and realized it must have been covered by the same canvas that had concealed the hatch. He almost asked what it was for, but then saw its purpose was obvious.

This was how supplies would get to him without having to be carried down the ladder.

It took Popova longer than Arbakov, but it was still just moments later when Popova found himself standing next to him at the ladder's bottom.

Only the area immediately around the ladder was lit. Popova could see a vast concrete expanse stretching off into the gloom. The air smelled a bit musty, but not too bad. Looking up, Popova could see a metal vent that was the source of the air he could feel ruffling his hair.

"What is this place?" Popova asked.

"A familiar space to me. Nuclear munitions used to be stored here, and I was in charge of their maintenance and storage. When orders came to destroy all the facilities on this base, I successfully argued it would be simpler to bury the entrances to this bunker and forget to tell the Americans about it," Arbakov said.

"Well, it's come in handy now," Popova said.

Arbakov shrugged. "It never occurred to me at the time that I might come back here. The front entrance we used to load and unload munitions is buried under tons of earth and rock. I had to use a metal detector to find this emergency escape hatch. I'm lucky they put just enough earth on top of the hatch to conceal it."

Popova pointed to a nearby air mattress. "I guess that's where I'll be sleeping?"

"Yes. As I told you before, there's no way to cook anything. It's good you didn't bring too much food, because the plumbing doesn't work. The bathroom's the first door on the right," Arbakov said, pointing towards a doorway barely visible in the gloom.

"Bring a flashlight when you go," Arbakov added.

"Power is from a generator?" Popova asked.

"Yes. I'm going to show you that next," Arbakov replied.

A few minutes later, they were standing in front of a generator. Though old, it appeared to be running without issues. Popova was glad to see the exhaust connected to a tube that led...somewhere.

Well, he couldn't smell the exhaust, and that's all that matters, Popova thought.

"It took me almost a day to get this generator working again, but it seems fine now. I've left you enough gas to keep it going for at least three days," Arbakov said.

Popova nodded. "I doubt I'll even need that long. I've already built the emulator based on the warhead I worked on for you. If it's identical, there should be no problems."

"Good," Arbakov said. "Let's go back to the entrance."

Once they were there, Arbakov pointed to an electrical outlet next to a small folding table and chair.

"This is the only outlet powered by the generator. It should work to recharge your laptop. We have now reached the end of the tour," Arbakov said wryly.

Popova laughed. "It will do fine. I appreciate the work you've done preparing this place."

"Well, without you, I'd have no arming code, so it seemed only fair. Now let's get your food and water down here. Wait here while I go back up and lower them on the tray. Tug at the rope once you're finished unloading," Arbakov said.

It didn't take long until all of Popova's supplies were in the bunker.

"Come on up," Arbakov called from on top of the ladder.

When Popova emerged, he could see Arbakov had already started his small forklift and used it to approach an object in his truck's bed. Popova watched silently as Arbakov slowly picked it up, and then even more slowly backed the forklift down his truck's ramp.

It only took a few minutes for Arbakov to transfer the warhead to Popova's truck.

Once the warhead was in place within Popova's apparatus, Arbakov backed his forklift off the truck. He said, "Please check and let me know if the warhead is fine where it is, or if I need to move it."

Popova climbed into the truck bed and looked over the metal container. It was now secured with a heavy padlock.

As Popova turned towards Arbakov and opened his mouth to speak, Arbakov shook his head and sent a metal key sailing through the air. Popova deftly caught it.

"Sorry. After all this effort, it would have been ridiculous to see it fail due to the lack of a simple key. The lock is no real security, of course. It's just for keeping out the curious during any stops you have to make between here and Dnipro," Arbakov said, and then hesitated.

"Anything else?" Popova prompted.

"Well, it's none of my business, but has it occurred to you that the authorities may have spotted my dark web notice about the warheads? By now, they've had time to investigate. Since you're one of the few SS-24 experts still living, they may have noticed your disappearance. They'll know about the grievance you have against Yuzhnoye. If they try to stop you before you reach Dnipro, what is your plan?" Arbakov asked.

Popova nodded. "Yes, the possibility of police interference did occur to me. I've arranged to meet some gunmen in Lubny. A man I trust hired them for me. From Lubny, it should only take about four hours to get to Dnipro on the M03 and P52 highways."

"Very well," Arbakov said. "Now, let's get this canvas cover on your truck. The cover won't interfere with your work, will it?"

"No," Popova replied. "We'll just get the cover in place over the hood and cab, and then I can stretch it back the rest of the way on my own once I'm done with the emulator."

"That should work," Arbakov said, nodding. A few minutes later, the cover was in place.

"Now that I see the cover over the truck, I understand why you sent me that picture and told me to match the color when I had the cover made. The picture was a close up of the grass here, right?" Popova asked.

"Right," Arbakov replied nodding. "Seemed like an obvious trick. With so many drones and satellites out there, you have to assume someone will look here. I think the few hours we've just spent was safe enough. I don't think a few days would be."

Popova stuck out his hand. "Thanks again. Good luck with your mission." Whatever that might be, he added to himself silently. Arbakov hadn't volunteered the information, and Popova hadn't asked.

The truth was, Popova didn't care. He'd be dead anyway.

Arbakov shook his hand and grinned, though Popova saw there was no real amusement there. Just grim determination.

"Good luck to you, too," Arbakov said.

"Let's make them pay."

Chapter Twenty-Three

9 Kilometers North of Nova Basan, Ukraine

Marko Zavod cursed as the black SUV they were following suddenly veered off the road.

Zavod ran his right hand over his bald, bullet-shaped head. His black eyes glittered as he worked to control his breathing and his temper. The years of physical and mental discipline required for Spetsnaz service came to his aid, and he was able to think.

When they'd first fallen in behind it, Zavod had hoped the SUV just happened to be going in the same direction. As a routine precaution, he had texted the license plate number to one of his few remaining Ukrainian contacts.

The response would have been meaningless to most. For someone with Zavod's history in the Ukrainian military, though, it meant bad news.

The SUV was leased to a Russian government front company.

Which meant the men in the SUV were Russian government agents.

Almost certainly armed agents.

The three other men in his SUV were armed too. But with the minimal notice Litvin had given him, they were far from the best he'd ever worked with.

They were just the best he could get right now to carry out Tarasenko's kidnapping.

And there was no way to know how many armed men could already be waiting at Tarasenko's house.

Zavod had only an instant to decide.

"Keep going," Zavod told the driver sitting next to him.

The man had been expecting to follow the black SUV but shrugged and kept their SUV on the road.

With those agents behind them now, they could quickly drive right up to Tarasenko's house. Then, dispose of anyone who might be there and grab Tarasenko.

Zavod cursed even more bitterly when he saw the metal gate barring the way to Tarasenko's house.

Exit their vehicle in front of the gate, and take on whoever might be in the house, while armed Russian agents were hard on their heels?

No.

"Keep going," Zavod told the driver.

The man's eyebrows rose, but he just shrugged again and kept driving straight.

After a few kilometers, Zavod saw a turnoff ahead.

"Make a U-turn," he told the driver.

By the time the gate to Tarasenko's house was once again in view, Zavod could see the parked black SUV they'd been following.

It was empty.

"Pull over," Zavod ordered.

So, probably no Russian agents already at Tarasenko's house, since they hadn't opened the gate.

Zavod briefly considered assaulting the house but rejected the idea almost immediately.

Defenders inside a structure always had the advantage. More important was that Zavod knew a stray round fired into the house could kill Tarasenko.

You couldn't kidnap a dead man.

Zavod reached inside his combat pack and extracted a tracking device.

Handing it to the driver, he pointed at the black SUV.

"Put it out of sight under the vehicle," Zavod said.

The driver nodded and did as he was told.

Zavod rolled down his window and covered the driver with his Fort-221, a licensed version of the Tavor-21 Israeli bullpup assault rifle produced for the sole use of Ukrainian special forces.

It was one of the few items Zavod had been able to take with him when he defected to Novorossiya.

But nothing happened, and the driver returned without incident. Zavod checked his cell phone and saw a map display with a red dot blinking in the middle.

The tracker was working.

"You remember the dirt road where that vehicle turned off?" Zavod asked.

The driver nodded.

"Good. Turn there, then go down far enough that we won't be visible from this road. Then make a U-turn and keep the engine running. We'll come up behind them," Zavod said.

Tarasenko pointed at the SS-24 warhead schematic he'd been reviewing and said, "I've realized that if someone had a warhead lying open before them, there is another approach that might work. One that doesn't involve the nuclear arming circuitry."

Grishkov interrupted. "Somebody's coming up behind us fast. I think it's that same SUV."

Vasilyev looked behind them and nodded. "I think you're right. Can you make this thing go any faster?"

Grishkov shrugged. "Not and be sure of keeping it on the road. I suggest you let our visitors know they're not welcome."

Vasilyev rolled down his window, undid his seat belt, and looked back. Then he steadied his AK-74 against the door frame. Next, he checked traffic in both directions.

Nothing.

"When I signal, move sharp left and slow," Vasilyev said.

"Got it," Grishkov replied.

With luck, that would put the pursuing SUV right in his sights.

Assuming the other driver was slow to react.

Chapter Twenty-Four

Highway 2521
Fifteen Kilometers North of Nova Basan, Ukraine

Marko Zavod smiled as he saw the black SUV he was sure included Tarasenko speed up. Yes, the Russians with him had bought a little time by going north.

But it didn't matter. There was nowhere to run.

And now he knew for sure there were only three Russians with Tarasenko. This would be easy.

"Close the distance," Zavod told the driver.

Zavod lowered the window and steadied his Fort-221 assault rifle against the doorframe.

He switched the rifle to single-shot. Zavod was targeting the right rear tire, and at the enemy vehicle's high speed, he needed the tire flat, not disintegrated.

No, the SUV with Tarasenko needed to be disabled, not careening off the road.

Zavod glanced backward and said, "Hold fast. Once I get them stopped, you'll have plenty to do."

He saw looks of annoyance and resentment flash across both gun-men's faces, but they nodded sullenly.

Good. Zavod didn't need contentment, just compliance.

Zavod looked down his gunsight and squeezed off a single round. At this range, there was no way he could miss.

Nothing happened.

The black SUV in front of them kept driving as though he'd missed entirely.

Of course! Self-sealing tires. He should have expected that.

Zavod switched the rifle to semi-automatic fire. He'd still have to be careful, but knew he could defeat the self-sealing feature with a few more rounds.

What was that on the right?

One of the Russians was going to fire at them!

"Move left!" Zavod shouted, ducking down at the same moment.

The driver responded quickly, but not quite fast enough. Several rounds hit Zavod's vehicle, though a quick check confirmed that none had hit Zavod.

The gunman directly behind Zavod hadn't been so lucky. Everyone had bulletproof vests, but they were little help against a headshot.

At least the rest of them were still untouched, and their vehicle con-tinued to move forward.

Zavod snarled a curse and leaned back out his window, aiming his ri-fle again at the Russian SUV's right rear tire.

Time to end this.

Just as Zavod had the tire lined up, the enemy's rear window ex-ploded, and the SUV veered leftward.

At the same instant, a rush of air and the deafening noise from the other gunman's AK-74 told Zavod what had happened.

The surviving gunman in the rear seat had ignored Zavod's orders and fired indiscriminately at the target SUV.

Zavod didn't hesitate. One of the first skills he'd been taught in the Ukrainian Spetsnaz had been firing left-handed. Now he used that skill with the pistol holstered on his left hip.

The gunman who had fired wouldn't risk Zavod's mission again.

But now Zavod only had one gunman left to help him take on three armed Russians.

Zavod glanced at the driver, who shrugged.

"He had it coming," the driver said.

Good. At least they weren't all idiots.

And the driver had been able to close the range further, even while weaving to avoid the rounds one of the Russians continued to send their way.

Well, assuming Tarasenko was still alive, Zavod could still complete this mission successfully.

The enemy SUV's right rear tire filled his assault rifle's gunsight, and his finger closed on the trigger.

Highway 2521
Seventeen Kilometers North of Nova Basan, Ukraine

"Tarasenko's hit!" Neda Rhahbar yelled from the back seat as she pulled her scarf from her hair to try to stop his bleeding.

It wasn't working.

Mikhail Vasilyev snarled a curse as he fired again at the pursuing vehicle. It continued to weave unpredictably, while still moving closer. He didn't think he was hitting anything.

Tarasenko's eyes fluttered open, and his mouth opened. Neda continued to apply pressure to his wound and said, "Don't try to speak."

In a low, urgent voice, Neda said, "You've got to pull over so I can get to the first aid kit in the trunk. He's bleeding too fast."

Before Vasilyev could reply, Tarasenko whispered in a voice so low only Neda could hear it, "Ignore the nuclear arming circuits. Focus on the explosive charge..."

His eyes closed.

From the back seat, Vasilyev heard the curse he'd forbidden Neda to use.

He didn't blame her.

As Vasilyev changed the clip in his rifle, he was determined to make whoever was behind them pay for Tarasenko's death.

Several rounds struck their right rear tire, and Anatoly Grishkov had to fight to maintain control of the vehicle. But, after a few seconds, their path straightened.

As Vasilyev leaned out the window, he tried again to score a meaningful hit against their pursuer. But the continued movement of both vehicles made it very difficult.

Suddenly, the enemy vehicle spun and veered off the road! As it circled, Vasilyev could see that one of its rear tires was shredded, and its back window was gone. But how?

As the other SUV left the road and came to a smoking halt in the grass, Vasilyev saw the answer come roaring up behind it.

A low-slung silver sedan that effortlessly closed the distance with their SUV.

Grishkov looked in his rearview mirror and said dryly, "Alina has joined us."

There had been no traffic on the road during their firefight, but now an old pickup truck went past them. The driver's head stuck out. Grishkov could see his reaction to their vehicle's condition and the smoking SUV quickly receding from view behind them.

"It won't be long before local police are called," Grishkov said.

Vasilyev nodded. "Put your right turn signal on, and ease off the road."

Moments later, both their vehicle and Alina's had pulled off the highway.

Alina strode up to Vasilyev's door just as he opened it.

"How bad is it?" Alina asked.

"Tarasenko's dead. The rest of us are OK," Vasilyev said.

Alina nodded. "Move your things to my car. I'll get Tarasenko ready."

With that, Alina shook out one of the two body bags Vasilyev now noticed she'd had in her right hand.

Shaking his head, Vasilyev worked with Grishkov and Neda to move their weapons and documents to Alina's sedan.

As Vasilyev walked back to their SUV to help Alina move Tarasenko's body, he noticed the state of their right rear tire. It had been stripped of its exterior rubber, and underneath was revealed a massive round metal frame. Though not solid anywhere except the rims, it evidently was capable of supporting the SUV's weight well enough to let Grishkov keep it on the highway.

As far as Vasilyev knew, this wasn't standard FSB field equipment. Had Alina expected others to be interested in Tarasenko?

As they moved Tarasenko's body into Alina's trunk, she said, "We'll abandon your vehicle. There's a turnoff ahead. With luck, we can avoid dealing with the police."

Vasilyev nodded, but he couldn't keep one thought from running around and around in his head.

With Tarasenko dead, even if they found the warheads, how could they disarm them?

CHAPTER TWENTY-FIVE

Highway 2521
Nineteen Kilometers North of Nova Basan, Ukraine

Marko Zavod's head hit the door frame, and his assault rifle flew from his hands as their vehicle went into a spin. He heard the rear window shatter as his eyes began to lose focus.

Moments later, consciousness returned. Blood was dripping from a cut over his right eye. Smoke was rising from the engine.

The driver's fixed, open-eyed stare told Zavod he'd lost his last man.

Wiping the blood away from his face with his sleeve, Zavod squinted as he looked ahead. Two stationary vehicles were barely visible ahead.

Zavod opened the trunk and extracted his Zbroyar Z-10, a semi-automatic 7.62×51mm sniper rifle manufactured in Ukraine. Now that he'd lost his Fort-221 assault rifle, it was his last remaining weapon dating from his time with Ukrainian Spetsnaz.

Opening the driver's door, Zavod crouched down and steadied the rifle on the doorframe. Moments later, the scene ahead came into focus.

A man and a woman were entering a sedan. Another man and woman were moving a body bag to the sedan's open trunk.

Zavod cursed bitterly. Even from this distance, Zavod could see that neither man had the full head of silver hair visible on the photo of Tarasenko he'd been given for target identification.

No, thanks to the dead idiot in the seat behind him, Tarasenko must be the one in the body bag.

Zavod briefly considered firing on the two Russians still outside the sedan, but quickly rejected the idea. They were barely inside the Z-10's twelve-hundred-meter range, and he could easily miss.

Worse, even if Zavod killed them both, there were two other armed Russians inside the sedan. They could reach him in moments. Alone and on foot, he didn't look forward to facing them.

Besides, even killing all four of them wouldn't help accomplish his mission. Tarasenko was dead.

But Zavod had been given two names, with payment promised for either man's delivery. He had moved immediately on Tarasenko because that name came with an address.

Now that Tarasenko was dead, it was time to move on to the other name.

Fedir Popova.

En Route to FSB Safe House, Brovary, Ukraine

Alina glanced in her rearview mirror at Mikhail Vasilyev and Neda Rhahbar. Neda was immersed in her folder of SS-24 technical documents. Vasilyev was in deep thought about something.

As was Anatoly Grishkov in the seat beside her.

Probably about what they were going to do next.

Time to tell them what was coming.

"We're on Highway H07 about twenty minutes out from our safe house in Brovary. The safe house is about half an hour's drive east of the Embassy. We're going to link up there with some additional support personnel provided to us at Moscow's direction," Alina said.

Then she paused.

"I should tell you this step was approved by Director Smyslov himself since it's quite unusual. Ordinarily, he would have sent additional FSB agents, but given the current state of relations with Ukraine, that's impossible. The Ukrainians know something's up, and it took me a long time to get away from them," Alina said.

Shaking her head, she added, "I'm sorry I was too late to avoid losing Tarasenko."

"I'm sure you did your best," Grishkov said. "At least we three are still in one piece. Without your arrival, I'm not sure we'd be here talking."

"Agreed," Vasilyev said. "So, who's waiting for us at Brovary?"

"Several men led by Boris Kharlov. He's a former Russian Spetsnaz soldier turned Novorossiya warlord who's suffered some recent reverses. Kharlov has been a reliable FSB intelligence source, and we've even called on him a few times for help with...certain problems," Alina said.

Vasilyev and Grishkov exchanged glances at that. They both knew what sort of problems would get the FSB to call a Novorossiya warlord.

Ones that could be solved with a small quantity of lead.

"So, after those reverses I mentioned it was no surprise that Kharlov reached out to the FSB for help. He's been promised that assistance, on condition he first helps us with this problem," Alina said.

Vasilyev grunted and shook his head. "I'm not sure this is such a great bargain. How far do you think this Kharlov can be trusted?"

Alina shrugged. "Well, the FSB has been dealing with Kharlov for years, and he's always come through for us. If he fails this time, he knows there will be no help for him against his enemies in Novorossiya."

Then Alina smiled, but there was nothing warm or pleasant in it.

"And remember Kharlov used to be Spetsnaz. He knows better than most that the FSB does not tolerate betrayal," Alina said.

Vasilyev did his best to keep his expression impassive, but it wasn't easy. He hadn't been with the FSB that long.

But long enough to know, Alina wasn't exaggerating.

CHAPTER TWENTY-SIX

FSB Safe House
Brovary, Ukraine

Alina walked in the front door, with Mikhail Vasilyev right behind her. Alina was empty-handed. Vasilyev was not.

Boris Kharlov was sitting casually on a chair placed to the side of the sofa. The TV was tuned to a news channel with the sound muted. No one else was visible.

"So, the others are upstairs?" Alina asked.

Kharlov nodded. "I was given a key for the upstairs level entrance. I used it, so we will have no interruptions while we speak."

Vasilyev checked the kitchen and the ground floor bedrooms. Then he tried the door to the upstairs level.

Locked.

Vasilyev went to the front door and signaled. Anatoly Grishkov and Neda Rhahbar entered a few minutes later.

Grishkov's pistol was also drawn, and he looked inquiringly at Vasilyev.

Vasilyev looked at Kharlov and hesitated.

Smiling, Kharlov stood and slowly raised his arms until they were straight out.

Vasilyev holstered his pistol and quickly but thoroughly searched Kharlov.

Grishkov covered Vasilyev with his pistol, and his concentration never wavered.

Satisfied that Kharlov was unarmed, Vasilyev moved back and gestured for Grishkov to put his pistol away.

Alina introduced each of them, and then said, "Let's all sit. We've got a lot to discuss."

Vasilyev sat on the end of the sofa closest to Kharlov, and said quietly, "No offense."

Kharlov grinned. "On the contrary. It's good to see you have the sense to observe elementary security precautions. After all, I've been called a dangerous man."

Kharlov's grin disappeared. "And so I am. But not to my friends and allies."

Turning to Alina, Kharlov said, "I'm sure you've been told I'm working with you to get help in return against my enemies in Novorossiya. You can rely on me for the best of all possible motives. Self-interest."

Alina nodded. "I accept that. How sure are you of your men?"

"I employ dozens of armed men. I picked the best four, and trust them to have my back. I can give them no higher recommendation," Kharlov replied.

Then Kharlov looked at each of the others present carefully.

"I was told two men were our initial targets, and that a team was already attempting to secure one of them. I presume I'm looking at that team?" Kharlov asked.

Alina nodded.

THE END OF RUSSIA'S WAR IN UKRAINE · 193

"I was also given photos of each man, yet I see neither here. So, still missing or dead?" Kharlov asked.

"One is dead, and the other is still missing," Alina replied.

Kharlov nodded and held up his cell phone. "Just before you arrived, I received a text from one of my sources in Novorossiya. Marko Zavod is in Ukraine on an unknown mission. He works for Avel Karpenko, the man I'm hoping to eliminate with the FSB's help. Perhaps not a coincidence?"

"Zavod," Alina repeated, shaking her head.

Seeing the others' reactions, Alina added, "Ukrainian Spetsnaz. He defected to Novorossiya last year."

"I think we've probably already met him. And if someone like Zavod is here, he's not alone." Vasilyev said.

"Yes," Kharlov said. "He may not have had time to gather men before coming, but Karpenko has deep pockets. Zavod knows who to contact in Ukraine for hired guns. They are plentiful here. If not always high quality."

Vasilyev nodded thoughtfully and looked at Alina.

Alina hesitated and then shrugged. "Kharlov has useful information. Our chances are better if we share what we know."

Vasilyev looked at Kharlov, who also shrugged. "What you decide to tell me is up to you. But Alina is right. The more I know, the more useful I can be. If it helps, I have never done anything to hurt Russia. And I never will."

"Very well," Vasilyev said. "What you've said tracks with what we just experienced. We were attacked by a car full of shooters. One of our rear tires was hit by carefully aimed fire. Tarasenko, though, was killed by indiscriminate rounds."

Kharlov grunted. "If it's any consolation, whoever killed the mission target is certainly dead by Zavod's hand. Were you able to verify Zavod's death? He's bald, with a bullet-shaped head."

"No," Alina said, shaking her head. "I disabled his vehicle, but the priority was leaving the scene. As it was, we barely escaped police response."

"Understood. So, we must assume Zavod escaped as well," Kharlov said.

"And from what you're saying, that Zavod will hire more men to replace the ones he just lost," Vasilyev said.

"Certainly," Kharlov replied. "Just as sure is that with Tarasenko dead, Zavod will move on to the remaining target, Fedir Popova. Do we have any ideas on his location?"

Everyone shook their head.

Then Vasilyev said, "We've learned his target is Yuzhnoye headquarters in Dnipro. Also, that Popova is wealthy as the result of illegal sales of Yuzhnoye's technology. And dying of pancreatic cancer."

Kharlov nodded. "What weapon will he use to attack Yuzhnoye? If I know the method, I can try to anticipate how he will approach the target."

Vasilyev looked at Alina again, and this time her hesitation lasted considerably longer.

Finally, Alina nodded. "Best to know now if he is truly committed."

Kharlov's eyebrows rose, but he said nothing.

"The weapon targeted on Dnipro is an SS-24 warhead," Vasilyev said. "One of two. We're not yet sure where the other is targeted, but we think it is presently located near Chernobyl."

Kharlov shrugged. "I thought it had to be something like that. Nothing else would warrant this level of effort. And, of course, it explains why you're not just leaving this to the Ukrainians."

Then Kharlov snapped his fingers and smiled. "Wealthy. Well, our friend Popova certainly won't try to carry out this attack alone. Unless he's a fool, he'll guess that people like us will try to stop him. So, he'll use his money just as Zavod did, to hire gunmen."

Vasilyev frowned. "But would Popova know who to contact?"

"Not like Zavod, that's for sure," Kharlov replied. "Maybe whoever arranged for the sale of the technology he stole would be willing to broker a deal. That's both good and bad for us."

"How so?" Vasilyev asked.

"The good is that with more people involved in hiring gunmen, my contacts here may be able to help us locate Popova before he reaches Dnipro. I'm sure the FSB is already using their contacts to do the same," Kharlov replied.

Alina nodded.

"Also good is that whoever Popova hires will have no loyalty to him, and unlike Zavod's men won't fear him either. At the first sign of trouble, many are likely to bolt," Kharlov said.

"And the bad?" Vasilyev asked.

"Well, if Popova tries to stop any of the gunmen from leaving, they'll probably shoot him. We do want him alive, right?" Kharlov asked.

Vasilyev nodded.

"Some of Popova's hired guns may panic, and begin firing indiscriminately. I imagine it would be bad if any rounds hit the warhead?" Kharlov asked dryly.

"Yes. They probably wouldn't cause a nuclear detonation, but might set off the conventional explosives it contains while spreading its radioactive materials," Vasilyev replied.

Then Vasilyev looked at Neda and asked, "Did I get that right?"

Neda smiled and nodded.

Kharlov stood and pulled out his cell phone. "Let me get moving on this. I also have to think about what to tell my men. I can assure you 'SS-24' won't be part of the conversation."

Moments later, they could hear Kharlov in the kitchen speaking in low, urgent tones.

Alina pointed upstairs.

"The shower is that way, as well as the bedrooms. I'll take whichever one is left. You can sleep now, or after we eat. I have a man coming to retrieve Tarasenko."

Alina paused and shook her head. "Kharlov is right. I do have people checking to see whether Popova is hiring shooters. I hope he does because right now, I think it's our only chance of finding him."

Then Alina sighed. "And I have no idea how we're going to find Arbakov."

"Well, I think there's a way we might be able to get help finding both of them," Vasilyev said with a smile.

"But, we're going to need to call Director Smyslov," Vasilyev added.

CHAPTER TWENTY-SEVEN

The Kremlin
Moscow, Russia

Director Smyslov relaxed a bit as he saw he was being ushered into the President's working office. The furnishings and decorations here were on a par with a major company's chief executive officer, and a meeting in this setting would probably last more than a few minutes.

The President's ceremonial office included world-class art pieces and was designed to impress foreign leaders. Russian officials like Smyslov could be sure a meeting there would be short.

The last time he'd met the President had gone badly and ended with Smyslov offering his resignation.

The President had refused the offer, saying they would revisit the matter once the missing Russian nuclear warhead had been recovered.

Smyslov hadn't even been sure the President would agree to meet him, especially when he specified it was to make a request.

However, Smyslov knew he had two things in his favor. First was that the President had previously held Smyslov's job as FSB Director, and knew Smyslov would ask for nothing lightly.

Smyslov knew he also had the President's respect, even if they often disagreed on priorities and tactics. He had offered his resignation because the President insisted on the use of the same few agents again and again for the highest priority FSB missions, even after one of them had been badly wounded and another killed.

Well, that was a matter for another day.

First, they needed to navigate this crisis.

The President's jacket was off, and Smyslov could see tea and cookies on the coffee table.

Better and better.

Then, the President astonished Smyslov by standing and grabbing him in a bear hug that squeezed the breath out of him.

Releasing him, President growled, "Sit, sit! I know that sort of a hug is your trademark, but I wanted you to know I didn't like how we left things at our last meeting. Let's have some tea, and then you can tell me how I can help."

A few minutes later, the pile of cookies on the tray was noticeably shorter, and both men were finishing their second mug of tea.

"So, we know there are two missing warheads, not just one. And we think we know who has them, and for one of them the intended target. But we don't know where they are. Does that sum up the situation?" the President asked.

"It does. And it brings me to my request. You know that we have the means to locate a nuclear warhead with some precision," Smyslov said.

"Yes," the President said with a frown. "The Okhotnik drone. Its performance in Afghanistan was indeed impressive. But we can't risk its use in Ukraine while I'm trying to negotiate a settlement to the conflict there. It's certain to be spotted, and might even be shot down."

Smyslov nodded. "Agreed. And that is what I told the agent who brought me that request. But I have another approach in mind. First, I'll note that I've made sure our radiation detection instrument package is compatible with NATO-standard equipment."

The President's eyebrows rose. "You have? Why?"

Smyslov shrugged. "I had a couple of possibilities in mind. You know that we've succeeded several times in acquiring Western military technology. In fact, I can think of at least one time when you were in my job that the FSB did so."

The President relaxed and smiled. Smyslov could see he'd scored a hit.

"Yes, I remember. You're right. And if we managed to get our hands on a Western drone, it would be nice to put our equipment on it without delay. So, the other possibility?" the President asked.

"The Americans have a training mission underway in Ukraine for a reconnaissance drone they just sold the Ukrainians. The equipment package could be at our Embassy in Kyiv very quickly. I propose we ask the Americans to attach our equipment to their drone, and forward contact reports to our agents in the field without telling the Ukrainians," Smyslov said.

"Let me guess. The equipment package is already at the Embassy in Kyiv," the President said flatly.

Smyslov just shrugged.

"Well, when I had your job, I would have done the same thing," the President said with a sigh. "Of course, this will have to be a personal request from me to Hernandez. How do you think the American President will respond?"

"If I had to guess, I'd say he would agree that finding the warheads is crucial. I think the problem will be our request that he does not tell the Ukrainians. If we fail and one or, God forbid, both detonate the consequences would be severe," Smyslov said somberly.

"Severe. Yes. I've read the FSB's assessment of Hernandez. I've also talked with him several times, so I have my ideas about him. But I'd like your opinion. If one or both of the SS-24s detonate, what will he do?" the President asked.

"I've given that question much thought. Intense economic sanctions with full European support, cutting off diplomatic relations, inviting more Eastern and Central European countries to join NATO are probably the least we could expect from one explosion. Along with a return to a Cold War level arms buildup. But if both detonate..."

Smyslov shook his head.

"If both of our warheads detonate in Ukraine and result in mass casualties, Hernandez may feel obliged to strike a Russian military target in response," Smyslov said.

"Yes, I think that is possible as well. I would have no choice but to retaliate. That could only end one way," the President said.

Smyslov nodded but said nothing.

"So, how can we avoid that outcome?" the President asked.

"I think first you explain to Hernandez that we want to avoid telling the Ukrainians for several reasons besides avoiding embarrassment for losing the warheads. Though you should admit that, yes, we are embarrassed," Smyslov said.

"True enough," the President said.

"But point out to Hernandez that we must avoid mass panic. That could result in casualties even if we were able to recover both warheads. I would not say we want to avoid Ukrainian interference with our agents' efforts, true though that is. Or that we fear a countrywide untargeted search would just alert the men who have the warheads," Smyslov said.

The President shook his head. "If all I can say is that we must avoid panic, I think Hernandez will tell the Ukrainians."

"Agreed. That is why you must offer Hernandez something of value," Smyslov said carefully.

The President's eyes narrowed. "What, for example?"

"You could promise Hernandez we will never release our drone footage of the American missile that detonated the nuclear warhead the Taliban stole from Pakistan, which destroyed the Afghan town of Bagram. Of course, we know they did it to protect Bagram Airfield. And that if the Taliban had been allowed to proceed with a controlled detonation at the airfield's entrance at least twice as many would have died," Smyslov said.

"But we know how the world would react. Up to now, the Taliban have rightly shouldered the blame. The Americans would be condemned twice over, first for detonating the warhead with their missile and then for covering up their role," the President said, nodding.

Then he frowned. "I was hoping to save that footage, but..."

Seeing Smyslov's expression, the President had to laugh. "You're right. Preventing World War III is probably the best use I can make of this particular secret."

The President stood. "I will let you know how Hernandez replies. It should be later today."

Smyslov nodded and left.

The President sat back down and reached again for the teapot.

No, he thought and drew his hand back.

I think I could use something a bit stronger.

Chapter Twenty-Eight

Eight Kilometers From Chernobyl New Safe Confinement (NSC), Ukraine

Pofistal Arbakov had done his homework. The SS-24 warhead's detonation would create a fireball vaporizing everything within a kilometer.

But Arbakov didn't want the New Safe Containment (NSC) vaporized. He wanted its contents released.

At the time of the disaster in 1986, the Chernobyl number four reactor contained about one hundred ninety metric tons of uranium dioxide fuel and fission products. Somewhere between thirteen and thirty percent of those radioactive elements had escaped into the atmosphere, with catastrophic results.

Arbakov was going to release the rest.

Between one and about two kilometers from the detonation, there would be a blast wave measuring at least twenty pounds per square inch, that could be counted on to destroy almost all structures.

The NSC complicated Arbakov's task. Made of steel with polycarbonate inner panels by workers and specialists from over two dozen countries, it had taken nearly a decade to finish at a cost paid by the European Union of over two billion Euros. The NSC measured over a hundred meters tall and was designed to last a century from its completion in 2019.

Arbakov had calculated that he needed to be about fourteen hundred meters from the NSC to be sure of releasing its contents, without vaporizing them.

To maximize the disaster, Arbakov had decided to lower the warhead to the ground with the forklift in his truck before detonation. He had read that the weapon's contact with the ground would substantially increase the amount of fallout.

In 1986 over half of Chernobyl's released radioactive materials had blown north into Belarus. Cell phone Internet coverage was spotty within the Exclusion Zone, but good enough for Arbakov to be confident he could download the current weather.

If not, though, he had a compass and a simple metal wind vane.

This time, all the radioactive material from Chernobyl was going south to Kyiv. And Arbakov wasn't going to leave anything to chance.

The White House, Washington DC

President Hernandez looked up from the call transcript as Air Force Chief of Staff Robinson walked into the Oval Office.

Robinson knew to close the door behind him.

A former businessman, Hernandez had started his administration with little knowledge of or interest in foreign relations. After seeing the effect that America's crumbling infrastructure and sinking educational standards were having on his business, he'd decided he could no longer sit on the sidelines.

Whether he liked it or not, though, much of his time had been spent on putting out fires overseas. Yes, he'd been able to make a start on infrastructure. But making a dent in education was turning out to be harder than he'd thought.

So many of the people applying for work at his business had been functionally illiterate. Few had useful skills, so nearly all had to be trained at his expense.

And good luck to those who tried to obtain skills. In many states, the waiting list for community college courses in fields like HVAC technician stretched to over a year.

Why? Federal and state funding of higher education had been repeatedly slashed, so both instructors and classroom space simply weren't there.

And for those who did manage to take classes, skyrocketing tuition and fees meant student loan debt had ballooned. A growing number found that what they'd learned had no relevance to the labor market skills in actual demand. While some arguably had only themselves to blame, most were just the victims of labor requirements that now often shifted in months rather than years.

Many American companies, including the largest, refused to train American workers or provide relocation allowances to ones with needed skills living in other states. Instead, it was cheaper to bring in foreign workers in the nonimmigrant H category and the immigrant E category.

Addressing any of those issues required the cooperation of Congress. "Cooperative" was not the adjective that came to mind when Hernandez thought about politicians in either party.

Well, time to focus on the current problem.

"You've read the transcript," Hernandez said flatly.

Robinson nodded. He thought the record of the call between Hernandez and the Russian President was one of the most remarkable he'd seen.

No, scratch that. The most remarkable.

"OK, I have a lot of questions. First, do we believe him?" Hernandez asked.

"I think so, sir. I don't see what the Russians have to gain from lying. If either one or two SS-24 warheads exploded inside Ukraine, they must know that fallout analysis would establish the warhead's origin within hours. The Ukrainians will never believe the warheads were stolen," Robinson said.

"Why should we?" Hernandez asked.

"It just makes no sense, sir. It will turn Europe against Russia, and make any non-NATO European countries insist on joining. That's the last thing the Russians want. And as for taking over Ukraine, after one or two thermonuclear warheads detonate there, I'm not sure it would still be worth having," Robinson replied.

Hernandez grunted. "I saw the intel community assessment that the latest Russian peace proposal for ending the Ukraine conflict was genuine. What do you think?"

"I agree, sir. Russia's support for Ukraine's eastern separatists was popular at first. But as sanctions against Russia have dragged on, that support is no longer a plus for their President. It's hard to see how smuggling the warheads into Ukraine, if that's what Russia did, would work to their benefit," Robinson replied.

"Of course, the Russians may be hoping we'd end up having a conversation just like this one," Hernandez said, shaking his head.

Then Hernandez paused. "No. If the Russians detonate one or heaven forbid, two nuclear weapons in Ukraine, resulting in mass casualties, I need immediate military response options. Maybe one of our nuclear weapons targeting a nuclear missile silo in an unpopulated area of Russia," Hernandez said.

Robinson said carefully, "Sir, I will carry out your order and get you a list of military response options by this time tomorrow. But I think we should focus our efforts on preventing the use of the two Russian weapons in Ukraine. Regardless of whether the Russians are telling us the truth or not."

"Fine," Hernandez said with a sigh. "Let's say for argument's sake we believe the Russians. Here's a related question for you. Why do we keep having to worry about other country's nuclear warheads?"

Robinson shrugged. "Well, sir, I'd start with the fact that there are over fourteen thousand nuclear warheads out there. And the two we're worried about now date back to the Cold War when there were many more."

Hernandez stared at Robinson. "Over fourteen thousand! That's not the number I remember!"

"Yes, sir. You're thinking of the number of warheads deployed, which is under four thousand. But when you consider either number, though, I think the real surprise is that so far the number of incidents and deaths has been relatively low," Robinson said.

"Maybe so. Anyway, what do you think of the Russian proposal? I like the way their President started," Hernandez said bitterly.

"Yes, sir. He knew you could never bow to blackmail. But by promising that they had destroyed their drone's footage of the Bagram attack, he accomplished several things at once. He told you they know it was our missile that detonated the Taliban's stolen Pakistani nuclear warhead. By expressing sympathy for our choice without condoning it, he created a public explanation for why the Russians haven't released that footage - yet. Finally, he made it much more difficult for you to say that you must inform the Ukrainians about the current threat," Robinson said.

"Right. Because if I say that, the next question will be why didn't we warn the Afghans about the nuclear warheads the Taliban stole from Pakistan. Well, we didn't because we were afraid of casualties caused by mass panic. Exactly what the Russians are saying now," Hernandez said, and then paused.

"What about that, General? Is panic a legitimate concern?"

"I think so, sir. I doubt very much whether the Ukrainians would accept that as an explanation for failing to inform them, though," Robinson replied.

"And what do you think the chances are that the Russians did destroy that drone footage?" Hernandez asked.

"I think you know the answer to that, sir," Robinson replied quietly.

"Yes. So, let's say we do what the Russians want. Put their radiation detection package on one of the drones we just sold the Ukrainians. An American officer is doing the drone training, right?" Hernandez asked.

"That's right, sir," Robinson said.

Why did Robinson look so uncomfortable?

"Sir, the officer is Captain Pettigrew," Robinson said.

"Of course it is," Hernandez said, shaking his head. "The same officer whose drone fired the missile that detonated the nuclear warhead at Bagram."

"Well, sir, it's not such a coincidence. We don't have that many officers qualified to fly drones, and even fewer to conduct training," Robinson said.

"Right. And I remember now telling you to put him someplace quiet in Europe. I guess with the peace talks going well, you thought Ukraine was safe enough," Hernandez said.

"Yes, sir. Frankly, I also picked him because the mission is to train the Ukrainians to use an unarmed reconnaissance drone. He won't be firing any Hellfire missiles from the Blackjack, sir," Robinson said.

"Good. Now, the Russians say their equipment is compatible with our drone. Do you think that's true?" Hernandez asked.

Robinson frowned. "If they say so, it probably is. It also means we need to step up security around our drone programs. With so many private contractors involved, it's been a challenge to keep drones from being stolen, let alone safeguard their technical details."

"Agreed. So, the Russians say they have the same agents in Ukraine who were able to defuse one of the nuclear warheads stolen by the Taliban. Let's say we decide not to cooperate with the Russians. How long would it take us to get equally qualified people there?" Hernandez asked.

"At least a couple of days, sir. Also, as we saw in Afghanistan, their airborne nuclear detection technology is better than ours. Plus, the Russians say the warheads are theirs. I have to think their people would be the most capable of defusing them," Robinson said.

"OK. I don't like it, but I don't see any better options. So, how will we do it?" Hernandez asked.

"Well, sir, I've given that some thought..." Robinson said.

CHAPTER TWENTY-NINE

US Embassy
Kyiv, Ukraine

Captain Josh Pettigrew looked at the large LED screen that dominated the secure conference room.

It was blank. And the conference room was empty.

Pettigrew shook his head. It was all very odd.

Pettigrew had received a message to come to the Embassy and see the Defense Attaché. He was an Army Colonel who Pettigrew knew only from the pro forma greeting he'd given him upon arrival to Ukraine.

This time the Defense Attaché hadn't looked especially happy to see Pettigrew. After telling him, "Someone in DC wants to talk to you," he'd escorted Pettigrew to the secure conference room, and closed the door behind him.

The LED screen flickered to life. At least now, Pettigrew knew who was on the other end of the screen.

"Captain Pettigrew," General Robinson's voice growled from the screen. "I imagine you're wondering why I've called."

"Yes, sir," was all Pettigrew could manage.

"I'll begin by saying everything I'm about to tell you is classified as Sensitive Compartmented Information. For the record, do you understand SCI requirements as explained to you in your most recent SCI briefing, including the penalties for unauthorized disclosure of SCI in whole or in part?" Robinson asked.

"Yes, sir," Pettigrew replied.

"Also, for the record, do you understand that no one else in Ukraine, including the Ambassador and the Defense Attaché, are authorized access to the information classified SCI you will receive in this briefing?" Robinson asked.

"Yes, sir," Pettigrew replied, with a bit more hesitation.

Robinson's grim smile told Pettigrew he'd heard it.

"Yes, that's unusual. But by the time I'm finished, you'll understand the reasons for it," Robinson said.

"Yes, sir," Pettigrew replied.

"Captain, the Russians have advised us that two of their SS-24 thermonuclear warheads were stolen years ago. Each one has an explosive yield of five hundred kilotons. The Russians believe both warheads will be used in attacks within Ukraine within the next few days. They have asked that we not inform the Ukrainian government of this threat, and we have agreed," Robinson said.

"Sir, is that because we want to avoid casualties from mass panic?" Pettigrew asked.

"Correct, Captain. That means you must ensure your students suspect nothing as you use the Blackjack drones under your command to search for the warheads. Do you remember the Russian drone that assisted us in locating the stolen Pakistani nuclear warheads in Afghanistan?" Robinson asked.

"Yes, sir," Pettigrew replied.

"Well, the Russians are going to give you one of the radiation detection equipment packages used by their drones, Captain," Robinson said.

Pettigrew sat still for a moment and said, "They must be desperate to find those warheads, sir."

That earned him another grim smile from Robinson.

"I believe that's correct, Captain. The Russians have also sent the same agents they used in Afghanistan to help find and defuse them. If you locate one or both warheads, I am giving you direct authorization to notify those agents and the FSB station chief in Kyiv," Robinson said.

"Sir, I don't understand one thing. I thought the SS-24 was taken out of service, and all its warheads destroyed years ago. How are two of those warheads turning up now?" Pettigrew asked.

Robinson shrugged. "The Russians say the warheads were stolen years ago, and don't know why the thieves waited so long to use them. The bottom line is we can't see any reason why the Russians would lie about the threat. So, we've decided we have to take it seriously."

"Understood, sir. Will this Russian equipment be compatible with our drone?" Pettigrew asked.

"The Russians say it will be. If it's not, then let me know," Robinson said neutrally.

Pettigrew frowned. "Sir, if the equipment they're giving us is compatible, it means the Russians know a lot more about our drones than they should."

"You're right, Captain. I've already got people looking into that and tightening up security at our many contractor facilities. Even if we're closing the barn door, we have to start somewhere," Robinson said.

"Yes, sir. Do the Russians have any ideas about where we can start looking for these warheads?" Pettigrew asked.

"They do. The Russians also have the exact radioactive materials composition of the warheads, which should make them easier to spot.

You'll be briefed on all these details by the Russians when you pick up the equipment package. Did the Defense Attaché give you a secure cell phone?" Robinson asked.

"Yes, sir," Pettigrew replied.

"I'll send you the names of all the people authorized to receive information on the location of the SS-24 warheads and the equipment pickup address via text shortly. Your Russian contact will also provide you with equipment installation and operation instructions. I'm told the equipment should fit easily inside the trunk of your vehicle," Robinson said.

Pettigrew did his best to keep the doubt out of his voice as he replied, "Yes, sir."

A gravelly laugh from Robinson told Pettigrew his best hadn't been good enough.

"Yes, I know this is all highly irregular. This isn't how the Air Force normally operates. But working with the Russians is the best hope we have to avoid a simply unacceptable outcome. Can I count on you, Captain?" Robinson asked.

Robinson had found the right words, Pettigrew thought. Probably one of the reasons he was a General. There was only one answer he could give.

"Absolutely, sir."

CHAPTER THIRTY

FSB Safe House, Brovary, Ukraine

As Captain Josh Pettigrew walked towards the house, the front door swung open. He caught a glimpse of a blond-haired woman, and then an unmistakable gesture.

Come inside.

Well, at least it looked like he was at the right address. It had only taken an hour to get there from the Embassy. If this pickup was quick, he could do the drive from here to Myrhorod Air Base in daylight.

As soon as Pettigrew entered, the woman said, "Captain Pettigrew, my name is Alina. Please have a seat and review the documents on the table. I'll be right back."

With that, Alina slipped through the same door Pettigrew had just entered.

Right in front of him was a coffee table with papers neatly stacked on top of a yellow folder. Pettigrew sat on the sofa next to it and started reading.

Just a few minutes later, Alina was back. She sat in the chair across the table from Pettigrew.

"We had to rush the translation from Russian of these documents. Please let me know if you find any mistakes, or if anything is unclear," Alina said.

"Not so far," Pettigrew said. Then he gave Alina a sharp look. "It's obvious that whoever prepared this knows a lot about how our drones work. The Blackjack specifically, and our military drones generally."

Alina shrugged. "I understand why that would concern you. But ask yourself this question. Would you rather be good at stealing secrets? Or at creating secrets worth stealing?"

Pettigrew grunted but said nothing. He saw Alina's point.

But he still didn't like it.

Then Pettigrew pulled the keys to his SUV from his pocket. "When can we load the equipment?" he asked.

Alina smiled. "It's already in your vehicle," she replied.

Pettigrew frowned, and said, "But I was sure I locked..."

Then he stopped talking as he saw Alina's raised right eyebrow.

Yeah. People capable of stealing highly classified military secrets were probably not worried about car locks.

Shaking his head, Pettigrew kept reading. It didn't take him long to finish.

"This all seems clear enough," Pettigrew said. "Of course, I may have questions later. How can I contact you?"

Alina nodded and put two cell phones in front of Pettigrew.

"This black one has my number programmed. You may call or text with questions at any time, day or night. The silver one is set up so you may send a group text to our agents with the GPS coordinates of the warheads, once you find them," Alina said.

Pettigrew held up the silver cell phone. "What if I were to call one of your agents directly?"

Alina shrugged. "You could, and if you have information to pass them, I'd have no objection. But if you call to ask them to do something, they'd probably have to contact me for approval. Also, depending on who answers the call, their English may be good. But mine is better. Best to avoid misunderstandings, yes?"

Pettigrew nodded and said, "Fair enough. One last thing before I go. I was told the same agents who successfully defused one of the stolen Pakistani nuclear warheads are here."

"That's right," Alina said, looking at him curiously.

"Please pass my deep appreciation to them for their service. It means more to me than you can imagine," Pettigrew said.

Alina's eyes narrowed. "You can't possibly be..." she said, followed by something in Russian that Pettigrew didn't catch.

Shaking her head, Alina said, "I'm sorry. I was repeating something my mother used to say. Despite all the obstacles that existed in Soviet days, she was a firm believer in the Orthodox Church. And very disappointed that I didn't follow her in that faith. She always said God would give me signs as I grew older."

Alina paused and then said, "I won't ask whether you're the officer who had to stop the other nuclear warhead at Bagram. Or tell you that doing so saved more lives than it cost, which I'm sure you've heard already. I'll only say that my mother always believed there were people chosen by God to do his work. Maybe she was right, and it's not a coincidence you're here."

Pettigrew looked at Alina, and just shrugged as he put the documents in their folder and stood.

Alina stood and smiled. "And maybe Marx was right, and I'm becoming superstitious as I grow older. Either way, it can't hurt to say what my mother would in my place."

Alina grasped Pettigrew's right hand firmly with one hand, while she opened the front door with the other.

"Go with God," she said.

Mikhail Vasilyev and Neda Rhahbar had been asked to stay upstairs while Alina spoke with Captain Pettigrew. Unlike Anatoly Grishkov and Boris Kharlov, they had interpreted that instruction as meaning they should stay out of sight.

But not out of hearing.

So, Vasilyev and Neda sat quietly in the hallway next to the top of the stairs. Since they couldn't see either Alina or Captain Pettigrew, they were confident Alina's request had been obeyed.

Once Pettigrew left, Vasilyev and Neda returned to their bedroom.

Neda looked at Vasilyev curiously. "What did you think of what Alina said to Pettigrew at the end?"

Vasilyev shrugged. "I was surprised. She's the last person I'd have imagined might be superstitious. Although I have to admit, it's quite a coincidence that Pettigrew is the same officer who dealt with the second nuclear warhead in Afghanistan."

"Are you so sure it's just a coincidence? We haven't spoken much about religion, but I've told you I believe in God. I think Alina might be right about him," Neda said, and then paused.

"Did your father ever talk to you about religion?" Neda asked.

Vasilyev smiled. "Alexei? Yes, just once. He told me about a time he was working at our Embassy in Brussels, feeling sorry for himself on a particularly dark and rainy day. Alexei was thinking about how he'd lost touch with all the friends he had made growing up since joining the KGB. Because of the nature of our work, he hadn't made any real friends to replace them. Alexei's cover job at the Embassy was processing passport applications. Imagine his shock when in the stack of applications, he discovered one from his best friend from high school!"

"Really!" Neda exclaimed. "Out of all the millions of Russians, the odds against such a thing happening seem very high!"

Vasilyev nodded. "Correct. But that's only part of the story. You see, Russians applying for passports overseas are required to do so in person. Ordinarily, the applicant in the Embassy lobby would be compared to the photo they submitted with their application through thick, bullet-proof glass. In this case, though, Alexei had one of his staff tell his friend that 'the consul needed to speak with him.' So, the man was escorted back to Alexei's office by the staff member. Naturally, Alexei told him to say nothing to his friend about the consul's identity."

Neda shook her head. "Was he trying to give the poor man a heart attack?"

"It's funny you say that," Vasilyev replied with a laugh. "Alexei told me if his friend had been just a few years older, he thought the man would have died of shock on the spot. But coffee was followed by vodka, and his friend made a complete recovery."

"So, what was your father's conclusion?" Neda asked.

"I asked him the same question. Alexei replied that this was only one of several times that events in his life had happened where coincidence seemed to be an implausible explanation. He said he hadn't decided whether such events were proof of God's existence or not. As far as I know, when he died, he still hadn't made up his mind," Vasilyev said.

Neda smiled. "Well, you're aware that I have many issues with the religion I was raised in from birth. Especially nonsense added by men found nowhere in the Koran like 'women aren't allowed to ride bicycles.' But I still agree with Alina's approach. Calling on God's help when we're trying to prevent great evil can't hurt. I still say a prayer for you every night."

Vasilyev looked at Neda thoughtfully. "I didn't know that. Teach me how, and I'll say one for you too."

Myrhorod Air Base, Ukraine

Captain Josh Pettigrew looked around him at the Ukrainian Air Force officers busy with breaking down their latest Blackjack training deployment. He held up his right hand and was pleased to see that all activity stopped immediately, and they were all focused on him.

"You've all done very well so far with the hands-on portion of the training. I'm going to move up the most challenging portion, actual field operations outside this training base. In a way, you all helped me choose the location," Pettigrew said with a smile.

Lieutenant Bondar said hesitantly, "Poltava, sir?"

"Correct!" Pettigrew said. "The former Eastern Command Headquarters of US Strategic Air Forces during World War II. Since, as you know, it is still an active Ukrainian Air Force base, it was easy for me to obtain authorization."

Then Pettigrew pointed at Lieutenant Melnik. "I'm going to put you on the spot, Lieutenant. I'm going to make this stage of your training especially difficult by having all of you fly the Blackjack to the edge of its range and then search for a simulated target. Now, thinking logically, which direction will you fly the Blackjack from Poltava?"

Melnik looked thoughtful and said nothing immediately.

Good, Pettigrew thought approvingly. Think first, then speak.

"Well, sir, I'll take each direction in turn. Not north, which would put the Blackjack close to the Russian border. Not west, which would run the risk of interfering with commercial air traffic going into Kyiv. Not east, which would put us close to the conflict zone, which you wouldn't risk doing during training. That leaves south, towards Dnipro," Melnik concluded.

"Outstanding, Lieutenant. Correct on all counts. Now, I have another challenge for all of you. So far, you've been training on the most advanced standard Blackjack sensor configuration. For this exercise, though, you're going to be using a brand-new instrument package," Pettigrew said.

Lieutenant Bondar nodded. "One that has a capability our current sensors lack, yes?"

Pettigrew smiled. "Correct, Lieutenant. Now, who would like to guess which capability that might be?"

There was silence for the next few moments.

Then, Lieutenant Smirnova said, "Radiation detection, sir?"

Pettigrew clapped his hands. "You're all batting a thousand!"

Then Pettigrew stopped himself. "What I mean is..."

Smirnova stopped him with a smile. "We have baseball in Ukraine, sir. We know what you meant."

"Very good! Now, if I wanted to make this exercise more of a challenge, what two things could I do?" Pettigrew asked.

"Well, you could make the target mobile, sir," Bondar said.

"Correct, Lieutenant. And I have indeed done that. What else?" Pettigrew asked.

Smirnova shrugged. "If we're looking for a target based on radiation, you could shield it with lead or something similar. If you did it well enough, the target could be almost impossible to detect from the air."

Pettigrew shook his head. "You're right about the shielding, but I would never give you an impossible problem to solve. In fact, I'm going to give you one bit of information to make the exercise easier."

Every student was focused on what Pettigrew would say next, he saw with satisfaction.

"The exact materials composition of the target. That way, you can be sure it's your goal in the exercise, and not a shipment of nuclear waste," Pettigrew said.

"Sir, once we locate the target, do we do anything besides tell you?" Melnik asked.

"A good question, Lieutenant. For this exercise, the answer is no. Telling me is all you do. But in a future exercise, we'll simulate passing a notification up your chain of command. After all, the information you obtain using the Blackjack is useless if it doesn't get to the decision-makers, right?" Pettigrew asked.

All the heads around Pettigrew nodded.

"Great! Now, let's see how quickly you can break down the Blackjack's support equipment. With luck, I think we can make Poltava before nightfall," Pettigrew said.

CHAPTER THIRTY-ONE

Mariyinsky Palace
Kyiv, Ukraine

President Babich looked critically at SBU Director Shevchuk as he was shown into his office. Really, he'd have to speak to the man. Not only the same threadbare suit as last time, but it looked as though...

Hmmm. Maybe he was being too harsh towards his intelligence chief. If Shevchuk had stayed in his office long enough to fall asleep in the suit, that proved his dedication.

Well, let's see what he has to say, Babich thought.

Aloud, he said, "Welcome, Director. I understand you have something for me."

Shevchuk nodded tiredly and handed Babich a folder.

"The details we've been able to gather so far are there," Shevchuk said. "I'd also like to share some other thoughts I had on the way to see you."

"Please," Babich said. At the same time, he thought, this doesn't sound like the man I know at all.

"First, I have to be frank. I've underestimated you since your days heading Department K. Your election to this office should have been enough to make me see that. But to be honest, it was just when I got your note yesterday about those test warheads that it really hit me," Shevchuk said, shaking his head.

The man was exhausted, Babich thought.

Aloud he just said, "Yes, and what was that?"

"Well, you were right. The eight test warheads in the weapons locker that so interested our Russian friends at Vasylkiv Air Base came from an SS-24. But, the SS-24 carried ten independently targeted warheads. We ignored this difference because the inventory log said two warheads had been removed for disposal. But, you asked the right question," Shevchuk said and shook his head.

Then Shevchuk paused, clearly gathering his thoughts.

"Could the disposal of the two test warheads be independently confirmed? We quickly discovered the answer to that question was no. In fact, the central records office at Air Force headquarters tried to insist that all nuclear materials of every kind, test or otherwise, had been turned over to the Russians in the 1990s. The commanding officer there was genuinely astonished to hear otherwise," Shevchuk said.

"So, that led you to focus on who signed off on that inventory log," Babich said.

Shevchuk nodded. "Just as you suggested it should. The name wasn't in the report I gave you before, but it's in the one I just handed you. Pofistal Arbakov."

Babich gave an involuntary snort of laughter. "Pofistal? Seriously?"

"Yes, I had trouble believing it too. I thought by now everyone with a name praising Stalin would have changed it. Apparently not. Anyway, we did the obvious and started looking for him," Shevchuk said.

"No luck so far, I take it," Babich said.

Shevchuk shook his head. "But we have learned some interesting things. For a start, that we're not the first to look for Arbakov."

"Let me guess. These other people were Russian," Babich said.

"Yes. We also found out something curious when one of Arbakov's neighbors told our investigators Arbakov owned a 6x6 truck. No such truck was registered to Arbakov. One of our men thought to cross-check military sales where Arbakov had been stationed before he retired," Shevchuk said.

Babich nodded. "And Arbakov bought a military truck. Which he never bothered to register under his name."

"Correct," Shevchuk said. "But that's not all that was odd. When our investigator went to add a lookout notice on the truck, he found one was already there."

Babich grunted and shook his head. "Did you question the police officer who entered the lookout?"

"We tried," Shevchuk said grimly. "He's disappeared."

Babich reddened. "This is unacceptable! How many men do the Russians have in Ukraine working for them?"

"Apparently, far too many," Shevchuk said.

Then, he reached inside his jacket and removed a folded piece of paper, which he put in front of Babich.

"The responsibility is mine," Shevchuk said. "That is my resignation letter."

"No," Babich said immediately. "The Russians wouldn't be burning through their assets at such a clip unless they're after something vital. You'll stay until we find out what it is and what action we need to take. Do so soon enough, and you'll stay as long as I do."

Shevchuk nodded. "Very well, sir. Now we come to that thought I mentioned. I have no proof. But what if somehow Arbakov switched the two test warheads with real ones?"

Babich sat stock still for a moment.

"OK, that would explain all the activity by the Russians. They're trying to find their missing warheads. But did Arbakov have access to the real warheads?"

"Yes. Arbakov was in charge of the crews removing them from SS-24s in the 1990s and preparing them for shipment to Russia," Shevchuk replied.

"But why wait so long? And what is he going to do with them? Sell them?" Babich asked.

Now Shevchuk looked uncertain.

"I have to make it clear that what I'm about to tell you may have nothing to do with Arbakov. Over a month ago, we noted a dark web posting about two SS-24 warheads. Of course, there are such 'nukes for sale' notices constantly, and nearly all are attempts to dupe the gullible with no real weapons available," Shevchuk said.

"But," Babich prompted.

"Yes. But this was not a sale offer. It was a request for assistance in providing an arming code for one of the two warheads. Payment would be the other warhead," Shevchuk said.

For a moment, both men were silent.

"So, the implication is that at least one warhead is intended for use, not for sale. Let's say that the user would be Arbakov, and he can get help with an arming code. What would be his target?" Babich asked.

Shevchuk shook his head. "I can only offer speculation, with few facts to back it. According to our records, Arbakov has never left Ukraine. There is nothing to show any ideology has radicalized him. His military record before retirement showed solid, even outstanding performance. Though his promotion record slowed dramatically after independence."

"Well, unless you were one of the few who happened to be well connected, that was true for almost every soldier. Anything else?" Babich asked.

"His wife died recently after a long struggle with cancer," Shevchuk said quietly.

Babich winced. "That could explain why he held onto the warheads until now, but never did anything with them. He didn't want anything to happen to his wife."

Then Babich's eyes widened. "We should check to see how his wife was treated."

"I've already done that. There's no way to prove she was singled out for poor treatment. But my investigator reports a definite attitude at her hospital towards Russian speakers. It may have made no difference to her survival," Shevchuk said.

"But that's probably not how it felt to Arbakov. So, let's say he wants someone to pay. Who?" Babich asked.

"Hard to even guess. A five hundred kiloton weapon seems like radical overkill for a single hospital building. Plus, the hospital wasn't far from where he lived, so targeting it would also kill his neighbors. It appears he was on good terms with them," Shevchuk said.

"That leaves a strike against the government in general. Kyiv is the obvious target in that case. But I see what you mean. We're just guessing, with no real basis in fact," Babich said.

"There is another possibility to consider. Could this be a long-term contingency plan by the Russians, allowing them to attack us with nuclear weapons while shifting the blame to a rogue weapons technician?" Shevchuk asked.

"You don't really believe that, do you?" Babich asked.

"No. The Russians took a real chance going to Vasylkiv Air Base. They wouldn't have taken a risk like that just to make a denial of responsibility more plausible. But many Ukrainians will believe it. Since they seized Crimea, many Ukrainians are always willing to believe the worst about Russia. I'm usually one of them," Shevchuk said.

"But this time the evidence says the Russians are trying to find nuclear weapons stolen from them by a Ukrainian. So, what do we do?" Babich asked.

"I lay out options and recommendations at the end of that report. Possible courses of action include confronting the Russian government, breaking diplomatic relations and expelling all Russian staff including their many spies, and mobilizing a nationwide search for the nuclear warheads using all police and military resources," Shevchuk said.

"Yes. But you're not recommending any of that, are you?" Babich said with a smile.

"No. We must avoid mass panic. I have all my best people on this, ones I trust to keep their mouths shut while they gather information. We can't just act blindly," Shevchuk said.

"Agreed," Babich said. "There are so many unanswered questions. What is Arbakov's target? Has Arbakov obtained an arming code, and if so, does someone else now have the other warhead? What is that unknown person's target?"

"Yes. And maybe the most critical question. How long before Arbakov and his confederate are ready to attack?" Shevchuk asked quietly.

"I presume you've stepped up surveillance on the Russians," Babich said flatly.

Shevchuk nodded.

"Good. I know that you will have ordered your people only to observe and report," Babich said.

"Correct. Those are their orders," Shevchuk replied.

"Fine," Babich said. "Now add to those orders that they are to prevent local authorities from intervening to either help or hinder the Russians, no matter what happens."

Shevchuk's eyebrows flew upwards. "Are you sure, sir?"

Babich nodded. "I know I may regret this order. But city cops or highway patrolmen won't be able to tell one side from the other, and are just as likely to make things worse."

Babich paused, hesitated, and finally nodded again. "Yes. The Russians made this mess. We have to hope they can clean it up."

CHAPTER THIRTY-TWO

FSB Safe House
Brovary, Ukraine

"So, how long do you think it will take for the American drone to begin searching for our missing warheads?" Mikhail Vasilyev asked.

"I didn't ask," Alina replied. "Given the stakes, I'm sure the American captain will do his best."

Boris Kharlov stopped his pacing long enough to gesture towards Neda Rhahbar, who was at the kitchen table. Around her were crumpled pieces of paper and two half-finished cups of coffee.

Neda said nothing, and her expression gave nothing away. But everyone present could feel her frustration.

Kharlov said quietly, "Finding the warheads may do us no good if we can't defuse them. Is there any way we can get her some help?"

Alina shook her head. "The Ukrainians know we're up to something, though we hope so far they don't know what. Getting a diplomatic visa for another expert to come from Russia will be difficult or impossible. Also, the Director has been told by the President security is paramount for this operation. That means the fewer who know about it, the better. We will have to make do with the people we have."

Anatoly Grishkov glanced up from the map of the tunnels at Duga he had been studying.

Looking at Vasilyev, he said, "Maybe a few words of encouragement from her husband would help."

Vasilyev grunted. "Sometimes I forget you're the only one here who's been married a long time."

Walking up behind Neda, Vasilyev put his hands on her shoulders and began to massage her gently. Neda sighed and closed her eyes.

A few moments later, Neda opened her eyes and patted Vasilyev's left hand with her right.

"I appreciate it, but you have to stop, or I may go to sleep right here. I just wish I knew more about conventional explosives," Neda sighed.

Kharlov cocked his head and walked over from the living room. "Well, the Russian Army invested quite a bit in my explosives training. But how does that help you disarm a nuclear warhead?"

Neda looked at Kharlov thoughtfully. "Normally, it's not the approach I'd take. As long as I know how to find the nuclear arming circuit in a warhead, defusing it is fairly straightforward. But not the SS-24 warhead, which has multiple redundant nuclear arming circuits. That's why Tarasenko suggested I focus on the warhead's conventional explosive trigger instead."

Kharlov frowned. "I don't understand. If you don't defuse the nuclear arming circuit doesn't the explosive trigger detonate anyway?"

Neda shook her head. "No. This nuclear warhead and any other design I've ever seen require that the conventional and the nuclear arming circuits are both armed and operational. If either one isn't, the other will not function. An elementary safety precaution. Without it, I'm sure we would have had many accidental detonations before now."

"May I see the explosive component schematics?" Kharlov asked.

Neda silently handed them to Kharlov.

After several minutes, Kharlov drew in a deep breath and shook his head. "It's the same issue for the explosive circuits. Multiple arming pathways. You've correctly identified the possible breakpoints..."

Kharlov frowned and began looking at the schematics even more closely. Then he put them in front of Neda and began pointing.

"Look, here, here, and also here and here. We cut at these locations, and I think detonation would fail," Kharlov said.

Neda looked at the schematics and shrugged. "The cuts would need to be simultaneous, and I only have two hands."

"I cut a few wires in Chechnya, and I'm still here. Anyway, I think it's our best chance," Kharlov said.

Vasilyev asked quietly, "How would you define simultaneous?"

Neda tapped the schematics and frowned. "There's no way to know. A second? A fraction of a second? If this were a modern warhead, I doubt we'd have any chance. One built decades ago? The design tolerances might be more forgiving. Maybe."

Kharlov grinned. "Only one way to find out for sure!"

At the same moment, Kharlov's cell phone buzzed.

After a brief conversation, Kharlov's grin was gone.

A few seconds of silence later, Vasilyev asked, "So, some news?"

Kharlov nodded. "Yes. Some good, some bad. I'll start with the good. As I guessed, Popova did hire security. They aren't due to meet until tomorrow morning, so we have some time to deploy our forces."

"And the bad?" Vasilyev asked.

"The man he hired, Bondarenko, is much better than average. He is also one of six armed men, who are probably almost as capable. But that's not the worst news," Kharlov said and paused.

"I don't know their exact meeting place, just that it's north of Dnipro. Three major highways go to Dnipro from the north, and we don't have enough men to cover them all. So, we're going to have to rely on our American friends for final deployment," Kharlov said.

Grishkov held up the map he had been studying. "Well, speaking of deployments, we need to talk about who's going to cover the area near the old Duga radar array. I'm guessing that's where Arbakov will stage his attack on Kyiv. He'll use its tunnel system to hide the warhead in the meantime. I suggest I go there with one of Kharlov's men as backup while the rest of you go to Dnipro."

Vasilyev frowned. "Very generous of you. But why are you only taking one man?"

"We know the Dnipro attack is on for tomorrow. Neda and Kharlov are needed to defuse the warhead. You're facing six armed men. With luck, you'll be successful and can then meet me near Duga," Grishkov said.

"So, you assume I'll abandon my partner so easily?" Vasilyev asked.

Grishkov snorted with laughter. "Wife versus partner is no contest. Don't insult me by pretending otherwise. For my part, handsome as you are, I would always choose Arisha."

"You realize it will take us at least nine hours to get to you at Duga from somewhere near Dnipro, right?" Vasilyev asked.

Before Grishkov could answer, Kharlov said, "This talk of travel time raises a point. I agree that Duga would make sense as a staging area for Arbakov's attack on Kyiv since it's only two hours away. Plus, the abandoned tunnels there would make a perfect hiding spot. And the ambient radiation still in that area from the Chernobyl disaster would make picking out the warhead very difficult."

"So then?" Vasilyev asked.

"What if the target isn't Kyiv, but instead the reactor at Chernobyl?" Kharlov replied.

Vasilyev shook his head. "I thought of that, but a direct attack on Kyiv would kill far more. I think we're all agreed that Ukrainian government officials are his target, and they're in Kyiv, not Chernobyl."

"Maybe so, but think harder about this Arbakov and his grievance. It's that his wife suffered from cancer and didn't get the help she needed, and so finally died after a long and painful bout with the disease. Justice for him would be condemning as many Ukrainian government officials as possible to the same fate," Kharlov said.

"Fine. Let's consider the two alternatives. If Arbakov were staging an attack on Kyiv, then he would probably try to get help too, since his truck could easily be stopped if he's traveling alone. It almost certainly would be since we now have an all-points notice out on his truck. But Arbakov could already be at Duga, right next to the Chernobyl reactor. Why not attack it now if his goal is to spread its radioactive materials to Kyiv?" Vasilyev asked.

Kharlov pulled out his cell phone. "A good question. I have an idea about the answer."

A few minutes later, Kharlov nodded. "As I thought," he said, holding up his cell phone display.

"This shows the prevailing winds for Kyiv. Combat operations at Spetsnaz tempo always required all the information we could obtain for planning. For everything from a parachute drop to aiming a sniper rifle accurately, wind data was critical. This web site averages all wind data for the selected location from 2007 to now. It shows the prevailing wind direction for the target area is west-northwest," Kharlov said.

"Opposite from the direction Arbakov needs if he's going to get the released radioactive materials from Chernobyl to Kyiv," Vasilyev said.

"Yes. The forecast for this week says winds in Chernobyl are expected to blow northwest today and tomorrow, and then shift to the south-west. But wind forecasts are notoriously unreliable by comparison with rain. Just too many variables to calculate," Kharlov said.

Vasilyev grunted. "So maybe we'll have just enough time to all shift from Dnipro to Duga. And maybe we won't."

"That's it," Kharlov said. "Still, I agree with Grishkov. We need to put most of our resources on the more immediate threat."

Vasilyev turned to Alina. "Can we get any of your staff at the Embassy to help?"

Alina shook her head. "The Ukrainians have at least doubled and maybe tripled the number of people they have dedicated to our surveil-lance. They know we're up to something, and are determined to find out what that is. That's why I need to get back to the Embassy. As long as I'm out here with all of you, they won't stop looking for me. The last thing we want is the SBU showing up in the middle of this operation."

"Agreed," Vasilyev said. Turning to Kharlov, he asked, "Who will you send with Grishkov?"

"Kolesnik," Kharlov replied. "My best man, also former Spetsnaz. Though he's Russian, his mother was Ukrainian, so he speaks the language. He's also the only man I've ever met who can beat me on the pistol range."

Vasilyev looked at Grishkov, who simply nodded.

"Very well," Vasilyev said. "Everyone besides Grishkov and Kolesnik will get on the road to Dnipro. We can decide who covers which highway tonight."

Vasilyev looked at Grishkov and shook his head. It was apparent Vasilyev was still unhappy about sending Grishkov off without him.

"If at all possible, even if you locate Arbakov, try to wait for us to join you. Only act if you see Arbakov moving towards the Chernobyl reactor with the warhead. Or getting on the road for Kyiv," Vasilyev said.

Neda had been sketching furiously while the others had been talking, and now showed Grishkov her work.

"You see here the four points where the wires connected to the warhead's explosive component must be cut. As you heard, the cuts must be simultaneous," Neda said.

Grishkov nodded. "Understood. Well, that will give me motivation to keep Kolesnik alive."

Kharlov laughed. "That would be much appreciated."

Vasilyev shook Grishkov's hand and pounded him on the back. "We'll be there before you know it."

"I'm sure of it," Grishkov said with a smile.

CHAPTER THIRTY-THREE

En Route to Duga Radar Array, Ukraine

Anatoly Grishkov looked over from the passenger seat at the man who he still knew only as Kolesnik. Grishkov hadn't asked the man's first name, and he hadn't volunteered it.

Considering Kolesnik's line of work, probably not surprising, Grishkov thought. As was his apparent lack of interest in conversation.

So far, Kolesnik had only spoken when Grishkov had asked for the keys to the four-wheel-drive SUV. Shaking his head, Kolesnik had pointed out that he had a Ukrainian driver's license matching the vehicle's registration. And spoke Ukrainian.

Grishkov had to agree that if Ukrainian police stopped them for some reason, Kolesnik would probably do better in the driver's seat.

After over an hour of silent driving with plenty of time to go, though, Grishkov decided he'd waited long enough.

"So, how did you come to work for Kharlov?" Grishkov asked.

Kolesnik shrugged. "I left Spetsnaz after our war with Georgia in 2008. Fortunately, my enlistment term was up a few months after my unit's deployment there ended, so all I had to do was fail to re-up. I worked in several security jobs for the next six years, but none of them paid very well. Finally, a mutual friend put me in touch with Kharlov. He offered more than any employer in Russia."

"What did you think of the war in Georgia?" Grishkov asked.

Kolesnik was silent, and for a moment, Grishkov thought he wouldn't answer.

Then Kolesnik said bitterly, "Well, it sure wasn't Chechnya, where I also served."

"Interesting. I fought in Chechnya as well, though I left the Army well before the war in Georgia. How would you say they were different?" Grishkov asked.

"We never left Chechnya after the end of the Soviet Union. Chechnya has been part of Russia for over a century. When some Chechens decided they wanted independence, they used terror tactics from the start. And their attacks happened throughout Russia, including hostage-takings in Beslan and Moscow," Kolesnik said.

Grishkov nodded. "I remember. Over three hundred dead in Beslan, most children. Nearly two hundred killed in Moscow."

"Yes," Kolesnik said. "The two Georgian territories we targeted, South Ossetia and Abkhazia, had been governed as part of Georgia for a decade before the war. Nobody there was targeting Russia."

"But there were many Russians in both territories. I recall there were complaints of mistreatment by the Georgian government," Grishkov said.

"Yes. It reminded me of similar complaints made by a German chancellor about the treatment of their citizens by the Czech and Polish authorities," Kolesnik replied.

"Ouch. You mean Adolph Hitler in the 1930s." Grishkov said. "Is that really a fair comparison?"

"Show me how it's different," Kolesnik said.

"Well, I don't know enough about the Georgia conflict and its origins to do that, but I get your point. You didn't support how Russia was using its military, so when your enlistment was up, you left. I can respect that. But was then going to work for Kharlov just about money?" Grishkov asked.

"You're right. It wasn't. It was also about what Kharlov was doing with his money," Kolesnik replied.

Grishkov's eyebrows rose. "And what was that?"

Kolesnik hesitated and then shrugged. "Kharlov told me to come back with you, or not at all. If that's how he feels about you and this mission, I suppose I can tell you. Anyway, by now it's no longer much of a secret."

Kolesnik paused. Grishkov correctly guessed that he was thinking about the best way to explain why he had decided to work for Kharlov.

"I will start at the beginning for Kharlov, though it was only later that I learned it. That is, why he feels so strongly about protecting women and children. After we lost a man one day, we both drank far more than usual. Somehow, we ended up talking about our fathers. Kharlov said his father put away vast quantities of vodka daily and often beat his mother and sister when he was drunk," Kolesnik said.

Grishkov nodded. "I was a policeman for years. It's an all too familiar story in Russia."

"Well, Kharlov said once he was old enough, he put a stop to it," Kolesnik said flatly.

Grishkov shrugged. "Also, not a new story, though I'm surprised Kharlov was able to serve in the Army afterward. Wait, the way you said it, I thought Kharlov killed him. Did he?"

"No, sorry. I did think so at the time, though. I had a friend in the Moscow police check since I was worried about working for someone with such severe psychological trauma. I was relieved to learn his father died of alcohol poisoning in a city hundreds of kilometers away shortly after Kharlov joined the Army," Kolesnik said.

"So, Kharlov beat him badly enough to make him leave, and never come back," Grishkov said thoughtfully. "Again, not unknown. But very unusual. Using enough violence to frighten an alcoholic into leaving without killing him? Difficult. And at such a young age, truly remarkable. I can see how Kharlov ended up qualifying as Spetsnaz."

"Yes. It certainly helped me understand the missions we ran almost every month to free trafficked women and children," Kolesnik said.

Grishkov frowned. "I understand that the collapse of law and order in eastern Ukraine made it an attractive target for smuggling people. But if you were hitting the traffickers monthly, why didn't they just go somewhere else?"

"After we'd been doing it almost a year, I asked Kharlov the same question. He said people shipments moved weekly, not monthly. And that in countries with a functioning police force, they often caught more than one in four. But it still made no sense to me," Kolesnik replied.

"Really? Why not?" Grishkov asked.

"Because we didn't arrest the traffickers we captured," Kolesnik said flatly.

"Right. Well, again drawing on my police experience, I can say that the average criminal is not overly burdened by intelligence. Also, greed is a powerful motivator. It would certainly help someone ignore stories of what had happened to other traffickers," Grishkov said.

Kolesnik shrugged. "Maybe so. But though I thought our attacks made sense at first, after a year I changed my mind. It felt like trying to hold back the tide with a hand-built sand wall. Futile."

"So, why not a sustained campaign over a couple of months? Wouldn't that be more likely to make the traffickers go elsewhere?" Grishkov asked.

"A good question, and one I asked Kharlov myself. He told me the organization receiving the women and children we rescued could only handle one group a month. Most of its members were volunteers who years earlier had been trafficked themselves, but one way or another escaped. Kharlov said that if they were overwhelmed, the people we rescued could end up on the street or worse," Kolesnik replied.

"Well, if we can prevent a nuclear disaster, the conflict in eastern Ukraine looks likely to end soon. Once law and order are restored, both people trafficking and smuggling of all types look likely to be much less profitable. What will you do then?" Grishkov asked.

As someone who still thought of himself as a policeman, Grishkov ordinarily felt very little sympathy for the problems of criminals. This time, though, he surprised himself by being genuinely curious about how Kolesnik would respond.

"None of us expected to spend the rest of our lives in eastern Ukraine. If I can continue to work for Kharlov in whatever he decides to do next, that would be preferable. If not, I'll probably look for security work in Russia. I think the same is true for many of the other men. A few may try their luck outside Russia," Kolesnik replied.

Grishkov grunted. "Risky. Didn't I read that at least two dozen such security contractors have been killed in Syria? Other locations I've heard are available like Libya and the Central African Republic don't sound very appealing."

"Agreed. Honestly, I hope I can stick with Kharlov. At least I know I can trust him," Kolesnik said.

Grishkov simply nodded. He was glad to hear Kolesnik put such a high value on trust.

Now Grishkov felt better about his prospects in the challenge ahead.

CHAPTER THIRTY-FOUR

Poltava Air Base, Ukraine

Captain Josh Pettigrew had to work hard to keep a smile off his face as he watched the Ukrainian Air Force officers wrestle with the Blackjack's catapult launch system. At sixty-one kilograms, the Blackjack wasn't too heavy for the fit young men to move into position. However, its five-meter wingspan made handling the drone more than a little awkward.

The Ukrainians' first "hands-off" launch of the Blackjack at Myrhorod Air Base had gone off without a hitch, just as Pettigrew had expected. "Hands-off" was what Pettigrew called letting the Ukrainian officers handle all aspects of the launch on their own, as though he had declared their training complete and returned to the U.S.

Pettigrew had also anticipated that the second "hands-off" training mission wouldn't go as smoothly. It was just human nature, he'd thought. After the first success, people tended to relax.

As soon as the Blackjack launched, Pettigrew had seen the problem. One of the Ukrainian officers had failed to set the catapult's tension correctly. The result was that the drone's initial launch speed had been too slow.

Pettigrew hadn't said a word as the Blackjack clawed for altitude. He'd thought the drone might clear the trees that surrounded the base.

But probably not.

Lieutenant Bondar had been at the drone's controls, and he'd had only seconds to make a decision. Pettigrew had been pleased to see it was the right one.

Bondar had cut the drone's speed and sent it into a gentle descent. The Blackjack had only bounced once as it hit the ground and then slid through the grass as Bondar cut all power.

It was only after the drone finally came to a stop with its wings still attached that Pettigrew had remembered to breathe.

Part of the Blackjack's light weight had been achieved by dispensing with landing gear and a reinforced undercarriage. In short, it had never been designed to land.

Instead, one of the Blackjack's trailers contained the Skyhook recovery system. This required hooking the drone in midair on a vertical wire, a task that so far the Ukrainian officers had managed to make look easy.

Fortunately, the damage to the Blackjack from the forced landing had been minimal.

That experience, though, had convinced Pettigrew to bring two Blackjacks for today's mission. Considering the stakes, a backup appeared to be an obvious precaution.

So far, it looked like the backup would be unnecessary. This time the Blackjack's catapult launch went off flawlessly, and it was soon headed south towards Dnipro.

Pettigrew walked over to the control vehicle and saw that Lieutenant Smirnova was at the controls. For the first time, Pettigrew had allowed the students to select who would fly the Blackjack. He'd announced he would do so before finding out about the SS-24 warheads, and had briefly considered choosing the pilot himself instead.

Unfortunately, there was no way to do that without negative consequences. The students would see it as Pettigrew's having decided they couldn't be trusted with the selection. Much worse, it would arouse their suspicions.

Pettigrew knew there would already be plenty of grounds for suspicion before the day was out. Best not to add to those grounds from the start.

The point of letting the students select the pilot had been to see how they arrived at the choice. By seniority? By picking the officer with the best political connections?

Pettigrew had been relieved to see Lieutenant Smirnova at the controls because it told him two things. First, they had decided to choose the best pilot.

Just as important, the Ukrainian officers agreed with Pettigrew that Smirnova was that best pilot.

"Sir, you said that we're looking for a vehicle with radioactive cargo headed south towards Dnipro and that it could use one of several highways to do so. I've checked, and I believe the three most likely roads are the T0410, P52, and E105. This is the flight plan I've calculated for maximum coverage," Smirnova said, tapping one of the nearby digital displays.

Good, Pettigrew thought. The students had been told they were in charge of this mission, so Smirnova wasn't asking for approval.

But he was smart enough to give Pettigrew the chance to point out any obvious mistakes.

Smirnova's flight plan put the Blackjack at close to maximum altitude. Good. That would provide the best coverage.

It also had the Blackjack moving south like a snake, sliding east and west in an attempt to cover all three highways at least partially.

"Great job, Lieutenant. I don't think I could have done better myself," Pettigrew said, meaning every word.

Smirnova nodded stoically, but Pettigrew wasn't fooled. He could see Smirnova was pleased, and so were the other students within earshot.

The truth was, though, their coverage of the main highways headed south to Dnipro would have gaps.

And though they'd had no trouble installing the Russian instrument package, was it truly compatible with the Blackjack's electronics? There was no way to test the Russian technology, so they'd only know for sure once it detected a radioactive source.

Or failed to do so.

Well, Pettigrew thought, that put him in the rather odd position of rooting for the effectiveness of the Russian spies who'd been collecting information on America's military drones.

Pettigrew walked over to where a group of Ukrainian students was preparing the backup Blackjack for launch. He wished he could put it in the air now as well, but there was no point. For this training program, he only had one control vehicle. Others were on the way from the manufacturer but would arrive in Ukraine too late for this mission.

In a way, it was good that the second Blackjack launch had been a failure. There'd been no surprise that Pettigrew was no longer "hands-off" around the catapult. Far from being resentful, Pettigrew could see that the Ukrainians appreciated having their work checked.

That was good. Because whether the students liked it or not, Pettigrew wasn't taking any chances with this mission.

CHAPTER THIRTY-FIVE

Near Dytyatky, Ukraine

Anatoly Grishkov started awake as their SUV bucked over a hole in the road.

Wait a minute, Grishkov thought to himself. What road?

The moon was bright, but Grishkov was still impressed that Kolesnik was able to drive by its light alone.

"So, this is another reason you thought it best that you drive," Grishkov said.

Kolesnik nodded. "Yes. We smugglers know all the back ways. And it's not the first time I've driven this beast off road."

Grishkov snorted. "Really? If it were that easy, why would they bother staffing a checkpoint at Dytyatky? We can't be the first people who have wanted to reach Chernobyl without authorization or escort."

That earned him a thin smile from Kolesnik. "You're right. Years ago, Kharlov sent me to pick up some old Soviet military equipment that someone had salvaged from tunnels near Duga in the Exclusion Zone. The man said it was too risky to move it out himself. I went with another of Kharlov's men, who used to run missions in the Zone all the time. He had a terrible sense of humor."

Grishkov looked at Kolesnik curiously, and couldn't resist asking, "For example?"

Kolesnik shook his head with resignation. "What's the slogan of Chernobyl Farms Chicken?"

Grishkov shrugged, and replied, "No idea."

Kolesnik said, "Always an extra drumstick."

Grishkov groaned.

"You asked," Kolesnik said with a smile.

After a few seconds, Kolesnik smiled again. This time, though, it was bitter.

"So, why didn't Kharlov send this tunnel expert with you? Well, remember the man I said we lost?" Kolesnik asked.

Grishkov nodded. "That was him?"

"Yes," Kolesnik said shortly. "One of the very few we'd lost over the years, until Karpenko's recent attack. Kharlov is nearly always smarter than his opponents. Another reason I hope I can stay with him."

Kolesnik paused and then pointed. "There. We're now far enough past Dytyatky that it should be safe to get back on the road."

Moments later, a roar of power from the engine propelled them up the embankment and back onto the pavement.

"I see you're keeping the lights off," Grishkov said. "Are there roving patrols?"

Kolesnik shrugged. "After all these decades, just about anything worth stealing from the area around Chernobyl is long gone. The government has made what I believe is the right decision, and will only spend so much on saving the foolish from themselves. Still, it doesn't hurt to be careful."

"A wise philosophy, and one I share. You focus on the road, and I'll watch out for approaching headlights," Grishkov replied.

"Good. I'll let you know when we're getting close to the bridge crossing the Uzh River. I've always feared some enterprising young officer would have the bright idea to set up a roadblock there. This SUV can't swim, so the river is the only obstacle we can't avoid," Kolesnik said.

"Understood," Grishkov said. "Once we're over the river, it's not that far to Chernobyl, right?"

"Yes. But we'll be turning off before we reach Chernobyl since our objective is the tunnels near Duga. There is also a checkpoint we need to skirt called Leviv on the main road between Chernobyl and the Duga radar array. Fortunately, there are some badly maintained secondary roads we can use for that purpose. Going off-road isn't an option since the area near that checkpoint is heavily forested," Kolesnik replied.

Grishkov grunted. "Does 'badly maintained' mean 'not maintained at all,' or am I too pessimistic?"

"Your pessimism is altogether warranted," Kolesnik said with a smile. "To be fair, since nobody is supposed to be living in the Zone, the Ukrainians can hardly be blamed for failing to keep up all the roads."

'Supposed to be living here," Grishkov repeated. "Are you saying that people are living here in the Exclusion Zone?"

Kolesnik shrugged. "Yes. From about ten thousand in the late eighties, fewer than two hundred Samosely remain in the Zone, but illegal settlers almost certainly outnumber them."

Grishkov shook his head. "Samosely?"

"Sorry. Samosely is the name for people who either refused to leave the Zone during the original evacuation or returned afterward. Most are now in their sixties and seventies, and their number is shrinking rapidly," Kolesnik said.

"But what about illegal settlers? How many are there? And who would be desperate enough to settle in a high radiation area?" Grishkov asked.

"I've heard government estimates of the number of illegal settlers ranging as high as two thousand, but most people I've talked to think it's much lower. Maybe a few hundred. As for why they came, the answer is simple. Free housing," Kolesnik replied.

"Really? How many of the homes and apartment buildings here are still habitable?" Grishkov asked.

"It depends on how you define habitable. Many of the structures are still intact, and plenty of people have the skills needed to do things like replace the flooring. Utilities may not be available, but compared to living on the street, it still looks like a bargain to some," Kolesnik replied.

"I had no idea conditions were that difficult here in Ukraine," Grishkov said, shaking his head.

"Well, for most people in Ukraine, life isn't that bad. Many, maybe even most, of the illegal settlers here in the Zone now are refugees from the fighting in Donbas," Kolesnik said.

Grishkov scowled. "That again. I wonder if the people who started the fighting had any idea how much misery they were about to unleash."

Kolesnik shrugged. "Maybe a better question is whether they cared."

"Wait a minute," Grishkov said. "If there are so many people living around here, isn't there a good chance someone will report us?"

"Anything is possible," Kolesnik replied. "But the odds are with us. We're avoiding Chernobyl itself, which has the largest number of Samosely and illegal settlers. I'm also avoiding villages known to be inhabited. The best thing in our favor, though, is that nobody here wants anything to do with the authorities."

Grishkov reached into his pocket and pulled out his phone. Then he nodded.

"I see there is no cell service at the moment. That makes me feel even better about our chances of avoiding a report to the authorities since I imagine no utilities includes no landline phone service. But I am getting a working satellite signal."

"Good," Kolesnik said. "Of course, that won't last once we get down in the tunnels."

"I've looked at maps of the tunnels around Duga, but I'm worried that they won't have much to do with current reality," Grishkov said.

Kolesnik laughed. "I haven't spent that much time in them, but from what I've seen, you're right to be worried. Parts of some of the tunnels have collapsed. Some collapsed sections are still passable. Others are completely blocked. Of course, movement in any damaged tunnel risks further collapse."

Grishkov tapped the maps in his lap. "I understand we're going to check out one of the largest tunnels first."

"Yes. There are many tunnels around Duga, and most are large enough to conceal a truck the size of the one Arbakov is using to transport the weapon. Our first stop is one of them. If we come up empty there, that tunnel will still let us conceal our vehicle from view after daybreak. With the weapons we're carrying, we can't risk an encounter with police," Kolesnik said.

"Agreed," Grishkov said. "I don't think we could pass for either Samosely or illegal settlers."

"Now, you will have to redouble your vigilance. See the roundabout ahead?" Kolesnik asked.

"Yes," Grishkov replied.

"And the road leading off to the left?" Kolesnik asked.

Grishkov frowned with concentration. The moon might be bright, but so far, not bright enough.

Then as they drew closer, Grishkov saw it.

"Yes, but I think the term 'road' is a bit generous," Grishkov said.

"Just so," Kolesnik said. "That's why I need you to keep a sharp eye out. Fallen trees, large rocks, and deep potholes are just a few of the possible obstacles standing in our way. At worst, we could break an axle. Even the time needed to replace a blown tire might still leave us on the road at daybreak."

"Understood," Grishkov replied. "Believe me. You have my complete attention."

As though to drive home Kolesnik's point, no sooner had they made the turn onto the secondary road than a pothole brought Grishkov's teeth together with a sharp "clack."

"I saw that one," Kolesnik said. "The pothole to the left was even worse."

Grishkov leaned forward, determined to see whatever he could.

Their SUV ground slowly forward, with Grishkov occasionally calling out a warning.

Mostly in time.

Trees on both sides made the road, as bad as it was, the only option to move forward.

The sky was just beginning to lighten in the east.

At least so far, there had been no headlights approaching them. Or, for that matter, any other indication that someone else was in this part of the Zone.

Just as Grishkov was about to ask how much farther they had to go, Kolesnik gestured ahead.

Grishkov immediately noticed that the woods to their left were much lighter. As though at one point, they had been cut to the ground. Only now had a few trees begun to approach the size of the ones on the other side of the road.

Kolesnik gradually slowed the SUV, and finally parked it between two trees.

Now to their left, Grishkov could see a gap among the trees. He couldn't say he saw a tunnel entrance. Just deep darkness that suggested it might be there.

Kolesnik whispered, "I'm taking point. You cover me."

Grishkov didn't argue.

But he did raise an eyebrow.

Kolesnik smiled and whispered, "Kharlov said to keep you alive. Said you've defused nuclear weapons before. And that you've got a wife and kids."

Grishkov nodded and whispered back, "Remember that it will take both of us to defuse the warhead. Keep your head down."

A tight smile was Kolesnik's only answer. Then he reached up and switched off the SUV's internal light.

Right, Grishkov realized. Otherwise, it would have illuminated the interior as soon as one of them opened a door.

An elementary precaution Grishkov remembered dressing down a hapless Vladivostok detective for missing during a stakeout. And he had almost forgotten it himself.

Going all night with little sleep was making him sloppy. Luckily, I've got someone younger with me to prevent such mistakes.

Not that I'd ever tell him that, Grishkov thought.

Kolesnik moved forward quickly, yet quietly. Grishkov followed close behind with his rifle at the ready.

It looked like his guess about the tunnel entrance's location had been correct. Kolesnik headed straight for the patch of darkness to their left.

Then Kolesnik held up a clenched right fist.

Stop.

They both crouched silently for several minutes. Grishkov could see nothing, and the only sound came from a few nearby insects.

Finally, Kolesnik straightened and started to move forward again. Apparently, whatever he'd heard had been nothing.

Grishkov looked nervously at the lightening sky. Though so far, it wasn't helping them see forward, he knew that soon that would change.

They had to be out of sight before that happened.

What was that smell?

Now Grishkov could finally see the tunnel entrance. Kolesnik had been right. It was easily large enough to admit a truck.

When Grishkov had first researched the military tunnels in this area, he had been surprised by their size. Once he thought about it, though, it made more sense.

After all, the tunnels had been occupied by many soldiers, scientists, and technicians. That meant stockpiles of food, water and other supplies large enough to support them.

And how would such a stockpile make it inside each of the tunnels? Being able to drive inside would make the task far more manageable.

Grishkov's thoughts were cut short by the intensifying smell. What was causing it?

Once again, Kolesnik held up a clenched right fist. This time, though, he only waited a minute before they resumed.

Then, Kolesnik gestured for Grishkov to join him. Once Grishkov was next to him, Kolesnik whispered, "I don't believe any person or vehicle has been here in some time. I'm going to risk a light."

Grishkov nodded. With dawn fast approaching, the time for subtlety was over.

Kolesnik snapped on a small flashlight. It had a tight beam that illuminated just what was directly before it.

Within moments, it was clear that nothing was at the tunnel entrance. No vehicle, no equipment, no supplies.

Just bare cement, as far back as they could see.

"What is that smell?" Grishkov asked in a whisper.

In the same low voice, Kolesnik answered, "Mold. All the tunnels have it, some worse than others. It's the reason nobody has tried to occupy them."

Grishkov scowled. Why hadn't he thought of that?

Well, it didn't smell like any mold Grishkov had encountered before, for a start. It was sharper and more...bitter?

Grishkov also had to admit to himself that lack of sleep was also a factor. He just wasn't thinking that clearly.

Kolesnik glanced at him, and Grishkov wondered if he had the same thought.

Then Kolesnik aimed the flashlight straight down, and Grishkov saw that he'd been wrong about one thing.

It wasn't bare cement.

Dark streaks were crisscrossing the cement, that now Grishkov could see were the mold Kolesnik had given as the source of the rank smell.

Then Kolesnik played the flashlight over the area they had just passed to reach their current location.

Grishkov could see the marks of their progress without any difficulty.

"There's no need for us to go in any further. There's no way Arbakov could have come into this tunnel either in a vehicle or on foot without leaving clear signs he'd done so," Kolesnik said.

Grishkov nodded agreement. He also had no interest in venturing in any further. The smell had already intensified in the short distance they'd advanced, and Grishkov's eyes were beginning to water.

Kolesnik glanced at Grishkov again and appeared to realize he needed a break.

Kolesnik tossed Grishkov the SUV's keys. "Bring the SUV back as quickly as you can. I'm going to look around a bit more, just to make sure I haven't missed anything."

Grishkov wasted no time exiting the tunnel entrance. Without the need to worry about stealth, it took him only a few minutes to reach the SUV and back it into the tunnel entrance.

Kolesnik climbed into the vehicle beside him. "I knew about the mold problem from having been here before. So, I installed a special air filter before we left. We can run the air conditioner every few hours and should be safe. As I'm sure you've guessed, the mold doesn't just smell bad. It's also highly toxic."

"You mentioned someone who had sold Kharlov some Soviet military equipment they found in one of these tunnels. But you think now they've all been picked clean?" Grishkov asked.

Kolesnik shrugged. "It's been years since I heard of anything coming on the market from these tunnels. In any case, I wouldn't risk my lungs trying to find out."

Grishkov nodded emphatic agreement.

"I'm going to take the first watch," Kolesnik said. "Why don't you try to get some sleep."

Grishkov said nothing and just hit the switch reclining the seat as far back as it would go.

His last thought before sleep claimed him was about the Americans and their drone. There were so many tunnels to search.

Would they get any help from that drone, or would they have to spend night after night searching one tunnel after another?

CHAPTER THIRTY-SIX

Lubny, Ukraine

Fedir Popova looked at his surroundings with disdain. Ordinarily, he would never have lingered at a truck stop, but this was the only meeting place that made sense. He certainly didn't want to take his truck any distance off the highway.

Popova had been forced to clean the table where he was now sitting. There was little he could do about the floor.

It all reminded Popova of how he had ended up on the path that had led him here. Yuzhnoye had paid him well by Ukrainian standards. But not well enough for Popova to live the way he had seen on visits to London and Paris.

And undoubtedly not well enough to pay for a cleaning service. Popova detested the sort of dirt and filth that was now all around him. But not enough to grab a mop and bucket himself at home.

So he had betrayed his employers at Yuzhnoye. With the money Popova obtained from selling their trade secrets, he had been set for life and could afford to laugh when he was fired.

It was curious, though. Popova didn't need to work. But when Yuzhnoye got him blacklisted, it made him furious.

Popova was an engineer. It's who he was. He could feel the rage building in him again as he thought about what Yuzhnoye had done to him.

Regret for the actions that had led to his blacklisting never entered his mind.

The final irony was that "set for life" turned out to mean very little once Popova received his cancer diagnosis.

Well, he was going to use the money he had left to set things right with Yuzhnoye. And at the same time, guarantee an instantaneous and painless death, rather than the months of agony cancer would give him.

As soon as Popova saw the man in the black leather jacket walk in, he knew his wait was over. At least the man's slicked-back black hair went with his jacket, he thought sardonically.

Popova gestured for the man to sit at his table.

"So, you have contracted for security?" the man asked.

"Yes. Your name?" Popova asked.

"Bondarenko," he replied.

Popova nodded. It was the name his contact had given him, one of the most common in Ukraine and almost certainly an alias. Not that it mattered.

"Please check your account to make sure that the half payment you were promised is there," Popova said.

Bondarenko frowned. "There's no need. I've already confirmed your half payment, and understand that you will pay the other half when we arrive in Dnipro."

Popova smiled. "Humor me, please."

Bondarenko shrugged and pulled out his phone. Popova did the same.

A few moments later, Bondarenko's eyebrows flew up. "Did you just...?"

"That's right. I just paid you the agreed amount now in advance. And if I make it safely to Dnipro with my cargo, I will give you double the amount I just paid," Popova said.

Bondarenko sat back and looked at Popova more carefully. "You must have some precious cargo."

"Yes. To my company and its competitors, though it would be worthless to anyone else. I fear another firm may try to steal it. They might even bribe the police to try to stop me," Popova said.

Bondarenko frowned. "As agreed, I have two cars with three armed men in each. But we can't fight our way through a police roadblock."

"Of course not. I only mean a single police car might be bribed to pull me over, while men in another vehicle try to steal my cargo. Could you deal with that?" Popova asked.

Bondarenko glanced again at his phone and the new cash balance shown there before he answered.

"Yes. I'll be in the lead car, and the other car will follow you. You are sticking to the route I was given to Dnipro via the M03 and P52 highways?" Bondarenko asked.

"Correct. I want this trip to be over as quickly as possible," Popova replied.

Bondarenko grunted. "There, we are in complete agreement."

With that, both men rose and hurried to their vehicles.

Popova had no illusions about how reliable Bondarenko and his men would be if put to a real test. He did believe, though, that they would now at least make some effort to safeguard a payday they had every reason to think would be substantial.

Popova smiled to himself. If he made it to Dnipro and the warhead worked as it should, there would be no need to pay anything more to Bondarenko.

CHAPTER THIRTY-SEVEN

65 Kilometers North of Dnipro, Ukraine

Mikhail Vasilyev had to admit he was impressed. Boris Kharlov had said he had a plan to stop the truck carrying the SS-24 warhead but insisted it would be easier to show him than to explain it.

Kharlov's grin told Vasilyev the gleaming semitrailer that had just pulled into the truck stop was the centerpiece of his plan.

"So, a Mercedes. Smuggling must pay better than I imagined," Vasilyev said.

"Well, the truck is. But the trailer and container were both made in Russia," Kharlov said.

"Makes sense," Vasilyev said. "You have to save money somewhere."

Kharlov shook his head. "Not at all. The trailer is designed for off-road duty supporting oil production operations in the far north. The container is climate controlled and has multiple movable compartments. Including, of course, ones that would be very difficult for anyone to detect without special equipment. Neither were cheap."

"I can see how hidden compartments would come in handy in your business. Is that how you propose we get the warhead back to Russia?" Vasilyev asked.

"That's the backup plan," Kharlov replied. "But I doubt we'll be able to stop Popova and his armed escort without attracting attention. Including from the police. So, we'll need something faster to do the job."

"And that would be?" Vasilyev asked.

Kharlov grinned. "A Mil-26 Halo."

Neda had been leaning against their SUV once again reviewing her SS-24 technical documents, but now her head jerked upwards. "How did you manage to obtain a Halo?" she asked.

Kharlov's grin broadened. "Well, I certainly don't have enough money to buy one. But there is a European company willing to lease Halos for the right price. Not cheap, but its carrying capacity made it worth the expense. On paper, it's based in Russia, but in reality, I have it on standby not far from here."

Vasilyev frowned. "Will it be capable of moving the warhead? It's quite heavy."

Now it was Neda's turn to grin. Kharlov nodded and said, "You tell him."

"The most famous Halo missions were decades ago, and we reviewed them in the training I did when I joined the FSB. The first was in 1999. A Halo transported a woolly mammoth estimated to have been frozen for over twenty thousand years, plus the permafrost that had preserved it. The weight was estimated at over twenty-two thousand kilos. Now, have you heard of the American Chinook cargo helicopter?" Neda asked.

Vasilyev nodded. "So, if it can carry a mammoth, the Halo must be at least as capable."

Neda smiled. "More than that. In 2002 Halos flew two missions in Afghanistan. In each, they transported disabled Chinooks back to base for repair. One was carried from an altitude of two thousand six hundred meters."

"Very impressive. I'm surprised I hadn't heard of the Halo before," Vasilyev said.

Neda shrugged. "Those incidents were news long ago. There are only a few in civilian use outside Russia. That's why I was surprised to see our friend here had managed to get one, even on a lease. I only know about the Halo because I happened to get an instructor during training who had flown one."

Vasilyev gestured towards the semitrailer. "So, if that's just backup transport, it must have a different primary role in this plan. A rolling roadblock?"

"Exactly," Kharlov replied, nodding with approval. "As soon as we know Popova's location, we'll position this vehicle and one of the SUVs to cover both lanes in front of it. I will be with you and your colleagues in this second SUV. The rest of my men will be in the trailer, ready to deal with Popova's hired gunmen."

"We'd better get plenty of notice from our American friends. Either that or get lucky with Popova's road choice," Vasilyev said.

Kharlov shrugged. "True. But of Popova's three choices, this road is the most direct and best maintained. Everything I've seen in his file says this is not a patient man. Also, I doubt whatever pills he's taking are completely successful in masking the pain from his illness. I think Popova will drive straight on to his objective."

Vasilyev nodded absently. His attention was now on Neda, who he could see had gone back to poring over warhead schematics.

A small part of Vasilyev was honest enough to admit that he almost hoped the Americans would miss Popova's vehicle. Or that Popova would take another road after all.

Vasilyev had complete faith in Neda's abilities. But he barely knew Kharlov. The two of them simultaneously cutting the weapon's detonation circuit in four places sounded more than a little risky.

Still, the stakes were just too high. Thousands dead at Dnipro would be bad enough. But if the Americans decided Russia had asked for their help as an elaborate ruse to allow a devastating Russian attack on Ukraine, there could be much worse to come.

No. It didn't matter how much Vasilyev loved Neda. Vasilyev knew neither of them could live with the consequences of failure.

Vasilyev looked at the traffic passing by on the highway. It made this moment all the more frustrating to know there was nothing he could do but wait.

And hope Kharlov was right about Popova's choice.

CHAPTER THIRTY-EIGHT

10 Kilometers North of Lubny, Ukraine

Marko Zavod had come very close to missing his chance to find one of the warheads. But he was not a man accustomed to failure.

Zavod knew that anyone moving such a valuable cargo would hire security. There weren't many outfits capable of taking on such a job with little or no notice. And many of those would balk at guarding an unknown cargo on the move. As well as taking payment from an unknown individual.

After all, that might indicate something illegal was going on, Zavod thought to himself with a fierce grin. He looked around the SUV and nodded with satisfaction.

Zavod had used the time since the debacle with Tarasenko to correct his last mistake. Then he'd hired the first gunmen he could lay his hands on, and nearly paid for that error with his life.

This time, the SUV's driver and the two men in the back were three of the best hired guns available in Ukraine. His boss Avel Karpenko hadn't been happy with the amount necessary to hire them.

Finally, Zavod had asked Karpenko how important the warhead was to him. Then Karpenko had finally stopped complaining and agreed to wire Zavod the necessary funds.

Yes, the men he'd found were some of the best.

Almost as good as the men Popova had hired to guard a certain cargo en route to Dnipro.

Well, Zavod reminded himself, he couldn't complain too much. If Popova had hired ordinary street thugs instead of someone like Bondarenko, he might have never been able to track him down, and discover that Dnipro was his destination. At the level of Zavod and his Ukrainian contacts, common thugs barely registered.

Zavod smiled to himself as another thought came to him. He'd been frustrated at first to realize he was going to just miss catching Popova at his meeting with Bondarenko in Lubny.

Now, though, Zavod realized that it was just as well. At four guns to six, the odds would not have been in his favor at Lubny.

With more time to think, though, Zavod had realized that he almost certainly had an unexpected ally in his mission to obtain the warhead. The Russians who had nearly killed him when he tried to kidnap Tarasenko.

Yes, the Russians would almost certainly have obtained Popova's target location the same way he had. By keeping an eye on security contract hires.

The highway went straight south from Lubny to Dnipro. Somewhere along it, the Russians would strike. Zavod was sure of it.

And then Zavod would be there to pick up the pieces.

Zavod had obtained a photo of Popova and distributed it to all of his new hires. Popova was now the primary target.

For whatever reason, Popova wanted to set off the warhead in Dnipro. If, as Zavod expected, the Russians stopped the vehicle carrying the warhead before then, he was sure they would see Popova as the primary target as well.

With luck, the Russians would stop Popova from arming the weapon before Zavod arrived on the scene.

If Popova triggered the warhead, Zavod knew it would be impossible to escape from the blast radius.

Zavod sighed as he compulsively checked his AK-74 to make sure all was ready for the encounter ahead. He missed his Fort-221 assault rifle, lost in the last disastrous battle with the Russians.

Zavod told the driver to pick up speed a little. Not too much, though.

It wouldn't do to be pulled over for speeding.

Zavod absently tapped the AK-74. It would do the job.

Which was first, to succeed in his mission.

And, most importantly, to make the Russians pay.

CHAPTER THIRTY-NINE

Poltava Air Base, Ukraine

Captain Josh Pettigrew was doing his best not to hover. When he'd been at the controls of a drone, having a superior officer at his back for more than a few minutes at a time had made him uneasy at best.

At worst, Pettigrew was honest enough to admit that his performance suffered. He had no idea whether Lieutenant Smirnova would react the same way.

But today's mission was far too important to take that chance.

So, Pettigrew had occupied his time talking with the other students. He'd made a point of seeking out Lieutenant Bondar. Pettigrew wanted to be sure none of the other students thought his opinion of Bondar had dropped because of his decision to abort the last Blackjack landing.

Sure, Pettigrew had already said Bondar had done the right thing, and in front of all the other students.

In the real world, Pettigrew knew that wasn't good enough.

Besides, it gave Pettigrew something to do. Without that, he knew himself well enough to be sure his feet would take him to the control vehicle.

Where he'd hover.

"So, Lieutenant, in your opinion, what is the greatest challenge facing Ukrainian pilots today?" Pettigrew asked.

Bondar nodded to acknowledge hearing the question but took a moment to frame his reply.

Good, thought Pettigrew. The question deserved some thought.

Besides, Pettigrew saw that several other students had turned towards them. Now that they had an audience, Bondar was well advised to think hard about his answer.

"Our only real potential adversary is Russia, the world's second greatest air power. Their planes, such as the SU-30, SU-33, and SU-35, are better than our MiG-29s and SU-27s. Thankfully, they don't have many SU-57s deployed yet, but their advantage will increase even further when they do. We have only one hope of victory," Bondar said.

Pettigrew cocked his head curiously but said nothing. He was sure Bondar would continue.

"We have to fly better than the Russians. Above all, we have to take advantage of knowing our skies. We're not flying attacks into Russia. Our flying will be defensive. So, that means flying low enough to avoid Russian radar, and hitting the enemy before they know we're there," Bondar said.

Pettigrew nodded. "Your planes' bellies should be yellow from the sunflowers," he said.

Bondar smiled. "I see you have spoken already to one of our flight instructors. Yes, that's something we hear quite a bit in training. But flying low comes with many challenges."

"Yes. Very little time to react if something goes wrong with the plane. And no time to eject," Pettigrew said softly.

"Exactly. That's what they think happened when Colonel Ivan Petrenko and his co-pilot, Lieutenant Colonel Seth "Jethro" Nehring, were killed," Bondar said.

"I remember reading about that in 2018," Pettigrew said. "I didn't know Colonel Nehring, but I've heard of his unit, the U.S. National Guard's 144th Fighter Wing. Its history dates back to World War II."

"Both men were very experienced and capable pilots. But though their plane had been thoroughly checked before they flew the exercise mission, like all our planes, it was well over thirty years old. Every plane we have dates from Soviet days. Some we've updated, but realistically there's only so much we can do," Bondar said.

Pettigrew grinned. "Well, you're right that age can be a problem for aircraft. But someday I have to get you inside a B-52. They've been around for over seventy years. What's more impressive, though, is that the average age of a B-52 in service is about fifty-five years. That's older than any B-52 pilot I've ever met."

"I would very much like to see such an aircraft. I've heard they're very capable. But I doubt you'd try to do low-altitude flying in one," Bondar said with a smile.

Pettigrew smiled back. "No. You're right, of course, that age is a bigger issue for fighters than for bombers."

Before he could continue, Pettigrew saw that Lieutenant Melnik was frantically waving from outside the control vehicle.

Seconds later, Pettigrew was looking over Smirnova's shoulder at the drone's visual display. It showed red brackets around the front and back of a moving truck and the logo "Target Match."

At the bottom of the display, there were three small lines of text. The first showed the radiation signature they were seeking. The second showed what the Russian equipment had found.

Pettigrew could see immediately that the rows of radioactive elements and their percentages were almost identical.

The third line agreed with Pettigrew. It merely said, "MATCH" in capital letters.

Well, it appeared that the Russians' equipment was working as advertised.

Doing his best to control his excitement, Pettigrew said, "Good work, Lieutenant. For the next part of this exercise, please focus on the target vehicle at the Blackjack's maximum resolution and capture an image. Then, do the same for the two vehicles in front of that truck, as well as the two behind it. All clear?"

Smirnova was puzzled, but his training kept his curiosity in check. He just said, "Yes, sir."

"Good. Once you've done that, start to lower your altitude gradually. For bonus points, I want images that will give us the license plate numbers on all the five vehicles I've just designated," Pettigrew said.

For a second, Pettigrew thought Smirnova's curiosity was going to force a question out of him. Finally, though, he just nodded.

That was a relief. Pettigrew didn't have a good explanation to hand.

Next, Pettigrew took a picture of the display with his cell phone, focused on the two GPS coordinates recorded by the drone. One labeled as "Target" and the other as "Blackjack."

Smirnova was wholly focused on flying the drone, since dropping altitude while maintaining position and control relative to a moving target was not a simple task. As a result, he didn't notice Pettigrew taking the picture behind him.

Moments later, Pettigrew was in his sedan parked next to the command vehicle. A few seconds later, the picture had been texted to the only number stored in the cell phone's memory.

Pettigrew shook his head. Even with General Robinson ordering him to do it, sending data of any kind to FSB agents still felt wrong.

But if there were two five hundred kiloton nuclear warheads out there, Pettigrew supposed that he'd just have to ignore those feelings.

As he walked back into the command vehicle, a quick look at the display told Pettigrew that he had the right pilot at the controls for this mission. Smirnova had just finished leveling out the drone at its new lower altitude, and now the target vehicles filled the display.

"Outstanding flying, Lieutenant! I doubt I could have dropped altitude while staying on target any faster myself," Pettigrew said, meaning every word.

Though Smirnova just nodded impassively, Pettigrew could see he was pleased.

"Ready for image collection," Smirnova announced.

Pettigrew observed as one after the other, each of the target vehicles was selected, and their image captured. Smirnova had no trouble obtaining images showing each vehicle's license plate.

This time, though, with the drone in level flight, Pettigrew knew Smirnova would notice if he took a series of pictures. Fortunately, this time that wouldn't be necessary.

"Excellent work, Lieutenant. Now, I'm going to show you a Blackjack capability we haven't covered in class. Go to the 'Communications' menu. Good. At the menu's end, select 'Other.' Good. Now select 'cellular phone number.' Good. Now, send each of the images you've just collected to my number. You can read it from my screen," Pettigrew said, holding up his cell phone. He already had the phone displaying its number from the settings page.

Smirnova frowned but did as he was ordered.

Shortly, a series of pings announced the arrival of the images on Pettigrew's phone.

"So, Lieutenant, why do you think this capability was added to the Blackjack?" Pettigrew asked.

Smirnova frowned again, but this time thoughtfully. "In case Blackjack data or images need to reach troops in the field who either lack regular military communications gear, or whose equipment has been damaged."

"Exactly right, Lieutenant. Now, you'd seen the Blackjack communications screen before in class. Why hadn't you noticed a cell phone option before?" Pettigrew asked.

At first, Smirnova looked startled. And then, puzzled. Finally, he smiled.

"Because in class, I was logged on to the software as a student, meaning as an ordinary operator. But today I saw you logged in to this equipment yourself, which meant with full supervisory access. Which includes the ability to send data and images to a cell phone," Smirnova replied.

"Very good," Pettigrew said. "As I'm sure you'll have realized, there are serious security implications to allowing data from a drone to be sent to a cell phone. But experience has taught us that, as long as precautions are observed, the capability is worth the risk."

"Understood, sir," Smirnova said.

"Continue to observe the target vehicles. I'll be back in a few minutes to check on your progress," Pettigrew said.

"Yes, sir," Smirnova replied.

A few moments later, Pettigrew was back in his sedan, and the vehicle images were on their way to the Russians.

Well, Pettigrew thought, I've done what I could.

Without conscious thought, Pettigrew's head swiveled south. A few seconds later, he caught himself and chuckled ruefully.

At this distance, Pettigrew doubted an explosion, if there were one, would be visible.

Then he realized he had no idea how far away a five hundred kiloton blast could be seen.

Nobody Pettigrew knew had ever witnessed a thermonuclear explosion. He frowned as he realized he had no idea how long it had been since one had been tested above ground.

A quick search on his phone answered the question.

1962.

That explained why nobody now serving in the Air Force talked about having seen the test of a thermonuclear weapon.

As he read further, Pettigrew winced as he saw that the 1962 test had knocked out streetlights and telephones in Hawaii.

Almost two thousand kilometers from the test site.

Pettigrew's eyes narrowed as he looked at the southern horizon.

He sincerely hoped he'd see nothing of interest there in the coming hours.

CHAPTER FORTY

65 Kilometers North of Dnipro, Ukraine

Mikhail Vasilyev rapidly highlighted the GPS coordinates from the text and copied them into his cell phone's browser. They instantly displayed a map position that showed Popova's truck with the warhead was on this very highway.

And Popova was still north of their position. For just a moment, Vasilyev had an odd feeling.

Could Alina, or more properly Alina's mother, have been right? Did all this good luck have a divine hand behind it?

Vasilyev quickly shook off the sensation, as he looked at Boris Kharlov cleaning and checking his weapon nearby. No, this wasn't the time for superstition. Hard work and good luck were enough of an explanation.

Though if they were successful in stopping both warheads, Vasilyev thought to himself, I would be happy to stop by an Orthodox church and say a prayer of thanks.

A very sincere, heartfelt prayer.

Vasilyev held the cell phone aloft and turned the display towards Kharlov. "We have a position for the warhead," he said.

Kharlov was beside him and looking at the display in seconds. "Excellent!" Kharlov said. "The time stamp on this image is from just five minutes ago. We can deploy our vehicles as planned with at least..." Kharlov checked his watch.

"Four minutes to spare!" With that, Kharlov began giving orders to his men. In moments, they were all in their vehicles and ready to move at his command.

Vasilyev hurried to their SUV, looking in the backseat where Neda Rhahbar had glanced up from her weapons schematics.

"They've been spotted?" Neda asked.

Vasilyev nodded. "Not far north of here. We still have time to intercept them as planned."

He looked in the rearview mirror, checking that Neda's ballistic vest was in place, and her seat belt buckled.

A wry smile told Vasilyev that his look's purpose had been understood. Fortunately for him, Neda didn't think Vasilyev was checking because he doubted her abilities.

Instead, Neda correctly thought Vasilyev was doing it because he cared about her.

Kharlov slid into the passenger seat next to Vasilyev. "By my reckoning, I think it's time to go."

Vasilyev nodded. He could see that the semitrailer was already in motion, closely followed by the SUV containing the rest of Kharlov's men.

Kharlov looked backward and could see no sign of the weapon he'd placed on the floor by Neda. "I hope my friend isn't bothering you back there," he said.

Neda laughed. "No, he's very quiet. I'm glad you put the talkative end inside a case."

Kharlov grinned and nodded.

Then he punched Vasilyev in the shoulder. It was his way of saying, "You've got a good woman there."

Vasilyev grunted and handed Kharlov his cell phone. "I've just received images of the vehicles immediately in front of and behind Popova's truck. We can't be sure they're all occupied by members of his security detail, but if vehicles with those license plates are still around the truck by the time we see them, I say that's enough reason to take them out."

"Agreed," Kharlov said immediately.

Vasilyev glanced back and saw the frown he'd expected on Neda's face, but she said nothing. She'd voiced her objections before to this approach, but accepted it when Vasilyev overruled them.

Given the stakes, Vasilyev wasn't going to wait for Popova's men to fire first, or even to be sure that a particular vehicle was part of his security detail.

No. Instead, they were going to hit Popova and his men hard, before they had any idea they were in danger.

And with luck, before Popova had the opportunity to arm the warhead.

Poltava Air Base, Ukraine

Captain Josh Pettigrew looked down at his buzzing phone and quickly read the text message it displayed. It was the one he'd been expecting. It said the Russian team had received his messages, and needed no further information on this target.

It also asked him to begin searching for the second target as soon as possible.

"Lieutenant, this exercise is now concluded. I need you to switch the display to the terrain immediately in front of the Blackjack," Pettigrew said.

Lieutenant Smirnova was puzzled by the abrupt change but didn't hesitate. In seconds, the display had switched from surveillance to active flight mode.

"Now, I'm going to give you a new course. Its purpose is to move the Blackjack towards our new control location at Vasylkiv Air Base," Pettigrew said.

"Yes, sir," Smirnova replied automatically.

"I'm setting you a new challenge. We're going to move towards the drone's new station point, which includes you and this control vehicle. The flight control software is going to try to compensate for the fact that you'll be moving at almost the same speed as the Blackjack. Do you understand that the key word I just used is 'try'?" Pettigrew asked.

Smirnova nodded vigorously. "Yes, sir. You can count on me to remain alert."

"Good, Lieutenant. I expected nothing less. The point of this stage in the exercise is to reproduce the stress of real-world combat operations. Ideally, you would always recover the Blackjack before moving to a new location. Combat is often anything but ideal," Pettigrew said.

"Yes, sir. First, I will calculate the best recovery point as close as possible to Vasylkiv Air Base based on the new course you've just given me. Then, we will all travel to recover the Blackjack. Finally, we will move on to Vasylkiv Air Base. Do I understand all that correctly, sir?" Smirnova asked.

"You do, Lieutenant," Pettigrew said with a smile.

Smirnova smiled back. "Sir, I think I speak for all the men when I say that this training has been much more challenging than we expected."

Now Pettigrew laughed. "Oh, Lieutenant, I'm just getting started. Wait till we get to Vasylkiv!"

Where, no matter what the students think, I may need to make some changes to the flight roster.

CHAPTER FORTY-ONE

60 Kilometers North of Dnipro, Ukraine

Fedir Popova scowled and could feel his grip involuntarily tightening on the truck's steering wheel. Then, he took a deep breath.

Calm down, Popova told himself. After all, his progress to Dnipro and his revenge was so far entirely on track. In less than an hour, Popova would be able to set off the warhead and make all his former coworkers at Yuzhnoye regret...

No, scratch that, Popova thought with a thin smile. They wouldn't have time to regret anything.

But none of them would outlive him, either.

The truth was, Popova was ready to stop living. His cancer had progressed to the point that pain medication could only do so much to allow him to function. Even one more day might have left Popova unable to obtain the revenge he craved.

Well, soon, the pain would be over.

Bondarenko had been in the SUV directly in front of him since they'd left Lubny. The other SUV with the rest of Bondarenko's men was right behind Popova's truck. They were all in the right lane driving a few kilometers per hour under the speed limit, and so far there had been no trouble staying together.

Fortunately, most Ukrainian drivers were only concerned about the speed limit when the highway police appeared. So far, Popova had noticed no police of any kind.

So, nearly all other vehicles had whizzed past them on the left, leaving Popova and his security detail to continue their slow but steady progress to Dnipro.

Until now. This blasted semitrailer was in the lane right in front of Bondarenko, and at first, it hadn't been a problem. It was also going a bit slower than the speed limit, so they had all just slowed down a fraction.

And then the semitrailer slowed down a little more. Bondarenko put on his turn signal, and Popova prepared to follow him around the semitrailer.

Then Bondarenko's SUV veered back into the right lane behind the semitrailer, and Popova heard his cell phone buzz.

The text Popova read made his heart begin to race.

"Vehicle blocking left lane. Prepare for possible attack."

This could just be a coincidence, Popova thought. He'd seen two vehicles rolling down the highway side by side before. The last time a woman had been in the left lane vehicle and had been texting.

It had just taken a blast from Bondarenko's horn, though, to get her attention. Popova remembered thinking she was quite pretty as he was finally able to pass her.

Though there was nothing attractive about the gesture she used as he went by.

Popova was jolted back to the present as he heard two loud sounds behind him. What were they?

Popova looked in his rearview mirror and was horrified to see that the most recent sound was the SUV behind him, leaving the road and flipping over.

The sound Popova had heard just before that had been the automatic weapons fire used to shoot out the SUV's tires.

At the same time, Popova saw something in front of him that made no sense.

The back door of the semitrailer was rising. And Popova could see little flashes of light at the very bottom of the space revealed by the opening door.

As the sound hit his ears an instant later, Popova understood what was happening. Men were lying on the floor of the truck and firing at Bondarenko's SUV!

And hitting it too. But so far, they hadn't managed to hit its tires or the driver.

Then Popova saw a small round object fly through the air from the SUV's passenger side, right into the back of the semitrailer.

Popova had only a second to guess that Bondarenko had just thrown a grenade.

There was a flash of light immediately followed by a loud bang.

Then everything was chaos.

The semitrailer driver reflexively braked, startled by the impact behind him.

Bondarenko's driver tried frantically to brake as well, but couldn't react in time.

The front of the SUV crumpled into the semitrailer, destroying the massive vehicle's right rear tire.

Despite its driver's best efforts, the semitrailer lurched left.

Popova briefly saw a blur to his left as the SUV Bondarenko had said was blocking the left lane departed the road. It looked like it was turning over and over.

But Popova had no time to worry about that.

Because what was left of Bondarenko's SUV was now rapidly filling his windshield.

Popova had been frantically pressing on the truck's brake pedal without even realizing it as he tried to keep track of everything that was happening.

But it wasn't enough.

Popova's last thought before everything went black was intensely bitter.

I was so close.

56.5 Kilometers North of Dnipro, Ukraine

Marko Zavod looked through his binoculars at the scene ahead. He had pulled his SUV off the highway and could see all the drivers behind him had done the same.

And no wonder. Even from this distance, everyone could see the semitrailer jackknifed and spread over both southbound lanes. Smoke was rising from it, but Zavod couldn't see any flames.

That was more than could be said for two other vehicles he could see nearby. One was in the median to the left of the semitrailer and the other directly behind it. Zavod winced as the fire blazing on the vehicle in the median reached its gas tank, and the resulting explosion sent it lurching skywards.

Its flight didn't last long. The flaming debris that was left was no longer recognizable as a vehicle.

Zavod trained his binoculars on the other flaming vehicle, the one directly behind the semitrailer. No movement there.

That left the truck behind the second damaged vehicle, and an SUV with no visible damage about twenty meters behind the truck. The truck was still lined up correctly on the highway, but the SUV had spun around so that the driver's side was now facing Zavod. Both were stationary, and though he could see they were occupied, Zavod could spot no movement.

No, wait.

It looked like the man on the front passenger side of the undamaged SUV was still alive. Zavod thought he could see him trying to rouse the driver, though it didn't look like he was having any luck.

Luck. Zavod drew his lips back in a humorless grin. Yes, it looked like luck was indeed with him today.

Zavod was nearly sure the truck in front of him carried the warhead. Its guards and the Russians appeared to have killed each other, with no more than a survivor or two.

This was going to be a lot easier than he'd thought, as long as they acted before the police showed up.

Or Popova armed the warhead.

Zavod told the men with him to ready their weapons.

It was time to collect his prize.

CHAPTER FORTY-TWO

56 Kilometers North of Dnipro, Ukraine

Boris Kharlov's head was aching, and it took a real effort of will to open his eyes. As consciousness flooded back, he realized survival would depend on how quickly he acted in the next few minutes.

First, Kharlov tried to rouse Mikhail Vasilyev in the driver's seat.

Nothing.

Well, Vasilyev was still breathing, at least. So was Neda Rhahbar, but she was also unconscious.

A flash of light from a silver SUV behind them caught the corner of Kharlov's eye.

Binoculars.

A curious motorist?

Or, more likely, someone else interested in Popova's cargo.

Staying low, Kharlov eased open the door on his side and slid out. Then, he opened the door behind his. Kharlov saw with relief that the case with the warhead and the launcher were on the floor right where he'd left them.

The RPG-7D3 was the improved paratrooper version of the venerable RPG-7, which had been around for decades and produced in the millions. Its key improvement was the folding stock that had let him position the launcher at Neda's feet.

Kharlov opened the case to the warhead and smiled. The TBG-7V, a 105mm thermobaric rocket, had not been cheap.

But Kharlov was hoping that if its explosive radius were as wide as advertised, it would be worth it.

In moments Kharlov had unfolded the launcher and attached the warhead. Staying as low as he could, he inched his way to the SUV's back rear corner.

Peeking around the corner, Kharlov saw one of the doors of the silver SUV starting to open.

As the door swung wide, he could see the man beginning to exit was holding a rifle.

Now he had to overcome the key disadvantage of this launcher. The rocket was unguided.

And he only had one warhead.

Well, Kharlov thought, I'd better not miss.

In a single fluid motion that Kharlov had practiced many times as a Spetsnaz soldier, he lifted the launcher to his shoulder, aimed and fired.

The result was everything he could have hoped.

The silver SUV leaped in the air, propelled by a ball of fire from the warhead's explosion. As it started to come back down, the gas tank ignited.

Flaming fragments of the SUV were scattered over dozens of meters. The force of the explosion rocked their vehicle but caused no damage.

All the vehicles in view behind the destroyed SUV did whatever was necessary to exit the area. Some crossed the median and headed back in the other direction. Others turned around and drove back on the shoulder.

Very soon, no vehicles were visible behind them.

But Kharlov wasn't satisfied.

He hadn't seen what had happened to the man who had been exiting the SUV with his rifle.

Kharlov was nearly sure that he had been thrown some distance by the explosion, and if he was right, then the concussive force of the blast had probably killed the man.

Indeed, he could see no movement anywhere in the area where the silver SUV had been.

Movement. Well, there was none where he'd been looking, but Kharlov was delighted to see some in the vehicle next to him.

Their entire vehicle's rocking had done what Kharlov's gentle shakes had failed to accomplish. Both Vasilyev and Neda were moving.

Vasilyev gingerly turned his head backward to look at Neda. He was relieved to see her looking back at him.

"Are you OK?" Vasilyev asked.

"I think so," Neda replied, carefully moving her arms and legs. "A few aches and pains, but nothing serious. Is anybody moving in that truck?"

"Not as far as I can see," Vasilyev replied. Then he turned his head as the passenger door opened, admitting Kharlov's burly form.

"Glad to see you two sleeping beauties are awake!" Kharlov said. "Are we ready to finish this?"

Vasilyev frowned. "I see nobody moving in the truck. But are we sure there's no opposition left?"

Kharlov nodded. "Glad to hear you say so. I was about to ask you to stay with the vehicle and provide rear security while I go with Neda to defuse this bomb. The burning wreckage behind us is what's left of a vehicle that I think belonged to Zavod and whatever men he hired."

"But you think someone got clear," Vasilyev said flatly.

"Yes. And my money's on Zavod. If I'm right and he is alive, I'm also pretty sure he's injured. That makes him more dangerous, not less. The bottom line is simple. If anything behind us moves, shoot it," Kharlov said.

Vasilyev glanced at Neda, who was checking to make sure she had all the tools they'd need to defuse the warhead.

"Count on it," Vasilyev said.

56.5 Kilometers North of Dnipro, Ukraine

The moment Marko Zavod opened his eyes, he wished they'd stayed closed. He'd experienced pain many times before.

But not like this.

Zavod looked at the pool of blood around him and grunted. So, this wasn't going to be survivable.

Next, he saw that his rifle was lying just out of reach.

So, was there any reason to make an effort to pick it up?

Zavod realized he was going to have to move at least a bit to answer that question. Where he was now, a large chunk of flaming metal was blocking his view of the road ahead. If he moved right...

Yes. Zavod could accomplish both objectives. See the road ahead, as well as reach his rifle.

Some instinct, though, told Zavod to be careful. Whoever had destroyed his vehicle and mortally wounded him was still out there.

Zavod inched slowly towards the rifle, every movement agony. Once he stopped and closed his eyes, and almost decided to give up then and there.

No. Maybe I can at least repay whoever did this to me, Zavod thought.

CHAPTER FORTY-THREE

56 Kilometers North of Dnipro, Ukraine

At first, Fedir Popova didn't know where he was or what he was doing. His head was spinning, and he felt blood dripping into his eyes from a cut in his scalp.

Popova waited a moment for the dizziness and nausea to subside.

Then he wiped the blood from his eyes with his sleeve. Now he could see a small pocket knife in his lap.

Popova grimaced. Now he remembered putting the knife on the dashboard at the truck stop. It was lucky he'd at least closed it first, or it might have done worse than smack him in the head.

Looking ahead, Popova could see there'd be no going forward. Not before someone moved that semitrailer.

To his left, Popova saw that burning vehicle pieces occupied the median. He wasn't going that way.

Can I back up?

No sooner had Popova had the thought than he looked at his rearview mirror.

The dark-haired woman carrying a case of some kind didn't concern Popova. He was sure the pistol he now pulled from the center storage compartment could take care of her.

A woman carrying a case could mean only one thing, though. They were going to try to defuse the warhead.

The engineer in Popova was stirred to curiosity. Had he missed something? Was defusing the warhead even possible? Popova hadn't spent time on the question since it wasn't anything he'd have reason to do.

Quite the contrary.

Popova shook his head. Well, all that mattered was that they thought the warhead could be defused.

The hulking brute walking beside her was a more pressing concern. Not only was he carrying an automatic rifle of some type. One look was all Popova needed to be sure he knew how to use it.

Trading his slow, painful death from cancer for instant nuclear vaporization had been one of the main reasons Popova had spent his remaining money and time on obtaining and arming the warhead.

Getting shot might be a quick death too. On the other hand, it might not.

Another goal had been getting revenge against the top people at Yuzhnoye.

Too bad that now that wasn't going to happen.

But he could, at least, take the people who had foiled his plan with him.

Popova smiled as he pulled the warhead's radio trigger from his vest pocket. Big and bad, the man with the rifle might be.

But Popova thought any man alive would hesitate when faced with a dead man's switch to a nuclear warhead.

Popova pressed the trigger.

So, now the warhead was armed. Popova knew that actual detonation would take place whenever the warhead had been programmed to reach its target. For closer destinations, perhaps twenty minutes. For the farthest, maybe thirty-five.

Could he keep the advancing pair talking that long?

Only one way to find out.

Popova slowly opened the truck's door, keeping it between him and the man and woman who were now only a dozen meters away.

"Stop!" Popova shouted, holding up the radio transmitter high over the door with his left hand while keeping the hand holding the pistol out of sight. "Do you know what happens if I drop this?"

"The warhead will be armed," the man said calmly.

"That's right," Popova replied. "Now, I want you to drive a car next to this truck that I can use to get out of here. I'll leave the warhead behind."

The man shrugged. "If all you want to do is leave, why didn't you do it in the truck?"

Popova sighed with genuine exasperation. "Maybe you could have found a way to drive a vehicle this size through all these wrecks. I don't see one. But I'm sure I can do it in a car. So, do we have a deal?"

"Just a minute," the man said.

"Take your time," Popova replied acidly.

In fact, though, Popova was pleased with how the exchange had gone so far. If they agreed, by the time they had a vehicle placed nearby, the warhead might already have had enough time to detonate. Even if it hadn't, whatever few minutes were left would never be enough to defuse the warhead.

Popova could see the man talking to the woman, but their voices were too low for him to hear what they were saying.

It didn't matter. They just needed to keep talking a little while longer.

CHAPTER FORTY-FOUR

56.5 Kilometers North of Dnipro, Ukraine

Marko Zavod sighed as he lifted his AK-74 rifle into position. It was good that he'd taken the time to fit a scope to it, though he hadn't expected to use it. The AK-74 was perfectly capable that way, but Zavod had thought combat in this mission would be close range.

Well, he'd been wrong. Now, though, the scope could give him a better view of what was on the road ahead. In particular, where the people who had wounded him were hiding.

The first thing Zavod saw was that two of them weren't hiding at all. They were walking openly towards the truck.

Hmmm. There was an SUV between him and the truck. Hadn't he just seen movement beside it?

The door to the truck swung open, and Zavod immediately switched his view back there. Zavod could see part of an arm holding something over the door, and heard the man yelling something.

It had to be Popova, Zavod thought. He was too far away for Zavod to hear him clearly, but close enough to understand his intent.

If Zavod hadn't been in so much pain, he would have laughed. Wasn't it evident that Popova had already activated the warhead? After going to all this trouble, who would just leave a nuclear warhead behind?

Popova is playing for time, Zavod realized. He's worried that those two will defuse the warhead.

Zavod also realized that if he was right, all he had to do was sit tight and watch the show. Once the warhead detonated, revenge on the people who had mortally wounded him would be accomplished.

Zavod glanced over at the other side of the highway. It was jammed with vehicles. Many had crossed the median from his side to escape the fires and explosions.

As he swept his scope over the scene, Zavod could see many women and children.

Zavod grit his teeth, fighting to remain conscious as a wave of nausea swept over him.

Whatever he was going to do, Zavod realized he had to do it quickly.

Zavod took careful aim and fired.

Yes! Popova was no longer behind the truck door and was instead now visible sprawled out beside it. Zavod had been concerned that from this range, the AK-74 round wouldn't penetrate the truck door, but obviously, it had.

Next, Zavod found himself looking up at the blue sky. How had that happened?

Zavod couldn't move. Or feel anything.

It was hard to breathe.

I must have been shot again.

It was Zavod's final thought before his eyes closed for the last time.

56 Kilometers North of Dnipro, Ukraine

Fedir Popova had been living with steadily increasing pain for months as his cancer progressed. It was now to the point that even the most potent painkillers were barely enough to let him function.

So, Popova thought he knew all about pain.

He was wrong.

Zavod's bullet had punched through the truck door but lost most of its velocity in the process. So, when it hit his stomach, it didn't pass through.

Instead, it lodged there.

The pain was worse than anything Popova had ever imagined.

He could hear the man and woman approaching the truck.

Popova knew neither of them had fired the shot that had left him prone and writhing in agony. He had been looking right at them when he'd been shot. Neither of them had been pointing a weapon.

He didn't care. Someone was going to pay.

Moving was out of the question. Popova was going to have to hope that one or both of them would come to him.

His right hand was still clutching the pistol. And Popova was ready to use it.

So ready.

The walking sounds came closer. Just a little nearer...

For an instant, the pain was so blinding that Popova imagined the warhead had exploded.

And then everything turned black.

CHAPTER FORTY-FIVE

56 Kilometers North of Dnipro, Ukraine

Boris Kharlov kicked the pistol away from Popova's hand, and then picked it up.

You never knew when a spare weapon might come in handy.

Kharlov quickly walked around the side of the truck to where Neda Rhahbar was waiting.

"Is he dead?" Neda asked.

Kharlov nodded. "Never leave a snake unwatched behind you," he said, holding up Popova's pistol.

"Here, let me give you a hand up," Kharlov added as he picked Neda up and deposited her in the truck bed.

Kharlov was about to follow her when he heard Neda hiss in dismay. "There's a case back here that I'm sure covers the warhead. It's closed with a padlock!"

Kharlov swore and lifted the radio from his belt. "Vasilyev! We need the bolt cutter right away!"

Seconds later, their vehicle roared towards them. Vasilyev leaped from the driver's seat and raced to the trunk.

Kharlov jumped into the back of the truck and had his arms outstretched for the bolt cutter when Vasilyev came running up.

"Keep an eye out behind us," Kharlov said, as he hurried to the warhead case.

Moments later, the case was open, and Neda was pulling tools from her bag. It took her several minutes, but finally, the interior wiring was exposed.

Neda breathed a sigh of relief.

"At least I see no surprises. It looks exactly like the diagrams I showed you," Neda said, as she handed Kharlov two wire cutters.

"You remember the locations?" Neda said nervously as she picked up two more wire cutters from the bag and positioned them over her side of the case.

Kharlov simply nodded, and gently placed the wires he intended to cut inside the open jaws of each wire cutter.

Neda peered over at Kharlov's side and smiled. "Very good," she said and placed the wires on her side inside her cutters.

"Now, on three," Neda said.

Kharlov nodded, entirely focused on the cutters he was holding.

"One. Two. Cut," Neda said.

Neda and Kharlov cut the wires simultaneously.

Or at least, they hoped they did.

Both Neda and Kharlov stood stock still after cutting the wires.

Finally, Kharlov exhaled and straightened. "Well, it appears we're still here."

Neda took a step back and shook her head. "I'm still not certain that the warhead is defused. If the target happened to be one of the most distant, there could still be time to go before detonation."

Kharlov looked at his watch and shrugged. "Understood. But every passing minute moves the odds further in our favor. In any case, I am calling the weapon's transport."

"Yes, I agree. The warhead must be removed before the authorities arrive. I'm surprised they're not here already," Neda said.

Kharlov keyed his radio and began speaking rapidly.

Next, he called out, "Vasilyev! Any sign we have company?"

Vasilyev had moved to the back right corner of their vehicle. There, he could see the road behind them more clearly, while still receiving some cover.

"Nothing!" Vasilyev shouted back.

Kharlov shook his head and looked at Neda. "You're right. The police should have been here by now."

A few minutes later, a small dot appeared in the sky that grew steadily larger. Very quickly, they could hear the helicopter as well.

Once it was overhead, the noise was deafening.

Kharlov leaned over to Neda and shouted, "Best that you're not here for this next part."

With that, Kharlov gently lifted Neda and lowered her to the ground next to the truck. Then, he pointed towards Vasilyev's position.

Neda nodded her understanding and was soon out of sight.

Kharlov grunted his appreciation as he examined the mechanism Popova had devised to secure the warhead and its case more closely. Mad he had indeed been, but a competent engineer.

Now all Kharlov had to do was press a button to activate the motor that released the metal plate holding the case in place.

Kharlov had already seen that the case was thankfully held up from the truck bed within metal brackets.

Two metal cables with large spring snap links at each end snaked down from the helicopter. Using a technique Kharlov had practiced several times on deployment with the Russian military, he looped the chains around the warhead's case. Next, he used the snap spring links to secure each side, making sure the weight was balanced.

Once he was done, Kharlov waved up at the helicopter crew.

At first slowly, and then faster as the warhead cleared the truck, the cables were rewound into the helicopter.

In just a few minutes, the warhead was in the helicopter, which then receded in the distance even faster than it had arrived.

Kharlov smiled to himself. Yes, that made sense. If he'd been the pilot, he would have made sure the flight was over as quickly as possible.

Jumping down from the truck bed, Kharlov ran to their SUV. Neda was back in the rear seat, visibly exhausted.

Well, Kharlov had to acknowledge, it had been a stressful day. At least the three good men he'd just lost had died helping to save thousands of lives. And their deaths had been avenged.

Vasilyev was just where he was supposed to be, crouched beside the vehicle, and sweeping the area behind them with his rifle for threats.

It looked like there were none left.

Kharlov tossed Vasilyev the keys. "I need you to drive us out of here."

Vasilyev caught the keys left-handed, which earned him an approving smile from Kharlov.

"I think the only way out is across the median, then beside the roadway out of the traffic until we can get back on going north. This SUV has a four-wheel-drive, so it should be possible. I'm going to be on the radio," Kharlov said.

Vasilyev simply nodded, and moments later, they were headed across the median.

It took Vasilyev some time to find a gap between vehicles large enough to let him reach the shoulder on the other side. Once he located one, the nearby drivers expressed their recognition of his accomplishment with a chorus of horns and gestures that Neda found intolerable.

Neda rolled down her window and unleashed a volley of Farsi invective channeling all the stress that had been building up in her for days. The words were accompanied by hand and arm motions that might have been specific to Iran.

But they were delivered with an emphasis that made their intent unmistakable.

As they emerged onto the other side of the highway, Kharlov put down his radio for a moment and glanced in the rearview mirror.

Neda, arms folded, glared back at him.

Kharlov looked over at Vasilyev, who was frowning with concentration as he weaved his way forward. Though he stayed on the shoulder as much as possible, he frequently had to take their SUV off the road to avoid obstacles and other vehicles doing the same thing they were.

They had already passed several overturned and stuck cars that showed focus was indeed required.

Still, Kharlov couldn't resist saying it.

"You're a lucky man," he said quietly.

Vasilyev's gaze never wavered from the road ahead.

But he did smile as he replied, "I know."

CHAPTER FORTY-SIX

Vasylkiv Air Base, Ukraine

Captain Josh Pettigrew smiled as he surveyed the busy but well-organized scene before him. The Ukrainian officers had responded well to the challenges he'd posed so far.

Now to see if they'd do as well with one even more difficult.

Pettigrew walked into the control vehicle and saw Lieutenant Bondar was at his station and ready to fly the drone.

"Everything's ready for launch, Lieutenant. You've had a chance to read the mission brief. Any questions?" Pettigrew asked.

"Just one, sir. I understand that the vehicle carrying the radioactive materials in today's exercise will be somewhere in the Chernobyl Exclusion Zone. It may even be in a tunnel within the Zone. Is that right, sir?" Bondar asked.

"It is, Lieutenant," Pettigrew replied.

Bondar shook his head. "Well, then, my question is whether the instruments on this drone are sensitive enough to pick out this truck and its cargo. With all the radiation already present throughout the Zone and the truck possibly being in a tunnel, do we really have a chance to find it?" Bondar asked.

"Absolutely, Lieutenant. Now, yesterday the drone's software put a big red 'match' around the truck. That made Lieutenant Smirnova's job a lot easier," Pettigrew replied.

"Yes, sir," Bondar said glumly. "But it's not going to be so easy for me, is it?"

Pettigrew laughed. "No, Lieutenant, it won't. On the left side of the screen, you see the radioactive elements we're seeking listed. You won't see a 'match' declared by the software until all the elements are detected in the proportions that confirm you've found the target."

Bondar nodded. "So, I have to look for any of these elements. Once I find one, I will tighten my search pattern, hoping that the additional elements present in the target appear. If they don't, then I will widen my search pattern again."

Pettigrew nodded. "An excellent approach, Lieutenant. I'll let the rest of the detachment know that they're cleared for launch."

A few minutes later, the Blackjack was on its way to the Chernobyl Exclusion Zone.

Pettigrew watched as the drone rapidly shrunk to a dot, and then disappeared from view.

Well, intercepting the first warhead headed for Dnipro had gone perfectly. Rather than inspiring confidence, though, that performance worried Pettigrew deeply.

Like many soldiers, Pettigrew had an ambiguous attitude towards luck. On the one hand, he would never dream of trusting any mission to chance.

If asked, Pettigrew would always say that any decent officer made his luck through hard work.

On the other hand, though, Pettigrew had an unstated belief that any mission's supply of good luck was finite.

So, a perfect performance with the first warhead's interception worried Pettigrew.

A lot.

Pettigrew shook his head vigorously, as though he could shake such thoughts free. They weren't helping, and he had to focus.

As he walked back to the command vehicle, Pettigrew remembered they weren't the only ones who could make this mission a success. The Russians were supposed to have people on the ground looking for the second warhead.

Pettigrew smiled wryly at the next thought that came into his head almost immediately.

I wonder how their luck is holding out?

Duga Complex Tunnel 8, Ukraine

Pofistal Arbakov took in deep breaths of clean air. It was amazing how good it felt. Something you normally took for granted.

Arbakov had checked several other tunnels before finally settling on this one. It was a little better than the others but still infested with mold.

At least it didn't have bats. Or booby traps.

It wasn't the first time Arbakov had dealt with military tunnels, so the mold was a problem he'd anticipated. He had outfitted his truck with a special air filter and had a respirator.

But Arbakov was running through respirator filters faster than he'd expected. And the weather hadn't cooperated. Winds had remained stubbornly northward, towards Belarus and away from Kyiv.

This had left Arbakov stuck hiding in the tunnel, trying fitfully to sleep. He wasn't sure which was worse. The nightmares, or the thoughts that occupied his mind while he was awake.

Sometimes he even doubted whether what he was doing made sense.

But then he thought again about his poor dead wife, and how much Natalia had suffered as cancer ate her from the inside over months.

And how little the Ukrainian doctors and nurses had done to help her.

Nobody ever came right out and said Natalia was being treated poorly because she was a Russian speaker. That's not how it worked.

Arbakov, though, heard the comments the doctors and nurses made when they thought he was out of earshot.

Things they would have never dared say to his face.

Arbakov had thought seriously about detonating the warhead at the hospital where his wife had suffered for so long. Indeed, the doctors and nurses there deserved death many times over.

But what about the patients? Many of them were just helpless victims, even as Natalia had been.

Then he realized that he didn't live that far away from the hospital. The blast radius and fallout would quickly kill his neighbors. They, too, were blameless.

And he knew them.

Arbakov had finally settled on his present plan because there was no doubt the snake's head was in Kyiv. The poisonous, "Ukraine for the Ukrainian-speakers" politicians. The ones who not only allowed but actively encouraged discrimination against Russian-speakers.

Cracking open the Chernobyl reactor's containment vessel and letting the wind spread its poison over Kyiv had the great advantage of ensuring those politicians wouldn't just die.

They would suffer. The same way his beloved wife had.

There would be no quick nuclear incineration for them. No, their death would be long and lingering, just as Natalia's had been.

There was a small but persistent voice in the back of his head, though.

It asked about the people living in Kyiv who weren't politicians.

It asked about Kyiv's children.

Arbakov had done his best to ignore that voice. After all, pity and sympathy were all well and good.

But where had they been for his wife?

No. Revenge always required sacrifice.

And he was going to wreak vengeance on those who were ultimately responsible for Natalia's suffering.

Arbakov's upbringing had replaced belief in religion with unquestioning faith in the State. And, of course, Stalin.

His wife had quietly followed the Orthodox faith, though she had never tried to force it on Arbakov.

Well, if Natalia had been right, then surely God would stop him now.

So far, though, everything had gone perfectly. Arbakov had breezed through the checkpoint at Dytyatky in broad daylight. Much of the work had been done by his obviously military truck, with its military plates.

Fortunately, the contract security guards staffing the checkpoint weren't aware that they were long-expired military plates.

Arbakov had a lifetime of shouting orders to privates to fall back on when dealing with the guards at the checkpoint. He waved a clipboard holding a form as he said in a loud voice that he was carrying maintenance supplies needed in Chernobyl.

Then, Arbakov pointedly asked the guards why they weren't expecting his arrival.

Next, Arbakov had pulled out his cell phone and told the guards to wait while he called headquarters to "get to the bottom of this."

The man in charge at the checkpoint had hurriedly assured Arbakov that they knew all about him and his vehicle. They'd just had to check to make sure his plates matched the notice they'd received.

Arbakov would have been highly amused if he'd known that there was a nationwide lookout for his plates. Fortunately, the lookout notice hadn't been provided to the contract security guards at Dytyatky.

After all, now that the containment vessel's construction was complete, there was no real reason to worry.

Was there?

On his way to checking out the first tunnel on his list, Arbakov had driven right past the Duga radar array. After all these decades, he'd expected it to have collapsed.

Well, maybe part of it had. But what Arbakov could see still looked very impressive. Towering over the nearby trees, the radar array continued to face towards Russia's enemies.

Arbakov knew the array hadn't been operational for decades. Looking at it, though, he felt a wave of pride that reminded him of why he'd joined the Soviet military in his youth.

Then Arbakov had smiled as he'd thought back to the day he had first seen an SS-24 ready for a test flight on the launch pad. He had been so sure the Soviet Union was invincible. How could a country that could build such a missile, one capable of raining death and destruction on ten different cities at once, ever fall?

Yet fall it had. And now one of those SS-24 warheads was secured in the truck behind him.

Arbakov had scowled and shaken his head, pulling his truck over. Now he was determined to get a closer look at the array.

It hadn't taken long for Arbakov to reach its base. He had been struck with two equally strong, yet contradictory impressions.

Up close, the scale and complexity of the array had been even more impressive. Thousands of different components, assembled in one precise way over a span reaching as far as he could see for a single great purpose. Providing early warning of an American nuclear attack.

It was the sort of thing that would have been wonderful to see with his father. Growing up, the only times he had ever seen his father happy had been while watching a spectacle like a Soviet space rocket launch.

Those had also been the only times Arbakov could remember his father being glad he was present to share in the event.

It had been a long time since he'd been able to remember his father as being happy.

But here and there, pieces of the array were falling off. Rust had been visible on many sections, particularly the ones closest to the ground.

Arbakov sighed, returning to the present. The weather forecast said that the winds would finally shift to the south later in the day, probably by mid-afternoon.

He could finally end this and have peace.

Driving the truck out of the tunnel, even at night, was a risk. Arbakov knew that. Drones and satellites could see in the dark, and there was no telling when a random security patrol might drive by.

But the desire to breathe clean air had just been too strong.

Now that he'd done it, Arbakov was sure it had been the right decision. There was no hint of movement anywhere nearby, and no lights were visible either.

His head felt much clearer now that he'd been able to breathe some fresh air. Rolling down the windows once he'd left the tunnel had let him flush out the ever-present smell of mold, and replace it with the clean air of the surrounding forest.

Yes, Arbakov thought to himself. Driving the truck outside the tunnel had been the right thing to do.

But now caution had to take priority. After all of Arbakov's work, it wouldn't do for it to all be undone by a passing patrol.

Ever so slowly, Arbakov backed the truck into the tunnel until it was no longer visible from outside. Leaving the engine running, Arbakov walked outside the vehicle.

Shining a flashlight down the tunnel, Arbakov checked his memory of the way back. He wasn't going back much further, but he didn't want to risk an accident now.

Satisfied, Arbakov returned to the truck and backed it up a bit further.

There. Arbakov shut off the engine.

Only a handful of hours to go, Arbakov thought.

If the wind will just cooperate.

CHAPTER FORTY-SEVEN

10 Kilometers Northwest of Ivankiv, Ukraine

Lieutenant Bondar peered intently at the display. The entire area around Chernobyl was contaminated with uranium.

But not the specific uranium isotope used in the SS-24 warhead.

Bondar knew the instrument package Captain Pettigrew had installed had worked perfectly in the first supposed exercise. Then, it had detected the correct isotope without difficulty. Would it be able to do as well when faced with the nearly universal presence of a practically identical element?

When Bondar had taken the assignment to report on Captain Pettigrew to Ukraine's internal intelligence agency, the SBU, it had been for two reasons. The first had been straightforward.

He could use the extra money.

The second was that Bondar agreed with the assignment's purpose. Did he want the training that Pettigrew offered? Absolutely. Had he been impressed with the capabilities of the Blackjack, and Pettigrew's ability as an instructor? Certainly.

But was keeping a close eye on foreign military officers in his country a good idea? Even if they were supposed to be allies?

Well, yes.

The truth was that Bondar hadn't expected much to come of this assignment besides a paycheck. He trusted his instincts, and they all told him Pettigrew sincerely wanted Bondar and the other students to be thoroughly trained in everything the Blackjack had to offer.

So, when Lieutenant Smirnova had come to him as they were preparing to leave Vasylkiv Air Base, it had been a shock on many levels.

It had never occurred to Bondar that the SBU would have had more than one agent in this small training detachment. Once he'd heard what Smirnova had to say, though, he had to admit that it had been a good idea.

According to Smirnova, this was no exercise. The SBU believed the Americans were working with Russians to recover two SS-24 warheads.

Which each had a payload of five hundred kilotons.

Smirnova said the SBU believed the so-called practice target they had detected north of Dnipro had been one of those two warheads.

And now they were after the second one.

After they had launched the first Blackjack sortie, they had moved north from Vasylkiv to reduce the range to their patrol area around Chernobyl.

If Bondar hadn't talked to Smirnova, he would have been impressed with the real-world difficulties posed by Pettigrew. Hurried movement. Sequential operation of two drones to provide nearly continuous coverage.

Smirnova had been sent to a bunk at Vasylkiv Air Base with orders to join them only after he'd had a full eight hours of sleep. Then he was due to replace Bondar.

Hearing those orders had helped to convince Bondar that Smirnova and the SBU were right, and this was no training exercise. Why keep just the two of them at the controls?

There was only one answer that made sense. Pettigrew wanted to make sure the best pilots were flying. That was the opposite of what Bondar would expect from a training mission.

Undoubtedly, the weakest pilots were the ones who needed time in the air to improve their skills.

But if they were looking for real warheads, then keeping the two best pilots in the group at the controls was just what Bondar would expect.

Bondar would have never said so within the hearing of any other officer. Still, he knew it was true. Just as he knew every other pilot in the detachment would have agreed with his assessment.

Bondar was roused from his thoughts by white letters scrolling across the left side of the display. This time, no red "Match" appeared on the screen.

It was the right uranium isotope, though it was barely enough to register. Bondar was about to dismiss it when another target element appeared as "detected."

Tritium.

So far, among the many radioactive elements Bondar had found in the Chernobyl Exclusion Zone, tritium had been notably absent.

The hydrogen isotope tritium was, though, a critical component of all thermonuclear weapons. So much so, that thermonuclear weapons were commonly called "hydrogen bombs."

Bondar was about to call for Pettigrew when he walked into the command vehicle.

How did he do that?

"So, Lieutenant, do we have something?" Pettigrew asked, pointing at the display.

Bondar nodded. "I think so, sir. I was just about to call you. There's both the right uranium isotope as well as tritium."

"Tritium," Pettigrew repeated thoughtfully. "Have you picked up any other tritium readings before this?"

"No, sir," Bondar replied. "Just about every other radioactive isotope imaginable, but not tritium."

"Good work, Lieutenant," Pettigrew said. Then he did something that took Bondar by surprise.

Pettigrew took his cell phone from his pocket and took a picture of the display!

Then Pettigrew put the phone back in his pocket and calmly said, "It occurred to me that this display image would make a good slide for my next lecture. After all, most of your classmates will never see tritium listed on a Blackjack display."

It took everything Bondar had just to say, "I'm sure you're right, sir."

What galled Bondar was that if Smirnova hadn't spoken to him, he knew he would have accepted Pettigrew's explanation.

"Let's make sure you've found the objective," Pettigrew said. "Drop altitude and close range to target. Don't worry about detection, since there's little chance of spotting the Blackjack even in the daytime. Now at night, that chance drops to zero."

"Yes, sir," Bondar said. "The only structures nearby that pose any collision hazard are the Chernobyl reactor containment vessel and the Duga radar array. Both are well outside my planned flight path."

"Excellent," Pettigrew said.

As suddenly as they had appeared, the matching uranium and tritium element readings vanished.

"Sir, the readings have disappeared," Bondar said.

Pettigrew appeared unconcerned, as though this was nothing more than an exercise. Could Smirnova have been wrong?

"Understood," Pettigrew said. "For now, maintain station in the area where the readings were last spotted. If they don't return, we'll reassess later on."

"Yes, sir," Bondar replied.

Then Pettigrew sat down.

Bondar kept his expression impassive, but internally he groaned. How was he supposed to report what was happening to the SBU with Pettigrew sitting a few feet away?

And for that matter, where was the SBU anyway? Smirnova had assured Bondar he'd reported everything that had happened north of Dnipro.

Bondar had to work hard to keep the scowl he felt from reaching his face.

Was anyone in Kyiv paying attention to what was happening out here?

CHAPTER FORTY-EIGHT

Duga Complex Tunnel 11, Ukraine

Anatoly Grishkov's nose prickled as they approached the entrance to yet another tunnel. So far, mold had been the only thing they'd had in common.

The first tunnel they'd checked that evening had collapsed about a dozen meters in from the entrance.

The next had a bat colony established close enough to the tunnel entrance to give the smell of mold some real competition. The thick and undisturbed layer of bat guano at the entrance showed that Arbakov hadn't been anywhere near.

Grishkov froze as Kolesnik made the clenched fist "hold fast" signal. Had he heard something?

Next came the arm signal moving down. Take cover.

Grishkov hugged the ground, grateful that unlike Kolesnik, he wasn't quite to the entrance yet. Shoving his nose against the mold he could already smell was growing on the entrance floor might be survivable.

But Grishkov thought he'd prefer taking his chances against whatever might be hidden in the tunnel.

What was Kolesnik doing? Whatever it was, he was certainly taking his time about it.

Finally, Kolesnik moved quickly and quietly next to Grishkov. Leaning next to his ear, Kolesnik whispered, "Booby trap. I disarmed it."

Grishkov's pulse quickened. A booby trap meant there was something in this tunnel worth protecting. And a career soldier like Arbakov would know how to set one.

Maybe they could finally end this.

"Any movement?" Grishkov asked quietly.

Kolesnik shook his head and got up, as did Grishkov.

Moments later, they were at the entrance with Kolesnik again in the lead.

Kolesnik snapped on his flashlight, playing it over the concrete floor. This time the mold growing on the surface showed ample evidence that men and at least one vehicle had been this way.

So far, though, there was no sound or movement at all. Just concrete floor, walls and ceilings. All covered with mold.

Maybe Arbakov was deeper inside the tunnel?

Only one way to find out.

They hadn't moved far down the tunnel before the smell of mold became nearly overpowering. Maybe Arbakov had a respirator?

Or more likely, he'd hidden the truck with the warhead here and then gone somewhere nearby to wait for favorable winds.

Though Kolesnik wasn't that far ahead, it was far enough that he could see around the next bend in the tunnel before Grishkov.

In the dim glow of Kolesnik's flashlight, Grishkov could see him stop. And then shake his head in...disgust?

Grishkov hurried up to Kolesnik's position and immediately saw what had provoked the reaction. At least two dozen wooden crates, all with markings stenciled on their sides.

If the markings were accurate, there was a fortune in weapons and explosives hidden in this tunnel.

So, now they knew what had accounted for the booby trap and the vehicle tracks. And it had nothing to do with Arbakov.

Grishkov looked at Kolesnik, who nodded. Without a word, they both hurried as fast as they could out of the tunnel.

Just as they reached their SUV, Grishkov's satellite phone buzzed. A quick look at the screen made Grishkov grunt with satisfaction.

As he reached for the GPS mounted on the dashboard, Grishkov said, "The Americans have a possible location for the warhead."

"Good," Kolesnik replied. "I am beginning to fear the mold in these tunnels more than I do a live nuclear warhead."

Grishkov laughed and replaced the GPS on the dashboard. "There, we are in complete agreement, my friend."

Moments later, they were underway. Grishkov checked the GPS and smiled. Driving slowly in the dark without headlights meant its projected arrival time was too optimistic. Even so, Grishkov calculated they would still reach the tunnel flagged by the Americans before dawn.

Yes. Time to end this.

CHAPTER FORTY-NINE

Mariyinsky Palace
Kyiv, Ukraine

President Babich smiled to himself as SBU Director Shevchuk entered his office. If Shevchuk's threadbare suit wasn't the same as the one he'd worn on his last visit, then it was its twin.

Shevchuk put a slim folder in front of Babich, and said, "Mr. President, thank you for seeing me at such an early hour. We have another report from our agents with the American officer. As you know, that American has been training our officers in the use of the new Blackjack drones we just purchased."

Babich grunted. "I'm sure this report will be just as interesting as the last one. But first, I understand you have a video to show me?"

"Yes, sir," Shevchuk replied, opening the laptop he was carrying and setting it on Babich's desk. "The footage you are about to see was collected by one of the Bayraktar drones we purchased from Turkey in 2019. As you know, we bought the Bayraktars to give us a remote strike capability that didn't risk our pilots. Not primarily for surveillance. That's why we just obtained the Blackjacks from the Americans."

"So, don't be disappointed in the video quality," Babich said with a smile.

"Yes, sir. We routed the Bayraktar into position once we were notified by one of our agents with the Blackjack. This video doesn't last long, but only one portion has been edited. It took several minutes for the cargo helicopter to arrive at the end, so that part has been cut," Shevchuk said.

Babich nodded. "Yes, the one you believe took one of the warheads back to Russia."

"That's right, sir. I appreciate your approving my recommendation to let it go," Shevchuk said.

Babich shrugged. "I certainly don't want the cursed thing. Besides, you told me later this video will be all the proof we need that the Russians have been involved. I'm curious to see why you think so."

Shevchuk smiled, and Babich realized with a start that he had rarely seen a genuine smile on Shevchuk's face before.

"You will see, sir," Shevchuk said, and tapped a few keys. At first, all Babich saw was a perfectly ordinary Ukrainian highway filled with traffic in both directions.

That changed quickly.

Babich swore as one vehicle after another collided with another, flipped, or exploded.

"You told me that only a few Ukrainian citizens were hurt in all this, and nobody was killed," Babich said. "Looking at this video, I find that hard to believe."

Shevchuk frowned. "I'm sorry if I wasn't clear, sir. I said no Ukrainian civilians were killed. You will remember from your time with Department K that..."

Babich didn't give him time to finish. "We don't consider criminals to be civilians. Especially ones who are carrying firearms. So, we're satisfied that all the victims I'm seeing now were such criminals?"

"Yes, sir," Shevchuk replied. "We've matched several bodies to their files, including a man going by the alias 'Bondarenko,' one of the most feared gunmen in Ukraine. We believe many of the other dead shooters worked for Marko Zavod."

"What! Zavod! The only soldier to ever desert from our special forces! Did you find him among the bodies?" Babich asked.

"We did," Shevchuk replied. "Now, you see the truck that has become the drone operator's focus?"

Babich nodded.

"Next to it, we found the body of Fedir Popova, another man I don't consider an uninvolved civilian. He was a nuclear engineer who had been fired from Yuzhnoye," Shevchuk said.

"Yuzhnoye. The company that used to build nuclear missiles for the Russians when we were still part of the Soviet Union," Babich said.

"Correct, sir. Including the SS-24. We think he's the one who found a way to arm both warheads. Popova was headed south to Dnipro, where Yuzhnoye has its headquarters. We think that was probably his target," Shevchuk said.

"Right in the middle of a city with a million Ukrainians. Well, then, I'm not going to shed any tears for him," Babich said, and then paused.

"Wait a minute, do you see those three people moving in and around the truck?"

Shevchuk nodded. "In a moment, you will see one of them more clearly."

The camera zoomed in as one of the men reached the back of the truck, and handed something to a large man inside it.

When the man did so, he looked up at the large man in the truck.

Shevchuk hit a key on the laptop that paused the video and handed Babich a grainy photo.

"The man you are looking at is Mikhail Vasilyev, one of the FSB's top agents."

Babich shook his head. "But how can you be so sure of this?"

Two genuine smiles from Shevchuk in one day. Well, if he was right, he had good reason to be pleased with himself, Babich thought.

"You told me you weren't happy with how many agents Russia has infiltrated into Ukraine, and you were right to feel that way. But it works both ways. We have a few people working for us in Russia. Some of them have been there for a long time," Shevchuk said.

"I'm impressed. I'm also surprised that I've never heard we have sources in Russia," Babich said.

Shevchuk nodded. "Understood, sir. But as a former intelligence chief yourself, I'm sure you realize I would never discuss their presence in Russia unless it were necessary."

Babich frowned but finally nodded. "You're right. I know how important such secrets are, and would never deliberately share them with anyone. But we've both seen people slip inadvertently, usually by referring to information that could have come from only one source."

Shevchuk pressed a key on the laptop that let playback resume, and pointed to a woman with long dark hair in the truck bed. "The woman never looks up, so we don't know who she is. All I can say about her for sure is that she's not the FSB station chief in Kyiv because she's too short."

"And the large man?" Babich asked.

Shevchuk handed Babich another grainy photo, and said, "We haven't reached the point in the video where he looks up, but we soon will. That happens while he's preparing the warhead for transport. His name is Boris Kharlov."

"I know that name. Isn't Kharlov one of the warlords in Donbas? What's he doing so far west?" Babich asked.

"We know Marko Zavod was working for Avel Karpenko, and so Zavod was probably there to get the warhead for Karpenko. Kharlov may have seen a nuclear-armed rival in Donbas as an unacceptable threat. But there's another, simpler explanation for his presence at that truck," Shevchuk said.

Babich arched an eyebrow, waiting for Shevchuk to continue.

"Kharlov was Spetsnaz for years before he went into business for himself in Donbas. We've heard that he regularly feeds intelligence to the Russians. So, maybe he's been on Russia's payroll all along," Shevchuk said.

Babich grunted. "Well, he's certainly working for them now," he said, as the drone's camera showed Kharlov wrapping what looked like two metal chains around the warhead. Next, they watched as the warhead was lifted into a hovering cargo helicopter.

"Well, the Russians have managed to locate, defuse and return one of their warheads to Russia. It looks like we're well rid of the only Ukrainians to be killed in the process. I hope the report from your agent with the American officer relates to the other warhead," Babich said.

Shevchuk nodded. "It does, sir. He believes the warhead has been located. In a tunnel near the Duga radar array."

"The Duga radar array? But that's been out of commission for decades. Wait a minute. Duga is right next to Chernobyl!" Babich exclaimed.

"Yes, sir. We think the damaged reactor and the radioactive material it contains are the targets Arbakov has selected. Our experts say the warhead could easily breach the new containment vessel and distribute the radioactive material inside," Shevchuk said.

"Incredible! Two billion Euros spent on that containment vessel for nothing! And where will the fallout go?" Babich asked.

"The winds are due to shift southwards by this afternoon, sir. That would send the fallout straight to us here in Kyiv," Shevchuk replied.

Babich stiffened and fell silent. Shevchuk said nothing and gave Babich time to think.

Finally, Babich said, "We must prevent tons of radioactive poison from reaching Kyiv. Your recommendation?"

"I have coordinated with the military to prepare orders for your approval to send our special forces to the area. Those forces can be in place within the next few hours, and well before the winds are predicted to shift south. However, I recommend ordering them to wait nearby until then," Shevchuk said.

Babich frowned. "You are hoping that the Russians will retrieve this warhead as well?"

"Yes. My concern is this. There is no way to approach a tunnel unobserved, which is probably one reason Arbakov chose it. As soon as he sees our troops, he can be expected to trigger the warhead. And then, drive the truck out of the tunnel. Our experts say where the truck is right now, the warhead might be able to breach the containment vessel."

"And you hope that if the Russians could disarm one warhead, they can do the same with the other," Babich said flatly.

"Yes, sir. But if they don't manage it by this afternoon, then I think we will have to use our forces, and hope for the best," Shevchuk said.

Babich chewed his lower lip and sat silently for several moments. Then he opened the folder Shevchuk had brought and signed the orders.

"Get our forces moving. But make sure their commander understands the Russians are to be given every opportunity to take care of this themselves. As I've said before, this is the Russians' mess to clean up. For that matter, so is Chernobyl," Babich said bitterly.

"Yes, sir," Shevchuk said. "I'm sure the special forces commander would prefer that too."

Chapter Fifty

Outside Duga Complex Tunnel 8, Ukraine

Kolesnik had attached an infrared scope to his rifle, and now he looked through it at the tunnel entrance. He saw nothing to mark it as any different than the other tunnels they'd seen so far.

Well, Kolesnik had to admit this one showed no signs of collapse. And from here, he could see no bats.

Fine. No different than the other ordinary tunnels.

Grishkov had tried to insist on taking point this time, saying it was "his turn."

Kolesnik had flatly refused, pointing out again that unlike Grishkov, he had no wife and children. He had also meant it when he reminded Grishkov that he didn't want to face Kharlov if he failed to keep Grishkov alive.

Kolesnik was prone and had made his approach to the tunnel entrance as carefully and quietly as possible. If he couldn't see anyone, there was no reason to believe anyone could see him.

So why did he feel a prickling on the back of his neck, and have an overwhelming urge to run?

One of his first combat instructors had told him - no, scratch that - yelled at him to listen to his instincts. That's what kept your ancestors alive when all they had was rocks and their hands, he'd shouted.

Kolesnik could still remember his trainer's voice.

He'd paid attention then. He needed to do it again now.

Kolesnik slowly began to move back the same way he had come.

Duga Complex Tunnel 8, Ukraine

There were a few changes in perspective that came with embarking on a trip you knew was strictly one-way. For example, the value of money had changed for Pofistal Arbakov.

Before his wife Natalia's death, Arbakov had spent years paying down the mortgage on their home. It hadn't been easy to get the mortgage, and he'd been forced to pay an interest rate that in a Western country would have been considered ridiculously high.

Arbakov had even made extra payments, and had been looking forward to the day he could have a "mortgage burning" party. By the time Natalia had been diagnosed with cancer, Arbakov had calculated he had less than a year to go.

He'd have spent all the money he had to keep Natalia alive. Even though Arbakov was told repeatedly that spending more wouldn't help, he refused to believe it.

Natalia did. She had forbidden Arbakov to "waste" money on any treatment besides what the government-run hospital provided.

Arbakov had still tried to get a second mortgage based on his home's considerable equity to move his wife to a private clinic. The bank manager had been all smiles until the issue of Natalia's signature came up.

Arbakov had pointed out that the home's current mortgage, with only a small amount left to pay, had only his name.

Ah yes, the bank manager had said, but what about the deed?

Arbakov had to admit that the deed was in both their names at his insistence.

So, there was no problem with putting the second mortgage in his name alone, the manager said. But Natalia had to sign the mortgage application.

Arbakov saw the point. He would be taking out debt on property she partly owned.

Desperate, Arbakov had said Natalia was in the hospital. The manager had said it didn't matter. As long as she was alive, he needed her notarized signature.

After Natalia died, Arbakov had thought seriously about trying to sell the house. He knew he would have obtained more money that way than from a second mortgage.

But selling the house would have taken time. By then, Arbakov had already decided to use the warheads he had stolen so many years before. And he didn't want to wait.

So, Arbakov had gone back to the same bank. And had silently slid Natalia's death certificate across the bank manager's desk.

The man did have the grace to be embarrassed and had hastily offered his condolences. And yes, of course, there'd be no need to redo the paperwork he'd already submitted.

In less than a week, Arbakov had all the money he thought he would need.

As long as he had told no one about the warheads, Arbakov had not been worried about defending them. But once Arbakov had realized he would need help to arm the warheads, he also understood that others would try to find them.

As a nuclear technician, Arbakov's combat training had received little emphasis. Besides basic training, he had been required to spend little time holding a rifle.

Fortunately, while in basic training, Arbakov had discovered he wasn't just a good shot. He enjoyed practicing with a rifle.

The Soviet Union and later Ukraine only allowed hunters to use smoothbore shotguns. As a civilian, Arbakov would have had no opportunity to practice shooting a rifle.

But as a soldier, there were no such restrictions for Arbakov. And every military base had a shooting range and an armory.

Arbakov spent enough time at ranges and armories that he had become friends with both the range master and the armorer at one base after another.

One day, Arbakov had complained to the armorer that he knew he could improve on his already impressive scores at the range if he could stick with the same weapon. Standard practice was to check out a random rifle, adjust its sights, and start shooting.

But Arbakov always had to fire the rifle several times to get the sights adjusted correctly. That affected his score since those first shots were invariably poor.

This mattered to no one but Arbakov, which the armorer knew very well.

Still, he liked Arbakov. And he liked money even more.

So, the armorer had proposed a solution.

He'd pointed to several AK-74s in various stages of disassembly and explained that they had all been recorded as no longer functional. He had planned to salvage a few parts, and then destroy what remained.

In fact, the armorer said their destruction had already been recorded.

So, if Arbakov were willing to pay him for his trouble, the armorer would use the best parts from the rifles slated for destruction to produce one gun. That rifle would be held apart from the others in the armory as defective and would be for Arbakov's sole use.

Arbakov had eagerly agreed.

Months later, as Arbakov had been walking back to the armory to return the rifle after a session at the shooting range, he'd seen an ambulance rush past him.

It had stopped in front of the armory.

Without conscious thought, Arbakov had ducked around the corner of the nearest building.

After a few minutes, the two men who had hurried into the armory had emerged carrying a man on a stretcher.

The man had been covered with a sheet.

Arbakov had known that the man could have been anyone. But some instinct had told him it was the armorer. Maybe the apparent effort it had taken for the two men to get the stretcher to the ambulance.

The armorer had enjoyed food even more than money.

By now, everyone in sight had gathered near the ambulance and were asking what had happened.

Arbakov had looked behind him at the parking lot where his car was less than a dozen meters away.

As far as he could tell, no one was looking at him. And it was now dusk, so spotting what he was about to do would not be too easy.

In a few strides, Arbakov had been at his car's trunk, and moments later, the AK-74 was buried underneath the tools and rags he had stored there.

Arbakov's heart had been racing. He'd more than half expected to hear a shout from a window, or from someone just turning the corner.

But no. There'd been nothing.

Arbakov had hurried to join the crowd around the ambulance, which was just leaving. He'd asked who had been in the ambulance, dreading to hear it had been anyone other than the armorer.

But no. It had been him.

Almost all the guards at the front gate knew Arbakov, and they hardly ever bothered to search his vehicle when he left the base. Every now and then, though, a newly assigned guard did.

Arbakov had waited in the line of vehicles at the gate, praying that luck would be with him.

It had been. The guard had been someone Arbakov knew, and he waved him through.

So, Arbakov already had a rifle. But the few bullets he'd been able to smuggle out of military ranges before his retirement he had long since used.

Arbakov had also realized that he might have to defend the warhead at night.

The same friend who had instructed Arbakov in the use of the dark web had put him in touch with a man he said could help him with both issues.

Indeed, once the arms merchant had understood that Arbakov wanted a high-quality night vision scope, he'd offered to throw in a case of AK-74 ammunition for "free."

The price that the man had quoted for the scope took Arbakov's breath away. The scope was supposed to be "third generation," whatever that meant.

When Arbakov had hesitated, the man had offered to let him have the case of bullets upfront at no charge. He'd asked Arbakov to give him the AK-74, to which he would mount and calibrate the scope. Then Arbakov could try shooting it at night, and decide whether it was worth the money.

If Arbakov decided against the scope, he could still keep the bullets.

Impressed with the man's confidence, Arbakov had agreed.

After trying the scope that evening, Arbakov had to agree the man's confidence had been warranted.

Now that AK-74 with its "third-generation" night vision scope was in Arbakov's hands as he lay prone on the tunnel floor.

At first, Arbakov didn't know what had woken him. Dawn was still well off.

But some instinct had told Arbakov he was in danger.

As he slowly swept the scope back and forth, Arbakov wondered how long he could stay prone. He couldn't wear his respirator and accurately aim the rifle with the scope mounted.

The smell of mold was overpowering, and Arbakov's head was spinning.

There! Just at the limit of his scope's range.

The man was inching closer and was also holding a rifle with a scope.

It was pointed right at him.

Arbakov held his breath and willed his head to stop spinning. Just as he regained his focus, the man did the last thing he'd expected.

He started to move backward.

Arbakov realized he had only seconds before the man would be out of view.

He fired.

Arbakov could no longer see the man. Had he hit him?

Was the tunnel ringed with soldiers getting ready to move in?

Arbakov hurried back to his truck.

He had to get out of this tunnel.

Wind or no wind, it was time. Arbakov knew that man hadn't been alone.

Right now, he wasn't close enough to Chernobyl. But in minutes, he could be.

Arbakov started the truck's engine and put it in gear. It responded as faithfully as ever.

Moments later, Arbakov drove the truck out of the tunnel.

CHAPTER FIFTY-ONE

90 Kilometers North of Dnipro, Ukraine

Online mapping tools had said that Mikhail Vasilyev, Neda Rhahbar, and Boris Kharlov would be approaching Anatoly Grishkov's location by now.

Unfortunately, those tools had no way to account for the reality they had been dealing with in the hours after defusing the first warhead.

It had taken quite a while to get clear of the chaos they had helped to cause with automatic weapons and a grenade launcher. That was no surprise.

Even after escaping the immediate vicinity, though, they'd found the traffic congestion they thought they had left behind persisted. Night had fallen hours ago, and at this rate, they wouldn't reach Grishkov until late the next morning.

"I thought this was going to work," Vasilyev said, shaking his head at the traffic before them.

"Yes, it is puzzling," Kharlov replied. "We saw no police at all responding to explosions, gunfire, and multiple crashed vehicles. Now that we are some distance from all that, though, we keep running into random roadblocks, and local police who seem confused by what's happening."

Kharlov paused and shook his head. "It's as though some police had been advised specifically to leave us alone, and others were told nothing. Is it possible the Ukrainians know what we're doing, and have decided not to interfere?"

"Maybe. It seems too much to expect of our luck," Vasilyev said. "Even if you're right, though, we can't afford an encounter with local police who haven't been told about us. I think our weapons would be difficult to explain."

"Agreed," Kharlov said with a shrug.

"OK, you said you had a backup plan to get to Grishkov, but that I wouldn't like it. Let's have it," Vasilyev said.

"Very well," Kharlov replied. "The calls I made earlier were to prepare payment for an emergency helicopter transport to Grishkov's location."

Vasilyev stared at Kharlov in disbelief. "How many helicopters do you have on-call?"

Kharlov laughed and shook his head. "You misunderstand. It's not my helicopter at all. It's an emergency air ambulance service that just started this year. It has two brand-new VRT 500 helicopters. Not only are they expensive, but the company also demands a large deposit on top of advance payment for transport."

"A deposit? Why?" Vasilyev asked with a frown.

Kharlov grinned and replied, "Well, because it's occurred to someone at the company that someone might try to steal one of their shiny new helicopters."

Vasilyev sighed and shook his head. "You mean, like us. So, I suppose you know how to fly this VRT 500."

Kharlov shrugged. "I've flown many different types of helicopters. I'm sure I can figure out how to fly this one."

"I'm starting to see why you didn't think I'd like this plan," Vasilyev said with a frown.

Kharlov raised his eyebrows. "No, I'm still not to the part I thought you'd like least. You will not be able to accompany me."

"Really? Just how small is this helicopter?" Vasilyev asked.

"It's not that it's so small. From the factory, it could seat six," Kharlov replied. "It's that in the air ambulance configuration, much of the space is dedicated to medical equipment. And, of course, for the patient to be carried prone on a stretcher. So, ordinarily, there is just room for the pilot and paramedic."

"Plus, the patient," Vasilyev pointed out.

"True," Kharlov said with a nod. "However, unless we took the time to reconfigure the space, the third person would have to fly flat on his back." Seeing Vasilyev was about to object, Kharlov raised his hand.

"Agreed, more an annoyance than a real obstacle. There are, though, two other factors to consider."

"Yes?" Vasilyev asked with a scowl.

Unperturbed, Kharlov continued. "An extra person will slow us down. Maybe not much, but every second may count. More importantly, though, once we relieve the pilot and paramedic of their helicopter, they will need to be kept under guard until we return. Do you wish to leave that task to Neda by herself?"

Kharlov paused. "Particularly if, for whatever reason, we fail to return."

Both Neda and Vasilyev began to speak.

And then both stopped and looked at each other.

They had both understood what Kharlov was really saying.

That it would be best for Vasilyev to avoid the risk of joining the rescue, since speed would almost certainly count for more than an extra gun.

"I think he's right," Neda said quietly. "I'd like you to stay and help me guard those men."

Vasilyev nodded, impressed. He knew how hard it had been for Neda to say those words. Guarding two unarmed civilians was nothing for her, compared to the countless other dangers she'd faced during her past two missions.

She wanted to give Vasilyev the chance to stay without guilt.

Vasilyev knew there was no time for hesitation. He had to decide now. Was staying cowardice? Or would going just be for the benefit of his conscience, while at the same time slowing Grishkov's rescue?

"I'll stay," Vasilyev said. "Call for the helicopter."

Kharlov nodded, but then said, "Not quite yet. There are a few things we must do to prepare for its arrival. Take the next turn on the right," he said, pointing to a dirt road a short distance ahead.

After driving on the road for about a kilometer, Kharlov nodded and said, "This will do. Pull off the road here."

Once Vasilyev had stopped the SUV, Kharlov jumped out and went to the back. Then he pulled out the jack and the first aid kit from the SUV's storage compartment.

"You'll both want to be out of the vehicle for this next part," Kharlov said.

Once they were beside him, Kharlov handed the jack to Vasilyev and the first aid kit to Neda.

"Just a moment while I make the call," Kharlov said, as he punched a number into his cell phone, and gave rapid instructions.

"That's done," Kharlov said. Holding up his cell phone, he said, "The helicopter has our approximate position, but just to be sure will home in on the GPS signal in this cell phone. I'm also leaving the headlights on. The payment has been confirmed so that it will be here soon. We need to hurry."

Gesturing for Vasilyev to follow, Kharlov walked a few steps into the meadow adjacent to the road. "Good, put the jack upright there," he said.

Vasilyev knew better than to ask questions, and simply did as he was told.

Kharlov looked at their SUV, and then at the jack. Nodding, he attached the jack's handle and stood back.

"It's more an art than a science, but I've done this a few times before," Kharlov said with a grin.

Neda exchanged a look with Vasilyev that said, "Done what?"

Vasilyev's answering shrug said, "I think we'll soon find out."

Sure enough, Kharlov walked to the far side of the SUV, gesturing for Vasilyev to join him. Then he told Neda, "Please stand clear," pointing to the other side of the dirt road.

Kharlov grabbed the vehicle's roof on one side, and said, "We're going to rock it back and forth until we flip it on its side. The goal is to have it land on the jack with the handle still accessible."

Understanding dawned. "You're going to make it look like we've been in an accident," Vasilyev said.

Kharlov nodded. "An old ambush tactic dating from my Spetsnaz days. When the helicopter sees the vehicle on its side with an injured man lying next to it, the sight should overcome any hesitation the pilot may have about landing."

"And the jack will make it easier to right the SUV once we're ready to leave," Vasilyev said as he grabbed the other side of the roof.

"Correct," Kharlov said. "Now, on three."

Vasilyev had to admit that Kharlov was doing most of the work, even though he was doing his best to put his back into the task.

It only took a moment before the SUV was lying on its side. Kharlov walked around the vehicle and confirmed with an upheld thumb that the jack's handle could be reached. Then, he gestured for Neda to join them.

Pointing to the first aid kit and then nodding towards Vasilyev, Kharlov said with a smile, "I have a patient for you. I think a heavily bandaged head wound would look most impressive from the air."

Shaking her head, Neda got to work. A few minutes later, Vasilyev indeed appeared to need immediate medical attention.

Kharlov looked at the results and frowned. "Good, but it needs something...". Then he rummaged in the first aid kit, finally holding a bottle aloft in triumph. "Lucky we have an old-school medical kit!" he exclaimed.

Then Kharlov gestured for Vasilyev to turn his head to the side. "Close your eyes," he warned him. Then, Kharlov poured some of the bottle's contents onto the bandages and stepped back to observe the results.

"Iodine," Kharlov said, nodding. "Not quite the same shade as blood, but close enough, especially in the dark."

Then Kharlov pointed to a patch of grass next to the SUV and said to Vasilyev, "Please lie there. It shouldn't be long."

Indeed, it was only minutes before they could hear the helicopter approaching. Once it was in sight, Kharlov and Neda waved frantically, pointing at Vasilyev's still, bandaged form lying next to the vehicle.

The helicopter turned on a large searchlight, which was bright enough to turn night into day throughout the meadow.

Kharlov nodded to himself. Not exactly standard equipment for an air ambulance, but then most services didn't advertise twenty-four-hour availability. He mentally apologized for thinking the service's price outrageous, and revised it to simply "high."

The helicopter then hovered for a moment, while its occupants assessed what they saw. Was it convincing enough for them to land?

Yes! Kharlov was delighted to see that not only did the helicopter land, but it also did so as close as it safely could.

That would make the next stage much easier.

A man wearing a paramedic uniform came running out from the helicopter, holding a stretcher. He yelled to Kharlov over the still turning rotors' noise, "Can you help me get him into the helicopter?"

Kharlov had to fight hard to keep a smile off his face and instead just say seriously, "I'll do anything I can to help."

The paramedic leaned over Vasilyev, and moments later looked up at Kharlov with a relieved expression. "Respiration and pulse are fine. Please help me get him on the stretcher."

Neda stood to one side crying, in what Kharlov thought was an excellent performance.

As they put Vasilyev in the stretcher, the paramedic called to her, "Don't worry, ma'am. We'll have him in a hospital in minutes."

Neda buried her face in her hands and gave a quick nod in response.

Less than a minute later, they were next to the helicopter with heads ducked low. Kharlov was impressed with the helicopter's efficient design. In its air ambulance configuration, an extensive plexiglass section swung wide to admit the paramedic and the stretcher without the contortions he was all too familiar with from his military career.

After Kharlov helped the paramedic put the stretcher inside, he then jumped into the paramedic's seat while the man was still securing the litter. The pilot started to object, but then found himself looking into the barrel of Kharlov's pistol.

The pilot looked up at Kharlov and then again at his pistol and shook his head in disgust. Turning his head towards the paramedic, he said, "My gut told me there was something wrong. I should have never listened to you."

Kharlov smiled and asked the pilot, "Former Russian Army?"

The pilot nodded.

"Well, you're right," Kharlov said. "You should always listen to your instincts. The good news is that today, the price for failing to do so will be light. I am only going to borrow your helicopter, and plan to bring it back directly with a passenger. I will then return it to you, I very much hope none the worse for wear."

The pilot shrugged. "I can only hope you're telling the truth." He hesitated, and then asked, "You are also former Russian Army?"

Kharlov nodded.

"Very well," the pilot said and unstrapped his flight harness. As he stepped down, Kharlov asked, "Anything I should know?"

The pilot looked at him and visibly decided it was best to hope Kharlov really would return the helicopter.

"The collective pulls a little to the left," he said.

"Thank you," Kharlov replied gravely.

The paramedic saw that Vasilyev was sitting upright on the stretcher, and removing the restraints he had just fastened. Now it was the paramedic's turn to shake his head in disgust. "Of course," he muttered.

Kharlov said, "Both of you, please walk towards the pretty lady."

Neda was no longer crying. Instead, having seen that Kharlov was holding a gun on the helicopter's occupants, she now had a pistol in her right hand.

Vasilyev climbed off the stretcher to follow the two men. Then he looked back at Kharlov, whose hands were already busy flipping switches.

"Good luck," Vasilyev said.

Kharlov nodded absently. "I should be back soon. I suggest you all wait out of sight of the road, in case someone happens to drive by. Fortunately, it seems to be little used."

Moments later, the helicopter rose into the sky and was soon out of sight.

Vasilyev looked at Neda, who he saw was expressionlessly covering the two men with her pistol.

As he retrieved his rifle from the SUV to take over that task, Vasilyev couldn't help wondering whether staying had been the right decision.

Pointless to wonder, he realized. Soon enough, Kharlov would return with Grishkov, and Vasilyev would be proved right.

Or Kharlov and Grishkov would never be seen again, and he wouldn't.

10 Kilometers Northwest of Ivankiv, Ukraine

Lieutenant Bondar looked up from the display screen and called out, "Sir, I have the same radiation signature as before, but much stronger now."

Captain Josh Pettigrew had been in and out of the control vehicle ever since Bondar's first sighting, and for some time now, it had looked like a dry hole. He had even been tempted to order Bondar to widen the search area, rather than continuing to circle around the spot of the last radiation sighting.

It looked like staying put had been the right call.

"Lieutenant, put the drone on autopilot and focus the Blackjack's infrared sensor on the source of that radiation signature," Pettigrew said.

"Yes, sir," Bondar replied.

Moments later, an image appeared on the display screen. It was a truck, moving without headlights. Probably as a result, it wasn't moving very fast.

"Where is it going at this hour?" Pettigrew wondered aloud.

Bondar pointed at the target heading display on the screen. "Sir, it is heading straight for Chernobyl."

Pettigrew had to fight hard to keep the realization off his expression. That was the target. The tons of radioactive material inside the damaged reactor at Chernobyl.

A nuclear warhead would crack open the new European-built containment vessel like an eggshell.

But how could he stop it?

The Blackjack had no weapons of any kind.

Then Pettigrew had an idea. Maybe he couldn't stop it.

But he might be able to slow it down.

Then Pettigrew looked at Bondar and froze.

How was he going to explain what he wanted to do to a Ukrainian officer?

As though reading his mind, Bondar said carefully, "Sir, I know this is not an exercise. If that truck is carrying a nuclear device of some kind towards Chernobyl, it can have only one purpose. What can we do to stop it? Can I fly the Blackjack into the truck?"

A wave of jumbled thoughts and emotions washed over Pettigrew. How did Bondar know? How long had he known?

Did the other Ukrainian officers know too?

Pettigrew immediately realized there was no time for any of those questions.

He was also certain crashing the drone into the truck would be a bad idea. Pettigrew still had nightmares about the missile he had sent into another vehicle carrying a nuclear weapon, and the aftermath of that decision.

Aloud, Pettigrew said, "No. I want you to fly the Blackjack right in front of that truck. You're going to have to do some careful calculations to make that work. You won't get a second chance."

Bondar nodded grimly. "I understand. At this angle and velocity, there's no way I'll be able to recover the Blackjack."

Pettigrew simply nodded, and let Bondar get on with it.

Bondar was right. If he did manage to fly the drone in front of the truck, it would undoubtedly crash very shortly afterward.

Pettigrew sat down at the console next to Bondar and began typing rapidly. Bondar glanced quizzically in his direction.

To get Bondar's attention back on flying the drone, Pettigrew realized he needed to explain.

"One reason I'm not taking the controls is that I have to disable the flight safety protocols so you can do what we discussed. You don't have the clearance or the experience needed to do that," Pettigrew said.

Bondar nodded and shifted his full attention back to flying the drone.

Pettigrew completed his task just in time. The truck was rapidly growing larger in the display.

For a sickening moment, Pettigrew thought Bondar had miscalculated and was going to fly the Blackjack straight into the truck.

But no! The drone flew right in front of the truck, and for just an instant, Pettigrew could see the truck swerve.

And then the display screen went black.

"Great job," Pettigrew said, patting Bondar on the shoulder.

Two thoughts kept running around and around in Pettigrew's head.

Who else knows what I've really been doing with these drones?

And - How long do I have to get out of Ukraine?

CHAPTER FIFTY-TWO

Outside Duga Complex Tunnel 8, Ukraine

Pofistal Arbakov swore as an enormous shape flew in front of him, and without conscious thought, he yanked at the steering wheel to avoid it.

Avoid it he did. But there was a forest on both sides of the road.

It was nothing short of a miracle that he could brake in time to avoid ramming the truck into a tree. But he was well and truly off the road.

There was a bright flash not far away, and then Arbakov heard the sound of an explosion.

Not a huge explosion. But loud enough to be heard for some distance.

It must be whatever flew past me.

That must have been a drone, Arbakov thought.

I'm going to have company very soon.

Arbakov swore again as he looked at the truck's odometer. He'd made his calculations hours ago, and knew how much farther he had to go to be sure of breaching the reactor's new containment vessel.

He wasn't close enough yet to be sure.

Very well, Arbakov thought. After all the work to get this far, it was worth a bit more to get the job done right.

He surveyed the truck's position and calculated the best path back to the road. Fortunately, it didn't look like the truck was stuck, and there wasn't too much vegetation in his way.

Not for the first time, Arbakov gave thanks that his truck had all-wheel drive, and had been designed for challenging missions just like this one.

Well, Arbakov thought with a grim smile, maybe not exactly like this one.

Arbakov's full attention was on driving the truck carefully back onto the road when it happened.

A series of what felt like hammer blows all over his body.

He heard a series of sharp cracks that he recognized as rifle fire.

I've been shot!

Then Arbakov briefly lost consciousness.

When he came to seconds later, he didn't feel pain. He felt cold and wet. And numb.

Looking down, Arbakov realized he was bleeding rapidly. He didn't have much time left.

He was just able to reach the arming switch.

The last image Arbakov had in his mind before his eyes closed forever was Natalia's face. She was smiling.

But the smile looked so sad.

Outside Duga Complex Tunnel 8, Ukraine

Anatoly Grishkov cursed as the sound of the rifle shot was immediately followed by Kolesnik's backward movement...stopping.

Even before Grishkov reached Kolesnik, he knew what he'd find. He'd seen that sort of absolute stillness too often in Chechnya.

Just as he confirmed Kolesnik was beyond his help, Grishkov heard the unmistakable sound of a truck engine starting.

The warhead.

Time to repay Kolesnik's killer.

Grishkov ran towards the truck, but it rounded a bend in the road before he could get off a decent shot.

But it wasn't going that fast. Probably because Arbakov was driving with his lights off.

Grishkov ran after the truck, hoping he could send a volley towards it once he was able to round the curve.

Just as the truck came into view and Grishkov was lifting his rifle, something flew right in front of the truck!

The truck veered out of its way, and in seconds was off the road and out of sight.

But Grishkov still had an idea where the truck had gone, and moved towards it.

There! The truck was slowly backing onto the road at an angle. Grishkov couldn't see the driver in the moonlight.

The truck's angle, though, put the driver's side window into clear view.

Grishkov fired multiple rounds into that window, sure he would hit the driver, who had to be Arbakov.

Then he ran to the truck and thrust his rifle through its shattered window, ready to fire again.

He could immediately see there was no need. Arbakov's body was just as still as Kolesnik's had been.

Then Grishkov saw it. A small metal device, with a blinking red light, on the seat next to Arbakov's body.

The trigger for the warhead. Did the blinking light just mean the trigger was operational or had Arbakov pressed the button before he died?

Grishkov quickly realized it didn't matter. He had to assume the warhead had been activated.

Without Kolesnik's pair of hands, he couldn't even attempt to defuse the warhead if it had been armed.

That left just one option.

Grishkov unceremoniously dumped Arbakov's body out of the truck and took his place in the driver's seat.

Next, he maneuvered the truck until it was facing the tunnel.

Then Grishkov turned on the truck's lights and stepped on the gas.

He was going to drive it into the tunnel as far as he could go.

Grishkov was surprised. It turned out to be much farther than he would have thought.

Even better, he seemed to be going down almost as fast as he was going forward.

Finally, Grishkov could go no further and switched off the engine. But he left the lights on.

Grishkov had no idea how deep he was, or how far he'd traveled from the tunnel entrance. But if the weapon had been armed, he thought it would do less damage here than on the surface.

Now, Grishkov's study of tunnel maps paid off. He knew that at several points in each tunnel, there were emergency exit ladders. Their position varied from one tunnel to another.

Except that every tunnel had one at the very end.

Sure enough. There was a metal ladder right in front of him.

Grishkov was so eager to make his exit from the tunnel that without thinking, he slung his rifle over his shoulder and began to make the climb.

And was almost immediately dumped onto the tunnel floor.

There had been blood all over the steering wheel, but Grishkov had been in such a hurry he had paid no attention.

The good news was that Grishkov had advanced only a short distance up the ladder, so he suffered no serious injury. The wind had been knocked out of him, but he was ready to give the ladder a second try in moments.

After this time, wiping his hands.

The bad news came from a "crack," Grishkov heard as he hit the concrete tunnel floor. A quick check confirmed his fear that it had been the satellite phone case, which was now partly split along one seam.

Another glance showed him that the display was still active. Well, no way to test it inside this tunnel.

One more reason to leave it as quickly as possible.

As though the toxic mold and the possibly armed thermonuclear weapon weren't reason enough, Grishkov thought with amusement.

Grishkov climbed. Now he had another smile, this time at his own expense.

He'd been so pleased to find how far down the tunnel went when all he'd been thinking about was the damage the warhead might do.

Now he realized that it also meant the climb up the ladder would be...difficult.

There was only one way to meet such a challenge.

One rung at a time.

Grishkov didn't know how long he'd been climbing.

He only knew that he'd better not fall off again.

While Grishkov had studied the tunnel maps, he'd thought hard about what he would need to make his way out. He'd settled on two decidedly low-tech items.

He had put on the first before starting his climb up the ladder. It was a small light mounted to an elastic strap that went around his head.

That light now showed him he'd reached the top of the ladder.

Directly above him was a metal hatch. Grishkov had seen many of them during his time in the Army. He knew his colleagues in the Navy saw far more.

That experience had prompted Grishkov to bring the second item, which he used now.

A can of petroleum-based spray lubricant.

Grishkov knew that even in the 1980s, the hatch would have been challenging to open. Now, he prayed it hadn't rusted shut completely.

After putting the can carefully back in his pocket, Grishkov tried to open the hatch.

It didn't budge.

Well, no surprise.

Grishkov put all his effort in first one direction, then the other.

There was no sign it had made any difference.

Grishkov sprayed the hatch again and repeated the procedure.

Still nothing.

Grishkov had expected the hatch to be a challenge, and so had brought the largest can of lubricant he could find.

But he knew he might not have much more time.

So, Grishkov emptied the rest of the can on the hatch's seal and mechanism. Then he let the can fall away into the darkness.

It took a long time for the sound of its impact on the tunnel floor to reach him.

No matter, Grishkov thought.

There's no way I'm going back down.

Drops of lubricant dripped down from the hatch onto his face. Keeping one hand on the hatch, he wiped his eyes with the other.

Back and forth, back and forth.

Finally, Grishkov felt a fraction of movement.

He smiled. A fraction was all he needed.

Grishkov's arms were burning like fire. But he ignored the pain and kept rocking the hatch's mechanism back and forth.

A shower of rust finally rewarded his efforts.

Cursing, Grishkov once again wiped his eyes with one hand. This time, no matter how much he rubbed and blinked, his eyes continued to burn.

Next time, he thought wryly, bring goggles.

More back and forth was still needed. But the hatch was finally ready to open.

With a final massive push, Grishkov opened the hatch.

He was rewarded by a blast of fresh air that felt wonderful in his lungs.

But it nearly made Grishkov lose his tenuous grip on the ladder.

After all the effort he'd made, though, there was no way Grishkov was going to fail now.

Regaining his grip, Grishkov pulled himself up the last few rungs to freedom.

Low clouds concealed the breaking dawn, but there was now enough light that Grishkov could see he'd emerged on the top of a hill.

He knew how important it was to move as far away as he could, as quickly as possible.

At the moment, though, Grishkov's body had been pushed to its limit and refused to obey. For several minutes he remained flat on his back, drawing in great lungfuls of clean pine-scented air.

Finally, though, an image of his wife Arisha came into his head.

Yes. Grishkov had to get moving, no matter how much his body might protest.

But move where? Certainly not back to his vehicle near the tunnel entrance, assuming he could even reach it from here.

A small voice in the back of his head said it didn't matter which way he went. He had no chance of outrunning the blast radius of a five hundred kiloton bomb on foot, even if it was buried underground.

The hill where Grishkov found himself wasn't very tall, but it did let him see over the trees below. In the distance, he saw a clearing.

Maybe a helicopter pickup?

Grishkov pulled out his satellite phone. As before, the display showed there was no cell phone signal.

Next, Grishkov tried to text a message.

But now the satellite connection appeared to be out as well.

Grishkov sighed. Apparently, dropping the phone on cement from a height affected its functionality.

Logic said he might as well sit down and relax during his last minutes.

Grishkov began to move down the hill at the best pace he thought he could sustain, headed for the distant clearing.

At least the ground was reasonably even, he thought as he jogged downhill. It would be a bad time for a sprained ankle.

Grishkov had no idea how long it had been since Arbakov had triggered the warhead if indeed he had done so.

His memory was also fuzzy about how long it would take the warhead to detonate if it had been armed.

Grishkov thought he remembered it would be at least half an hour, but might well be longer.

He thought back as he jogged through the trees. Driving to the end of the tunnel hadn't taken long.

Neither had climbing the ladder.

But opening the hatch...

Yes. That had taken a while.

Grishkov smiled to himself. None of this mattered. He would either survive or not.

What was that sound?

Grishkov's heart quickened as he recognized it.

It was a helicopter.

But was it his team coming to rescue him? Or Ukrainian authorities coming to put him under arrest?

Grishkov smiled again as he continued to jog towards where memory said the clearing had to be.

Arrest was undoubtedly preferable to incineration.

Whichever it was, by his reckoning, the helicopter was making for the same clearing he was.

There! Grishkov burst through the trees, to emerge into a meadow filled with waist-high grass and a few low bushes.

He thought the helicopter in its center, blades still rotating, might have been the most beautiful thing he'd ever seen.

Grishkov ducked his head and ran towards it, wondering as he did who he'd find inside. From here, he couldn't see any kind of insignia or weaponry, which was good as far as it went.

Once he drew closer, though, Grishkov could see that the man at the controls was Boris Kharlov.

He felt a wave of relief wash over him that surprised him with its intensity.

Grishkov realized that he hadn't really feared arrest. Instead, he'd worried that the time needed to explain the situation was time he didn't have.

Not a problem with Kharlov.

Grishkov leaped into the passenger seat, and as he was fastening his flight harness said, "Back the way you came, as fast as you can."

Kharlov said nothing but instead began flipping switches. Moments later, they were airborne.

Only then did Kharlov look in Grishkov's direction. "The weapon is armed?" he asked.

Grishkov shrugged. "Probably. The triggering switch was blinking. Arbakov wasn't alive to ask whether that just meant the switch was working, or that the weapon was armed."

"Good," Kharlov said simply.

Grishkov looked at him, confused.

Kharlov smiled. "Not good that you don't know whether the warhead is armed. Good that you avenged Kolesnik's death. I knew if he were still alive, he'd be with you."

Grishkov nodded. "If he hadn't insisted on taking point, it would be me lying dead back there. Arbakov was waiting for us."

"Kolesnik knew the risks. And he died a hero, saving thousands of lives. When my time comes, I only hope I die as well," Kharlov said soberly.

The helicopter was angled forward, and Grishkov could hear the engine straining. The treetops seemed alarmingly close.

Grishkov had been in helicopters many times, first with the Army and then with the police.

He had never been in one flying this fast before.

"Where did you leave the warhead?" Kharlov asked.

"As we'd guessed, Arbakov was hiding in a tunnel with the warhead in his truck. I drove it to the end of the tunnel, and then made my way out the emergency exit," Grishkov replied.

Kharlov grunted approval. "Good man," he said. "I'd been wondering whether we really had a chance of escape. I'm pretty sure Arbakov did trigger the warhead. Underground, its impact should be greatly reduced. There is one other factor that may be in our favor."

"Please, let's hear it!" Grishkov exclaimed.

"One responsibility of Spetsnaz forces was the protection and recovery of nuclear weapons. We received detailed background briefings in their maintenance and operation. In particular, thermonuclear weapons require periodic replenishment of the tritium that allows the fusion reaction to occur."

Grishkov slowly exhaled. "Arbakov held on to that warhead for decades, and I doubt very much he had the materials or equipment to perform maintenance. So, there's a chance the warhead won't work?"

Kharlov shook his head. "No. The best case is that only the atomic fission trigger will function. It is more likely that fusion will be achieved, but due to an inadequate tritium level, it will fail to reach the full five hundred kiloton design yield."

Grishkov looked out of the cockpit at the landscape passing by in a blur. He fought against the small bit of optimism he felt as Kharlov spoke.

Yes, the warhead was underground.

Yes, it might fail to achieve its full yield.

But it was still a thermonuclear warhead.

And they were in a helicopter, not a supersonic fighter.

As though in agreement, Grishkov could now see that the landscape below them was not just lit by the sun rising before them in the east.

It was also lit from the west. Behind them.

Neither of them turned around.

The helicopter continued to move forward, and for a few seconds, Grishkov dared to hope they were out of range of the warhead's shock wave.

Then it felt as though a giant hand had decided to swat them from the sky.

Kharlov did his best to keep them flying. But Grishkov could see almost at once it wouldn't be enough.

"Brace yourself," Kharlov said.

It was the last thing Grishkov could remember hearing before everything went black.

Chapter Fifty-Three

The White House
Washington DC

President Hernandez looked up from his briefing papers as General Robinson walked into the Oval Office.

"I hope you've got more than I just finished reading here," Hernandez said, pointing at the briefing papers with disgust.

"Basically, they say 'something sure did happen, but we're not really sure what.' Please tell me you've got more than that," Hernandez said.

"Yes, sir. Since that brief was prepared, I've spoken with Captain Pettigrew. We've also had a chance to analyze satellite coverage of the incident," Robinson said.

"The incident, huh? So that's what we're going to call it?" Hernandez growled.

Robinson shrugged. "You can blame me, sir. I think we want to deemphasize the importance of what happened near Chernobyl. The Ukrainians have confirmed that the new containment vessel built around the reactor that melted down in the 80s is intact. Most of the fallout from the explosion was blown north towards areas of Belarus that are lightly populated. Evacuation of the area is underway."

"Casualties from the explosion?" Hernandez asked.

"The Ukrainians aren't saying, sir. The blast radius was confined to the Chernobyl Exclusion Zone, so very few people were authorized to be there. We understand that there were illegal settlers, though," Robinson replied.

"Really, General? Who would want to live in an area famous for radioactive contamination?" Hernandez asked.

"Many of the structures abandoned in the 80s are still intact, sir. And some people believed enough time had passed that the radiation should no longer be an issue," Robinson replied.

Hernandez shook his head. "Well, whether that was true or not before, it's sure not now. Do we have an estimate for the size of the explosion?"

"Not yet, sir. Analysis has been made more difficult by the fact that the explosion took place underground. But there's no doubt the impact on the surrounding area was greatly reduced as a result. There is one thing we know for sure, though," Robinson said with a frown.

"Yes, General?" Hernandez asked impatiently.

"This was a thermonuclear explosion. Analysis of the radioactive elements leaves no doubt of that. Details on that analysis and many other aspects of this incident are in this report, sir," Robinson said.

With that, Robinson leaned over and placed a folder on front of Hernandez.

Hernandez nodded. "I understand the Russians provided Captain Pettigrew with specific elements to search for, and that their instrument package was able to find them twice. I suppose you've checked them against what we know of Russian thermonuclear weapons?"

"Yes, sir. They were a match for warheads carried by a Russian ICBM model decommissioned long ago. I think the Russians were telling the truth about the warheads having been stolen," Robinson said.

"Maybe so, General. Too bad they weren't able to defuse and recover the second one the way they did the first. Do you think the Russian cover story will hold?" Hernandez asked.

"It might," Robinson replied. "Though it was thermonuclear, the warhead didn't achieve its designed yield. Since it hadn't been maintained for decades, that's no surprise. So, the claim that it was a tactical nuclear weapon missed in the hurried Russian evacuation of their forces from Ukraine after the Soviet Union's collapse could be believable."

Hernandez grunted. "Maybe easier to believe than what really happened. Has Babich left for Moscow?"

"Actually, sir, that's one of the things I wanted to discuss with you. President Babich asked to speak with you before he goes on that flight," Robinson said.

"OK. Do we know what he wants?" Hernandez asked.

"Well, sir, first I should tell you that based on my conversation with Pettigrew, the Ukrainians know all about our involvement with the warhead recovery effort. It looks like they know about the role the Russians played, too, though maybe not all the details," Robinson said.

Hernandez swore and slapped his hand on the desk. "How did that happen, General? Don't tell me Pettigrew told the Ukrainians!"

"Pettigrew says no, sir, and I believe him. He told me that it's actually a good thing the Ukrainians knew, or the second warhead might have reached its target. The details are in that report," Robinson said.

Hernandez shook his head. "I suppose it doesn't really matter how the Ukrainians found out, just that they know. So, I suppose now the Ukrainians will expect us to sell them armed drones?"

Robinson shrugged. "They already have the Bayraktars from the Turks, sir. Maybe not as good as ours, but good enough. They're already in talks with the Turks about getting the Anka-2, a new drone that's even more capable than the Bayraktar."

Hernandez scowled. "OK, so what do you think they'll want to keep quiet about this?"

"Fighter jets, sir. Everything the Ukrainians are flying now is a leftover from the Soviet days. When the Russians seized Crimea, the Ukrainians lost some of those planes, too. Even with the best maintenance, the remaining planes don't have many flying years left," Robinson said.

"Fine. But I hope you're not suggesting we sell the Ukrainians F-35s," Hernandez said.

"No, sir. I agree that would be too provocative to the Russians. I suggest a mix of F-16s and F-15s. That will give them a credible deterrent, and at the same time prepare them for possible integration into NATO at some future date," Robinson said.

Hernandez's eyebrows rose. "A date that I'm sure the Russians expect to be far in the future, right?"

"Yes, sir. Instead I expect President Babich to press the Russians hard to back off their objections to Ukraine's membership in the European Union," Robinson said.

Hernandez grunted thoughtfully. "Yes, that makes sense. OK, I'll propose selling him the fighters and offer him support for Ukraine's EU membership. Maybe if I do it fast enough, I can avoid an awkward discussion about our role in the big smoking hole near Chernobyl."

Then Hernandez paused. "I know you're the one here discussing this because of Pettigrew's involvement, and the plane sale. I also know I've offered you the job before, and you turned it down. But I really think you should reconsider becoming my National Security Advisor."

Robinson shook his head firmly. "During your campaign you spoke out clearly against military officers in Cabinet positions, especially as Defense Secretary and National Security Advisor. What you said made sense, and I agreed with you. I still do."

Hernandez pursed his lips ruefully. "Yes, you said that before too. Well, I guess we'll have to leave things as they are."

Robinson smiled. "I'm just as happy to stay under the radar, sir. Every time I see you talking with reporters I'm reminded that's the way to go."

Hernandez laughed, and said, "Well, I guess I can't argue with that, General."

CHAPTER FIFTY-FOUR

Mariyinsky Palace
Kyiv, Ukraine

President Babich's eyebrows flew up as SBU Director Shevchuk walked into his office. A new suit! And a pretty nice one, at that.

Well, at least he could cross improving Shevchuk's appearance off his to-do list!

"Welcome back, Mr. President. I understand congratulations are in order," Shevchuk said.

Babich shrugged. "I don't know about that. We'll have to see how well the cleanup effort goes. How much progress have the Russians made so far?"

Shevchuk placed a folder on Babich's desk. "I feel comfortable saying that no significant additional fallout should reach Kyiv or other population centers in Ukraine. The same can't yet be said for Belarus, but that's not our problem. Our resources are concentrated on removing contamination from fallout reaching areas in Ukraine outside the Exclusion Zone on the day of the explosion."

"Yes. And how is our progress there?" Babich asked.

"It's been going quite well. The fact that the warhead detonated well underground helped, of course. Our experts also believe it did not detonate with as much power as called for in its original design. Probably because of its age. In short, it could have been much worse," Shevchuk said.

"Do we have any idea yet of casualties in the Exclusion Zone?" Babich asked quietly.

"All we can say for sure is that people certainly died. Some are known for a fact. For example, guards operating checkpoints in the Zone who were killed outright by the blast. We're still receiving inquiries about people believed to have been living illegally within the Zone. Unless we can eventually account for them, they're almost certainly casualties as well," Shevchuk replied.

"Understood. And how many injured?" Babich asked.

"Not many, and I think by now we've found all there were to find. Fortunately, our special forces troops had just arrived in the area and were available for search and rescue. Because they knew of the threat, they had the appropriate gear," Shevchuk replied.

"We have sent the Russian they found unconscious in a downed helicopter to Moscow as I directed?" Babich asked.

"Yes, sir. I was surprised by your order, but of course, obeyed it. There's still no sign of the other man our troops thought they spotted near the helicopter," Shevchuk said.

"Did the Russian regain consciousness before you put him on the medevac flight?" Babich asked.

"No, sir. There were quite a few questions I would have liked to ask him if he had. The crashed helicopter had been outfitted as an air ambulance, and its supplies had been put to good use. Probably by the mystery man our soldiers say they saw, but who then disappeared. Our doctors say the man he treated was lucky to survive, even so. May I ask why you decided to send him back to Russia?" Shevchuk asked.

Babich shrugged. "It's the only request the Russian President made. Considering my long list, it seemed only fair."

"From the press reports, it sounds like he agreed to just about everything on your list, sir. Did the reporters get it right this time?" Shevchuk said.

Babich nodded. "Of course, we still have to see whether agreement translates to facts on the ground. What can you tell me about Russian forces in Donbas?"

"Gone, as promised. The so-called advisors, and even the supposed volunteers. And it looks like they took their equipment with them. I'd be surprised if everything they brought into Donbas ended up back in Russia. Still, everything we can easily check with drones like armor and anti-aircraft systems is gone," Shevchuk replied.

"You are monitoring the election preparations?" Babich asked.

"Of course, sir. I was never happy about leaving those traitors in place in Donbas. Now that you got the Russians to agree to our holding elections there, I hope that some of them will get tossed out by the voters," Shevchuk said with a scowl.

Babich nodded. "Agreed. Are you satisfied that disbanding the militias is complete?"

Shevchuk rocked his hand back and forth. "Heavy weapons like tanks, yes. We've had a lot of old rifles handed over, but not so many new ones. Many of the militias were just glorified criminal bands, like the one led by Avel Karpenko. At least one of those criminal organizations, though, seems to have melted away. The one led by Boris Kharlov."

"Kharlov. The most important so-called warlord in Donbas, and the man we spotted near Dnipro getting one of the warheads on a cargo helicopter and out of Ukraine," Babich said.

"That's right, sir. He's gone without a trace, along with all of his men. We had a report recently that he'd been attacked successfully in Donbas by Karpenko's forces. Plus, Kharlov isn't just a Russian-speaker. He's actually from Russia. Maybe he and his men just went home," Shevchuk said.

"Well, if so, good riddance. Now, I understand the American officer who was training our drone pilots is gone?" Babich asked.

"Yes, sir. As soon as the warhead detonated, he drove directly to Kyiv and boarded the first available Lufthansa flight to Germany, with an onward connection to America. I was notified, but decided not to detain him," Shevchuk said.

Babich frowned, and started to say something, but then stopped.

"I was about to say you should have stopped the American officer and let me decide, but you were right. I obtained everything I wanted from the American President, and part of that may have been gratitude that we both kept quiet about their role in this and let the officer go," Babich said.

Shevchuk asked, "Is it true, sir, that Hernandez has agreed to sell us American fighter jets?"

"Yes. Even more important, the Russians will not object," Babich replied.

"And the Russians have dropped their objection to our membership in the EU?" Shevchuk asked.

"Yes," Babich replied. "But membership won't happen overnight. The Europeans have never fully recovered from the coronavirus pandemic. That goes for their economies as well as their finances. Ironically, though, our best hope of EU acceptance is thanks to both the coronavirus and the British."

Shevchuk stared at Babich in confusion. "How is that, sir?" he asked.

Babich laughed. "Yes, I can understand how that would be puzzling. The German Chancellor told me yesterday that there's still a lot of unhappiness in the EU at how the British left. Many EU members are in the mood to show that their union is still a going concern, even after coronavirus and the British departure. The Chancellor told me taking in a country like Ukraine twice victimized by Russia would appeal to many Europeans."

Shevchuk sat still for a moment and then said thoughtfully, "I certainly hope the Chancellor is right. Fighter jets are good. NATO membership would be even better. But joining the EU is the best we could hope for to secure Ukraine's future."

Babich nodded. "Yes. If it happens, at least the poor souls consumed by that Russian warhead won't have died in vain."

CHAPTER FIFTY-FIVE

Gospital Fsb Na Shchukinskoy,
Moscow, Russia

Anatoly Grishkov opened his eyes and immediately realized he was in a hospital.

Again.

It looked like the same one as last time.

Grishkov shook his head. It would be a while before anyone talked him into a helicopter again.

Then he smiled to himself. If he were again offered the sole alternative of nuclear incineration, Grishkov imagined he'd board a winged dragon.

No sooner had he completed the thought than a familiar face appeared at the door.

"Dr. Kotov. Good to see you again," Grishkov said.

"Polite of you to say so, though I think we can both agree it should have been under better circumstances. I will also say that you should more properly address me as Director Kotov," he said with a wide smile.

"Congratulations, Director," Grishkov said with all sincerity.

"I have you to thank for being put in charge of this hospital. I don't know who you spoke to after your last stay, but I was made Director almost immediately. We have been able to reduce addiction rates from pain medications dramatically, and it would have never happened without your support," Kotov said.

Then he paused. "But first things first. You have been unconscious or asleep for quite a while, which has given your body a chance to recover in part from serious trauma. During part of that time, painkillers were administered to you to ensure you did not wake before I judged you ready to do so. Only you, though, can tell me if our treatment has been successful. So, how are you feeling?"

Grishkov looked down at his right leg, which was in a cast. Some throbbing there, but not too bad.

Otherwise a few aches here and there, but nothing serious.

"I think two aspirin will do it," Grishkov said.

Kotov's smile was even wider than before. "Excellent! When they brought you in, I wasn't sure we could save your leg. But our tests suggest you could regain full mobility after therapy, once the bones have had a chance to knit."

Grishkov grunted. "Bones, plural?"

Kotov nodded. "Yes, I'm afraid two separate bones in your right leg were broken, but X-rays show that they are healing cleanly. You are very fortunate that the helicopter you were on carried medical equipment and someone competent in its use."

Grishkov nodded. "So, the helicopter pilot survived?"

"Mr. Kharlov? Yes, indeed, he did. He was briefly a patient here, though there wasn't much we could do for his cracked ribs. He'd also done a good job of removing radioactive contamination, but we took care of what little was left," Kotov said.

Grishkov shook his head. "And how affected was I by the radiation?"

Kotov patted his shoulder. "You were very fortunate there. Your initial treatment took place inside the helicopter. Though it had crashed, it was still largely intact. The Ukrainian troops who then collected you appear to have known radiation could be an issue since they had the proper protective gear to transport you to one of their facilities for further treatment. You were not there long, though, before being flown here."

"So, Director, how long has it been since I was injured?" Grishkov asked.

Kotov hesitated, and finally said, "Almost three weeks."

Grishkov frowned. "So, you were not exaggerating when you said my injuries were serious."

"No, I was not. But as I said, your recovery prospects are excellent. I believe you could return to light duty in less than a year if your therapy progresses as well as I expect," Kotov said.

Grishkov didn't like what he was hearing at all and was about to ask more questions when Kotov's smile returned.

"But come," he said, "we can discuss the details of your therapy later. Right now, though, you have some visitors who are very anxious to see you."

No sooner had he said that than his wife Arisha and his sons Sasha and Misha came running into the room.

Kotov grinned, and beat a hasty retreat.

"Tolya! I am so happy to see you awake!" Arisha said. Then she kissed and hugged Grishkov so hard he was fighting for air.

He didn't mind at all.

Arisha was the only person who had ever called him Tolya besides his mother. It was good to hear the name on her lips again.

Misha asked, "Father, can I draw on your cast?"

Sasha, the elder brother by two years, immediately scowled and said, "Certainly not! He has been in a serious accident and can't be distracted by such foolishness! Don't you understand he was in a helicopter that fell from the sky?"

Misha's eyes got large, and Grishkov knew he was about to start crying. Hurriedly, he said, "Now Sasha, don't frighten your brother. It wasn't as bad as all that. I'll be up and dancing with your mother again before you know it!"

That did the trick, as Grishkov knew it would. Both Sasha and Misha laughed at the idea of their father dancing. They had never seen their always-serious father dancing and rightly thought they never would.

"We're going to be seeing a lot more of your father, boys. The doctor says we'll be able to bring him home in a few days, and then he'll be with us for months while he does physical therapy," Arisha said.

Grishkov smiled, and he could see both of his sons were pleased by the news.

"Even better, your father's not going to be going on any more trips out of the country. He'll be staying right here in Moscow, where it's safe," Arisha said.

The look in her eye told Grishkov this wasn't the right time to ask her exactly what she meant by "no more trips." Or to point out that being a police officer, even a Captain, in Moscow wasn't exactly "safe."

Well, compared to what he'd been doing recently, it probably was.

"Now, your father has other visitors, so we need to go home now. Soon we'll have him all to ourselves," Arisha said.

Then she leaned over to Grishkov, whispered, "Rest up," and gently bit his ear.

Grishkov blushed, but before he could say anything in response, Arisha had hustled the children out of the room.

Very quickly, a bearded figure hurled through the door and launched itself at Grishkov. He barely had time to identify it as Director Smyslov before he found himself once again fighting for air.

This time, the fight was more unequal, and there was little Grishkov could do but hope for mercy.

Finally, Grishkov could hear laughter, and the pressure eased as he heard Neda's voice say, "Director, you mustn't undo the hard work of all these doctors!"

Smyslov grinned and released his grip, though still holding Grishkov by the shoulders.

"You are looking well! I was glad to be able to let you see your wife and sons first this time. You have a family to be proud of, my friend!" Smyslov exclaimed.

Grishkov smiled and nodded. He certainly wasn't going to argue the point.

Now Grishkov heard Neda's voice again. "You must let us see him, too!" she said.

"Of course, of course, my dear! I know you're just as happy to see him as I am!" Smyslov said.

Smyslov moved aside, and now Grishkov could see Neda, Vasilyev, and Kharlov standing behind him. Neda leaned forward and kissed him on the cheek, while Grishkov could see Vasilyev and Kharlov looking at his cast.

"I am guessing one of your sons was the artist?" Vasilyev asked, pointing at Grishkov's cast.

Now that he had the chance to look, Grishkov could see a smiling face had been drawn about halfway down the cast.

Shaking his head with resignation, Grishkov said ruefully, "That would have been Misha. He's always saying I should smile more."

"Well, let me come straight to the news that should make that happen," Smyslov said. "First, you will all be receiving a one million US dollar cash bonus for your performance on this mission, paid for from the President's personal funds."

The truth was, for the first time, Smyslov had been forced to plead with the President to continue his practice of paying such a bonus. The President had not been happy with the outcome of his meeting with Babich. Smyslov had finally persuaded the President that without the agents' intervention, the outcome could have been far worse.

There was a chorus of thanks from everyone in the room, including Kharlov. There was a look of amusement on Kharlov's face, which made Smyslov look at him with a raised, questioning eyebrow.

"I just thought that it's not warlord pay, but much better than I'd expected," Kharlov said with a smile.

To himself, Smyslov thought Kharlov didn't know how close he'd come to getting nothing. Aloud, he said, "On behalf of the Russian state, I will promise that no one will burn down whatever Moscow residence you purchase with your bonus."

"Ouch!" Kharlov said, while all the others laughed. "You are, of course, right that the life of a warlord, while lucrative, does carry certain risks."

"You are fortunate that both the helicopter you, let's say borrowed, and the company that operated it were Russian. As a result, the President has authorized me to reimburse the company for the cost of their lost helicopter. Once that payment has been processed, you will receive a refund of your deposit, which I understand was quite substantial," Smyslov said.

"Yes, it was," Kharlov said. "I'm very grateful. I'd never expected to see that money again."

"Because of your service to Russia both before and during this mission, the President has also pardoned you for the crime of desertion and approved changing your military records to reflect your honorable discharge. He has also approved my request to appoint you as an agent in the FSB. Of course, you will still be expected to complete FSB training successfully," Smyslov said.

On all these counts, Kharlov had no idea how lucky he was. The President had been explicit that he would have approved none of these steps if Kharlov had not risked his life to save Grishkov.

"How bad was the damage from the blast?" Grishkov asked quietly.

"First, the impact was reduced very substantially by your action in moving the warhead far underground. Our experts also say the warhead's yield was well under its designed five hundred kilotons. This was almost certainly due to the decades that had passed since the warhead had been properly maintained," Smyslov said.

Grishkov nodded. "But still strong enough to knock our helicopter out of the sky."

Smyslov shrugged. "Yes. And of course, strong enough to kill anyone in the immediate vicinity. Fortunately, that number appears to have been fairly small. Most of the illegal residents in the Exclusion Zone were in and around Chernobyl itself, and the blast didn't reach that far. Hundreds are being treated by the Ukrainians for radiation sickness, but most are expected to survive."

"How have the Americans responded?" Grishkov asked.

"So far, they have not publicly challenged our cover story that the explosion was caused by a tactical nuclear weapon missed during the hurried pullout of our forces from Ukraine when the Soviet Union collapsed. Of course, they know better," Smyslov said.

Grishkov nodded. Since an American officer had overseen the aerial search for the stolen warheads, that much was certain.

"And the Ukrainians?" Grishkov asked.

Smyslov scowled. "They are milking this incident for everything it's worth. And maybe a bit more."

Grishkov looked down at his cast and raised one eyebrow, but said nothing.

Smyslov's scowl gave way to a rueful smile. "Well, yes, being on the receiving end of a nuclear weapon would make anyone unhappy. The principal consequence is that negotiations over our pullout from Donbas were ended on terms that could hardly have been more favorable to Ukraine. Our forces have withdrawn, and all militias have been disbanded. It doesn't matter much, though. We'd already decided to leave anyway."

Grishkov nodded but said nothing. It was apparent from Smyslov's expression that he was putting a brave face on the outcome, but they all knew it could have been far worse.

"So, what crisis do we have to look forward to next? It seems that one just follows another," Grishkov said.

Smyslov laughed and shook his head. "First, any further crises will no longer be your problem. The doctor tells me that it will take months of physical therapy for you to regain full mobility in that leg, once the bones have had a chance to knit," he said, pointing at Grishkov's cast.

"Also, even then, you are unlikely to meet the FSB's demanding standards for overseas deployment. Of course, the doctor tells me that duty as a captain with the Moscow police should be no issue. Captains are free to decide whether they will leave their desk, and under what circumstances," Smyslov said and then paused.

He could see Grishkov was about to object and raised his hand.

"In any case, even if you were to make a full recovery against all expectations, there is another consideration. The details of your missions are, of course, highly classified. But their broad outlines are well known within the FSB. Where you have become something of a legend. For morale purposes, I have decided it best that we end your story with us as a *living* legend," Smyslov said.

Grishkov was plainly not convinced and gestured towards Vasilyev. "And who will see after him? Tell me you're not sending him to the field without a partner!"

Turning to Neda, he quickly added, "No offense meant, I'm sure you know."

Neda smiled. "I do. My job is nuclear weapons. I can't defuse one and watch my husband's back at the same time."

Kharlov nodded. "But I can watch his back in your place," he said.

That made Grishkov think. Finally, he shrugged. "Well, I certainly can't complain about your performance so far. If you hadn't come for me, I wouldn't be here now. And just for the record, I understand why you left when the Ukrainian soldiers showed up. You couldn't fight them all off, and you couldn't move me. All that would have happened if you'd stayed is that the Ukrainians would have had someone to question who was conscious and able to answer."

Kharlov smiled. "I'm glad you understand. Just as I'd hoped from a soldier who served in Chechnya."

Grishkov frowned and turned to Smyslov. "But Director, you haven't answered my question about the next crisis. Surely the world hasn't gone quiet!"

"As a matter of fact, for the moment it has. There is no crisis, pending or otherwise. Kharlov, here, will have plenty of time to complete his training," Smyslov said.

Neda touched his arm and said, "The doctor says you will be allowed to go home soon. We will visit you there often, so you can see for yourself that we are not having fun without you."

Grishkov snorted. "Fun! Yes, that's the right word for it!"

They all laughed, and finally, Grishkov shrugged, and looked at Kharlov. "Very well. At least I know my partner is in good hands."

Once they had all said their goodbyes, Vasilyev stopped Kharlov as they got onto the elevator.

"Would you like us to give you a ride? I know you haven't had time to buy a car yet," Vasilyev said.

Kharlov shook his head. "Thanks, but I'll take a cab. I have to make a phone call first."

Vasilyev shrugged, and shortly Kharlov was alone in front of the hospital.

Kharlov smiled. He had Smyslov's comment about militias disbanding to thank for reminding him of some unfinished business.

He was going to enjoy this.

CHAPTER FIFTY-SIX

Donetsk, Ukraine

Avel Karpenko cursed as he watched the latest online news broadcast. The details matched what he had already learned from a variety of sources.

The Russians were gone. And it was no game this time.

Advisors. Volunteers. Weapons.

All of it.

All militias, including his, had been officially disbanded and forced to hand over all their heavy weapons. In theory, they were supposed to hand over their small arms as well, but Karpenko had played that game before. All they gave the authorities was junk.

Ukrainians from the central government in Kyiv were already here, and organizing elections. There were no more "People's Republics" in either Donetsk or Luhansk. Soon the authorities that had been his allies would become an armed nuisance.

They were likely even to reestablish a functioning police force.

Karpenko shook his head. If the Russians had just bought Shulga's operation with the Javelins as a real Ukrainian attack.

Or even better, if he'd only been able to get his hands on a nuclear warhead...

His sources in Ukraine said that Boris Kharlov had played a role in stopping Marko Zavod from doing just that.

Well, maybe it was no use worrying about what might have been.

But he could certainly make sure Kharlov never interfered with his plans again.

They were undoubtedly plans Kharlov wouldn't like, Karpenko thought with a thin smile.

Karpenko had decided to traffic as many women and children through the territory he controlled as possible. Before he didn't control it anymore.

At least without Kharlov's ambushes to worry about, he could do enough volume to make all the money he'd need to leave Ukraine for good.

His sources in Russia had just told him that Kharlov had been spotted in Moscow, and confirmed his location at a hotel.

That was excellent news for Karpenko. There were plenty of guns for hire in Moscow, and a big, busy city like that was the perfect setting for an assassination.

They happened there all the time.

Karpenko glanced at the cell phone sitting on his desk and smiled. At least one good thing had come from Kharlov. The high-end phone his men had retrieved from Kharlov's mansion, still in its original shrink-wrapped packaging, was still not yet available in Ukrainian stores.

It was the best one Karpenko had ever used.

Of course, Karpenko had heard the story about Kharlov and the Chechen terrorist he had assassinated with a cell phone.

And he knew it wasn't so hard to make a package look like it hadn't been opened. He'd done it himself.

So, Karpenko had tested the phone with the help of a security guard, who, of course, wasn't told the real reason he was answering the phone alone in a separate room.

Karpenko had called the guard over a dozen times to "test reception," each time half expecting to hear an explosion. But it never came.

At first, Karpenko had been cautious about using the phone, even then. He had set it well back on his desk and used it on speaker rather than pressing it against his head as he preferred for privacy.

His deputy, Osip Litvin, had suggested he use a Bluetooth earpiece, but Karpenko had always disliked the way they felt in his ear.

Instead, he had settled on the most elementary precaution of all. Karpenko used the phone to make calls to anyone he liked, with the outgoing number blocked.

But he only answered calls on the phone from Litvin, and he was the only person Karpenko trusted with the number. Litvin was one of the few people Karpenko wanted to hear from anyway.

Like now. Litvin was the man he could trust to arrange for Kharlov's liquidation.

And now, as though Litvin had been summoned by his thoughts, the phone was ringing!

Karpenko put the phone to his head and grinned. It was a good omen.

Yes, maybe things hadn't been going his way for a while. But that was about to change.

Moscow, Russia

Boris Kharlov tapped on the screen of his phone, activating an app he had purchased at a price he'd found surprisingly reasonable. Probably because multiple apps provided the same service.

Competition was great for driving down prices.

The phone number he entered into the app next had been more expensive to obtain. Not surprising, since someone being bribed to provide information theoretically unavailable to the public ran a risk.

If they were caught, they could be fired. And lose the job that gave them a salary, as well as access to information worth a bribe.

The call connected.

A voice boomed over the phone, "Litvin! Great that you called. I have something for you to do right away. I want you to arrange the assassination of Boris Kharlov. I've just learned where he's staying in Moscow."

Kharlov smiled and said, "Dasvidaniya."

At the same moment, he pressed the number on the phone's virtual keypad that signaled the software controlling the explosive charge in Karpenko's phone.

Kharlov heard what sounded like the beginning of the word, "No" before the call was cut off.

Yes, the app to make Litvin's number display on Karpenko's phone when Kharlov called had cost some money. And the bribe to obtain the numbers of Karpenko and Litvin from the cell phone service provider had cost even more.

But it was money well spent.

Kharlov's smile grew wider. Yes.

Never leave a snake unwatched behind you.

CHAPTER FIFTY-SEVEN

The Kremlin
Moscow, Russia

FSB Director Smyslov knew the President was still unhappy with the outcome in Ukraine. Even though they both knew it could have been much worse.

Well, Smyslov thought, he would have to get over it.

And move on to the next crisis.

If Smyslov could just convince the President that this was, indeed, a crisis.

"So, what do you think of the requests made by our friend in Kazakhstan?" the President asked.

Smyslov scowled. "Sir, those read like demands, not requests. I think we should tell him to..."

The President's raised eyebrows stopped him. Smyslov knew he didn't care for profanity.

Usually, neither did Smyslov.

But the new dictator of Kazakhstan made him so angry.

Well, he'd just have to get hold of his temper.

Smyslov finished his sentence with, "reconsider whether his requests are reasonable."

The President smiled. "I think our friend isn't the type to do much 'reconsidering.' And besides, he thinks we have to agree with what he wants, yes?"

Smyslov's scowl was back. Even deeper this time.

"If you would approve my plan, we could get rid of Sadykov's leverage. And then we could get rid of him, too," Smyslov added darkly.

The President's smile broadened. "Really! It's been quite a while since I've heard you so...bloodthirsty. You're usually the one holding me back."

Smyslov shook his head. "The man is a menace. Islamic fundamentalism is one thing. But he's talking openly about united all the neighboring Muslim countries under his banner. Remember what happened the last time we heard talk like that?"

The President's smile disappeared. "Yes. ISIS. But, look at what's happened to them. Their leader dead. His followers scattered. The territory they control, a few patches of desert in Syria. Why worry about them?"

"Because their most important asset is their ideology and the thousands who follow it around the world. Also, recall that forty tons of the gold ISIS stole from the central bank in Mosul was never recovered. That's more than enough money to pay for some real trouble," Smyslov replied.

The President was still obviously unconvinced. "Fine, but Sadykov isn't claiming to lead ISIS. As far as I know, he's never even publicly mentioned them."

Smyslov sighed. "That is true."

"Very well. Look, I understand how you feel. I don't like blackmail either. But this is a card the Kazakhs have been playing for decades now. This new fellow is just playing it a bit more aggressively. So, let's agree to what he wants," the President said.

Seeing Smyslov's expression, the President held up his hand. "And go ahead with preparations for your plan. From what I read, it will take quite some time to prepare all its elements, yes?"

Smyslov drew a deep breath and visibly collected himself. "Yes, Mr. President. Of course, we will not execute the plan without your direct order."

The President nodded. "I would expect nothing less," he said approvingly. "Now, I presume you'll put the new FSB station chief there in charge of plan preparations? The one you just moved from Ukraine?"

Smyslov did his best to hide his astonishment but knew he was failing when he saw the President's smile.

Yes, the President had been in his job before he became President. And still kept a close eye on what was happening at the FSB.

Who knew how many of Smyslov's people were reporting directly to the President?

Aloud, Smyslov just said, "Yes, sir. I think she did well in Ukraine."

"Agreed," the President said. "Besides," he added, "I think most of what Sadykov wants will work for us, anyway. And after all this time, who knows if the missiles even work anymore."

Smyslov disagreed with the President's first statement but knew better than to argue the point. An old-school politician, the President was too inclined to think anything bad for the West in general, and the Americans, in particular, was good for Russia.

Smyslov believed first and foremost in stability. With so many nuclear powers in the world, he considered any other priority entirely secondary.

In his bones, Smyslov knew Sadykov was terrible for stability.

But he couldn't let the second statement stand.

"You are correct that the potency of the warheads has probably degraded over time. In particular, it's likely the Kazakhs haven't replenished the tritium required for optimal performance. But, as we recently saw in Ukraine, those old warheads are still capable of doing great damage. We are fortunate that our agent could place the one that detonated deep underground," Smyslov said.

Then he paused.

"In fact, I wonder if it's a coincidence that we received this list of new and fairly bold demands so soon after the explosion in Ukraine. Which we said publicly was of a weapon dating back to Soviet days," Smyslov said.

The President grunted, and his eyes narrowed. Smyslov could see that this point had not, in fact, occurred to him.

"Very well," the President finally said. "You may be right. But Sadykov can only push the missile threat so far. He has to know that any attempt to use them on us would be met by a response that would leave him dead and his country a radioactive wasteland."

"Yes, sir. Always assuming that Sadykov is a rational actor. His most recent speeches are moving in an alarming direction. I think he's starting to believe in his own rhetoric. That he is divinely ordained to unite Muslims in his region under a single leader. Him," Smyslov said.

The President was clearly unmoved. "What about the Pakistanis, Muslims who have a much larger and completely modern nuclear arsenal, and no interest in being led by Sadykov?"

Smyslov nodded. "You're right, sir, that the Pakistanis are entirely focused on the Indian nuclear threat. But that works both ways. I agree they would never join Sadykov. But I also doubt they would do anything to stop him."

"Agreed," the President said. "Let me know when preparations for your plan are complete. I'll decide whether to proceed, depending on what happens in the meantime. Like more requests from Sadykov, for example."

"Yes, Mr. President," Smyslov said and rose to leave.

It was only when Smyslov was in the car headed back to his office that the image came to him.

As quickly as it appeared, Smyslov tried to push it away mentally.

Futile, Smyslov thought with a sigh. He could keep it out of his head during the day with work, but he knew the image would come back to haunt his dreams.

Or more accurately, his nightmares.

The image of three SS-18 missiles in flight, painted with the black flag of ISIS.

First, thanks very much for reading my book! I sincerely hope you enjoyed it. If you did, I'd really appreciate it if you could leave a review - even a short one - on Amazon.

If in spite of the best efforts of my editor (and me!) you found a typo or some other error, please let me know with details. I will fix it!

If you have questions, please send those to me too. You can reach me at my blog, https://thesecondkoreanwar.wordpress.com or on Twitter at https://Twitter.com/TedHalstead18

Or if all else fails, you can e-mail me directly at thalstead2018@gmail.com

I'll answer a few questions now that I received after my first three books. I'll start with the newest questions, and then repeat answers to a few old ones, in case this is the only one of my books you've read.

Is any of the information in your books classified?

For the benefit of anyone in the national security apparatus of which I used to be a part, the short answer is an emphatic NO.

Now, the longer and more detailed answer.

I was aware when I started writing these books of the danger that I might inadvertently include classified information. Of course, that danger has receded as time has marched on since my retirement. But it's still there.

The way I dealt with it was simple. I made sure that absolutely every detail that could possibly have been classified when I learned of it has since made it into public knowledge. In short, if I could find out about it through Google, I could put it in the book.

For instance, I first read about the idea of arming US subs with anti-aircraft missiles long ago. But before I included it as a near-future capability in my first book, I did a Google search. Here's what I found in an article from an editor at Time's "The War Zone":

"During the late 2000s, the US Navy, Raytheon and Northrop Grumman worked to migrate the highly flexible AIM-9X short-range air-to-air missile to the undersea world under the Littoral Warfare Weapon program. The AIM-9X would be vertically launched in a canister from a submarine, then the missile would climb into the sky when the canister broke the surface, locking onto its target after launch.

Tests during the mid 2000s had the AIM-9X fired from a vertical launcher as a proof of concept demonstration. A few years later, an AIM-9X was launched from an actual submarine as part of a series of integration tests. Since then the program seems to have disappeared from public view, but it's likely development has continued on in the classified world—especially considering that submarine-launched unmanned aircraft have been an operational reality within America's nuclear submarine fleet for some time."

In one of the book's first reviews, I was called out by a reviewer who said:

"The author could have done a little research using Google. A Virginia class submarine with stern tubes that carry fire AIM-9 air to air missiles? Puhleaze...."

After I responded by posting the quote from the article I used as the basis for including a sub-launched AIM-9 in the book, later the same day another reader had this comment:

"Re: the author's reply: very nicely done. You just sold another copy of your book."

Satisfying? Well, yes!

Information about the Soviet SS-24 test involving anti-tank mines described in this book was indeed classified when it happened almost thirty years ago. Reports of the test made quite an impression on me at the time, and I always thought the SS-24 would make a great element to include in a novel.

And of course, now all the details about that incident are available to anyone with Internet access.

What inspires you to write these books?

Sometimes it's 100% personal experience. I worked in Seoul for four years, and almost every day at the US Embassy we had reason to think about what would happen if the North Koreans attacked.

Also, every day at work I talked to South Koreans applying to immigrate to America, in numbers that made Korea one of the top ten source countries at the time. Why were they leaving, when Korea was already an economic powerhouse and future prospects seemed to be bright?

Applicants were blunt when we asked them. They were worried about the prospect of a North Korean attack for themselves. They were even more worried for their children.

So, I had the ideas that eventually became *The Second Korean War* in my head for a long time.

Are any of the stories in the books from my own experience, and if so which ones?

You can usually apply common sense to answer that one.

In my first book, *The Second Korean War:*

Characters set mines, throw grenades, and attempt to defuse nuclear weapons.

None of that was me.

Characters describe kicking up tear "gas" powder on a Seoul subway platform and not enjoying the results, and dealing with poorly aimed golf balls hit by American military officers landing in their yard at Yongsan Army Base in Seoul.

Yes, that was me.

In my second book, *The Saudi-Iranian War:*

Characters fire rockets, and drive a truck off a pier.

Not me.

Characters in Saudi Arabia go through traffic experiences themselves, and recount others. They describe the treatment of women in Saudi Arabia. Hulk Hogan makes an unexpected appearance in the narrative.

All from my experience, all true.

Sometimes, though, it's a bit trickier. In my third book *The End of America's War in Afghanistan* one character describes a person nearly being bisected by the wing of a Harrier jump jet. Looking back, it's hard to believe it, but that really was me!

Many readers have asked questions along the lines of "why would the Russians want to help." I think the answer is simple. Like citizens of all countries, Russians want first and foremost to help themselves.

In each book, I've tried to lay out what I believe is a compelling case for the Russians to take action. I think it's also important to remember what the Russians are actually risking in these books - the lives of a few agents, and a plane here, a drone there.

So, each time Russia may not stand to gain that much. But the risk/reward ratio is always very, very favorable. To me, that makes Russia's actions in the books credible.

Do I think Russia is our friend?

Well, no. First the Soviet Union and then Russia have nearly always seen America as a threat to its interests, and even to its very existence. Particularly since the development of nuclear weapons, America has seen Russia the same way.

That's not the basis for friendship.

Russia's belief that America is a threat has deep roots. In 1918, as the Communists were trying to establish control over all of what would become the Soviet Union, President Wilson sent eight thousand soldiers to Vladivostok. It was called the American Expeditionary Force, Siberia. They stayed until 1920.

At the same time, Wilson sent another five thousand troops to Archangelsk, a major port on the White Sea, in what was called the Polar Bear Expedition.

Few Americans know anything about these events.

Nearly all Russians do.

It's true that in WWII we were allies, because we faced a threat in Nazi Germany that we both correctly saw as an even greater threat than each other. But that alliance ended as soon as we defeated the Nazis.

A few years after that alliance ended, we deployed nuclear weapons at each other. America built them first after a massive research and development effort called the Manhattan Project.

How did the Soviet Union get nuclear weapons so quickly, with no such effort? By stealing our nuclear weapon designs with the help of Julius and Ethel Rosenberg, two American citizens. In 1953, the Rosenbergs became the last Americans to be executed for espionage.

Before long, the power of those nuclear weapons was enough to end each other's existence. That's still true today.

And Russian espionage targeting America didn't stop with the Rosenbergs. The Walker family spy ring, Aldrich Ames, and Robert Hanssen were just a few of the many spies who sold American military and intelligence secrets to Russia.

America has plenty of evidence to show that it remains Russia's primary target abroad.

That doesn't mean, though, that our interests and Russia's can never coincide. In the 1970s, for example, both countries decided it would be useful for spacecraft to be able to rescue one another in the event of an emergency. This led to joint design of a docking module, leading in 1975 to the successful docking of a Soviet Soyuz and an American Apollo spacecraft.

From 1993 to 2013 the Megatons to Megawatts Program mentioned in this book sent 500 tons of Russian weapons-grade uranium from scrapped weapons to America after being reprocessed into 15,000 tons of reactor fuel. The 500 tons was the equivalent of about 20,000 nuclear warheads.

About ten percent of all electricity produced in the United States from 1993 to 2013 came from this program. Power that was, incidentally, carbon-free.

More recently Russia and America have sent each other equipment and supplies to address the coronavirus pandemic. In a world with global travel and trade, it's clear we have a shared interest with all other countries in first reducing and eventually eliminating this pandemic.

Could occasional shared interests ever result in our working together as we do in these books? Maybe. I'd like to hope so, since the alternative isn't pleasant to contemplate.

I've set these books in the near future in part to make such cooperation a bit more credible.

Again, as also noted on the book listing page all of my books are set in the near future, not the present. Please keep that in mind when deciding whether the technology described in this book is plausible. If you still think not, remember that not so long ago widespread GPS capability in cars and phones wouldn't have been just science fiction. It would have been not very credible science fiction.

Thanks again for reading my book, and I hope you will enjoy my next one in 2021!

CAST OF CHARACTERS
ALPHABETICAL ORDER BY NATIONALITY
MOST IMPORTANT CHARACTERS IN BOLD

Ukrainian Citizens

Sergeant Pofistal Arbakov, ex-soldier who stole two SS-24 warheads

Ukrainian President **Babich**

Bondarenko, hired criminal working for Popova

Avel Karpenko, Novorossiya organized crime boss and militia leader

Colonel Klimenko, munitions commander, Vasylkiv Air Base

The widow Kulik, Arbakov's neighbor

Osip Litvin, Karpenko's deputy

Fedir Popova, former SS-24 engineer

SBU Director **Shevchuk**

Danya Shulga, ex-soldier and commander of Karpenko's militia

Olek Tarasenko, former SS-24 engineer

Marko Zavod, ex-soldier working for Karpenko

Russian Citizens

FSB Kyiv Station Chief Alina

Andreas Burmakin, worker, Russian Nuclear Weapons Disposal Plant

Vitaly Dreev, worker, Russian Nuclear Weapons Disposal Plant

Senior Academic Researcher Golovkin, Russian Strategic Rocket Headquarters, Moscow

Anatoly Grishkov, FSB agent, former Vladivostok homicide detective

Boris Kharlov, Novorossiya warlord

Kolesnik, ex-soldier working for Kharlov

Dr. Kotov, Gospital Fsb Na Shchukinskoy, Moscow

Neda Rhahbar, FSB agent, former Iranian citizen

Colonel Valery Rozum, Commander, Pervomaysk Strategic Rocket Base

Colonel Leonid Shipov, Kharlov's Russian Army commander

FSB Director **Smyslov**

Mikhail Vasilyev, FSB agent

American Citizens

U.S. President Hernandez

Captain Josh Pettigrew, Drone Training Officer, Ukraine

General Robinson, the Air Force Chief of Staff

Made in the USA
Columbia, SC
23 May 2022

60799717R00233